AN OUTRAGE

"I have a business arrangement for you." She couldn't believe the steadiness of her voice.

He arched a brow. "Now I am even more intrigued."

"You shouldn't be." She made a sweeping gesture with her hand, taking in his room in all its opulence. "You are known as a man of many skills, greatly favored at court. I am in need of one of your talents."

"Indeed?" He narrowed his eyes, no longer bemused. "And what might that be?"

"I require your amatory skills." Mirabelle kept her chin raised. "I want you to ruin me."

...AND HER NOVELS

SEDUCTION OF A HIGHLAND WARRIOR

"4½ stars! This is Welfonder at her finest. The well-paced, intricate plot brings life to a highly sensual and emotional romance populated by unforgettable characters. The romance is steeped in rich lore and legend, adding a fairy-tale dimension that will have readers sighing with happiness."

—*RT Book Reviews*

"Sue-Ellen Welfonder takes the reader away from the mundane and gives her an emotional journey that floods the senses and makes the heart pound with both hope and fear... This one kept me up late and was worth every minute.

—LongandShortReviews.com

TEMPTATION OF A HIGHLAND SCOUNDREL

"4½ stars! Welfonder's second installment in the Highland Warriors trilogy is even better than the first! This finely crafted, highly emotional romance is populated by heroes whose lives are defined by the concept of honor and strong-willed heroines who don't accept surrender as a possibility."

—*RT Book Reviews*

"Kendrew is quite the hero! Readers will love his rough ways, as much as they will love Isobel's fire and spirit...an enchanting mix of romance, history, and the smallest bit of paranormal."

—RomRevToday.com

"This series fulfills all of my Scottish historical romance requirements...fierce men with feisty women, magic everywhere, and the amazing landscape of Scotland. Ms. Welfonder is able to place the reader in Scotland with such accuracy you feel the mist upon your face and see the men in kilts standing on the hillside embracing the women they love."

—TheReadingReviewer.com

"Sizzling...This story was magical...I look forward to reading the next book in the series."

—SeducedByABook.com

SINS OF A HIGHLAND DEVIL

"4½ stars! Top Pick! The first installment in Welfonder's Highland Warriors trilogy continues a long tradition of well-written, highly emotional romances. This marvelous novel is rich in love and legend, populated by characters steeped in honor, to make for a sensual and emotional read."

—*RT Book Reviews*

"Sue-Ellen Welfonder has truly brought legends and love to life...I cannot wait for the next two."

—FreshFiction.com

"A richly enjoyable story. Welfonder is a master storyteller."

—ARomanceReview.com

"One of the finest books I've read in a long time. The characters are so rich and vibrant, and Sue-Ellen Welfonder writes the most realistic descriptions of Highland battles. I was transported to the Glen and could almost smell the forest and the peat fires in the castles...I'm looking forward to the next story in the series!"

—OnceUponARomance.net

A HIGHLANDER'S TEMPTATION

"[Welfonder] continues to weave magical tales of redemption, love, and loyalty in glorious, perilous mid-fourteenth-century Scotland."

—Booklist

"4 stars! A fascinating, intriguing story that will definitely stand the test of time."

—RT Book Reviews

SEDUCING A SCOTTISH BRIDE

"4½ stars! Welfonder sweeps readers into a tale brimming with witty banter between a feisty heroine and a stalwart hero... The added paranormal elements and sensuality turn this into an intriguing page-turner that fans of Scottish romance will adore."

—RT Book Reviews

"A great paranormal historical romance... Fans will read this in one delightful sitting so set aside the time."

—Midwest Book Review

BRIDE FOR A KNIGHT

"Once again, Welfonder's careful scholarship and attention to detail vividly re-create the lusty, brawling days of medieval Scotland with larger-than-life chivalrous heroes and the dainty but spirited maidens."

—Booklist

ONLY FOR A KNIGHT

"4½ stars! Enthralling... Welfonder brings the Highlands to life with her vibrant characters, impassioned stories, and vivid description."
—*RT Book Reviews*

WEDDING FOR A KNIGHT

"A very romantic story... extremely sexy. I recommend this book to anyone who loves the era and Scotland."
—*TheBestReviews.com*

MASTER OF THE HIGHLANDS

"Welfonder does it again, bringing readers another powerful, emotional, highly romantic medieval that steals your heart and keeps you turning the pages."
—*RT Book Reviews*

DEVIL IN A KILT

"A lovely gem of a book. Wonderful characters and a true sense of place make this a keeper."
—Patricia Potter, author of *The Heart Queen*

TO LOVE A HIGHLANDER

SUE-ELLEN WELFONDER

FOREVER

NEW YORK   BOSTON

Forever
Hachette Book Group
237 Park Avenue
New York, NY 10017

www.HachetteBookGroup.com

Printed in the United States of America

First edition: April 2014
10 9 8 7 6 5 4 3 2 1

OPM

Forever is an imprint of Grand Central Publishing.
The Forever name and logo are trademarks of Hachette Book Group, Inc.

The Hachette Speakers Bureau provides a wide range of authors for speaking events. To find out more, go to www.hachettespeakersbureau.com or call (866) 376-6591.

The publisher is not responsible for websites (or their content) that are not owned by the publisher.

To honor the "real" Little Heart, a tiny gray tabby kitten who should have enjoyed a long and happy life in a loving forever home, had he not met the sad fate that claimed him at only seven weeks.

Little Heart was a stray, and his story touched me so deeply that I was compelled to write him into this book, letting Mirabelle find, adopt, and adore him, giving him the happy ending I so wish he'd had in real life.

Heartfelt thanks and appreciation to everyone who helps stray and feral cats and kittens. How I wish they could all be saved and loved.

Little Heart, you aren't forgotten.

Acknowledgments

The spark for my Scandalous Scots series was ignited by my fascination with the Scottish medieval hero Alexander Stewart, Lord of Badenoch and Earl of Buchan. Son of Scotland's King Robert II, brother to King Robert III, "Alex" was most famously known as the Wolf of Badenoch.

To many, he was a villain, the quintessential bad boy. One reason for his notoriety was his burning of Elgin Cathedral in June 1390. Of course, the Wolf had reasons for everything he did, and he made his own rules. He was a larger than life man of his time and, as the King's Justiciar of the North, he governed the Highlands with an iron fist. Bold and charismatic, he is said to have been six feet four and dashingly handsome. He was also known for his grand passions.

I have deep personal and family ties to his longtime mistress, Mariota de Athyn (Clan Mackay), with whom he had five sons. Because of my interest in the Wolf and Mariota, I've visited many sites in Scotland that were significant to these medieval lovers. In some such places, especially the more remote ones, it is still possible to feel their presence. I suspect that will always be so, even hundreds of years from now. Such vibrant and colorful personages leave an indelible mark on history, regardless of how you view them.

So when I decided to write a series about Highland bad boys, genuine rogues and rascals who would be bastards at the royal court of Stirling Castle, I knew exactly who I wanted as their "ringleader": my own lifelong hero, Alexander Stewart, the Wolf of Badenoch.

He was a real-life legend and loving him as I do, I really enjoyed weaving him into Scandalous Scots. If he could read his appearances in the story, I hope he'd approve of how I portrayed him.

Special thanks to my best friend and agent, Roberta Brown. She'll know why I'm also giving a nod to Horatio, Hercules, and the gang.

Much love and appreciation to my very handsome husband, Manfred, who married a stewardess and ended up with a cranky writer. He surely preferred free flying privileges to suffering my deadlines, but he makes the best of it. As always, the whole of my heart to my little Jack Russell, Em. I could write a million words and not convey how much I love him. Hopefully he knows.

TO LOVE A
HIGHLANDER

It isn't the plaid that makes a Highlander, but the man whose shoulder it graces.

—An old Scottish proverb

The Damning of Clan MacNab

❧

Since time immemorial, kings have surrounded themselves with a lively, colorful throng. The Stewart kings of medieval Scotland kept a particularly glittering court. And of these privileged worthies, the King's bard held a place of highest honor.

Archibald MacNab was one such fortunate tale-teller.

A laughing-eyed, roguish Highlander, he charmed and entertained, his silvered tongue gaining him royal trust and affection. With song and wit, he also won the adoration of all who heard his magical voice, rumored so beautiful that birds envied him.

Few men enjoyed such favor.

Unfortunately, the King's grace wasn't the only boon bestowed on him.

Privileged ladies, Lowlanders mostly, were enchanted by Archie's dashing good looks and his status as a Highland chieftain, hailing from a wild and remote region far from the civilities of court. It was no secret that Highlanders were rugged and dangerous men, their deep, buttery-rich voices making them irresistible.

And when their tongues were so masterful...

It followed that Archie rarely slept alone.

At night, when the hall quieted and torches guttered, the court lovelies beat a path to his door. Eager to discover if the whispered praise about the carnality of wild Highland men was true, these women often undressed as soon as they stepped over Archie's threshold.

They also did other things. Some arrived bearing flagons of headiest wine. Others brought scented oils to bathe and massage him. All plied him with silken kisses and skilled embraces, rousing him with their smooth and creamy naked- ness, their rosy-crested breasts, and the tempting shadows between their thighs. As a well-lusted, hot-blooded man, he gladly surrendered to the pleasure.

Life was good.

Young, virile, and unabashedly fond of women, Archie appreciated such bounty, enjoying the gifts offered to him. In turn, he did his best to prove the prowess of Highland men. This was easy, for his amatory skills were as extraordi- nary as his storytelling.

His only weakness was saying no.

And so it came that he accepted the wrong ladies into his bed.

In quick succession, he tasted the sweetness of the King's four most cherished mistresses.

Fine lovers indeed, and beautiful enough to stop a man's heart, Archie understood why the King held them in such high esteem.

Soon he learned that the King also distrusted them.

Even though he'd left their beds of late, lavishing his royal attention on a new, much younger temptress, his four favorites were still watched carefully, their every move reported to the sovereign.

When these ladies started falling ill in the morning and their shapely figures began to thicken, tongues wagged and fingers pointed. Envious court women were quick to share things they'd seen, suspicions that led to the King's roguish, laughing-eyed bard.

Archie's fall from grace was swift and hard.

Now as maligned as he was once loved, he was banished to Duncreag Castle, his stony, clifftop home in the Highlands. But exile wasn't enough to satisfy the King's wrath. Death was considered, but such punishment was believed too kind.

Something more galling was desired.

So a marriage was arranged, pairing the lusty Highlander with a most unattractive female of royal choosing. Archie was also threatened with losing his land and title if he ever again approached court, or his four bastards, so long as he lived.

The same fate would befall him if he spoke of their mothers.

Archie left court disgraced.

In time, he put his amorous past behind him, even falling in love with his wife. She played the harp beautifully, her music a perfect accompaniment to his silvered words. They raised a fine brood of sons and daughters, many as gifted as their talented parents. Archie's youthful scandals were eventually forgotten. To his great delight, Duncreag Castle came to be known as a place of happiness and laughter.

Yet one should never rile a King.

Such transgressions follow a man always, their effects reappearing when least expected and even when royal attention has long since turned elsewhere.

The gods remember and exact vengeance.

So those with long memories weren't surprised when tragedy struck Duncreag. A band of clanless men, greed-driven and dark-hearted, attacked the stronghold hoping to claim the riches rumored to be hidden there. Never warlike, Archie and his men were overcome with ease, their doom sealed when the raiders refused to believe a treasure hoard didn't exist. Failing to gain the wealth they'd desired, the dastards stole what Duncreag could offer: the lives of Archie's kin.

Nearly all of them perished that day, including Archie's beloved wife.

Help soon came when warriors from a neighboring glen rode in to oust the marauders. But even the fiercest fighting men are not able to journey quickly across such wild and rugged terrain. By the time the rescuers arrived at Duncreag, the worst damage was done. Archie had been robbed of everything he held most dear.

Alone in his empty, echoing stronghold, he became a broken man.

Yet he wasn't entirely friendless.

Those who cared for him remembered distant rumors, hushed tales of Archie's days at the royal Stewart court when his scandals took seed.

Somewhere in Scotland, his four bastards lived and thrived.

Unbeknownst to Archie, someone means to find them.

A pity doing so will only damn Archie the more.

The Beginning

❧

The Great Hall at Stirling Castle
Summer 1386

I'll have a kiss from the dark-eyed lass before the night is done." Sorley, baseborn and proud, swelled his youthful chest, his gaze on a comely maid dancing vigorously to the skirl of pipes. She wore a richly embroidered gown of deep red, its bodice cut to display her breasts, while her jeweled belt dipped suggestively low. She held her chin high and her raven hair shone in the torchlight.

Smitten, Sorley stepped out of the shadows at the hall's edge. His pulse quickened. "She has fire in her veins, that one."

"So do the kitchen maids." Roag, the lad beside him, slid an appreciative glance at the swaying hips of a passing serving lass. "Suchlike willnae run crying to their fathers after you taste their charms."

Sorley crossed his arms, his mind set. "I'd rather sample thon lass."

As if she heard, the red-gowned girl twirled with even greater abandon. Her skirts flew, revealing shapely calves and trim ankles. Her breasts bounced, her bodice laces temptingly undone. Equally enticing, her hair spilled to her hips, a skein of glossy black curls. Daughter of a lesser knight, she was several years older than Sorley's own four-and-ten summers. Her flirtatious eyes and bright smile were pure invitation, hinting she'd welcome kisses and more.

Wanting her badly, Sorley flashed his most roguish smile.

The one he'd used to attract so many bonnie serving wenches. In the center of the hall, the dark-haired vixen appeared similarly captivated. She tilted her head, looking at him from beneath her lashes, her own smile deepening.

Sorley grinned and cracked his knuckles.

"Go kiss her then." Roag gave him a shove, pushing him forward. "See how fast you feel the back of her hand. That's all she'll be giving you."

"Say you." Sorley spun about, grabbing Roag's wrist and leaning in. "Be glad my mind's on a lass this night and no' on fighting."

"It makes no' difference." Caelen, another lad, snorted. "The lordies willnae let you near her."

"They'll do more than that. They'll skewer you with their swords." Andrew, a fourth boy, looked pleased by the notion. "You dinnae even have a good dirk. They'll—"

"They'll run if I glare at them." Sorley's tone dared the other lads to deny it. His narrowed eyes warned what he'd do if any of them tried. The day before, he'd won an archery contest. He might not yet wield steel, but he could put an arrow into a foe's backside.

If he wished, he could pierce more tender places.

His rivals knew not to tempt him.

So he stared hard at all three. Like him, they were of questionable birth, unable to name father or mother. Roag had the most swagger, and a scar on his left cheekbone proved he enjoyed using his fists. Caelen deserved a smashed nose, if only because his good looks and silvered tongue made him a great favorite with court ladies. Andrew annoyed because he fancied himself above the rest, aye claiming he was the King's own by-blow.

Sorley knew better.

Royal bastards weren't left to sleep where they could and didn't wear cast-off clothes. Their shoes were of softest leather and didn't have holes. They ate at bright, candlelit tables in the hall. Not in shadow and dark niches in the corners.

Unsavory places Sorley knew well.

As did his rivals, Roag, Caelen, and Andrew, with all four lads of like age and roughly the same height and weight. Excepting blue-eyed, auburn-haired Caelen, they were swarthy boys with inky black hair and dark eyes. Each one boasted a fine, strong face.

To Sorley's irritation, they also shared dimples.

Women appreciated dimpled smiles.

And no one could employ such a desired feature to better advantage than Sorley. He wasn't about to share the trick with his rivals. He did step closer, giving Caelan, in particular, a slow, knowing smile.

"My dirk serves well enough." He dropped a glance to the blade's hilt, peeking up from his boot. "Someday soon"—he knew it was true—"I'll carry my own sword and swing it with greater skill than any lord."

An unimpressed smile spread over Caelan's bonnie face. "Aye, and the stale ale we're served at dinner will turn to nectar."

"The King will employ me to deflower the fairest court maids." Roag laughed and sketched a curvaceous shape in the air. "They shall vie for my services," he added, winking at the other lads. "Eager to—"

"You shall be the first to taste the bite of my steel." Sorley went toe-to-toe with Roag. "The day will come, be warned."

"You willnae live so long, eyeing the gels of lordies." Roag's voice was full of amusement.

When he elbowed Caelan and Andrew, earning their

laughter, Sorley showed them his back. Closing his ears, he looked again to the hall's dance space.

A ring of tall, iron-mounted torches edged the area, the blaze of light shimmering across the dancers. They were a colorful lot, all nobles, dressed in finery and jewels. Many were unsteady on their feet, lurching and weaving rather than properly dancing. They also had red-glowing faces, their eyes bright from wine. A good number of women were scantily clad, their gowns slipping down their shoulders. Smooth and creamy female flesh was everywhere to be seen. But only one maid interested Sorley.

He wanted the knight's daughter.

Ignoring the lads behind him, he felt his mouth curve in a smile that was more wicked than charming. He also stood taller, squared shoulders already hinting at the strapping man he'd soon be.

In truth, he already was a man.

He certainly knew how to pleasure a lady.

He couldn't say the same of his companions. He did note that they also couldn't take their gazes off the dark-haired enchantress. They watched her every twirl and sway, caught in her spell as she bewitched them from the center of the smoky, torchlit hall.

When her gown slipped to her waist, freeing her breasts, Sorley's entire body tightened. She danced nearer then, tempting him with hot, brazen glances so that his heart pounded fiercely. His young, virile loins throbbed, quickening with sharp, potent desire.

He started forward, grateful for the "new" plaid slung across his shoulder. A bit threadbare, the wool well-worn and the colors indistinguishable, the tartan was nevertheless clean. It was also a gift from Alexander Stewart, Lord of Badenoch and Earl of Buchan, the King's boldest, most outspoken son. Above all, the plaid gave Sorley a welcome edge of bravura.

The other court bastards had only received handed-down linen tunics.

Proud, Sorley put back his shoulders. He was glad he'd taken the trouble to polish the battered bronze pin that'd come with the cast-off tartan.

Rarely had he looked so fine.

"She's toying with you," Roag warned behind him.

"Making him an arse, more like," Caelan agreed.

"That, he already is." Andrew gave a bark of laughter.

"No more than you." Sorley shot Andrew a dark look. "Your arse is where you'll land if you say the like again."

"Or you," Andrew returned the threat. Grinning, he leaned against the edge of a trestle table and crossed his arms, insolently. He also made a show of gazing up at the hall's dark, hammer-beamed ceiling.

Light from a torch fell across his face and Sorley almost felt sorry for him.

Andrew still carried a swollen, black eye he'd earned several days earlier when he'd dared to offer flowers to a scribe's daughter. Her brother, a young knight-in-training, walked away with worse bruises. But Andrew's victory was dampened by the cruel whisperings that soon spread through the castle.

Court bastards, while tolerated, should know their place.

It was a truth that rankled.

And one Sorley was not wont to accept.

Setting his jaw, he looked out across the crowded hall, eager to challenge any lordlings or knights' sons who dared to eye him crossly.

None did.

Sorley knew why.

With the King away at Dundonald Castle, one of his most favored residences, the hall had run wild. Loud and unruly, the notables of the land were filling their bellies with rich victuals and too much ale. The feasting had reached a pitch that dulled wits and blurred vision, even robbing some men of their dignity. More than one lofty slumped in a drunken stupor, babbling nonsense. Others sprawled face-first across the tables, heads on their arms as they slept, snoring loudly, oblivious to the pandemonium.

Not averse to taking advantage, Sorley strode into the circle of dancing nobles.

He made straight for the whirling, laughing-eyed temptress, encouraged when she stopped dancing at his approach. That she didn't bother to cover her breasts emboldened him all the more.

Seldom had he seen such perfection.

Her dark, thrusting nipples sent heat flashing through him, setting him like stone. His hands itched to reach for her, to plump and squeeze her full, lush bosom. He burned to touch her nipples, run his thumbs in circles around them, and then pluck them sweetly.

Truth was he wanted to devour her whole.

To that end, he bowed low, giving her his most practiced smile.

"One dance, fair lass." He deepened the smile as he straightened, knew his dimples would flash, delighting her. He held out his hands, confident. "I shall be the most envied lad in the hall."

"Think you?" She lifted a brow. Her tone was cold, her dark eyes chilling as she pulled up her gown, hiding her nakedness. "I say you are Sorley the bastard and greatly mistaken."

She gave him a tight, icy smile. "Be glad the King is away or I'd have him punish you for your impertinence.

"I may yet." She narrowed her eyes, looking at him as if he were a speck of mud on her shoe.

Sorley tried to speak, but words wouldn't come. His throat had closed, his mouth gone dry. The maid tossed her head, shaking back her rippling, raven curls before she sailed away into the throng, leaving him to stare after her.

Mortification sluiced through him.

The hall grayed, blurring around him. A loud buzzing filled his ears and a terrible, flaming heat raced up his neck, branding his cheeks. From a great distance, or so it seemed, he caught a glimpse of Roag, Andrew, and Caelan, gaping at him. The pity on their faces made him want to sink into the floor.

He swallowed hard, his heart hammering in shame.

Never had he been so humiliated.

Worse, he still stood with his hands extended. He couldn't lower his arms. They felt frozen, stiff and immoveable. Everything careened around him. The dancers and strutting pipers, the hurrying servants, and even the castle dogs, they all blended into a great whir, making him dizzy.

He blinked, certain he was about to die, when an angel appeared out of the spinning chaos and came forward to take his outstretched hands.

A hush fell over the hall, a stillness so loud it was deafening. Everyone turned to stare at Sorley and the startling beauty who gripped his hands so demonstratively. As fair and bright as the other lass had been dark, she was the most exquisite maid he'd ever seen. Her large blue eyes sparkled like sapphires. And her hair shone red-gold in the torchlight, her braids falling below her waist. Unquestionably of high birth, she wore amethyst silk and jewels, her delicate rose perfume scenting the air around her.

"I will dance with you." She laced her fingers with his, squeezing lightly. "If it pleases you?"

Sorley nodded, not trusting himself to speak. She looked at him with her great blue eyes, holding his gaze as if partnering him in the dance was the most natural thing for her to do.

He was certain he'd never seen her before.

Her accent told him why.

She spoke with a soft and pleasing lilt, the musical

sweetness of the Highlands flowing in her voice. He also noted that her eyes weren't just blue, but lavender-blue. And despite the brightness of her hair and her fair, creamy skin, she was graced with exceptionally long, black eyelashes. Though still tender in years, likely close to his own age, she already possessed the power to hold any man's heart in the palm of her hand.

His own heart beat wildly, the rest of the hall, the dancers and the bright ring of torches, fading away. Nothing existed except the racing of his pulse and the flame-haired lass with the beautiful eyes, her honeyed voice and dazzling smile.

She lit the hall as if a thousand suns had descended into their midst.

Sorley lifted her hand to his mouth and kissed her palm. He remembered too late that, because she was surely chaste, he should have touched his lips to the air above her knuckles, no more. Yet she didn't pull away. The warmth in her eyes remained, her face even softening as if she'd enjoyed his attentions.

"I am Mirabelle." Her sweet voice made his pulse leap. "My uncle is celebrating this e'en. He—"

"He'll be Murd MacLaren. Your father is Munro, chief of that clan." Sorley should've known. There'd been talk of the MacLaren's fetching daughter. The Highlanders were here because the King had granted Mirabelle's uncle a land charter and pension for his support and retinue service in last year's Anglo-Scottish war.

Her father had claimed his reward the year before.

The King's son and heir, John, had issued the charter, allowing the visiting clansmen to host the night's feasting and entertainments.

It was a reason Sorley wore his new cast-off plaid with such pride this e'en.

He felt drawn to Highlanders.

There was much to be said for men famed to be as fierce,

wild, and rugged as the soaring, mist-drenched hills of their homeland; women prized for their strength and beauty, the fiery passion known to heat a man's blood even on cold, dark nights when chill winds raced through the glens. Sorley had never been to the Highlands, but he'd heard the tales, seen the wonder, and envy, in the eyes of those who had. All claimed no land was more awe-inspiring, no people more proud.

Secretly, he believed his nameless sire was a great Highland chieftain. A man who'd allowed the splendor of his home and the glory of his deeds to swell his head so much that he didn't want the taint of a bastard son to besmirch the grandness of his name.

Sorley glanced toward the dais end of the hall, caught a glimpse of colorful plaid and bold, bearded faces. Men who sat at the high table, laughing loudly as they chinked wine cups with the King's sons.

His father would be such a man.

Someday...

He drew a breath, pushing aside such thoughts. Mirabelle's sparkling eyes, the gleam of her hair, and her light, flowery perfume made it hard to think of anything but her. Especially as she still held his hands, looking pleased to partner him in a dance.

"I have heard men speak of you. They say you are good with a bow. That you won yesterday's competition." Her lilting voice chased the last darkness from his mind. "You are Sorley." She spoke his name as if he were a prince, her praise doing strange things to his insides.

She lifted her chin toward the dancers, just starting a fast and furious Highland reel. "Can you dance to our hill music?"

"Better than anyone here." Sorley flashed his most confident smile and kept it in place when she took his arm, pulling him into the dance.

He'd never reeled in all his days.

But he'd dance a naked jig on a balefire for Mirabelle MacLaren.

Besides, so many revelers crowded the dancing space it was hard to even breathe, much less leap and whirl in a wild Highland reel.

No one would notice his lack of skill.

He saw only Mirabelle.

The scream of the pipes and the thunder of stamping feet made it difficult to talk, but speech wasn't needed for him to know that she liked him. Her sparkling eyes stayed on his and a fine blush colored her high, delicate cheekbones. Her braids swung about her shoulders, the brilliant strands golden in the firelight.

Slender as a wisp, she moved with fluid grace. Her braids began to unravel, her hair spilling loose and lustrous to her waist. Sorley's breath caught, her disarray giving him bold, wicked thoughts. His body heated, and not just from the dance. She laughed as if she knew, her merriment encouraging him. When she spun closer, her pert young breasts brushing his arm, he was sure of it.

"You can dance our reel." She twirled and her hip bumped his, sending a rush of pleasure through him.

His heart swelled. "I can do more."

This night he'd believe he could do anything. Uproot trees singlehandedly, move whole mountains, and swim the deepest, wildest seas. All he *wanted* to do was spend a few moments alone with Mirabelle.

He hoped to kiss her.

But he didn't trust himself to say so.

He did lift his chin toward the shadows of the tower stair. "Have you been up on the eastern battlements?"

"Nae, should I have been?" She followed his gaze. "I've not seen much of the castle except this hall and the ladies' bower."

"Then you've missed something grand." Sorley's smile widened. He raised his voice above the music, secretly proud that he wasn't short of breath. "The best view in the land is to be had from up there. Even your Highland peaks can be seen in the distance.

"Perhaps I can show you?" He'd love nothing more.

"I'd enjoy that." She glanced toward the dais as if she was about to say something else and then thought better of it. Turning back to him, she reached to touch the plaid he'd slung so proudly over his shoulder. "You dance our reel like a true Highlander."

Sorley grinned and swirled her in a circle.

He *was* dancing well. The reel's mad pace came natural to him, the wail of the pipes firing his blood. Something inside him split and cracked wide, freeing a surge of happiness such as he'd never known.

Somewhere in the hall, a Highlander began to sing. His voice was deep and strong, the song full of longing for the heathery hills of his homeland. Sorley took the man's words for a portent. A never-before sense of belonging rose inside him. He could almost see the great hills and wild, cloud-chased skies, smell the peat and broom. Truly moved, he drew Mirabelle close as the other dancers whirled past them. Her light, flowery perfume teased him and her silky hair slid against his arm. The ring of torches flamed bright, casting a reddish glow on the eddying throng. Above them, the hall's smoke-blackened rafters glistened, gleaming like the star-studded heavens. And Sorley danced with the fairest of maids.

He could believe an ancient magic was upon them.

It was a night like no other.

Until the crowd parted and a stern-faced matron sailed over to them, her mouth set in a tight, unsmiling line. A giant, bull-necked Highlander towered behind her, the MacLaren plaid swept boldly across his broad chest and shoulders. A deep scar scored his face, but it was his cold, expressionless stare that chilled Sorley's blood.

"Mirabelle!" The woman grasped Mirabelle's wrist. "So this is where you've been." She gave Sorley a sharp look, her lips compressing even more. "Your father will be livid. To think you—"

"She danced, no more." Sorley put back his shoulders, met the woman's gaze. He'd learned early on to stand against such disapproval, casting off slurs as a dog shakes rain from his fur. "She—"

"She is Lady Mirabelle to you." The woman's voice was like ice. She glanced at the guard, her look significant. "A well-born young lady doesn't—"

"Smile and laugh, my lady?" Sorley angled his head, challengingly. "Enjoy a quick turn at your own Highland reel?"

"You're a bonnie lad." The giant spoke then, coming forward to clamp his hand on Sorley's shoulder. "You'll no' be wanting your face ruined afore you're a man, eh?"

"And you'll be wishing to stay one?" Sorley bent, pulling the dirk from his boot, but the Highlander was faster, grabbing his arm in an iron grip.

Sorley's blade clattered to the floor.

The giant kicked the dirk aside and then released him. He dusted his hands demonstratively. "Think well, lad, before you're next so ambitious." He slid a telling look at Mirabelle. "No good comes o' those who dinnae ken their place."

Sorley bristled, felt heat surging into his cheeks. Even so, he couldn't let Mirabelle see him humiliated. Not twice in one night.

She liked him, he was sure.

Perhaps he'd see her again before the MacLaren party left Stirling. Hoping so, he turned to her, but her expression froze the words on his tongue. All the warmth was gone from her eyes. Her face was as cold and stony as the woman's, her stance rigid as the hulking giant beside her.

She looked at him as she would a stranger, a ragged beggar in the street.

"A good e'en," she offered him, speaking with stiff courtesy.

"That it was not." The old woman sniffed. "I'll hear the meaning of this."

"I wished to dance, that is all." Mirabelle shrugged, flicked at her sleeve. "It is over and done, forgotten."

"And so it shall remain." The old woman jerked her away, pulling her into the crowd, toward the dais where pipers were again strutting, blowing their vigorous tunes as if nothing had happened.

In truth, nothing had.

Except that everything she'd stirred in Sorley withered and died.

He stared after her, a strange buzzing in his ears.

Anger and resentment welled in his chest, chasing the pride and pleasure, and the magic he'd believed had spilled into the hall, casting an enchantment.

How could he have been so foolish?

He wouldn't ever again.

So he assumed his best look of defiance and strode from the dancing space, his shoulders straight, his head held high. He crossed the hall with purpose, winding his way through the crowd until he reached the stair tower. He felt a deep need to visit his special corner of the battlements, so he took the circular steps two at a time, frowning only when he pulled open the door at the top.

A surge of cold air and a swirl of mist greeted him, the night's fog-drenched grayness suiting his mood. He went straight to the battlements' eastern wall, where he braced his hands on the chill, damp stone. This late in summer, the night sky should've gleamed like silvered glass, offering him sweeping views of the broad plain beneath the castle, the winding band of the river, and—he clenched his fists against the uncaring stone of the wall—the distant peaks of the Highlands.

Instead, thick mist spoiled the view, drifting in sheets across the land, blowing in shimmering curtains past the battlements.

Not that he cared.

The Highlands were there, waiting for him, even if he couldn't see them.

They called to him more fiercely than ever.

Because now he knew beyond doubt that he *was* a Highlander.

Weren't they said to never forget a grievance? Knowing it was so, he leaned against the wall, narrowing his eyes to peer through the whirling gray. He fancied he could see the faint outline of hills. He knew they marked the start of a different world, a wondrous place unlike any other, where deep glens beckoned with quiet and cold, clean air. Granite mountains so stark, lonely, and beautiful, it was a physical pain to look upon them.

All that he'd known since he'd first glimpsed them from this, his special corner of the ramparts, a viewing place he had sought again and again, ever since he'd heard a visiting storyteller sing of his misty, heathered home in the hills.

The bard's song had spoken to him. Noticing his awe, the man hauled Sorley onto his broad, plaid-draped shoulders and carried him up to the battlements to see such wonders for himself, if only from afar. Sorley had been all of six, but he'd never forgotten.

Someday he'd find the Highland chieftain who'd sired him.

He'd claim the birthright he'd been denied.

He'd prove his Highland blood by avenging the wrongs done him. Vengeance would be his and it'd be as cold and gray as the mist swirling around him. He'd live for the day and he'd be ready when it came.

Nothing would stop him.

It was more than a matter of reckoning.

It was a point of pride.

Chapter One

✤

Stirling Castle
Summer 1399

Sorley the Hawk slept naked.

His bare-bottomed state was glaringly apparent, even to Lady Mirabelle MacLaren's innocent eyes. She should have known that a man with such an inordinate fondness for pleasures of the flesh would take to his bed unclothed. Still, it was a possibility she should've considered before sneaking into his privy quarters. She hadn't expected him to be in his room so early of an e'en. She'd hoped to catch him unawares, surprising him when he strode inside.

Now she was trapped.

She stood frozen, her heart racing as she glanced around his bedchamber. Even in the dimness, she could tell his quarters were boldly masculine and entirely too sumptuous for an ordinary court bastard. Exquisitely embroidered and richly colored tapestries hung from the walls and the floor was immaculate, the rushes fresh and scented with aromatic herbs. A heavily carved and polished trestle table held the remains of what had surely been a superb repast. Several iron-banded coffers drew her curiosity, making her wonder what treasures they contained. Above all, her eye was drawn to the large curtained bed at the far end of the room.

There, atop the massive four-poster, Sorley was stretched out on his back, one arm folded behind his head.

That he was nude stood without question.

What astonished her was her reaction to seeing him in such an intimate state.

Her mouth had gone dry and her heart beat too rapidly for comfort. She couldn't deny that she found herself strongly attracted to him. Yet to accomplish what she must, she required her wits.

Unfortunately, she also needed Sorley.

Sir John Sinclair, an oily-mannered noble she couldn't abide, was showing interest in her. Worse, he was wooing her father, a man who believed the best in others and didn't always catch the nuances that revealed their true nature. Castle tongue-waggers whispered that Sinclair desired a chaste bride, requiring a suitable wife to appease the King's wish that he live more quietly than was his wont. Mirabelle suspected he'd chosen her as his future consort.

She knew Sorley loathed Sinclair.

And that the bad blood was mutual.

No one was better suited to help her repel Sinclair's advances than Sorley the Hawk.

Time was also of the essence. Mirabelle's father's work at court wouldn't take much longer. As a scholar and herbalist, he'd tirelessly seen to his duties, assisting the royal scribes in deciphering Gaelic texts on healing. Soon, the MacLaren party would return home to the Highlands.

Mirabelle didn't want to remain behind as Sir John's betrothed. For that reason, she summoned all the strength she possessed to remain where she stood. It cost her great effort not to back from the room, disappearing whence she'd come. Harder still was not edging closer to the bed, then angling her head to better see Sorley.

He was magnificent.

Blessedly, the sheet reached to his waist, hiding a certain part of him. The rest of his big, strapping body was shockingly uncovered. Mirabelle's face heated to see the dusting of dark hair on his hard-muscled chest. She felt an irresistible urge to touch him. Well aware that she daren't, she did let her gaze drift over him. Light from an almost-guttered night candle flickered across his skin, revealing a few scars. His thick, shoulder-length hair was as inky-black as she remembered, the glossy strands gleaming in the dimness. Even asleep, he possessed a bold arrogance. Now that her eyes had adjusted to the shadows, she could see from the bulge outlined beneath the bedcovers that his masculinity was equally proud.

The observation made her belly flutter.

Unable to help herself, she let her gaze linger on his slumbering perfection. His darkly handsome face and oh-so-sensual mouth that, if all went well, would soon play expertly over hers, claiming her in passion.

The only problem was she'd rather make her proposition when he was fully clothed.

Confronting him now would only compound her troubles.

So she pressed a hand to her breast and retraced her steps to the door. It stood ajar, the passage beyond beckoning, urging escape. Scarce daring to breathe, she peered from one end of the corridor to the other. Nothing stirred except a cat scurrying along in the darkness and a poorly burning wall sconce that hissed and spit.

Or so she thought until two chattering laundresses sailed around a corner, their arms loaded with bed linens. A small lad followed in their wake, carrying a wicker basket brimming with candles.

They were heading her way.

"Botheration!" She felt a jolt of panic.

Nipping back into Sorley's bedchamber, she closed the door.

It fell into place with a distinct *knick*.

Before she could catch her breath, Sorley was behind her, gripping her shoulders with firm, strong fingers. He lowered his head, nuzzling her neck, his mouth brushing over her skin. She bit her lip as he slid his hands down her arms, pulling her back against him.

He was still naked.

She could feel the hot, hard length of him pressing into her.

Almost as bad, he was now rubbing his face in her hair, nipping her ear. His warm breath sent shivers rippling through her.

She gasped, her heart thundering.

"Sweet minx, I didnae expect a visitor this night." He chuckled and closed his hands more firmly around her wrists. "Followed me from the Red Lion, did you?"

"To be sure, I didn't!" Mirabelle found her tongue at his mention of the notorious tavern, an ill-famed place frequented by rogues and light-skirts. She jerked free, whirling to face him. "Nor am I a minx. I'm—"

"You are Lady Mirabelle." His voice chilled, his eyes narrowing as he looked her up and down. He stepped back, folding his arms.

He made no move to cover his nakedness.

"I'd heard you were at court." His gaze held hers, his face an unreadable mask. "Indeed, I've seen you in the hall a time or two. I didn't think to find you here, in my bedchamber."

"Neither did I." Her chin came up. "I lost my way."

"You're also a terrible liar." He angled his head, studying her. "You wouldn't be here without a reason. My quarters are no place for a lady." A corner of his mouth hitched up in a smile that didn't meet his eyes. "So tell me, to what do I owe the honor?"

Mirabelle drew a tight breath, the words lodging in her throat. The explanation, her carefully crafted plea for help, had slipped her mind. Vanishing as if she hadn't spent hours, even days and nights, practicing everything she'd meant to say to him.

"Sir, you're unclothed." Those words came easily. They also caused her cheeks to flame.

"So I am." He glanced down, seemingly unconcerned. Turning, he took a plaid and a shirt off a peg on the wall, donning both with a slow, lazy grace that embarrassed her almost as much as his nakedness.

"Now that I'm decent"—he placed himself between her and the door, crossing his arms again—"I'd know why you're here."

"I told you—"

"You told me a falsehood. I'd hear the truth."

Mirabelle wanted to sink into the floor. Unfortunately, such an escape wasn't possible, and as she prided herself on being of a practical nature, she kept her head raised and flicked a speck of lint from her sleeve. Her mind raced, seeking a plausible explanation. It came to her when the wind whistled past the long windows, the sound almost like the keening cry of a woman.

"I thought to see the castle's pink lady." She didn't turn a hair mentioning the ghost. Everyone knew she existed. Believed the wife of a man killed when England's Edward I captured the castle nearly a hundred years before, the poor woman was rumored to be beautiful, her luminous gown a lovely shade of rose.

Mirabelle had quite forgotten about her until now.

But she did believe in bogles.

Her own home, Knocking Tower, abounded with spirits. She'd even encountered a few. Not a one of them had disquieted her as much as the man now standing before her, his arms still folded and the most annoying look on his darkly rugged face.

He was entirely too virile.

He also had proved a much greater threat than any ghost.

"The pink lady walks the courtyard, last I heard." Sorley spoke with the masculine triumph of a man sure he knew better than the gullible female before him. His tone left no doubt that he didn't believe in the bogle. "You would not have met her in my privy chambers.

"Come, I'll show you where folk claim she prowls." He wrapped his hand around her wrist and led her across the room to one of the tall, arch-topped windows. "Look down into the bailey. Tell me if you see her."

"I won't. See her, I mean." Mirabelle tried to ignore how her skin tingled beneath his touch. "She's elusive. She doesn't appear simply because one peers out a window."

"Even so, I'd hear what you see." He stepped closer, so near the air around her filled with his scent.

Mirabelle set her lips in a tight, irritated line, doing her best not to notice how delicious he smelled. It was a bold, provocative mix of wool and leather, pure man and something exotic, perhaps sandalwood, the whole laced with a trace of peat smoke. Entirely too beguiling, the heady blend made her pulse race.

Furious that was so, she straightened her back, determined to focus on anything but him.

She failed miserably.

Awareness of him sped through her; a cascade of warm, tingly sensations that weakened her knees and warmed unmentionable places. His near-naked proximity also made it impossible to think. Never had she been in such a compromisingly intimate situation. She certainly hadn't experienced the like with a man so brazen, so devilishly attractive.

As if he knew she was uncomfortable, he placed his hand at the small of her back, urging her closer to the broad stone ledge of the window. "I'd have your answer, Lady Mirabelle. I am no' a patient man."

"Very well." Mirabelle leaned forward, pretending to

study the darkened courtyard below. A hard rain was falling and the bailey stood empty, the cobbles gleaming wetly.
Torches burned in the sheltered arcade circling the large,
open space. A few guards, spearmen, huddled in a corner
where a small brazier cast a red glow against the wall of a
pillared walkway. Nothing else stirred.

She drew a tight breath, wishing she hadn't mentioned
the ghost.

She turned to face her tormentor. "The pink lady is not
down there."

"I didnae expect she would be, prowling—"

"I'm sure she drifts or hovers." Mirabelle held his gaze.
"She's had her heart torn and is searching for her husband.
Such a soul wouldn't—"

"She wouldn't drift, hover, or prowl, because she isn't
real." He came closer, gripping her chin and tilting her face
upward. "The pink lady's existence is as unlikely as a flesh-
and-blood lady letting herself into my bedchamber. Even
women who are not of gentle birth only enter this room at
my invitation." He looked at her, his gaze steady and penetrating. "I do not recall extending such an offer to you.

"So I'll ask again." He slid his thumb over the corner of
her mouth, then along the curve of her bottom lip. "Why are
you here?"

Mirabelle shivered. She didn't know if it was because
of the way he was looking at her or if her body was simply
reacting to his touch.

Without question, he was the most dangerously handsome man at court.

She suspected in all the land.

He was also the man most suited to aid her.

So she stepped back, summoning all her courage. "You
know women well," she owned, her heartbeat quickening. "I
do have a reason for this visit. It has nothing to do with the
castle ghost."

"So we near the truth at last." He sounded amused. "I'll admit I am curious."

"I have a business arrangement for you." She couldn't believe the steadiness of her voice.

He arched a brow. "Now I am even more intrigued."

"You shouldn't be." She made a sweeping gesture with her hand, taking in his room in all its opulence. "You are known as a man of many skills, greatly favored at court. I am in need of one of your talents."

"Indeed?" He narrowed his eyes, no longer bemused. "And what might that be?"

"I require your amatory skills." Mirabelle kept her chin raised. "I want you to ruin me."

"Lady, I surely didn't hear you clearly." Sorley held her gaze, hoping his cold tone and steady stare would unnerve her into retracting her ridiculous request. "You wish me to despoil you?"

"Take my virtue, yes." She didn't turn a hair. Far from looking embarrassed, her lovely lavender-blue eyes sparked with challenge and determination. "I shall pay you well for your trouble."

Sorley almost choked.

He did his best to keep his jaw off the floor. It wasn't easy, so he went to the door, crossing his bedchamber in long, swift strides. He didn't want her to see his shock. Worse, how tempted he was to accept her offer. Not that he'd take coin for such pleasure. A shame he'd have to decline. Even one such as he had honor, his own brand of it, anyway.

Still, he was stunned. Her suggestion was the last thing he'd expected.

It was outrageous.

He could find no words.

Certain the world had run mad, he unlatched the door, flinging it wide. With surprising agility, Lady Mirabelle fair flew across the room and nipped around him, closing the door before he could stop her.

"A word is all I ask of you." She put out a hand to touch his chest. "Only that, and—"

"Do you believe maidens are ruined by words?"

"I meant just now, as well you know. Later..." She lowered her hand, giving him a look that was much too provocative for a virgin. "You will be generously recompensed."

"So you said." Sorley didn't say how much that offended him.

He also wished he could tear his gaze from her.

Regrettably, he couldn't.

A softly burning wall sconce limned her in glowing golden light, making her look like an angel. Her rose scent drifted about her, bewitching him now as it'd done so many years before. The heady fragrance was hers alone, an annoying intoxication he remembered well. A temptation he was determined to never fall prey to again.

He frowned. "I dinnae want or need your coin. I might be baseborn, but I'm no' a man in need of funds. And"—he let his gaze drop to her breasts, her hips—"the only trouble I wish is the kind I make myself. For naught in all broad Scotland would I touch you, a gently born lady."

A hint of color bloomed on her face. "Do not think I came here lightly." She drew a breath, her shoulders going back as she struggled to keep her composure. "It is not every day that a woman seeks to blacken her reputation."

"You've already damaged your good name by coming here, assuming someone might have seen you."

"No one did."

"Think you?" Sorley cocked a brow. "Are you so well-practiced at sneaking through the night, then? How many times have you crept down empty corridors, slipping into a man's bedchamber?"

"Never before, but—"

"You'll no' do the like again, if you're wise." Reaching around her, Sorley cracked the door and peered into the darkened passage. Seeing no one, he turned back to her, needing her gone before he reconsidered his options. An irritating twitch at his loins was making a damned persuasive argument.

He was also tempted simply because her remarkable eyes held nary a flicker of recognition.

She'd forgotten him.

And the knowledge annoyed him almost as much as the slight she'd shown him at her uncle's celebratory feast all those years ago.

The memory dashed the pleasurable stirrings at his groin.

With slow deliberation, he shut the door and leaned back against its solid, unyielding wood. He crossed his ankles and folded his arms, letting his stance show her that he was prepared to remain there until he had the answers he desired. He was a stubborn man.

Nor did he tire easily.

"So-o-o"—he gave her a slow smile, careful not to let it reach his eyes—"I'd hear why you came to me with such a fool request."

"Seeing you now, sir," she returned, her own voice as chilly, "I almost regret my folly."

"You should." He studied her face, feeling a scowl darken his own. If anything, she was even more fetching than he remembered. Her silky red-gold hair gleamed in the light of the wall sconce and her sparkling eyes were still the widest, loveliest he'd ever seen. Her small, upturned nose gave her an irksome air of innocence, while her mouth, so full and lush...

The pestiferous twitch at his loins returned.

He willed the stirrings away before she noticed and took advantage.

Praise the gods she wore a cloak that only hinted at the ripeness of her womanly curves.

She was no longer a girl.

And for sure, he wasn't a cocky, full-of-himself lad.

"You haven't answered me." He put just enough arrogance into his tone to prove it.

Her chin came up again, showing her own mettle. "I say I did. I am troubled by a matter of some delicacy and require a man's aid in—"

"Creating a scandal that will soil you," Sorley finished for her.

To her credit, she blushed. "It could be put that way, yes."

"That I understand." He knew exactly what her wish entailed. "I'd know why you'd give me such an honor?"

"Because it is rumored you are one of the Fenris Guards." She didn't blink. "Men the King employs when his noble, more fastidious warriors fail him." She tilted her head, her gaze bold. "Word is men of the Fenris will do anything. They are known to be fearless. Formidable fighters who"— her eyes took on an entirely too determined glint—"are also known for their legendary skill at seducing women."

Sorley laughed. "The Fenris *are* legend, my lady. Such men dinnae exist."

"I have heard you are one of them."

"All I am is a bastard. Though"—he flashed his most roguish smile—"I'll admit I enjoy tumbling comely, willing lasses. That includes ladies of quality so long as they are wed or widowed and looking for mutual pleasure. I do not lie with virgins."

"You speak bluntly." She glanced aside, the wall sconce revealing the high color blooming on her cheeks.

"I told you the truth, no more."

He was also damned glad to have shocked her. In his experience, just a hint of a man's baser nature was enough to send ladies running. Their fear of carnality filled their innocent minds, chasing all else. She wouldn't mention the Fenris again. And when he discovered who'd dared to breathe his name in connection with the band of secret warriors, there'd be hell to pay.

"Then I shall do the same." She looked back at him, now calm. "You spoke true and so you deserve to hear my fullest reasons." Her head high, she went back to the window arch across the room. When she turned to look at him, she might as well have kicked him in the gut.

Rarely had he seen a woman more bent on having her way.

Regrettably, he also hadn't ever gazed upon a female he found more desirable.

She clearly knew it, and she meant to take advantage.

Proving it, she moved to the small oaken table by the window where a ewer of finest wine and a jug of excellent heather ale waited almost conspiratorially amidst the remains of his evening repast. Equally annoying, as he truly did enjoy entertaining amiable women in his quarters, a half-score of ale cups and wine chalices stood at the ready, each one gleaming softly in the candlelight.

"You'll surely join me?" She glanced at him as she lifted the ewer, pouring two measures of wine. When he didn't move to accept her offering, she set his chalice on the table. Her gaze locking on his, she took a long, slow sip of the strong Rhenish wine.

"I think no'." Sorley frowned and pushed away from the door. "Drinking my wine is no' telling me why you're here, seeking a man to—" He snapped his mouth shut, his scowl deepening when he was unable to finish the fool sentence.

He did start pacing, taking care not to stride too near to her and the cloud of disturbingly enchanting rose perfume that wafted about her.

"Not any man." She touched the chalice to her lips, sipping slowly, provocatively. "I wish your aid, no one else's."

"Any man could perform such a deed." Sorley glared at her.

"Could, I certainly agree. But would they? I believe not." She set down the wine chalice. "Most men at court would decline out of respect for my father. Those of less noble birth would refuse because they'd fear the repercussions. My sire is a scholar, not a fighting man, but he employs a garrison of formidable warriors."

"I see." Sorley did, and her explanation riled him unreasonably. "You chose me because I'm known no' to stand in awe of my betters. And"—he couldn't keep the anger from his voice—"because it's rumored I'm wild and crazed enough to fear no man.

"Lastly, for the reason you already stated." He crossed to the table and tossed back the wine he'd refused. Setting down the empty chalice, he deliberately let his gaze slide over her from head to toe. "Everyone at court is aware of my appetite for comely women."

"Your appreciation of ladies was a consideration." She held his gaze, not flinching.

"I said women, no' ladies. There is a difference."

"I know that very well."

Sorley studied her with narrowed eyes. "Yet you wish to explore why that is so?"

"Would I be here otherwise?" She angled her head, her gaze as sharp as his. "I think not."

"I say you dinnae ken what you're asking." His temper fraying, Sorley stepped closer and braced his arms on either side of her. He splayed his hands against the wall so she was caught between him and a colorful unicorn tapestry. "Sweet lass, I am no' a weak-wristed, embroidered tunic-wearing courtier. A passionless man who likely beds his wife beneath the coverlet, all candles snuffed. If you had even the slightest idea of what it's like to couple with a man like me, you'd run screaming from this room."

Her chin came up. "I never scream. Nor do I cry. Not even when I wish I could."

On her words, Sorley felt like an arse.

But his pride cut deeper.

So he leaned in, wishing his every breath wasn't laced with her intoxicating rose scent. He touched his lips to the curve of her neck, nipped lightly. "I could make you cry out in pleasure, Lady Mirabelle.

"A pity I have no desire to do so." He stepped back, folded his arms. "I learned long ago that dallying with highborn lasses brings naught but grief."

Rather than color with indignation and sail from his room as he'd expected her to do, she simply lifted her hands to the jeweled clasp of her cloak and undid the pin so that her mantle fell open to reveal the outrageously provocative gown she wore beneath.

Surely designed to singe a man's eyes, the raiment's rich, emerald silk clung to her every dip and curve. Threads of deep bronze were woven into the fabric, an intricate pattern that glittered in the firelight. Her glossy red-gold hair shone to equal advantage, annoyingly lustrous against the jeweled tones of her dress. Worse, her bodice dipped low, offering tantalizing glimpses of her creamy skin and full, round breasts. A braided belt of golden cord circled her slim waist, the tasseled ends dangling suggestively near a very feminine place Sorley did not want to notice. More gold glittered along the delicate border edging the top of the gown, drawing his attention back to her lush bosom.

She looked like a living flame.

And damn if he didn't feel a powerful urge to be burned to a crisp.

Instead, he frowned, ignoring the heat spearing straight to the swelling hardness he was sure she could see.

Secretly, he now hoped she did.

He was that angry.

For truth, he could see the top crescents of her nipples! They were a lovely pink and puckered, peeking up above her bodice's gold-edged border.

"I'll no' deny you're lovely, my lady." He could hardly

speak. "Though along with erroneous judgment, I suspect your hearing is no' what it should be. I told you I am no' the man to fulfill your request."

"I did not err in coming here. You are the only man who can help me."

"You will easily find another." Sorley turned his back on her to stare out into the cold, wet night. He didn't like the way just looking at her did funny things to his chest. Elsewhere, he was setting like granite, curse the lass. "You found your way in here. You can leave by the same door."

"I thought you were a man who courts danger." She joined him at the window. "Was I mistaken? Are you not as daring as everyone says?"

"I am that and more, sweetness. What I am no', is a fool. And I'm no' of a mind to make myself one by tearing that fine gown off of you and initiating you in the pleasures of carnal passion.

"I'll leave that honor to a man less wise." He fixed his gaze on the misty drizzle, the darkly gleaming cobbles of the bailey far below. "There's nothing you can say to sway me otherwise."

"Not even if I told you helping me would enrage John Sinclair?"

Sorley stiffened, the name chilling his innards. He closed his eyes and took a long breath of the cold, damp air. Lady Mirabelle's mention of the much-lauded, sneakily treacherous noble struck him like a fist in the ribs.

Sinclair was his greatest enemy.

Even if the dastard didn't know Sorley was aware of his crimes. That one of the innocent young bastard women he'd once raped and tormented had been a lass Sorley loved as strongly as if she'd been his sister. Now she was no more and hadn't been for many years. The courtier's twisted pleasures had caused her to drown herself, ending her shame in the cold waters of the River Forth.

It was a death Sorley meant to avenge.

He was only waiting for the best opportunity.

"I see I guessed rightly." Lady Mirabelle touched his arm. "You do not care for Sir John?"

"There are some who dinnae admire the man. I am one of them, aye." Sorley tamped down the revulsion surging through him. He turned to meet Mirabelle's gaze. "What does he have to do with you?"

Sorley had a good idea, but wanted to hear the words from her.

"He's been making overtures." She spoke plainly. "Enough so that I believe he intends to ask for my hand. As my father is"—she paused, drew a tight breath—"more accustomed to peering at his precious books than into the character of men, I fear he will accept such an offer. I am determined to avoid his bid at all costs."

"So that is the way of it." Sorley now understood why she wanted to be rid of her virginity. "You are hoping Sinclair will no' want soiled goods?"

"I am certain he will not." She looked up at him from beneath thick, surprisingly dark lashes.

"There are many ladies at court who welcome his interest." Sorley wished it wasn't true. "The King has aye held him in high esteem."

"With all respect, the King is a Lowlander. I am Highland born and bred." She lifted her chin, her pride unmistakable. "With some exceptions"—she blushed, clearly thinking of her scholarly sire—"we are not easily fooled. I also put out discreet enquiries."

"Many women wouldn't have bothered." Sorley went back to the table, helping himself to another measure of wine. "They see only—"

"I am not 'other women.' I am myself, always." She followed him across the room, boldly putting herself in his path when he would've started pacing again. "I am not blinded by golden torques and beringed fingers, raiments adorned with jewels.

"Nor do I care for arrogance." She put her hands on her hips, her determination and wit beginning to delight him as much as her other, more obvious charms. "I do not trust Sir John's smile. I'm also not fond of his eyes.

"Such things are more telling than words." She flipped back her hair. "That is why I asked a trusted servant to befriend those working in the castle kitchens. Such people often know more about a person's true nature than anyone sitting at the high table."

"Is that so?"

"I believe you know that it is."

"Indeed, I do." Sorley squelched the smile tugging at his lips.

The last thing he wanted was for her to guess how much he admired her good sense. Most ladies at court fawned all over Sir John Sinclair.

It scarce mattered that the noble's underhanded dealings and treachery had cost him lands and wealth. Or that he'd also lost esteem in the eyes of a few. Those worthies who looked beyond Sinclair's slick, oiled hair and handsome face; the shining mail and lavish clothes he favored. Somehow he managed to dress himself extravagantly even when reputed to have lost much of his coin.

Despite it all, he stayed within the bounds allowed him, craftily avoiding royal wrath.

By comparison, Sorley wasn't half as skilled at self-preservation.

He rubbed the back of his neck, uncomfortably aware that he couldn't possibly keep hiding how appealing he found Lady Mirabelle.

He wanted to despise her.

As if she sensed his approaching capitulation, she came forward, her bewitching perfume floating with her. The fragrance swirled about him, teasing and tempting him, the delicate rose scent forming a trap more inescapable than bars of hot-forged iron.

"So you agree?" She stopped right before him, so near he couldn't breathe.

"I share your opinion of Sinclair." He regretted the words as soon as they left his mouth.

She pounced, the flare of hope in her eyes almost persuading him. "If he believes I am no longer—"

"Sweet lass, I regret spoiling your plans, but they won't work. No' with Sinclair." His voice hardened just thinking of the man. "A woman's purity matters naught to him. He isn't a fastidious sort. No' in that regard."

"Perhaps not," she agreed. "But he is fiercely proud."

"No' that proud." Sorley let his gaze again dip to her breasts. Looking up again, he smoothed the backs of his fingers down her cheek, brushed his thumb over the corner of her lips. "If he wants you, which isn't surprising, he'll no' leave you be until he's had you.

"And there'll be hell to pay if you resist him." Sorley knew it well. "John Sinclair is no' a man you'd wish to rile, my lady."

"If you help me, that won't be necessary."

"Have you Heiland bog cotton in your ears, lass? Sinclair won't care a whit if you're soiled or pure. Not that lecherous bastard."

To Sorley's surprise, she glanced aside, color once again blooming on her cheeks. When she looked back at him, he could almost feel the embarrassment rolling off her. But she stood tall, her shoulders straight and her head raised. Whatever her faults—and he knew she had them—her courage delighted and fascinated him.

She moistened her lips. "My servant also asked around about you."

Sorley's brow went up. "Is that so?"

"It was necessary." She held his gaze, her voice strong. "I learned there's bad blood between you and Sir John. If you help me, you'd benefit as well."

Sorley almost choked. "Any man would enjoy taking you to his bed."

He just wasn't that man.

"Aside from the obvious"—he gripped her chin, his gaze fierce—"how would such an association favor me?"

"It is known at court that Sir John reviles you as much as you dislike him." She spoke as if she'd rehearsed her arguments. "He considers any woman touched by you as tainted goods. They are no longer worth his esteem.

"You've never been in a position to challenge him before his peers." She looked at him with those sparkling eyes, speaking easily of his lowly birth. "Now you have the chance to thwart him, spoiling his plans."

For a heartbeat, Sorley was tempted.

Greatly so.

But he knew Sinclair too well.

So he went to the door, setting his hand on the latch. "Sir John's fury would be terrible, my lady. I dinnae care for myself, but he would—"

"He won't lay a hand on me." She joined him at the door, touched his elbow. "I'll be home to Knocking Tower before he'd have the chance. Besides"—she gave him a smile that went straight to his heart, almost convincing him—"the Highlands are no place for a Lowland noble. He wouldn't find me there if he tried.

"So, please…" She squeezed his arm. "Will you not agree to help me?"

"I will consider it." He wouldn't, but she needn't know that. "Meet me in the castle chapel tomorrow e'en and I'll give you my answer. If anyone questions you, you can say you're hoping to catch a glimpse of the pink lady. That's where she is most frequently seen."

"I will be there." She lifted on her toes and kissed his cheek. "Thank you."

"I've no' yet agreed." He was determined to say no.

Placing a hand on the small of her back, he urged her out the door. Once it was closed again, he leaned his back against the wood, a smile curving his lips. Perhaps there was a way he could assist her and scratch an itch that had plagued him for years.

Sometimes the gods did favor a man, and who was he to refuse their gifts?

Pushing away from the door, he went to the window and braced his hands on the cold, damp stone of the ledge. As if the fates truly were tempting him, he was in time to see Lady Mirabelle crossing the bailey. A thin drizzle still fell and an enormous moon drifted in and out of the clouds. Wind blew sheets of mist across the courtyard, but Mirabelle strode through the rain as if she was made for such weather.

His smile deepened as he watched her.

She paused before the sheltered arcade on the far side of the bailey and tipped back her head as if she savored the misty damp on her face. Sorley's pulse quickened, a whirl of heated images filling his mind. In his experience, women who appreciated rough weather were equally wild and passionate in a man's arms.

He'd enjoy discovering if the same was true of Lady Mirabelle.

His blood ran hot at the thought, pure masculine anticipation surging through him as she disappeared into the shadows of the arcade. Rarely had a woman roused such an intense response in him. And never had he been more inclined to ignore such yearnings.

What a shame he knew he wouldn't.

Chapter Two

❧

The rain had stopped by the time Sorley wakened early the next morning. Through his window arch he could see a clear gray sky and a scattering of stars. Wind howled round the tower and the predawn air had turned so cold he almost expected to find a dusting of frost on the bailey cobbles. Not that he was eager to leave the warmth of his bed and trudge across the room to confirm his suspicions. Doing so would require braving a floor that rolled like waves on the sea and suffering the sight of walls that appeared to breathe.

Even so, he pushed up on his elbows to glare at the toppled ewer of wine lying on the floor rushes in the middle of his bedchamber.

It swam in and out of view, as did the equally empty ale jug on the table.

In truth, there were a few other discarded ale and wine vessels littering the quarters he usually kept as tidy as possible.

He knew because he'd downed the contents of each one.

Now he was paying for his folly.

Rarely had his head pained him so greatly.

"Devil take the lass," he snarled the curse, the effort only worsening the thunder at his temples. He glowered into his room's dark and chilly shadows, furious he'd felt such a need to banish certain images from his mind. But what man could find sleep when the memory of Lady Mirabelle's pert nipples wouldn't give him any peace?

Praise be he'd only glimpsed their puckered upper crests.

Had he seen more . . .

He pulled a hand down over his face, not wanting to imagine. Never before had a woman driven him to such madness. His head pounded, he felt queasy, and he doubted if he had the strength to crawl from his bed, much less stand and face the morning.

And wasn't this the worst day to find himself in such a state?

Duty called. Fenris business he'd been tending for ages and with the intricate care required of one of his sort. Bringing down any man for shady, villainous maneuvers was aye a pleasure. But when the blackguard counted himself among the highest in the land, such outlawry had to be handled with especial caution. In this case, severity, the Fenris having been urged to stretch punishment to the farthest reach of their efficiency.

And few Fenris were as hardened, proud, and skilled as Sorley.

Never yet had he disappointed his King.

He wouldn't now either.

So he bit back a groan, threw aside the bed covers, and pushed to his feet. The room careened around him, but he grumbled his way across the rushes to the one ewer he hadn't touched. Feeling queasy, he bent over his wash basin and poured the jug's icy water onto his head.

"Satan's arse!" Spluttering, he straightened and grabbed a drying cloth, rubbing briskly at his drenched hair and aching eyes.

The shock helped some, but the room still spun.

He quirked a small smile on noting that, despite his wretched condition, he'd remembered to place his weapons by the door before he'd slept.

When he reached his destination, a hard and rough hamlet on the River Forth, near to the ruined Abbey of St. Mary, he'd have need of his sword and dirk. For good measure, he'd even added a broad-bladed war ax. He eyed the arms now as he dragged on his clothes, having the greatest struggle with his tall, soft-leathered journeying-boots. The truth was, as foul as he felt, he might forgo weapons and use his bare hands to have done with the miscreant known to be sharing the King's secrets with the English enemy.

Relishing the possibility, he somehow managed to tug on his boots, buckle his sword-belt low about his hips, and even stuff a ratty, moth-eaten pilgrim's cloak into a large leather satchel. His war ax followed. A man with a sword at his hip wasn't an unusual sight about Stirling, but a fighting ax would draw unwanted attention.

He'd retrieve the weapon when he donned the wayfarer's mantle. For now, all he needed was to rid himself of the pain ripping through his head.

The wretched pounding was worse than a hammer on a forge anvil.

Blessedly, he knew a cure.

Frowning because a scowl also helped soothe a raging ale-head, he slung the leather pouch over his shoulder and left his room, hoping the wall torches in the corridor weren't burning too brightly.

The gods were kind.

Most of the passage was steeped in darkness. Only a few sconces flickered, their light too feeble to stab his hurting eyes.

Grateful for such small mercies, he strode down the corridor and then took the winding stair up to the battlements.

When he reached the top and opened the door, a blast of chill air hit him. The cold stung his eyes and helped clear his aching, ale-fuzzed head. Knowing the view from his special corner of the ramparts would do the rest, giving him the strength he needed to start his day, he stepped into the icy wind and turned toward the eastern wall.

He stopped short after only a few steps.

Lady Mirabelle stood near his favorite spot, her lovely face turned to the wind, her red-gold hair tumbling loose about her shoulders.

"By all that's holy," Sorley swore, glaring at her as the pain in his head returned with a vengeance.

"You!" She spun about at once, her eyes flying wide. "What are you doing here so early of a morn?"

"I might ask the same of you." Sorley strolled over to her, retreat no longer an option. "Myself, I greet each new day up here. The brisk, clean air and the view"—he swung out an arm, indicating the broad spread of rich farmland, misty hills, and the distant peaks of the Highlands—"is one of the few pleasures I allow myself."

Her cheeks colored most becomingly on the word *pleasures*.

Selfishly pleased to have unsettled her, Sorley stepped around her and braced his hands on a merlon. He fixed his gaze on the winding path of the river, knowing she'd join him.

When she did, he glanced at her. "Truth is, sweetness, I've been visiting this viewpoint nearly every morn since I was all of six years. How is it that you, a visitor to the castle, would seek such an out-of-the-way spot?" He held her gaze, hoping to see a flash of guilt.

Hadn't he once offered to bring her here?

All those long years ago when she'd come to Stirling with her father and her uncle?

If she remembered, she showed no sign.

Her forgetfulness added a sharp jab of annoyance to the ills already plaguing him that morning.

"I always miss the hills when I'm away." She turned her gaze back to the far-off mountains that were just beginning to glow with hints of the coming dawn. "Most of all, I yearn for my home, Knocking Tower. Someone at the high table yestere'en mentioned one can see clear to the Highlands from up here. I wanted to look."

"The view is exceptional this morn." Sorley put just enough suggestiveness into his tone to rattle her. He also slanted her a glance that left no doubt to his meaning.

When her blush deepened, he almost regretted the taunt, but it bothered him more than it should that she had no recollection of their youthful encounter.

She brought out the worst in him.

So much so that he straightened, turning away from the wall to glance boldly down the length of her body and back up again. He took special delight in allowing his gaze to linger where she clutched her cloak together over the swell of her luscious breasts.

Not dressed as splendidly as the night before, she wore a simple mantle of deep blue, its edges fluttering in the wind to reveal a plain gown of the same hue beneath. Her hair shone, silky and lustrous in the pale morning sun. The shining strands minded him of richly hued autumn leaves. And weren't her great blue eyes bright, the high color on her cheekbones flattering, and—something inside him twisted with annoyance—her ripe lips as red as rowan berries? He was certain no fairer maid walked the land.

Despite all reason, he wanted to devour her whole.

Her chin came up as if she knew. "You are not looking at the view."

"Aye, I am." He gave her a slow, lazy smile. "I've ne'er seen aught finer."

A slight lifting of her brow indicated she knew exactly

what he meant. "If that is so, are you now willing to help me?"

"You'll have my answer this e'en in the chapel, as we agreed." He cupped her cheek in one hand, unable to resist. "As yet, I'm undecided."

It was a bald-faced lie.

Regrettably, the hammering in his head and her ability to scatter his wits drove him to share his misery. He couldn't tamp down the powerful urge to unsettle her as much as she did him.

"Then I shall hope you decide in my favor." She looked up at him, speaking as calmly as if she'd commented on the weather and not something as scandalous as her wish for him to deflower her.

He almost told her the truth; that he'd enjoy nothing more, taking great pleasure in the deed. Sakes, even with the cold morning wind racing over the battlements, he could almost feel the heat of her as if she were already in his arms.

Somehow his fingers went to her hair, touching glossy strands as if the devil himself wouldn't allow him to lower this hand. In truth, the fiend had nothing to do with his lack of willpower. It was her. She was simply breathtaking in the soft morning light.

He frowned, not wanting her to guess how fetching he found her. "Lady, I'd have thought a good night's sleep would put such nonsense from your mind."

"To me, the matter is most serious." Annoyance flickered over her face. "Will you not even consider it?"

He'd thought of nothing else since he'd wakened to find her in his bedchamber.

A truth he was not about to share with her.

"I make no promises." His tone was harsher than he'd have wished, but she rode him like a sharp-clawed, ring-tailed she-devil.

Nae, a vixen of the very kind he sought to avoid at all costs.

She was a cunning and devious minx, brazen, provocative, and entirely too alluring. She was also a lady of good breeding, her lineage beyond question, her virginity equally so.

He stepped away from her at last, leaning against the wall with all the casualness he could muster. He crossed his arms, his mind racing for a way to be rid of her. A look, a phrase, anything he could avail himself of that would send her fleeing from the ramparts, away from his special place. Above all, out of his sight.

"So-o-o, sweetness…" He looked at her with hooded eyes, putting just enough arrogance into his tone to rile her. "Did you hope to catch a glimpse of the pink lady up here? Or were you truly only after gazing toward your distant homeland? If you're pining so fiercely for the hills, surely you can persuade your father to take you back to Knocking Tower?"

"Where are you heading this fine morn?" Ignoring his questions, she glanced pointedly at the bulky leather pouch he'd left beside the stair tower door. When she looked at him again, she angled her head, her gaze challenging. "Can it be you're off to visit ladies, pink or otherwise?"

"I'm on my way to the Red Lion." He spoke true, just not mentioning that he intended to pay a call at the popular tavern not this morning, but much later, after he'd met with her in the chapel. He meant to slake his need for her with the comeliest, most wanton joy woman tending her trade at the Red Lion that night.

Only so, by thoroughly taking the edge off his raging desire for Lady Mirabelle, could he keep to the offer he intended to make her.

She glanced again at his travel pouch. "You must have a most expensive lady in mind if you need such a large bag to carry her payment."

"I ne'er have need of coin for such delights." He pushed away from the wall, guilt pinching him when his words put a deep flush on her face.

A pity his irritation weighed more than shame for speaking so plainly. "If you'd hear the right of it, many are the bonnie lasses who come freely to my bed. Others, such as your own lovely self, offer recompense for my attentions.

"No' that I accept such boons." He hooked his thumbs in his sword-belt, well aware he'd gone too far but unable to curb his tongue.

She annoyed him that greatly.

So he leaned in, giving her a wink. "The ladies' *favor* is payment enough."

Her eyes rounded. "You, sir, are insufferable."

"So many say." He flashed his most roguish smile. "But you err in calling me sir. Surely you've not forgotten my nameless birth?"

"I've forgotten nothing." Her temper flaring, she narrowed her gaze at him.

Sorley shrugged, feigning indifference.

In truth, she made him damned uncomfortable.

What a shame that even now, aware of her perfidy as he was, just standing so close to her hit him like a punch to the gut. She made him feel four and ten summers again, young and vulnerable. He didn't like the feeling. Yet for some inexplicable reason, he couldn't summon the will to turn and leave her standing alone, to stroll away with just enough swagger to put another maidenly flush on her face. He did brace a hand on the rampart wall, careful to keep his gaze on the distant hills.

"If you've forgotten nothing, fair lady,"—he spoke without looking at her—"you'll remember from last night that I am no' a man to be taken off guard. If you thought to sway my decision by waiting for me up here—"

"I did not come here to meet with you." The truth in her denial was vexing.

"So you did hope to see the pink lady?" Sorley glanced at her, cocking a brow. "No' wish to corner a lowly court bastard, use your womanly wiles to persuade him to do your biding?" He reached to trace a finger along the softness of her cheek. "And here I thought—"

"You thought wrong." She captured his wrist, lowering his hand before he could comb his fingers through her hair as he'd been about to do.

Instead, he set his jaw, struggled to keep his arms at his sides. He should be glad for her prickliness. Touching her silken tresses would've distracted him, provoking him beyond measure.

Mirabelle's heart hammered. His caress fuzzed her mind, chasing her wits and sending the most distracting tingles all through her. She couldn't think with his hands on her. His proximity was trying enough, his brazen masculinity and air of roguishness appealing to her in ways she shouldn't allow.

He was much too good-looking, his gaze too hot and knowing. Even the way he moved revealed how powerfully virile he was, how strong and able. In his arms, a woman would melt, losing all control, and gladly so. He was that intense—also wicked she was sure. No, he was predacious and surely sparked a thrill of desire in every woman he met.

Heaven help her if he did agree to her wishes.

She'd be spoiled for all men.

And not in the manner she intended.

How could she ever want another man after lying in his arms, letting him initiate her to carnal acts, enjoying the passion she knew would blaze so hotly between them?

She felt that fire now, the heightened awareness prickling in her veins. Feminine anticipation that pooled deep, it was a soft, slow melting low in her belly, exciting sensations that were entirely new to her and much more enjoyable than she would have believed.

Not wanting him to guess, she stood as straight as she could. Pride kept her from pushing the wind-whipped hair from her face. Trying to ignore how much he intrigued and disquieted her, she took pleasure in the morn's chilly rawness, a delight she doubted he'd understand. Highlanders appreciated wild weather.

Sorley the Hawk was only interested in wild women.

And—she drew an annoyed breath—he found amusement in her belief in ghosts.

Mirabelle stiffened, knowing well that bogles existed.

"You asked if I wished to glimpse the pink lady, sir." She emphasized the courtesy title. She wasn't about to comment on his bastardy. He'd reminded her simply to provoke her, she knew. Spirits were a safer topic. "It's a shame you cannot accept the possibilities of ghosts. We of the Highlands know they are real."

"I would not know, my lady." The brusqueness of his tone surprised her.

She'd expected him to quirk a smile, making fun of her.

Instead his face closed, a muscle jumping in his jaw. Equally telling, he stiffened, his hands even fisting before he caught himself and once again tucked his thumbs in his sword-belt.

Bogles were clearly a sore point with him.

Mirabelle felt her brow pleating. She also couldn't help but defend her beliefs. So she stepped closer to him and placed a hand on his arm. "If you were a Highlander, you'd feel differently."

He looked at her, his expression even darker than before. "I have better things to do than consider such nonsense."

"I could tell you tales..." Mirabelle let her voice tail off, knowing he'd only scoff at her stories.

Still, she slid her fingers down his arm, touching his hand lightly before she turned back to the wall and the magnificent view beyond.

Steep and craggy, nearly the whole range of the Highlands stretched along the horizon, every fissure and corrie
standing out in the low morning light, a scarf of cloud veiling the summits. Just gazing at the scudding mists and age-
less rock caused the sweetest warmth to bloom in her breast,
a sensation entirely different from the feelings Sorley stirred
in her. Not quite ready to meet his dark, intent eyes, she let
her own light briefly on the sparkling bend of the river, so
much nearer than her beloved hills.

"Would you hear of my home?" She didn't look at him as
she spoke.

And she took his silence for a yes.

Pleased to have won even a small battle, she breathed
deeply of the cold morning air, wonder already filling her to
think of her clan's proud ancestral seat.

"Knocking Tower was named to appease the long-dead
souls who made a racket when my ancestors built the stronghold." She cast a sideling glance at Sorley, immediately
wishing she hadn't.

He wasn't listening.

He'd fixed his gaze on the hills, his back straight and his
jaw hard-set.

Even so, Mirabelle continued. "Clan legend claims
stones for the castle were taken from the remains of a nearby
fortress. A sacred place that belonged to the Old Ones who
lived in times so dim only the tumbled and lichened rocks of
their ruined homes remember them."

She paused, expecting him to say something. When he
didn't, she bit back a sigh. "It's not surprising they objected
to seeing the weathered stones so violated. They played mischief with the builders, causing thorn bushes to grow over
newly laid walkways and foundations, even tearing down
just-started walls at night when the men slept.

"Once the stronghold stood, they made their displeasure
known in other ways." Her heart gave a lurch, sympathy for

the spirits of her home beating fiercely inside her. "They took up hammers of their own, pounding on the walls and wailing through the stair towers so that my ancestors couldn't enjoy a single night's rest.

"And then"—her voice caught, her favorite part of the tale misting her eyes—"the lady of the castle, my great-great-great-grandmother and then some, declared that we should do the ghosts honor and keep a long table in the hall always set for them, allowing no one to sit there so the spirits would know the place was theirs and they were welcome. That we revered them and the ancient stone they allowed us to use.

"This great lady insisted the ghosts' nightly ruckus was their way of showing approval and goodwill." Mirabelle dabbed discreetly at her cheek. "It was she who decided the new stronghold should be called Knocking so they'd aye know we understood."

"Did they?" Sorley's voice was gruff, so low she scarce heard him.

"Our storytellers say they did, because the noises stopped." She paused, her breath hitching. "An air of peace and contentment descended, and it remains so to this day, felt and appreciated by us all."

"It is a touching tale, my lady." He still didn't look at her. "I am sure your hills abound with such fables."

"There is truth behind every legend." Mirabelle flicked at her sleeve, speaking lightly. "Of this tale, I believe every word."

"I am sure you do."

"You do not?"

"I believe that you believe." He turned to her, his expression unreadable. "I can also understand why Stirling's pink lady fascinates you."

"She does." Mirabelle's heart started racing again, and for reasons that had nothing to do with ghosts and everything to do with the man standing so near. "I hope to see her some-day. But I did not come up here searching for her. It will be some days before my father's transcribing work for the King is finished. He is helping the royal scribes decipher an ancient Gaelic book on medicine and healing."

"Such work is tedious and takes time." She touched a hand to her breast, drank deep of the brisk morning air. "And so"—she glanced again at the breathtaking vista before them—"I felt a need to gaze in the direction of my home. As I told you, that's the reason I came up here."

"You miss your hills so much?" His voice carried an edge.

"Any Highlander would." Mirabelle wished he wasn't standing so near. He truly was imposing. Wind tossed his thick, dark hair, the ends dancing across his broad shoulders. Thanks to the same wind, his warm, sandalwood scent drifted over her, its headiness proving a great distraction. The fierce look on his face disturbed her even more.

Could it be he disliked the Highlands?

Turning back to the view, she lifted her chin, sure that wasn't possible.

He simply didn't care for her.

She placed her hands on the same merlon he'd leaned against moments ago, taking strength from the stone's cold, damp solidity.

"A Highlander is aye deeply attached to the land." She kept her gaze on the River Forth rather than her beloved hills. She didn't want emotion to thicken her voice and that would happen if she spoke such truths while looking on her home when separated by miles from its embrace. "Our hearts shrivel, our souls withering when we must be away. The yearning to return is a terrible ache inside us."

"Indeed?" He came to stand beside her, his voice even harder than before. "I would not know."

Mirabelle glanced at him. "Have you never been there then? If you had, you'd understand."

"Stirling is my home. I've ne'er journeyed so far north as your hills. I—" he broke off when two guardsmen rounded a corner, striding past them on their morning circuit of the battlements.

As if the patrol's arrival heralded the true beginning of the day, the sound of garrison men practicing arms reached them from the training ground then, the burst of noise quickly followed by the laughter of kitchen women at the castle well. Somewhere a cart rumbled over cobbles and a horn blast signaled that visitors had been spotted nearing the gates. Before the flourish faded away, a woman's angry voice rose, scolding someone about a spilled barrel of oats. Soon, Mirabelle knew, the cacophony would worsen.

She lifted her face into the wind, trying not to wince.

"All I wish is here, lady." Sorley leaned against the wall and crossed his ankles. "For truth, I cannae see the lure of a place so remote and empty that the only sound is the wind across the moors and the fall of rain on stone. Or, saints forbid, the lonely echo of one's own footsteps halloing through a deserted glen.

"Indeed"—he folded his arms—"a man must be mad to dwell in such a place."

Mirabelle held her peace, refusing to let him bait her. "I would say it is astonishing that anyone could resist living there."

Something like annoyance flashed over Sorley's features. "I'm sure every Highlander believes that is so."

Mirabelle's chin came up. "We know it is."

"And I must be gone." He pushed away from the wall, adjusted his thick calfskin jerkin.

"I've kept you, haven't I?" Mirabelle glanced at his travel pouch over by the tower stair. "You were on your way to the Red Lion."

"Aye, so I am."

"Do you always carry so many weapons when visiting

an alehouse?" She flicked a look at his sword, then the dirk tucked beneath his belt. She couldn't be sure, but suspected he also had a dagger in his boot. "Have you more arms in thon leather bag? You already said it doesn't contain coin for the tavern wenches."

"Are you aye so inquisitive, sweetness?" He leaned in, so close that his breath warmed her cheek. "Curiosity is no' a safe habit."

"Highlanders are a curious folk."

"That they are." He smiled, clearly pleased to twist her words.

"You know what I meant." Mirabelle studied him, noting the irritation behind his levity. "You dislike Highlanders, don't you?" She tilted her head, tapping her chin. "I wonder why that is when, as you say, you have never traveled north to visit our hills?"

"I've no need to go there." He turned away from her, again bracing his hands on the wall. "Enough Highlanders come to court for me to know them well. A man needn't walk a folk's heather to ken the make of them."

"I see." Mirabelle went to stand beside him. "A Highlander hurt you."

"Nae, one of the devils sired me." He glanced at her, his voice like ice. "Leastways, I suspect as much."

"Oh. I am sorry." Mirabelle was.

She wanted to sink into the stone slabs of the battlement. She should've known there was a deeper reason for his resentment of her people. The hills and moorlands that, most times, stole a man's breath, stilling his heart with their haunting beauty. Yet he'd claimed he sought this spot every morning, "allowing himself the pleasure of the view..."

Mirabelle understood then, and the knowledge broke her heart.

She stepped forward, hoping he'd think the chill wind

and not sympathy misted her eyes. "Do you know who the man was? Have you ever tried speaking to him?"

"Nae, lady, I dinnae even ken his name. Nor do I wish to. I've no desire to meet him."

"And if ever you did?"

"That isn't likely." He cupped her chin, lifting her face to his. "More important is that you meet me in the chapel this e'en. I'll be there no' long after gloaming. I'll give you my answer then."

"About your father or me?"

"Concerning the 'matter of delicacy' we spoke of yestere'en. My father doesn't interest me in the slightest. Nor do gently bred ladies." He released her and bowed slightly. "Crazed as it is, I'm mightily tempted to make an exception for you."

Before Mirabelle could respond, he strode away, heading toward the tower stair. At the door, he picked up his satchel and looked back at her.

"Because I ken how curious Highlanders are, I'll give you one answer now, Lady Mirabelle." He set his hand on the latch, his dark eyes hard. "If ever I do meet my sire, it will be a day like no other."

Then he was gone, disappearing into the shadows of the stairwell. A hint of his sandalwood scent remained behind. And the knowledge that Sorley the Hawk was not a man to be trifled with.

He was bold and dangerous.

Much more sensually appealing by the light of day than she'd realized in the dimness of his bedchamber. She also knew that if he agreed to do as she'd bid him, he'd do more than ruin her.

He'd steal her heart.

She strongly suspected she wouldn't be able to do a thing to stop him.

Worse, she doubted she'd want to.

Chapter Three

❖

Sorley didn't care for men said to possess the devil's own temper.

Restraint was aye the better way. A surer means to achieve one's goals. Yet just now, as he strode past the cottages that marked the end of Stirling town, he had the unpleasant feeling that the dark one himself had climbed up from his fiery pit to blast him with brimstone and sulfur, fouling his mood and stealing the roguish charm that never failed to attract the ladies.

He also knew who was responsible for calling the fiend into his world.

Worst of all, she loosened his tongue.

Frowning, he quickened his pace past the cottages. Little more than hovels, these homes were thick-walled and heavy with thatch, each one set close to the narrow road.

They belonged to the poorest of the poor. Good, hard-working folk. Many were the times he secretly dropped a cloth-wrapped packet of foodstuffs on the door stoops. Sometimes cold, generously sliced roasted meat, other times a handful of the castle cooks' prized cheese pasties. Now and then, he'd leave a castoff tunic or length of linen, given to him by a Stirling laundress. On feast days, he set flasks of uisge beatha on the deep-cut window ledges, knowing well that all Scotsmen appreciated a nip of the strong Highland spirits.

This day, he hoped no one noticed his passage.

Some of the tenseness left his shoulders as he neared the wood at the town's edge. The pines were dense, their scent already reaching him. He breathed deep, appreciating the cooling mist that chased the heat from his face, the back of his neck.

If he didn't know better he'd swear someone had strapped a furnace on his back. His blood boiled that hotly, making him more certain than ever that Lady Mirabelle had cast a witchy spell on him, an incantation to dash his wits.

How else could she have used a single glance from her great lavender-blue eyes to persuade him to blurt his most private secret?

Praise the gods he hadn't expounded on his suspicions, admitting he was certain his father wasn't just a Highlander, but a chieftain.

His gut told him so.

Only a Highland man in a position of power would ever find himself at the royal court, after all. In his experience with courtiers, Highlanders and otherwise, only such men possessed the arrogance to leave their unwanted seed planted deeply in the bellies of castle lovelies. Long-nosed as Mirabelle was, if she guessed his thoughts, she'd no doubt begin peppering chieftains and lairds about their amorous pasts upon her return to her bluidy hills.

He couldn't allow such probing into his affairs.

When the day came for him to face his sire, the dastard wouldn't have a jot of warning.

His errant sire could wait.

This morn, he had Fenris matters to attend to, an urgent

mission for the crown that already had his sword hand itching to reach for steel. Sir Henry Lockhart, traitor to King
and country, would never guess his fate when he approached
him garbed as a penniless wayfarer riding an equally
decrepit nag.

Sorley excelled at such disguises.

Few warriors, even among his secret band of Fenris brothers, could carry off such messy work without letting even a
drop of blood soil King Robert's hands. Lockhart deserved
a particularly unpleasant end. Savoring the moment the bastard sensed his doom, Sorley welcomed the bend in the road
that signaled the approach to the Red Lion. Set conveniently
at a crossroads, the rambling old inn offered a greater selection of sway-backed, long-toothed horses than the stables at
Stirling Castle.

Better yet, the Red Lion was run by William Wyldes,
a rough-hewn giant of a man who never saw anything and
spoke of even less. He enjoyed laughter and song, bonnie
lasses, and making a profit. As long as a body paid for his ale
and victuals, didn't cause too much of a ruckus or tear up the
rooms, all was good in Wyldes's world.

He also demanded that the tavern wenches be treated
with respect.

If a man broke his rules...

For the first time that morning, a smile curved Sorley's
lips. Sir John Sinclair had only visited the inn once, to his
knowledge. Taking offense at something the noble said to a
serving lass, Wyldes tossed out the courtier, making sure his
richly garbed arse landed in the mud. Sorley's smile broad-
ened at the memory of how the innkeeper had warned Sinclair he'd leave minus his best piece if he dared to return.

Sorley appreciated a man who kept order, taking care of
his own.

He strode faster when the inn came into view. Old before
he was even born, the inn was rumored to have been built

on the site of a pagan sacred well, popular even in ancient times with travelers seeking blessings and refreshment. These days, thick stone walls greeted guests, and a sloping slate roof, the tiles laced with lichen and moss, ensured that a fire would be unlikely to spread.

Thick piney woods protected the inn's back, while the front looked out upon pleasantly rolling countryside. Villagers and farmers were frequent guests. And the river was close enough to attract those who journeyed by water.

A reputation for good, homey food and excellent ale did the rest, pulling in trade from near and far. If some came because of the friendliness of the well-made, aye cheerful tavern lasses, that was only to be expected. William Wyldes sought to please all patrons.

Eager to please his King, Sorley pushed open the heavy oak door and stepped into the inn's low-beamed long room. The air was thick with the smell of stew and ale, and peats glimmered in the fine stone fireplace. But the scarred tables were empty. A few oil lanterns burned, their smoky light not enough to banish the corner shadows. The clatter of plates and ale cups came from the kitchen, the noise breaking the silence that hung so heavy in the public room.

Sorley remained where he stood, letting his eyes adjust to the dimness, not liking the stillness.

He knew why when a hand clamped down on his shoulder and a familiar voice boomed behind him, "You're losing your touch, letting a beautiful woman leave your bedchamber after less time than it takes to properly kiss a lass.

"Or"—his archfiend, Roag the Bear, stepped around him, grinning—"did she run after discovering you dinnae even know how to kiss?"

"What have you done?" Sorley glanced around the empty long room. "Downed all of Wydes's ale so that your wits are addled? I slept alone last night, no' that it's aught to you."

"That I know!" Roag's grin widened. "The lady would've

sliced you with her razor-sharp tongue had you tried to keep her any longer.

"She cannae abide you, that one." Roag dropped onto a chair and stretched his long legs toward the fire. "We've known that since we were lads, what?"

"You're talking nonsense." Sorley remained standing, the other man's cheek making his head ache again. "I ne'er have aught to do with ladies, as well you know."

"Whate'er." Roag shrugged, his damnable grin appearing permanent.

Roag, too, was an agent of the crown. A Fenris Guard, much as Roag's membership in the secret brotherhood sometimes irked Sorley. For sure, he didn't recall any mention of the lout's participation in dealing with the unpleasantness that was Sir Henry Lockhart.

Hoping he hadn't erred, Sorley did rake the arse with a narrow-eyed stare. A great hulk of a man, hence his by-name, Bear, Roag enjoyed the same dark good looks as Sorley, much to his annoyance. Even more galling, the thin knife-slash that arced across Roag's left cheekbone gave him a dashing, roguish air that appealed strongly to women.

Sorley couldn't stand him.

So he crossed his arms, ignoring the chair Roag pulled out for him.

"What are you doing here?" Sorley glanced across the room, not surprised to see a fetching dark-haired lass peering at them from behind the kitchen door. She was Maili, a cheery, plump-breasted castle laundress who enjoyed earning a bit of extra coin at the Red Lion.

Sorley suspected she simply had a taste for men and took delight in lifting her skirts. She did put her heart into each amorous adventure, as he knew well.

Roag especially favored her. But Sorley's gut warned that the buxom lass wasn't the bastard's only reason for being at the inn.

Following Sorley's gaze, Roag winked at the maid before turning back to Sorley. "I ken you've sampled her charms, so dinnae tell me you wonder what drew me here. There's no' a sweeter tumble for miles. Unless"—his grin returned, flashing boldly—"you tame Lady Mirabelle. I'll wager she'd set the heather ablaze."

"The lady's amorous abilities are of no interest to me," Sorley lied. "If she even possesses such skills, which I doubt."

Roag snorted. "And Wyldes will turn out his stable of comely, well-made tavern wenches and hire shriveled, grizzle-haired crones to serve his patrons. Those with breasts hanging to their knees will claim the highest price."

"You deserve such a female."

"There speaks a man soured because he cannae enjoy the MacLaren minx in the heather."

"You're a bastard, spawned on the hottest hob of hell."

"So I am." Roag shrugged, looking amused.

Furious because his archrival had struck a nerve, Sorley tore his gaze from the lout's grinning face before he planted his fist in the middle of it. Resisting the urge, he glanced at the shadowed doorway to the kitchen and then the fire burning low in the grate.

Roag leaned back in his chair, lifting his arms to hook his fingers behind his neck. "Lady Mirabelle scorched you once years ago." The humor left his face, the flicker of sympathy in his eyes annoying Sorley more than his devilry. "Dinnae let a second mistake turn into something that will fry you to a crisp. That lass—"

"What mistake?" Sorley's tone was his lowest, his most deadly.

Unimpressed, Roag raised his arms over his head and cracked his knuckles. "Allowing her into your bedchamber, that's what. A fool would know you thought she'd leap into your embrace, now that all the court ladies adore you." He lowered his arms and shook his head. "A shame; from the way she left so soon, it was clear she wanted none of you.

"Now if she'd been with me..." He let the words tail off, his levity returning. "I'd have shown her—"

"Hold your tongue is what you'll do." Sorley was on him in a beat, leaning across the table, his hands braced on the well-scrubbed surface. "Dinnae push me too far," he warned. "Have done with such prattle and tell me why you're following me about. And speak plain. I can see your lies at a hundred paces. This close, they're as conspicuous as a three-eyed troll."

"You wound me." Roag clapped a hand to his heart.

"Nae, I ken you."

Before Roag could respond, a deep voice boomed behind them, "And I ken there's a fine north wind blowing this morn."

On hearing the secret Fenris greeting, both men turned to see William Wyldes striding toward them, carrying two brimming cups of ale.

"Is there indeed?" Sorley lifted a brow when the innkeeper stopped before the table.

"Aye, and it'll worsen before the day is o'er," Wyldes gave the required answer, letting Sorley and Roag know they could speak freely, the inn hiding no one with peeled ears and, worse, a flapping tongue.

"I also ken, as should you, that I dinnae allow fighting in my public room." The innkeeper plunked down the ale cups and then planted his hands on his hips. A big man, he equaled Sorley and Roag in height and muscle, but had a shock of unruly auburn hair that he wore tied back at his nape. His beard was just as bushy and wild, and he had light blue eyes that always smiled. And although he kept the Red Lion ruckus-free, there was no man better to have at your side in a fight.

Just now he looked Sorley and Roag up and down. "You ken the rules," he reminded them. "No brawling. Unless"— he winked—"it's a fight I start myself."

"Understood." Sorley clapped him on the shoulder and then pulled back a chair, reaching for one of the ale cups after he took a seat. "I'll just call on our long friendship and ask you to take a swing at this bastard." He turned a significant look on Roag. "I'll do the rest."

"Try and you'll meet the cutting edge of my sword." Roag tossed back his ale and slapped the empty cup on the table. "The blade already has your name on it."

"As mine carries yours." Sorley glared at him.

Wyldes laughed. "Someday the two of you will kill each other. When it happens"—he grabbed an ale jug from another table and refilled Roag's cup—"I'll be filling my purse taking wagers, not jumping into the fray. If I did that, I'd be obliged to have done with both of you and then wouldn't the King be after me?"

"True enough." Sorley took a healthy gulp of his own ale, secretly annoyed that Roag also held a place in the King's graces. "Though I cannae believe our good Robert set Roag on my tail this morn.

"He has other reasons for making a nuisance of himself." Sorley glanced at him, sure of it. "He thinks I'm hoping to bed a gently bred lady."

"Are you?" Wyldes looked amused. "I'd no' bet on it."

"Rightly so." Sorley lifted his cup in salute. "Here's to a man who kens me well."

"Let's no' forget the man who kens Wyldes better than you." Roag reached across the table, knocking his ale cup against Sorley's. "William!"—he looked at the innkeeper, using his given name—"why is this den o' madmen so empty? The floor swept and the tables scrubbed cleaner than a bairn's behind?"

"Why would any man go to such trouble?" Wyldes pulled back a chair, joining them. "Word came that a party of lofties are riding in later this morn. I wasn't told if they'll be staying the night or just wanting a good, warm meal and my best heather ale.

"So-o-o!" He brought his hand down on the table, striking the wood so hard the ale cups jumped. "I've warned my patrons to stay away. The lasses are cleaning the rooms, should they be needed."

"Worthies, eh?" Roag cocked a brow. "Good to take care then. Suchlike are the same the world o'er. A dust mote twirling the wrong way and they'll be for demanding your head. Or"—he slid a wolfish look at Sorley—"are they bringing along ladies? If so, my friend here—"

"I am no' your friend, you buffoon." Sorley didn't allow him to finish.

For the oddest reason, his gut had tightened when the innkeeper mentioned visiting nobles. Worse, the fine hairs on his nape lifted, and that was a sign he never ignored. His instincts served him well.

"Do you ken who these gentlefolk are?" He kept his gaze on Wyldes, not daring to look at Roag lest the blackguard guess his thoughts.

For that reason, he didn't dare ask if the guests were Highlanders.

"Nae, no one saw fit to tell me their names." Wyldes shrugged, seemingly unconcerned. "You needn't worry you'll miss a delectable lass." He winked at Roag. "The men are scholars. Most learned, by the sound of it. Scribes, clerks, and that ilk, I'm sure. Suchlike willnae have fetching misses with them."

"Quill-wielders and ink-fingers?" Roag nearly choked. "What would they want at the Red Lion?"

Wyldes gripped the table edge and leaned forward. "Queer folk, I say you." He lowered his voice, casting a glance at the inn's main door. "I was told they plan to climb on the roof to examine the lichen and moss up there. Odin only knows what they hope to discover."

"Odd, indeed." Roag waved a hand through a drift of smoke wafting past them from one of the lanterns.

"Whate'er, you'd best put fresh oil in the lamps before they arrive. On the other hand," he sounded amused, "if they're after slate moss and lichen rather than your ale and fine roasted meats, like as no' they'll no' notice a bit of candle grease and lamp smoke in the air.

"Eh, Hawk?" Roag half-rose from his chair to punch Sorley's arm. "Such fools could probably eat a plate of bog peat and no' ken what they're putting in their bellies. Nothing but their books and scrolls interests them."

Sorley scarce heard him.

He had caught Wyldes's calling the men learned.

Mirabelle's father was a known scholar. Hadn't she claimed they were in Stirling so he could assist the King's scribes in translating ancient Gaelic medicinal texts? Could lichen and moss be used for healing? Sorley was sure he'd heard the like somewhere.

With his luck of late, the party of nobles would be MacLarens. For sure, Lady Mirabelle would be along. Meeting her here, at the Red Lion, was the last thing he needed. He especially didn't want to run into her when he was leaving the inn.

Hoping to avoid such a disaster, he pushed back his chair and stood.

"I must be away." He shot a glance at a door in a corner of the inn. It led to the rear yard and stables. He turned to the innkeeper, hoping Roag would take his leave. "Have you readied a horse?"

"I've done better." The big man grinned, likewise pushing to his feet. "You'll find two of my sorriest nags saddled and waiting for you. And"—his deep voice took on a conspiratorial tone—"o'er by the well, there's a bucket of fresh-reeking muck. Horse and cow manure.

"If the smell doesn't convince Lockhart you're beggars or lepers, nothing will." Stepping back, he winked. Unfortunately, Sorley was anything but happy.

He'd planned to address the matter of Sir Henry Lockhart on his own

Before he could argue, Roag appeared at his elbow, stepping around him so that his bulk blocked Sorley's retreat.

Cocking his head to the side, he fixed Sorley with a determined stare. "When the wind whistles..." He let the code words trail away, waiting for Sorley to acknowledge that his reason for being here came from the crown.

Sorley glared at him.

He didn't want to answer.

Direct reference to Fenris the Wolf, their namesake in Norse mythology, was aye a serious matter. As son of the trickster god, Loki, the wolf was only mentioned when circumstances, and orders, brooked no argument.

So...

Sorley pulled a hand down over his chin and peered up at the smoke-blackened rafters.

He tried not to swear. It wasn't easy.

"When the wind whistles," he finally repeated the secret phrase, "a wolf is sharpening his teeth."

"Aye, so they say." Roag beamed and punched his arm again. "And those with reason to believe warn that Lockhart isn't acting alone."

"Traitors to their country usually do have helpers." Sorley knew it well. "I'll handle them on my own."

Roag shrugged. "Think you I wish to don an already rancid wayfarer's robe and then smear it and myself with dung?"

"Then stay here. I'll no' force you to ride with me."

"I will all the same." Roag leaned in, all mirth gone. "Truth is, for reasons I cannae explain, I'd go with you whether King Robert wished it or nae. No man should deal with a worm like Lockhart only to feel a dagger sinking into his back when he turns to ride away."

"Hummph." Sorley couldn't deny such a truth, so he

strode across the long room to where Wyldes stood by the door to the rear yard.

"Come, then." He glanced over his shoulder at Roag. "The day is aging and my fists are itching to crush bone, my blade calling for blood."

Roag joined him, shaking his head. "No blood will spill at all if Lockhart sees you and notices the bloodlust in your eye. He'll be away before—"

"You talk too much." Sorley grabbed Roag's elbow and pulled him through the door Wyldes held wide.

The reek from the muck barrel the innkeeper had prepared hit them at once, the stink almost blinding. As Wyldes had promised, the barrel stood near the well, as did two of the sorriest-looking horses Sorley had ever seen.

He doubted they'd make the few steps out of the stable-yard, much less the day's journey.

Sorley might not either with the perfume of manure clinging to him.

At least the weather was fine.

It was a bright morning, cold and crisp. The sun shone, its light dappling the cobbles where the rays slanted through the trees. Few clouds marred the brilliant blue of the sky and all that stood between Sorley and his day's work was the road that wound away through the piney woods and then across the open countryside to his destination, the ruined Abbey of St. Mary and the wee riverside village and wharf that belonged to the ancient holy site.

Much damaged in the wars with the English, their armies taking pleasure in violating sacred Scottish ground, it was a place that should never be soiled by the likes of Sir Henry and his perfidy.

Sorley's head began to pound again. A muscle jerked in his jaw and he felt his hands fisting. The King had plans to rebuild the once-magnificent abbey, but the site was now tainted. Every stone, still in place or tumbled to the ground, forever stained by an enemy's willful destruction. Sorley frowned, pushing away the anger at long-ago wrongs so he could concentrate on the task at hand.

He'd take especial delight in confronting the traitor Lockhart at St. Mary's.

Roag was an annoyance he hadn't expected.

He glared at him now, sure he enjoyed needling him.

"I'll no' have you hanging on my cloak when we reach the abbey village." He released Roag's arm, brushed at his sleeve. Behind them, Wyldes closed the door, no doubt returning to his innkeeper duties. "Why don't you go back inside and spend the day with Maili? She'd welcome your company."

"Such a good friend, you are." Roag retrieved a leather satchel, similar to Sorley's, that rested on the cobbles near the well. Opening it, he withdrew a hooded cloak just as threadbare and ratty as the one stashed in Sorley's travel bag. "With such friends, a man doesn't need—"

"I am no' your friend." Sorley watched his rival plunge the cloak into the barrel of muck. Not surprisingly, the lout flashed a wicked grin, as if he enjoyed thrusting his arms into steaming horse and cow dung. "I have ne'er liked you and dinnae plan on e'er doing so.

"If you ruin this day's work, there'll be no end to the reckoning I'll have from you." Grimacing, Sorley dipped his own cloak into the barrel. "I'll no' wear such reeking rags for naught."

"I'll be nowhere near you and Sir Henry." Roag straightened, shaking out his pilgrim's mantle before swirling it across his shoulders. "Though"—he rubbed a handful of muck on his arms—"I mean to keep close enough to see if anyone in the village makes a suspicious move. There's an old abbey watergate down by the river edge. That's where I'll be."

"See you stay there." Sorley watched him mount his

shaggy beast, irritated because he did so with such care. Not that Sorley would swing up onto the aged back of his steed with any less caution. But he didn't like being reminded of Roag's better side. The bastard was good to animals.

It was his only merit.

Even his sudden cough was irritating. Hacking and loud in the chill morning air, it grated on Sorley's nerves even more than the wretched cloak he'd just donned. Trying to close his ears, and his nose, he climbed onto his nag's back.

He saw the reason for Roag's coughing fit as soon as he settled himself in the saddle and turned his horse toward the road.

"Damnation!" Sorley's eyes widened, his heart almost stopping.

A terrible rushing sound roared in his ears as he stared at the small party of mounted Highlanders riding into the stableyard. Their tartan finery and the well-tooled broadswords hanging on elaborate shoulder-and-hip belts marked them as a chiefly entourage, as did the silver-buckled brogues on their feet. The over-large great dirks tucked beneath their sword-belts also screamed quality. Dark blue and green plaids, the wool shot through with thin lines of red and yellow, signaled them as men of Clan Labhran.

The MacLarens.

Lady Mirabelle rode at the head of the column, beside her father, Munro.

Sorley bit back a curse and pulled his cloak's hood lower down on his forehead. He was vaguely aware of a barely muffled noise that could only be Roag laughing. Ignoring him, Sorley felt his gut clench and his heart plummet nearly to his dung-encrusted toes, for hadn't he also smeared the muck on his arms and legs, hoping to make himself as unpalatable and beggarlike as possible?

Apparently he'd succeeded, because the MacLarens gave

him and Roag a wide berth as they approached each other near the inn's gateway to the road.

The Highland guards, big and burly to a man, rumpled their noses. They also kneed their horses, urging them to trot faster past the two men they clearly held for lepers or worse.

Munro MacLaren, graying, slight of build, and rather incongruous in his bold, chiefly raiments, looked at them with pity as he rode by.

Mirabelle eyed them with interest.

Or rather, her gaze sharpened on Sorley.

To his horror, she edged her horse closer, her eyes narrowing as she looked him up and down. "Good sir," she addressed him in her soft Highland voice, "can it be I've seen you at Stirling?"

"I think not, my lady," Sorley answered in the musical dialect of an Islesman, grateful not for the first time for his ability to adopt different accents. He also allowed his hood to slip farther down his face. "My like isnae welcome there."

"Is that so?" She lifted a brow. "I'm sure I've seen you somewhere. It will come to me."

"Belike you saw him here, fair lady." Roag rode between them, blocking her view of Sorley. "If you've halted at the Red Lion before.

"See you,"—he used the same Hebridean dialect as Sorley—"Dungal here empties the inn cesspit for a crust o' bread and ale.

"When I'm hungry meself, I help him." He flashed a look at Sorley, the muck smears on his face not dark enough to hide his amusement. "A good day to you, lady! The saints' blessings upon you."

Mirabelle opened her mouth to respond, but Roag whacked Sorley's nag on the rump so the poor beast bolted through the gate and onto the road. Roag followed swiftly, his laughter again disguised as a cough.

Sorley waited until they'd rounded a bend in the road

before he reined in and threw back his hood. Anger blazed in his veins and he'd swear a fine red haze tinted the rolling farmland and woods around them. For two pins, he'd whip out his sword and ensure that the ground ran red as well, drenched with Roag's spilled blood.

Roag was still laughing, nearly convulsed, and his tears made tracks in the dung on his face.

Sorley reached over, gripping the lout's arm. "Dinnae e'er do that again or I'll forget every rule I live by and make you a true reeking gangrel before you could catch your breath to run away."

"You could try." Roag grinned and thwacked Sorley's shoulder. "I'm thinking you should thank me. Thon lady knew you."

"A pig's eye, she did." Sorley knew she had.

Scowling, he drew a long, tight breath and started riding again.

Roag could take himself to hell, though Sorley knew he'd never have such luck. He also knew he'd be wise not to meet Mirabelle in the chapel later that night.

He should forget their rendezvous and put her from his mind.

But even as he acknowledged the wisdom of such a plan, he knew it was doomed to fail. As soon as he returned to Stirling from the hamlet of St. Mary's, he'd take a hot, cleansing bath, dress in his finest, and hie himself to the chapel like the fool he'd become.

Mirabelle would be there waiting.

And simply put, he couldn't resist her.

Chapter Four

❧

Lichen and moss such as gracing this inn's roof slates have long been prized for their remedial properties." Munro MacLaren's voice rang with enthusiasm as he paced the Red Lion's long room. A small man, slight of stature, but with piercing, intelligent blue eyes, he could scarcely contain his excitement. "A century ago, Bernard of Gordon praised them in his masterful work on healing, the *Lilium Medicinae*."

Standing near the door, Mirabelle recognized her father's fervor. She hoped he wouldn't start a long discourse, keeping them from their business here.

It wouldn't take hours for his men to help him onto the roof to examine and gather his samples.

But if he became carried away speaking of medicine and healing, they wouldn't be leaving the inn before nightfall, if then. Should rooms be secured, their return to the castle delayed until morning...

She'd miss meeting Sorley at the chapel.

Not wanting to consider such a possibility, Mirabelle stepped closer to the door, pretending to peer out at the inn's cobbled rear yard.

Behind her, her father had drawn a deep breath and was already extolling the virtues of the *Lilium Medicinae,* his favorite manuscript on healing.

Turning back to the room, Mirabelle's heart sank to see the familiar look on her father's face. The slight flush to his cheeks and the light in his eyes hinted that they could be here until the morrow.

If so, she'd find a way to return to Stirling on her own. A guardsman could be persuaded to escort her. She'd even walk if need be, leaving when no one was looking. If she must, she'd sprout wings and fly. Desperation made all things possible, didn't it?

Before they'd left the castle, she'd caught her father speaking with John Sinclair. She didn't know what they'd discussed, but she didn't like the look Sir John had given her when he'd left them.

Mirabelle shivered, the gossip she'd heard about the man making her stomach knot. Tales of castle serving wenches gone missing after having caught his eye. Whispers about the bruises seen on Stirling town's joy women whenever he'd spent time in the taverns where they plied their trade.

Many court worthies claimed envious lords spread the rumors, men who stood in Sinclair's debt and hoped to avoid returning coin he'd loaned them. If Sinclair fell from favor and was banished from the King's grace, such men could forget the monies due to him.

Straightening, she smoothed her skirts, not wanting anyone to note her discomfiture.

Above all, she was not going to miss her rendezvous with Sorley.

Most certainly not because of a hoary tome filled with cures that involved horses' teeth, dried adder heads, toads, newts, and even birds' windpipes. Mirabelle took a deep breath, silently willing her father to not lecture on the curative properties of suchlike.

He was pacing the long room again, his hands clasped behind him as he continued to pontificate on the much-revered *Lilium Medicinae.*

"I once saw a copy of that book." William Wyldes, the huge, red-haired innkeeper glanced at her father as he placed a large platter of delicious-smelling roasted meat on the table claimed by the MacLaren guards. "A party of Skye MacLeods stopped here for the night and they had one of the famed MacBeth healers with them. That man carried the *Lilium Medicinae* with him while his chief traveled by boat on the river.

"The book was so treasured by him and the MacLeod that they felt it was more secure journeying by land than on water." The innkeeper scratched his beard, then grinned. "It was that MacBeth healer who told me to wedge clubmoss between the roof slates.

"He said the moss protects travelers." Wyldes glanced up at the smoke-blackened rafters as if he could see the moss through the ceiling. "Running an inn for wayfarers, I was glad to take his advice. Though"—he shook his head—"I'm no' sure I'd go to the trouble of carrying round a book as if it were a coffer of gold."

"The *Lilium Medicinae* is precious." Munro now stood before the fire, rubbing his hands. "It's why I'm in Stirling. I'm helping the King's scribes translate the Gaelic text. The work is tedious, but greatly rewarding."

"So is mine." The innkeeper winked, pouring the guardsmen generous cups of ale. "Though this is the first time anyone has wished to climb onto my roof. Most men who come here have other desires."

Near the door, Mirabelle felt her face color. She knew exactly what kind of desires the innkeeper meant. The sudden snickering of her father's guardsmen proved she'd guessed rightly.

Men didn't come to the Red Lion strictly for ale and

victuals, a warm fire, and a roof over their heads on cold, wet nights.

They sought certain other comforts as well.

If her father noticed the sidelong glances and elbow nudges of his men, he said nothing. Mirabelle doubted such a thought even crossed his mind. Little else did when he expounded on his books or his lifelong interest in healing.

"You could earn extra coin with the crotal lichen on your roof slates." Munro followed the innkeeper across the room, clearly pleased to have a receptive audience. "Such lichens are good for more than making dye."

"Say you?" William Wyldes set down his ale jug, all ears.

"Och, aye." Munro rocked back on his heels, his chest swelling. "Have some of your kitchen lads scrape the lichen off the slates, then dry it and pound it into a fine powder.

"That"—his chest puffed even more—"you sell to weary travelers. If they place the powder inside their shoes, it'll protect their feet on long journeys, sparing them aches and blisters."

"Is that so?" The innkeeper's brows lifted.

"True as I'm standing here." Munro beamed.

Any other time, Mirabelle would've smiled as well. She loved her father dearly and enjoyed seeing him happy, his scholarly ways appreciated. Just now, though, she was certain she'd also seen Sorley the Hawk guised as a leprous beggar when they'd arrived at the inn.

Yet the man spoke like a Hebridean Islesman, and she hadn't caught a good look at his face. Dungal, the other man had called him. Mirabelle hadn't believed a word.

She had noted that the man, indeed both men, bore a hard, almost dangerous edge that no penniless wretch could possess. Even when the first man slumped in his saddle, she'd sensed the strength of him beneath his soiled and stinking mantle. It was the same bold, predaceous air that so attracted her to Sorley in his bedchamber.

The cloak also couldn't hide the *beggar's* powerful

shoulders, or his large frame, which she just knew would be well-muscled and magnificent, pure masculine perfection, when freed from the ratty cloak.

All that she'd noticed, her awareness of him unerring.

His beggar's hood had dipped too low for her to see his eyes clearly. If she had, she was certain they'd have been dark as peat, his gaze intense enough to make her heart beat faster. Her pulse raced now, just thinking of how Sorley looked at her, making her feel as if he wanted to devour her.

And wouldn't she enjoy such a feasting?

"Dear saints," she gasped when sweet, liquid warmth started pooling low in her belly, delicious tingles prickling the secret place between her thighs.

Was this desire?

The fierce bedding-lust she'd heard the kitchen wenches and serving lasses whisper about at Knocking? Pleasurable as the sensations were, she believed that was so. Only one man roused her thus.

Sorley the Hawk.

"Lady?"

Mirabelle turned to find a comely young woman smiling at her. Dark-haired and with warm brown eyes, she wore a simple gown of deep green, its laced bodice and the low-cut white blouse beneath flattering her shapeliness. An apron tied around her waist revealed her position while her friendly air put Mirabelle at ease.

She also struck her as vaguely familiar.

"Have we met?" Mirabelle returned her smile. "Have you been at Stirling of late? In the castle? I'm sure I've seen you there."

"You are observant, my lady." The girl's eyes sparkled, her smile deepening to reveal a dimple in her cheek. "I'm a laundress at the castle. And"—she gestured at the long room behind them—"I help out here as well. The Red Lion does a good trade."

"I'd thought the inn would be busier." Mirabelle glanced to where her father's retinue crowded four of the tables. No other guests were about, and she swiftly wished she hadn't looked at the guards, because rather than tending their trenchers of roasted meat and quaffing ale, or even listening to her father enthuse about the inn's roof lichen and moss, the men were eyeing the dark-haired maid with undisguised appreciation, seeming unable to take their gazes off her. Their thoughts were easy to guess, the nature of their speculation making Mirabelle take a deep breath and smooth her hands on her skirts.

Nowise discomfited, the serving lass aimed a dazzling smile at the guards. When she looked again to Mirabelle, she shrugged lightly.

"Men will be men, aye?" She winked, her high spirits lifting Mirabelle's own. "I am Maili," she declared, bobbing a curtsy. "And you truly are observant. The inn is quiet this morn. When William"—she glanced at the innkeeper—"learned your party would be riding in, he put out word for our regular patrons to stay away. We ken many nobles prefer privacy when they visit."

"My father wouldn't have minded a crowd." Mirabelle knew that was true. "He loves nothing more than speaking about books, healers, and healing."

"Aye, well." Maili flashed another smile. "If you'd prefer, we've a smaller, more comfortable room through there." She indicated an open archway not far from where they stood. "There's a light repast already set out for you and a small fire on the grate, if you'll come with me?"

She started forward, looking over her shoulder as she approached the archway. "You'll be alone there, and quite safe. No one will bother you."

"I wasn't worried." Mirabelle followed her into the other room.

Even more noticeably well-scrubbed than the long room, this one had the same low ceiling and age-blackened rafters, but there the similarity ended. A faint hint of ale and peat hung in the air, the peaty scent coming from a small, handsomely tiled hearth set against the far wall. White linens covered the tables and gleaming pewter plates lined a shelf that circled all four walls. Candles burned in wall sconces, their flickering light casting shadows across the tables and polished flagstone floor. A small basket of heather graced a corner table, as did a tempting selection of roasted sliced capon, several sorts of cheese, and a loaf of fresh-baked bread.

Mirabelle noted a dish of creamy fresh butter and a small pot of preserved gooseberries. Seeing the fare, she felt a stab of guilt as the girl led her across the room, clearly a private parlor.

Hadn't she resented this place when, during their early morning encounter on Stirling's battlements, Sorley mentioned his intent to come here?

Worse, she'd envied the women she was sure he'd meant to visit. She'd thought of them as harlots, brazen and amoral, catering to men only for the coin such performances would bring them.

Maili's warmth shamed her.

The girl had a glow of kindliness she'd seldom noticed on court ladies.

"You shouldn't have gone to so much trouble." Mirabelle touched the girl's arm when she pulled out a chair, gesturing she should sit. "But I do appreciate it. I hadn't realized how hungry I am. And"—she smiled, gratefully dropping into the chair—"I am tired."

She was.

She hadn't slept well. Her night rest was repeatedly disrupted by images of Sorley. How he'd looked naked in his bed before he'd wakened. Equally distracting, she hadn't been able to stop imagining all the deliciously wicked things he'd surely do to her if he agreed to help her. How much she'd enjoy his skillful attentions.

Mirabelle frowned and reached for the wine Maili set before her.

"Are you feeling faint, my lady?" Maili looked at her, her own brow pleating. "Would you prefer to rest in one of the rooms abovestairs? The beds are freshly made and—"

"I am fine, truly." Mirabelle took a sip of the morning wine, glad it was watered.

Unfortunately, it was excellent wine, weakened or not. Sweet and potent, it went straight to her head, loosening her tongue, emboldening her.

"I wouldn't keep you from your duties." She didn't want to trouble the girl. But she also hoped Maili might solve a riddle or two that continued to pester her. So she rushed on, before manners prevented her from being so plainspoken. "You had other visitors before we arrived. Pilgrims or beggars, two men. I saw them leave when we—"

"Beggars?" The girl blinked. "The only men who stopped in earlier were—"

"Loons who didnae bring me half as many peat bricks as they'd promised, eh?" William Wyldes loomed in the archway, his hands planted on his aproned hips. "No one else was here this morn. To be sure, no' bluidy beggars. Suchlike ne'er come to the Red Lion." He winked. "They ken I'll put 'em to work. Isn't that so, Maili?" He flicked a glance at the girl and then disappeared into the dimness of the long room before she could answer.

"William spoke true." Maili didn't look at her, intent on smoothing the linen on the next table. "The only two men who were here before you were farm lads bringing a cartload of peat."

Mirabelle set down her wine cup. "We passed two beggars as we turned into the inn's rear yard."

"You heard William." Maili didn't meet her eyes. "There weren't any such men here."

"I spoke with one of them."

Maili moved to another table, her wrinkle-straightening hands more busy than ever. She also kept her face averted. "Perhaps they were wayfarers? All sorts of travelers use the crossroads."

"The men were leaving the stableyard, riding two ancient horses." Mirabelle watched the girl closely. "They didn't look like any beggars I've ever seen. They were big, well-built men, burly and muscled."

"Many such men visit the Red Lion." Maili gestured toward the door arch, the smoky long room now filled with the rumble of deep, male voices. "Our patrons are farmers and their sons, smithies and thatchers, men from the town, and sailing men from the wharves along the river. Sometimes we see well-born parties like your father and his guardsmen.

"Everyone hereabouts knew not to look in this morn." She bobbed a curtsy. "If you've no further wishes, I'll leave you. There's a bell"—she lifted her chin toward a small ringer fastened to the wall near Mirabelle's table—"if you need me."

"I'm fine, although..." Mirabelle ran a finger around the edge of her wine cup, deliberately stalling to keep the girl with her.

She knew something Mirabelle didn't.

And the more she tried to hide it, the more Mirabelle wanted to know what it was.

So she willed herself to appear relaxed, spooned a dollop of gooseberry preserves on a thick slice of warm, crusty bread. She also decided on a different approach. "You said you work at the castle..." Mirabelle spread the preserves evenly. The Stirling connection was her best opening. "Do you know Sorley the Hawk?"

"Everyone knows him." Maili's face softened, her eyes turning dreamy in a way that pinched Mirabelle's heart. "Sorley and I go way back. We grew up together, mostly causing mischief in the castle kitchens."

"Oh." Mirabelle put down her spoon. "I didn't realize—"

"Och, I'm not someone's by-blow, my lady." The girl gave Mirabelle a smile. "Not that I'd be hanging my head if I was." She winked. "Truth is, most such bairns are born of love, or at the least, powerful desire. That's a very fine way to have been made if you ask me. I cannae say the same for many nobles."

"I do agree." Mirabelle did.

"That I knew, my lady. If you didn't, you wouldn't have met my eyes when I brought you in here, much less spoken to me. Some of the worthies at court don't see me at all, or they act as if I'm air.

"Sorley faced worse, not having a father in a place where blood and station matter over all else. Many were unkind..." She let the words trail away and smoothed the apron tied around her waist. "My mother worked in the castle kitchens and looked after him. Until she succumbed to a fever." She glanced aside, her gaze on the peats glowing softly on the grate. "My father passed when I was two summers and so I became an orphan, dependent on those with a heart, much like Sorley and other castle bastards."

"I am sorry for your losses." Mirabelle was. She liked Maili, admiring her goodness and her strength. She took a deep breath, forcing herself to speak her mind. There was so much she wanted to know. "Sorley's fortunes appear to have bettered. The court ladies speak highly of him."

"They would, wouldn't they? He's a bonnie man. He has the devil's own good looks, charm, and..." A wash of pink stole across Maili's cheekbones. "He's most popular at Stirling, aye.

"You've noticed him, too, my lady." She spoke bluntly, then reached down to pet a large gray tabby cat that'd slipped into the room and now leaned against her skirts. Straightening, she smiled. "Most women do."

Mirabelle took a sip of wine, considering. "Yet that

wasn't always so. You said he was treated poorly at court?" She hoped he'd forgotten the night of her uncle's celebratory feast, the Highland reel they'd danced and that had ended so cruelly. But what choice had she other than to walk away with her chaperone? The fierce guard, one of her father's most brutish warriors, who'd accompanied the woman, would've ripped Sorley's head off his neck had she stayed at his side.

Wishing she'd had the courage to have done so, she set down her wine cup. "Popular as Sorley is now, something must've changed."

"To be sure!" Maili's smile flashed again. "He saved King Robert's life. After that, he became a royal favorite. His reputation soared and almost overnight, those who'd shunned him sought his friendship. Such is the way among nobles."

As soon as the words left her lips, her smile vanished and she pressed a hand to her breast. "My pardon. I didn't mean to say—"

"I'm not offended." Mirabelle rushed to reassure her. "The royal court is much different from Highland halls. There are some men who could well be Lowland worthies, but they are few and not looked upon kindly. Our chieftains do swagger a bit and hold great power, but they are also a friend and protector to every clansman. All have the right to approach the chief at any time, knowing they'll be welcomed, their concerns taken seriously. Indeed, they think of themselves as his cousin, no matter how tenuous the bond. Our lairds call them such, so why shouldn't they?

"In clan society, all men are important and appreciated. The blood ties and"—Mirabelle's heart squeezed—"the love of our land bind us powerfully."

"I should like to have been of your Highlands, my lady."

"It is a privilege we cherish, calling our hills home."

Maili again reached down to pet the cat, who was now

batting at her hem. "I should leave you. You've only had a bite of gooseberry bread."

"It is good." Mirabelle glanced at the crusty loaf, scarcely seeing it. Her mind raced, her heart thumping at her daring. "If you have a moment, I'd love to hear how Sorley saved the King's life."

"Oh, it's a grand tale!" The girl beamed. "Perhaps even romantic enough to be sung in your Highland halls. It happened when Sorley was six-and-ten summers, during a royal procession to Holyrood Abbey in Edinburgh. The King and his party were riding in style, for the King loves Edinburgh and looked forward to returning there. In a joyous mood, no one paid any heed to the thick mists darkening the day. Great swirls of it blew across the heather, veiling outcrops and large swathes of whin and broom. Sorley—"

"He was in the royal entourage?" Mirabelle lifted a brow, doubtful.

"Aye, well…" Maili glanced at the door arch, lowering her voice. "He wasn't with the King's party. Some of the squires had been taunting him more than usual, claiming they'd win glory at an archery tournament to be held at Holyrood. Local archers were encouraged to enter the competition. Sorley followed the group, hoping to—"

"He wished to compete?" Mirabelle guessed, her heart squeezing for the bold lad she knew he'd been.

No boy should be jeered at by others. She understood his need to prove himself.

"Sorley excelled at anything he did." Maili went to stand before the fire, the gray tabby cat trailing after her. "He wasn't allowed to train with the squires, so he hid in the shadows and watched them. Later, when the castle slept, he'd sneak to a dark corner of the training ground and practice, mimicking what he'd seen. He quickly mastered sword work, but it was with a bow that he shone the brightest." Maili smiled, clearly reminiscing. "Not even the most seasoned castle archers shot better. His friends, the other lads in the kitchens and stableyards, swore he could split a hair at a hundred yards. That wasn't just boys' bluster, he truly was good."

"He proved it at the tournament?" Mirabelle was sure that was so.

"That he did, my lady. He took all prizes in his age group."

Mirabelle looked at her. The girl's face glowed and her eyes held admiration. Was it possible her affection for Sorley went deeper than the innocent relationship she'd described? If so, it was no concern of hers. So why did the possibility pinch her so fiercely?

Trying to ignore the sensation, she took a small piece of cheese.

"Will you not join me?" She offered the tray to the girl, pleased when she accepted a bit of green cheese and an oatcake.

Watching her, Mirabelle remembered something Maili had left out of her tale. It was her own fault for distracting the girl. And she felt a need to learn as much about Sorley the Hawk as possible. If he accepted the proposal she'd made him, they'd share great intimacies.

If she knew more about him, she'd be able to better relax when the time came.

She might be willing to lose her innocence, but the act was still a bit daunting, much as she was attracted to Sorley.

She also remained certain he was the man she'd encountered in the inn's rear yard. Likewise she was sure the innkeeper had looked into the private parlor to warn Maili against revealing Sorley's disguise.

Mirabelle took another sip of wine. Her Highland curiosity would give her no rest until she discovered the reasons behind such an intrigue.

So she set down her cup and turned her entire attention

on Maili. "You said Sorley saved the King on the journey to Holyrood?"

"He did, aye." Maili took a linen napkin from another table and dabbed at her mouth. "There was an ambush, planned by a small troop of English hunkering in a thicket of whin and broom. The underbrush and mist hid them well, but Sorley spotted them just as one of the archers aimed at King Robert. Before the assailant could loose his arrow, Sorley fired one of his own, piercing the man's wrist.

"The archer fell, his arrow flying wild and slamming into the heather." The girl's face lit, her excitement catching. "His men yelled and burst out of the thicket, armed with flails, light spears, and swords. But the King's men were warned and ready, making short work of the Sassenachs. By e'en, when the royal party reached Edinburgh, Sorley's feat was on all lips, his fame sealed. From that day onward, men called him Sorley the Hawk." Maili swiped at her cheek, her eyes glistening. "Had it not been for his keen eyesight and sharp aim, our good King might not have lived."

"It's a fine tale." Mirabelle found her throat thick, her voice not as steady as she would've wished. "I'm not surprised, given the high praise I've heard when castle folk speak of him. Tell me"—she had to know—"does he come to the Red Lion often?"

In a blink, the brightness slipped from Maili's face and she darted a glance at the archway. Men's voices could still be heard, Mirabelle's father's the most dominant as he continued to praise the virtues of the learned order of MacBeth physicians and Celtic medicine. The clatter of cutlery and the chink of ale cups proved that the men were still eating, not yet ready to clamber onto the inn's roof.

Turning back to Mirabelle, the serving girl drew a long breath. "Aye, well, Sorley does look in now and again. Most men hereabouts do, lest their womenfolk forbid them a cup or two of ale and..." She blushed, and then shrugged. "A bit of comfort such as they don't enjoy in their marriage bed, as you surely knew."

"I do." Mirabelle didn't lie. "All men need more than a plaid to warm their bones of a cold, dark night."

Maili's face warmed with a smile. "You are unlike any gentleborn lady I've ever met."

"I am myself, no more." Mirabelle flicked an oatcake crumb off the table linen. "Life can be hard in the Highlands. We don't have time or inclination to fool ourselves or put a gloss of nicety on things that simply are. Women learn early to accept the ways of men. They are all driven by desire." Mirabelle glanced at the room's one window, just catching the tail end of a horse riding by on the road. "Highlanders understand a man's need for a woman, his thirst for land, and the love of his own glen, the drive to protect kith and kin."

"I do not think Sorley cares about land, but he is well-lusted, my lady. Such a man is to be celebrated, if only because he joys in living." Maili moved to a nearby table, nipping its guttering candlewick. She waved away the rising smoke, then turned back to Mirabelle, her tone conspiratorial. "If I didn't think of him as a brother, I'd have lured him into my bed years ago. Word is one night in his arms spoils a lass for all other lovers."

"So I have heard." Mirabelle couldn't count the number of times she'd caught such whisperings.

"And you?" Maili peered at her with a considering eye. "Why are you interested in him?"

"Because"—Mirabelle decided to speak true—"I believe he is the beggar I spoke with when we arrived at the inn."

"Och, nae." Maili shook her head. "Sorley takes great pride in his appearance. His raiment is as fine as any courtier's. Ne'er would he slink about garbed in rags, no' after having to suffer wearing castoffs and worse as a lad."

"I don't know…" Mirabelle glanced at the fire, seeing more than the orange-glowing peats. "More than one

Highland chieftain has been known to walk his hills in a wayfarer's robe, the hood pulled low to hide his face. When trouble is about, sometimes a humble soul is able to see and hear more than could e'er be learned on a chiefly ride through the glen, pennants waving and pipes blaring.

"We of the hills and glens ken that much is not as it seems." She looked back at Maili, sensing she could trust her. "I believe Sorley is more than he appears. Indeed, I am sure—"

She went silent as the inn door banged open. Both women glanced at the archway just as a man called a good morn to the men in the long room.

"Ho, stranger!" William Wyldes greeted him, full of cheer and welcome. "Are you wanting a room or just ale and a warm meal? We've other comforts if you're cold and weary from your journey."

"I'll be needing a bed, aye," the man answered, his voice carrying. It was a deep voice, low and rich, thick with the lilting tones of the Highlands. "A few nights, mayhap more, I cannae say. An ale and some of that stew I'm smelling would suit me fine."

Maili glanced at Mirabelle. "A Highlander," she whispered, full of awe.

"Aye." Mirabelle's heart leapt at the soft dialect of her home.

"He sounds bonnie." Maili smiled.

Mirabelle watched her slip over to the archway and peer into the public room. She didn't tell her that even Highland graybeards and dotards spoke so beautifully.

"Saints a mercy!" Maili glanced back, her eyes round. "Ne'er have I seen such a man," she spoke low, her cheeks blushing. "Come take a peek."

Curious, Mirabelle stood and crossed the little room. She saw at once why the serving girl was so intrigued with the big Highlander sitting alone at a corner table near the long room's peat fire.

Mirabelle had never glimpsed such a man.

Big and burly as were many Highlanders, this one looked fierce. Clearly a fighting man, he had unusual smoke-gray eyes, wild black hair, and a great black beard, braided with silver beard rings Mirabelle knew warriors made from the weapons of slain enemies.

"Oh, my..." She gripped Maili's elbow. "He is a sight, isn't he?"

"If he weren't so dark, I'd think he was a Viking." Maili leaned in, whispering in her ear. "Don't they also wear wolf pelts slung around their shoulders? Isn't that a Thor's hammer at his neck?"

"It is." Mirabelle narrowed her eyes to better see the shining silver talisman that glinted against the warrior's mailed shirt. "Perhaps he's a mercenary, passing through?"

"I hope he's in a mood for company." Maili was eyeing him up and down, her excitement palpable. "I like a big, rough-looking man..." She let the words trail off, frowning when William Wyldes strode over to the newcomer's table, plunking down a steaming bowl of meaty stew and a large tankard of ale. "Botheration!"

Mirabelle understood the girl's frustration.

A large man himself, the innkeeper blocked their view of the huge, big-bearded Highlander.

Hovering in the shadows of the archway, the two women watched as the innkeeper stepped back, planting his hands on his leather-aproned hips. They still couldn't see much of the Highlander, only the edge of his broad, wolf-pelt-covered shoulders. The sword and war ax he'd propped against the wall behind his table, the weapons proving they'd guessed rightly that he was a warring man.

One who possessed the courtesy to remove his arms without having been asked, even if they remained within easy reach.

Mirabelle also spotted the top of dagger's hilt peeking up from his boot.

Still, something about the solemn-faced giant told her he wouldn't leap up and attack the innkeeper, or her father and his party.

Though rough-hewn, he was a good man.

That much she could tell.

"I should go offer to top his ale." Maili stood back, dusting her skirts, arranging her low-cut bodice to dip even more. "Suchlike as him will surely drain his tankard in one draw."

"Will you be having aught else?" William Wyldes's voice boomed then.

Maili paused, waiting just inside the door arch.

She slid a glance at Mirabelle, winking. "He'll be asking for a warmed bed. That means—"

"I hope so, for you." Mirabelle returned her smile, knowing well that a "warmed bed" at the Red Lion included a soft and naked female body to comfort the traveler.

"Aye, I'd have a word with you," the Highlander returned, not giving the innkeeper the response Maili desired.

"Later, fine." Wyldes thumped the table, good-naturedly. "I've business yet this day with thon group of nobles." He jerked his head toward Munro MacLaren and his guardsmen. "I'll sup with you at gloaming, what?"

"That's good enough." The Highlander lifted his tankard in salute. "I should be back at the inn by then."

"You've dealings hereabouts?" The innkeeper hovered.

"Aye, of sorts." The man set down the tankard, leaned back in his chair. "I'm Grim Mackintosh of Nought Castle in the Glen of Many Legends. I'm looking for a man rumored to frequent this inn."

"Who might that be?" Some of the friendliness left the innkeeper's voice.

"A Stirling man." The Highlander met Wyldes's gaze, his own calm and steady. "He's a court bastard by all accounts. His name is Sorley the Hawk."

Chapter Five

❦

"We part ways here, my friend."

Sorley gave Roag a look that brooked no argument as they drew their horses to a halt well before the string of hovels that were all that remained of the once-thriving riverside settlement belonging to the Abbey of St. Mary.

"So we do." Roag slipped down from his beast, stroked the aged horse's neck, and gave him a carrot. Glancing at Sorley, he flashed an annoying smile. "Dinnae think I'd have gone any farther."

"I'd no' have let you." Sorley glared at him, irked that he hadn't thought of bringing a treat for his horse. As always, Roag strove to outdo him.

Proving it, the lout fished a second carrot from inside a small pouch fastened to his saddle and sauntered over to offer it to Sorley's beast.

He didn't look at Sorley, his attention on feeding the horse. "Truth is, I'm no' riding any deeper into thon village because I prefer that as few folk as possible see me in these dung-rags. You, though..."

He stepped back from the horse, eyeing Sorley up and down. "I do believe they become you."

"I'll stuff them up your arse when we're finished here." Sorley slid off his own horse, taking the same care as Roag had done. Wyldes swore the creatures were sturdier than they looked, but he wasn't convinced.

He did know the abbey ruins and the sad little hamlet tore his heart.

Set in a broad loop of the River Forth, the ancient holy site was a maze of tumbled walls and rubble. Thorn bushes, bracken, and stinging nettles raged where magnificent arches and spires should've soared to the heavens. The marauding English had even savaged the sanctity of the abbey burial yard. Ornamental grave slabs were toppled everywhere, their highly carved surfaces barely visible through the thick deer grass choking the ground.

Proud effigies had fared no better, some of them defiled, missing sculpted heads and feet. Even several of the Celtic standing crosses had been knocked over, moss and mud marring their sacred stone.

"Hurts the eye, what?" Roag tucked his thumbs into the corded belt of his beggar's robe.

"For once I agree with you." Sorley felt anger brewing inside him and almost whipped back his own cloak to draw his sword, Dragon-Breath. Named for the man who'd gifted him with the blade, a battle-hardened knight who styled himself Dragon and aye had onion breath, the brand would serve Sorley well when he reached the traitor, Lockhart. The King trusted him to put a sure end to the faithless noble's treachery, and he would. Fenris work was swift and silent, always efficient. But until he went toe-to-toe with Lockhart, he'd keep his fury at bay.

This particular Fenris mission required a humble, sub-servient mien.

A shame he wanted to throw back his head and roar at the cloud-chased sky.

Roag strolled over to him and clapped a hand on his shoulder. For once, the lout knew better than to rile him. "Fiends didn't leave much of anything." Roag glanced toward the Forth, where a large stone slab slanted at a weird angle near the river's edge. In better times, it'd been part of the abbey's watergate. "I'm no' sure I want to wait there, seeing how thickly the nettles are growing o'er the ruins."

"You can hie yourself back to the Red Lion." Sorley let his gaze travel down the narrow beaten-earth road that curved through the hamlet. "Maili is aye glad for your attentions. You'll find no such comfort here."

"Must you aye think the worst of me?" Roag leaned round to peer into Sorley's face, affecting an expression of injury. "My bones tell me you'll be glad I'm along this day."

"Mine say if I cannae take a swing at the English, I sure can make Lockhart scream like a woman." Sorley spat in his palms and rubbed his hands together in anticipation. "Nae, make that ten women."

"See?" Roag straightened, sounding amused. "We are again of the same mind."

"A rare exception." Sorley kept his gaze on the low, rough-stoned cottages lining the road. Built of more turf than rock, they looked more like cow byres than anyone's home. He was sure herds of mice lived in the roof thatch. Worse, the wind had changed, bringing not just the smell of rain but the reek of the communal cesspit.

Still, enough folk went about their daily chores. He even noted trade on the rotting wharf. Several clunky, blunt-bowed cargo ships were tied to the remaining posts, their hulls rocking in the strong-flowing river.

Chickens and goats ran between the hovels and along the road. A cluster of stout, work-worn women carried wicker washing baskets down to the river. And a big-bellied, red-faced man hawked bowls of stewed mutton and ale, drawing a fair crowd to his little cart.

Sorley wished the man well.

He also knew the largest gathering would be around the bend in the road, near the old market cross where Sir Henry Lockhart plied his deceit, calling down miracles while passing on the King's secrets.

"Do you think he truly floats in the air?" Roag had his thumbs in his belt again, proving as so oft that he could read Sorley's mind. "Folk claim he's touched by the gods."

Sorley snorted. "The only thing that'll touch him this day is the cutting edge of Dragon-Breath."

"Many men have witnessed the wonder." Roag shrugged. "He may be a traitor, but he must also be a wizard."

"If he is, the beady red eyes of every pig in the land will turn into spears of flame and sear the first farmer who tries to make them bacon."

"Good men have said—"

"I say he's a crafty fraudster." Sorley flashed a glance at his archrival, amazed he'd allow that Sir Henry could sit in midair.

He wasn't about to share how Sir Henry hovered about the ground.

Or that he'd pried the answer from the sweet-bottomed daughter of an English ironsmith who lived just across the border from Scotland. The smith helped Sir Henry in interest of his own land and loyalties, making him blameless.

Sorley turned toward Roag. "If you dinnae interfere with my work, mayhap I'll show you how—"

He broke off, for Roag was already leading their horses to a patch of grass near one of the still-standing Celtic crosses. He watched as Roag tethered them, once again treating the beasts to a handful of carrots. Then he turned to Sorley and touched the rim of his beggar's hood, a half-smile on his face.

"Gods save me," Sorley swore beneath his breath as he

returned the salute, annoyed there were times he almost liked Roag.

Above all, he enjoyed righting wrongs.

Eager to begin, he tossed one last look at Roag.

True to his word, Roag was perched atop the slanting slab of stone that was once part of the abbey's watergate. He'd drawn up one leg and let the other dangle free, somehow managing to look like anything but the tatty-robed wretch he was supposed to portray.

Anyone would recognize him for what he was.

A cocky bastard.

Hoping he'd stay put, Sorley drew a deep breath and adjusted his cloak. Then he assumed his best humble mien and a suitably crooked posture and limped over to the road, easily melting into the crowd.

"Blessed saints, have mercy on these good folk. Lift their cares, cure their ills! I call upon your greatness Reach through the veil of mysteries to heal them, bringing wonders as only you can!"

Sorley stood at the edge of the crowd, paying scant heed to the ringing words of the raggedy-cloaked monk he recognized as Sir Henry Lockhart, traitor to the crown. The fiend had whitened his face, no doubt to better conceal his identity. Not that any of the clamoring villagers would guess he wasn't a wandering friar, gifted with God's ear. They'd never suspect he was a deep-pursed, land-rich courtier who allowed greed to govern his loyalty.

All they heard were promises of miracles.

What they saw convinced them he could deliver.

Why would anyone doubt when the noble appeared to sit in midair, floating high above a colorful tapestry spread across the muddied ground?

Guised as a monk, his hooded face lowered and his be-robed legs crossed, he clutched a long staff as if to steady himself against the wind. He did present an astonishing spectacle. If Sorley didn't know his trick, he'd have also found himself with his jaw on the ground.

Gullible country folk believed what their eyes showed them.

They were also tossing their hard-earned coin into a battered bronze cauldron Lockhart had set atop the brightly woven rug.

Sorley's blood boiled, watching him.

Deceiving and stealing from those who scratched a living out of the cold, bitter earth was a worse sin than selling the King's secrets to the English.

No king had to worry that his children went to sleep hungry at night.

His bile rising, Sorley willed the rage from his features and then began to limp forward, taking care to appear as bent and distressed as possible.

He dragged one leg, secretly proud of his inspiration to do so.

His best plans came when he was angry.

Rarely had he been so furious. He worked his way past hopeful villagers, many thrusting sickly bairns before them. Others fell to their knees, their arms raised in supplication.

"Gracious monk!" Sorley reached the edge of the rug and used the voice of a weary, pain-riddled man. "Can you heal a poor leper? I've lost toes dragging myself into your sainted presence."

As he'd hoped, his words sent the crowd running.

Even Lockhart appeared to blanch beneath the thick white paste he'd painted on his face. But he caught himself quickly, lifting his free hand, palm outward in the accepted gesture of a blessing.

"I can heal all men, even you." His voice boomed, surely so that his words would carry down the miserable little road, now so deserted. "It is not my power that casts out ills and

demons. The saints use my words and my breath, spending
their miracles with grace."

"Their grace must be great, as they allow you to fly."
Sorley huddled deeper in his cloak, letting his hand search
through the voluminous folds, seeking his sword hilt. "I
have ne'er seen such a sight."

Unaware of Sorley's loathing, Sir Henry tipped his
cowled head toward the river. "As thon waters roll, my son,
so does God's mercy. All things are possible when one is
chosen to perform His benefice."

In the shadows of his cloak's hood, Sorley felt his lips twist
hard. He turned briefly to the river, gliding silently past on the
far side of the sad little market square. If he faced Lockhart
now, the bastard would surely sense his anger and disgust.

And the King, in his goodness, had made him swear he
wouldn't act unless Lockhart's treachery was proven beyond
a doubt.

His guise as a floating monk would be forgiven, the
King's mercy generous.

Betraying Scotland to weight his own purse was unpardonable.

So Sorley schooled his features into a semblance of hope
and humility and limped closer to the colorful rug with its
coin-filled cauldron.

"Such as I dinnae have much," he murmured, dropping a
coin atop the others.

"Soon, lad, you'll have all you desire." Lockhart nodded
sagely, his free hand rising in another blessing. "Your health
restored, and your prosperity."

"I am grateful." Sorley nodded thanks, then moved
slowly around the carpet, limping less with each step. He
stopped in front of Lockhart, meeting his eyes with a gaze
that was steady and calm.

Sorley let a small smile quirk his lips, then lowered his
voice, speaking in the clipped tones of the English. "It is said

that heather blooms sweeter on the south side of the Tweed."
The damning words tasted bitter on his tongue. "And ale
flows more freely, the women..."

"Are a pleasure untold," Lockhart finished, the coded
answer sealing his fate.

Sorley just looked at him, not surprised the courtier recognized the secret phrases used for identification between
spies, men who acted in the name of their own English
crown and the Scottish vermin who served them, selling
their souls for coin.

"A shame you'll ne'er again know such delights." Sorley
switched to his own voice. "Your days are done." Stepping
closer, he threw back his hood, revealing his face. "The
King's wolves are hungry."

"You!" Lockhart jolted, his eyes rounding.

"Nae, the Fenris." Sorley gave a slight bow. "You have
heard the name?"

"See here..." Lockhart's demeanor changed, turning
sly. He glanced up and down the empty road, across the
deserted market square. "All know you appreciate good living. There's a fine sum for—"

"For what?" Sorley moved quickly, clamping his hand
over Lockhart's tight-fisted grip on the staff. "Posing as
a miracle-caster to meet with the English King's spies?
Betraying Scotland? Turning my back on the country I love
more than life itself?

"There is no recompense for such treachery. Less"—he
kicked the carpet, scattering coins—"for putting false hope
in the hearts of innocents. There is only one way to deal with
such perfidy." Sorley squeezed Lockhart's hand, stopping
just short of breaking the traitor's fingers. "It's the reason
King Robert keeps ravening wolves. Men known as the Fenris, my lord."

Lockhart's bravura faded. "You can't mean to..." He
didn't finish, clearly too cowardly to voice his doom.

"I can and shall." Sorley whipped aside his cloak, drawing Dragon-Breath.

Lockhart began to sweat, perspiration melting the white paste on his face. "Wait, hear me. We can work together, a collaboration to benefit—"

"Keep speaking and you'll only fire my urge to wade in your blood." Sorley lifted his sword, holding its tip to Lockhart's face. "Admit your villainies and I'll give you one mercy. A boon the King has granted you: that your innocent lady wife and family shall be told you fell from your horse, breaking your neck. Deny the charges and all Scotland will know of your treachery." Sorley narrowed his eyes, his gaze unblinking. "Your name forever damned, your lands and titles reverting to the crown."

"You're drawing a crowd." Lockhart glanced down the road, hope flickering in his eyes. "Lower your blade lest men challenge you for accosting a helpless monk."

"Think you?" Sorley pressed Dragon-Breath's tip more firmly against Lockhart's cheek. "The villagers won't near me. They'll want to keep their fingers and toes. Let them look, whoe'er they are."

But when he followed Lockhart's gaze, his heart almost stopped. A mounted party of three, two young women and a strapping, sword-hung Highlander, had halted in the village road, near the ruined gate to St. Mary's burial yard.

They were staring at Sorley and Lockhart, seeing, he hoped, only a beggar and a monk. Sorley prayed his broad back and voluminous robes would hide his sword and the airy space between Lockhart's perch and the ground.

Sorley saw the riders clearly. Only the red-faced, big-bellied man selling stewed mutton and ale loomed between them, having pulled his cart farther up the road. Even so, the newcomers stood out sharply against the rough-stoned cottages and the burial ground's crumbling gate.

They were Lady Mirabelle, Maili, and a MacLaren guardsman.

A large basket of flowers affixed to the Highlander's saddle hinted Mirabelle hoped to lay blooms at someone's grave. Shadows hid her face, but suspicion rolled off her in waves. She recognized Sorley.

Maili also knew, clearly. Working with William Wyldes she was privy to much, and sworn to secrecy.

The MacLaren guardsman, apparently sensing trouble, rode forward, placing himself before the two young women. He tossed back his plaid and was about to reach for his sword hilt when a large, hulking shape lurched into the road from the direction of the abbey's watergate.

Staggering drunkenly, the cloaked wretch drew up before the mounted Highlander. He grasped the man's leg, appearing to babble. Whatever he said must've alarmed the Highlander, because he roared and shoved him away. As quickly, he jerked his horse around and snatched the reins of the other two beasts, leading them swiftly into the burial ground, out of sight of the market square and men he surely deemed unfit company for the two young women he escorted.

When they disappeared, Roag wheeled about, now standing tall and straight. He touched his robe's cowl in a salute before he sauntered away down the muddied road.

Sorley would take any bet Roag was grinning. Rarely had he put on a better performance.

"Thon folk are gone." Sorley returned his attention to Lockhart, his sword tip still at the traitor's face. He didn't let on he'd recognized Mirabelle and her party. He hoped they wouldn't reappear. The last thing he wanted was having her near when he cut Lockhart to ribbons.

But that was what he was here to do.

So he jiggled his blade, drawing a bead of blood from Lockhart's cheekbone. "I gave you a choice." He met the noble's eye. "Admit your treacheries or deny them."

Lockhart set his jaw, saying nothing.

"Speak true, and your family will no' suffer for your evil deeds."

Lockhart only stared at him.

Sorley slid his sword tip from the noble's face to his throat. "I shall count to three…"

"I deny naught," Lockhart spat the words. "My wife, my family—"

"They will aye remain in the King's good graces. You…" Sorley drew Dragon-Breath along Lockhart's shoulder, then down his sleeve, slicing the cloth, exposing the iron-worked frame that held his perch aloft.

Just as the English ironmonger's daughter had sworn, the contraption was cleverly crafted. The monk's staff, heavy iron painted to look like wood, bent at the top, the curve hidden by Lockhart's hand. The iron then disappeared inside his robe's sleeve, forming a metal frame that provided a stable seat. The massive base stayed out of sight beneath the colorful carpet and bronze cauldron.

Once it was in place, the monk's robes carefully draped, anyone sitting in such a structure would appear to float high above the ground, unless the robes were cut away to reveal the trickery, as Sorley now did with great pleasure.

He gave Lockhart a cold look as the cloak fell to the ground. "Spare yourself the shame of me dragging you away. Come now."

"The hell I will." Lockhart sprang from his perch, darting between two close-lying cottages.

Sorley threw off his beggar's cloak and tore after him, leaping over a low stone wall to catch up with him in a kale patch behind the hovels. "That's where you're headed, aye." Sorley lunged, using the flat side of his sword to strike Lockhart behind the knees. Lockhart's feet flew out from beneath him and he landed hard, grunting as his breath left him. "A shame your journey there will be a long one."

"You'll not cut down an unarmed man?" Lockhart gasped the words, glaring up at Sorley from where he sprawled in the dirt. The linen tunic he wore beneath the now-gone monk's robe fluttered in the rising wind. "Even you will have that much honor."

"Dinnae sully such a fine word on your fouled tongue." Sorley slammed his sword into the ground, rested his hands on the vibrating hilt. "I should lop off your head and leave it dripping on thon wall." He jerked his chin toward the mossy stones that were all remaining of the village boundary. "King Robert gave me leave to have done with you any way I wish. As I'm thinking your sword is back in the square, hidden beneath your magical carpet, I'll fight you with dirks. I'll hasten no man to hell without giving him a chance to send me there first." Leaning down, Sorley grabbed Lockhart's arm and yanked him to his feet. "After I'm done with you, for I've no taste to die this day, I'll fetch your blade if a village man hasn't claimed it. If it's still there, your lady will receive it."

"You can't do this." Lockhart blanched. "I'm a lord—"

"You disgraced the privilege." Sorley pulled Dragon-Breath from the ground and wiped her blade on his jerkin, then sheathed her. "Be a man and die with courage."

Lockhart glanced toward the village road. "Wait—"

"I have waited, longer than you deserve." Sorley pulled him out of the kale patch and down to the river. "The Forth is thirsty." He made for a stand of birches that would shield them from the village. "Your blood will quench that need."

As they neared the water, Lockhart stumbled, his feet catching in the knee-high grass. He began to pray. Sorley ignored him, sure the gods, by any name, didn't look kindly on traitors.

Sorley stopped near a jumble of rocks, once part of the abbey's outer wall.

It seemed a good place for a turncoat to die.

Lockhart shrieked when Sorley released him. Backing away, he held out his hands, palms outward, his eyes terror-filled.

"This is crazed."

"I say it is the King's due." Sorley pulled a dirk from beneath his belt and plucked another from his boot, tossing it to Lockhart. "Fight well and I'll make your end faster."

Lockhart ignored the dagger when it dropped by his foot.

Sorley retrieved the blade, pressing its hilt into the noble's hand. "Have you no belly for bloodletting?"

"Dirks make clumsy killings."

Sorley shrugged. "You should've thought of that before you hid your sword beneath your gypsy-rug. Though"—he eyed the dirk in his hand—"a quick knife thrust through the ribs is fair painless.

"If a man pierces the heart," he added, taking up a fighting stance. "I'm only oath-sworn to kill you, I cannae promise such mercy."

The threat worked, causing Lockhart to leap at him, slashing wildly. "You are dirt beneath my feet," he screamed, his blade slicing air.

"So some say." Sorley countered Lockhart's frantic swipes effortlessly, backing him to the river's edge. "Loving Scotland as I do, I see no slur in being likened to our blessed soil."

Lockhart leapt at him, his dagger high. "You should've been dashed against the hearthstone at birth!"

"Perhaps." Sorley sidestepped him.

In that moment, somewhere in the distance, a woman screamed. Sorley tensed, his amusement gone. The cry came from the village.

The voice sounded like Mirabelle's.

Terrible images flashed across his mind, turning his world red and tilting the earth beneath his feet. He whirled about, glancing through the trees, seeing nothing beyond their bounds but the slow-rising slope of the water meadows and a few scrawny sheep munching grass.

No further cries rose, but one was enough.

Lockhart dashed away. Sorley wheeled about to see him running along the river's shingled beach. The tide was out and he'd hitched up his long tunic to scramble over the rotten, waterlogged planks of a ruined quay. He didn't look back, racing as if the devil were on his heels.

Sorley sprinted after him, sure he could run even faster.

Gaining on him swiftly, Sorley leapt over a seaweed-draped piece of the old wharf and caught Lockhart by the scruff of his neck and the back of his tunic, tossing him roughly into the shallow water.

"Aggggh!" Lockhart shrieked, scrabbling backward across the shingle.

Sorley tackled him, pressing his dirk hard against the noble's gullet. They grappled, rolling over the wet stone and mud at the river's edge. Lockhart raised his arm, Sorley's spare dirk still clutched in his fist. Sorley let him draw blood, even welcomed the glancing slice across his shoulder. It was no more than a flesh wound, but enough to redden his sleeve.

To stem the guilt he'd have felt otherwise.

He never struck down a man who wouldn't fight.

No matter his sins.

And Sir Henry Lockhart's were great. The King wanted his head. Or rather, he wished Lockhart removed from the land of the living.

How that happened, he'd left to Sorley.

So-o-o...

He glanced up at the clouded heavens, the silence of the village loud in his ears as he thrust his dirk point deeper, Lockhart's blood red on the blade.

"I'll give you my sword," the noble pleaded, shaking. "My oath—"

"As you swore to King Robert?" Sorley remained hard.

"I think no'. I will make this swift. You can thank a lady for that mercy," he vowed, arcing the long blade, letting it plunge downward to spear the traitor's throat. "Without her scream, I'd no' be so kind."

A terrible gurgling answered him, the soul's last cry when it leaves this earth.

Lockhart's blood fled, too. Hot, red, and streaming, it poured forth to drench the shingle and stain the muddied water at the tide line. Repulsed—such was never a fair sight—Sorley jerked his blade free and cleaned it on a mossy rock. He leapt to his feet, leaving the King's enemy to be claimed by the river's swift-running current.

Mirabelle was in trouble and now naught else mattered.

So he tore down the narrow foreshore, almost flew up the river's slippery bank, and then ran across the water meadows and through the birches, not stopping until he reached the deserted village road.

Lady Mirabelle was nowhere. Sorley frowned, glancing about. The burly MacLaren guardsman and Maili were also gone.

The village appeared emptied, nothing stirring except the cold, damp wind off the river and the ever-present gulls wheeling above. Somewhere a sheep baaed, and a few chickens pecked near someone's doorstep.

"Mother of all the gods!" Sorley shoved a hand through his hair, not caring that his fingers were covered in blood.

Breathing hard, his chest on fire, he bent forward, resting his hands on his thighs. His heart thundering, he glanced up and down the road, hoping he'd imagined Mirabelle's cry, trying to believe a cat had yowled or that the shrill tone had come from a troubled ewe.

He discarded the possibilities as soon as they crossed his mind.

His gut told him who had screamed.

The knowledge chilled his blood as he sprinted down

the road, making for the watergate and the bastard he'd tear apart with his bare hands if he'd witnessed Mirabelle's distress and done nothing.

"Damnation!" Sorley ran faster, barreling around the bend in the road only to skid to a halt before the body of the big-bellied, red-faced man who'd been selling stewed mutton and ale. Clearly dead, the wretch was sprawled face-down in a pool of blood, his toppled cart a few paces away, resting at a weird angle against a cottage wall.

It was then that Sorley heard a grunt and the clank of steel on steel.

He also caught a curse, recognizing the voice as Roag's in the same moment the fiend burst into view, sword in hand and fighting a man Sorley didn't recognize.

They were evenly matched.

And Sorley knew Roag wouldn't appreciate his interference.

He also knew his archrival would win.

But there was one thing he didn't know.

"The lady!" Sorley shouted above the clashing steel. "Where is she?"

"No' here!" Roag waved his free hand in Sorley's direction, as if brushing off his concern. "She's safe," he yelled, leaping aside when his opponent slashed forward in a lightning-quick arc meant to kill.

Roag lunged at the other man, striking him in the side with such brute strength that blood plumed in a red fountain and his body swung away into the shattered stew cart.

"English devil!" Roag had nearly sliced him in two.

He sheathed his bloodied sword. Then he spat on the ground, grinned, and swaggered up to Sorley, brazen as ever.

"Did I no' say you'd be glad for my company?" He punched Sorley's arm, his grin spreading. "Thon fiend was unloading fish at the wharf. When you took off with

Lockhart, he leapt o'er a barrel of eels and drew a sword, chasing after you. He was Lockhart's man, a lookout—"

"Mirabelle, what of her?" Sorley grabbed Roag's arms, gripping tight. Blood pumped through his veins, hot and rushing. The air thinned around him, making it hard to breathe. "Where is she? Who attacked her?"

"Nary a soul." Roag shook free, his words letting Sorley's heart slow again. "She—"

"I heard her scream."

He had. And now she'd vanished like a curl of mist, her father's man and Maili with her.

"So she did." Roag swiped his arm across his brow. A steel-gray drizzle was beginning to fall, a fine mist rolling along the narrow road. "But she didnae cry out because of the eel-reeking Sassenach.

"He ate steel later. It was the other one who made her scream." He glanced to the dead mutton-stew-and-ale purveyor and back again. "She and her party came trotting out of the abbey burial ground just as—"

Sorley raised a hand, silencing him. "Dinnae tell me she saw you skewer a hapless hawker." He eyed the poor man's back, the blood surrounding him like a scarlet robe. He could see Roag chasing the Englishman, blade drawn and not paying any heed to a bumbling, big-bellied man and his stew cart, trundling along the road. "He'll haunt you all your days."

"I think no'."

"He should."

"Nae, you ought to thank me for cutting him down." Roag swelled his chest. "Truth is, it was seeing him pull his blade from beneath the straw of his peddler's wagon that made Lady Mirabelle scream. The cart was near the gate to the burial ground when she and her party rode into the road." Roag shook his head, remembering. "Imagine the lady's fright to see a lowly stew-and-ale hawker whip out a longsword, transforming himself into a warrior before her startled, gently-bred eyes? Her guard drew his blade, but he soon saw the man wasn't interested in his lady or Maili.

"The Highlander slewed his horse about, slapped the rumps of the ladies' steeds, and they thundered away. The hawker..." He pulled a hand down over his chin. "He shook his blade at their backs and then took off after you."

"He wasn't fit to lift a sword, much less swing one." Sorley glanced at the man again, still seeing no more than a pitiful peddler. "He was fat," he added, turning an accusatory look on Roag.

"Aye, he was, but no' from too much ale." Roag strolled to the toppled cart, pulling a sword from under its shattered side. Tossing a glance at Sorley, he used the blade's tip to lift something from the road's edge.

It was a well-stuffed linen sack, about the size of the hawker's belly.

"This was the man's girth." Roag jiggled the sword, sending goose feathers into the air. "If I hadn't caught him, and his English pal, you'd have been fighting three against one down by the river."

"I saw him earlier, selling his stew." Sorley shook his head, astounded. "He looked more like a pig farmer than any fighting man."

Roag shrugged. "If you dinnae believe me, roll him onto his back. You'll see he's as hard-muscled as we are. Or he was." He flicked the sword, letting the feather sack slip to the ground.

The blade he flipped into the air, catching the hilt as it dropped. "I've done you two favors this day. And you"—he began tying the sword to his belt, using a spare length of leather—"have forgotten one of the Fenris's basic credos.

"It's times of trouble that prove a man's mettle." He looked up, the new sword hanging at his hip. "Peril and hardship—"

"Reveal friend or foe." Sorley took a whisky flask from a belt at his own hip and handed it to Roag. He nodded gruffly when Roag tipped the flask to his lips, drinking deeply.

Roag wiped his mouth and returned the flask to Sorley. "I'd hoped to take Maili abovestairs at the Red Lion this e'en, but now she's heading to Stirling with your lady and her guardsman. So-o-o"—he winked—"what say you we hie ourselves back to the inn and see what other lovelies Wyldes has working tonight?"

"I'm no' in the mood." Sorley wasn't. The thought didn't cause the slightest stirring in his loins.

"Och, come." Roag sketched a female form in the air. "A bit of female comfort will do you good, help you sleep."

"Nae." Sorley swung up onto his saddle. "The last thing I want is a wench in my bed this e'en."

He couldn't believe how smoothly the lie fell from his tongue.

He did desire a woman, and badly.

The problem was that he didn't ache for just any female's charms. He wanted Mirabelle. He burned to ravish her, devouring her whole.

He doubted he'd be able to keep his hands off her when they met in the castle chapel later that night.

As he was feeling now, he'd pounce on her. Lowborn as he was, he was more than capable of such predaceous behavior, especially when he wanted something as fiercely as he desired Mirabelle.

She should never have come to him.

But she had.

When they parted ways, he would be the one left empty-handed, his heart ripped asunder.

Even so, he could scarce control the thrum of anticipation inside him, didn't know how he'd manage the long ride back to the castle, the necessity of a much-needed bath, and then the waiting until she opened the chapel door, joining him in the dimly lit privacy he'd make sure they'd have. He might even kiss her, there before God and sundry saints.

He frowned, now feeling most definite stirrings.

What did that say about him?

He knew, and it was a challenge he wasn't of a mind to deny.

Chapter Six

❧

Much later that evening, Mirabelle stood outside Stirling Castle's small stone chapel and did her best to hold on to her composure. The truth was she'd felt the weight of her actions bearing down on her more heavily with every step she'd taken across the courtyard. She didn't know whether that was because of excitement or nerves. She wasn't a fearful person. Indeed, many at Knocking called her spirited and bold. But it wasn't every day that she considered such an outrageous plan, giving herself to a man she scarcely knew.

She *was* attracted to him.

And why not?

He was darkly handsome, strapping and tall, with broad shoulders. And he had a roguish air that drew her. He was celebrated in courtly and common circles, reaping admiration because he'd earned every bit of his fame.

Few men could rise to such adulation from Sorley's lowly beginnings.

He truly was a man apart.

And while she might be known for her fiery temperament, her skill at convincing her father of Sir John's true nature had proved lacking. Adept at presenting himself as a gallant, prosperous and polished, the noble held the confidence of even the most astute courtiers. Any whisperings against him were discarded as the grumblings of the envious. Mirabelle's objections fell on deaf ears.

In truth, nothing could be proven against him.

Still, Mirabelle trusted the feeling that washed over her when he was near.

If he looked at her...

She shivered, her skin prickling. Sir John need only enter a room and a shadow seemed to spread out from him, dimming the light, darkening his surroundings. Unfortunately, few others at court noticed.

Sorley did.

Heat swirled low in her belly and she shivered again, this time for very different reasons. "Oh, dear saints." She took a deep breath of the night's chill air, needing to calm herself.

Her emotions raged, unleashed and tumultuous. The only thing remaining between her and ruination was the thickness of a door. She had only to open it and step inside to learn if Sorley the Hawk would accept her offer.

If he'd despoil her as only he could, using darkly seductive skills she knew would be deeply carnal, dangerously lascivious, and maddeningly addictive.

Instinct told her he'd agree.

Her heart warned she'd be in trouble if he did.

She was also sure he was the beggar she'd met in the stableyard of the Red Lion Inn. No other man could wear such rags and still possess an air of blatant, almost savage masculinity. His cloak's hood had shadowed much of his face, including his eyes. But she'd felt him looking at her, sensed his searing gaze, so much bolder than any simple wayfarer would have dared to turn on her.

Sorley was a notorious rogue.

He'd stare down the devil if it pleased him.

He might stand high in the King's favor, but he took pride in shunning the rules and strictures of courtly behavior. His appetite for carnal delights was legend. Ladies of high birth blushed on hearing his name, even vied for his attention. Word was they often fought each other to land in his arms. They didn't care that he ruined reputations with one dark glance, a meaningful nod toward the shadows of a quiet stairwell.

Everyone knew what then transpired. In the stair tower, against the wall, or—Mirabelle bit her lower lip and inhaled—atop the silken sheets of a massive four-poster bed in a noblewoman's privy quarters.

No doubt his sumptuous bedchamber had witnessed many scandals, the tapestried walls echoing with the cries of lust-crazed females.

Forbidden pleasures were his specialty.

Mirabelle pressed closer to the chapel door. The night was turning colder, the wind cutting like a knife. She felt as hot as a balefire. Visions of wild orgies and all manner of debauchery gave her no peace. Each heated image made her heart beat faster.

Was this what it meant to be wanton?

She was sure that was so.

She was also certain she wouldn't remember a word of the carefully crafted arguments she'd prepared should Sorley refuse to ravish her.

In truth, he already had—seducing her in his bedchamber with the dark, decadent heat of his peat-brown eyes.

In the shadowy gloom, she'd imagined his hands on her, even hoped for his kiss.

Worse, she'd tingled.

And in a place no well-bred and proper young lady should acknowledge.

It was madness to tryst with him in the close confines of a candlelit chapel where the saints were sure to scowl down at her for her reckless, scandalous behavior.

Yet...

What red-blooded female could resist such a devilishly handsome scoundrel?

She certainly couldn't.

His appeal might prove dangerous, but his oh-so-intimate gazes melted her. She already knew that his touch stirred forbidden desires so thrilling any woman would gladly surrender to his lovemaking.

And...

She'd seen him naked.

She'd stood before him when he was in such a state, less than a hand's breadth separating her from all that magnificent masculinity.

His powerfully intense virility was known to her. How easily she'd succumbed, his stunning maleness taking her breath, even charging the air around them. She'd been unable to look away, not caring about the wicked tales whispered about him. The cast-aside bedmates rumored to spend their days pining for him. The married ladies who'd risked everything for the expertise of his amorous attentions.

Soon she'd join their ranks.

But first she lifted a hand to her throat, felt the racing of her pulse. A still-hesitant part of her couldn't believe her daring. Yet now that she was so close to the culmination of her plan, a fresh rush of delicious, shivery excitement swept her, proving she'd welcome his attentions, even pure and inexperienced as she was.

Hoping she wouldn't remain so much longer, she glanced across the deserted bailey. A light drizzle had been falling for hours, keeping most castle dwellers inside the warm, firelit hall. Guards did patrol the battlements, but their gaze was turned outward, watching the night-darkened hills and the surrounding countryside. Here in the stronghold's heart, little stirred. Drifts of fine, chill mist blurred the edges of the soaring castle walls and outbuildings, the fog dampening any voices and evening revelry that might've otherwise escaped the keep.

The chapel was equally silent, a tiny ancient-walled structure, humble for all its royal connections; an even older place of worship had once stood on the site.

Few remains existed of the place where, according to castle tongue-waggers, long-ago Druids worshipped the sun and pagans sacrificed virgins to bloodthirsty Celtic deities. But there were a few faint etchings in some of the stones that supported the chapel's foundation. Embellishments that would've been bold and handsome in their day, the carvings consisted of mythical beasts and strange swirling lines and interlaced circles that no one now living could decipher.

Some claimed raucous couplings once took place atop the chapel's altar stone, a large piece of unusually smooth granite said to have sparkled brilliantly when pagan lovers found their release.

The notion sent a flood of heat to Mirabelle's cheeks and she took another calming breath of the chill air. She let her gaze flick over the courtyard's enclosing arcade to be sure she was unobserved.

On her way to the chapel, she'd thought she'd caught a glimpse of Sir John Sinclair watching her from the shadows behind one of the arcade's pillars.

Blessedly, she saw no one now.

The arcaded walkways appeared deserted.

So she pushed open the door and stepped into the chapel. The air was cold and damp, smelling of old stone, candle wax, and smoky-sweet incense. Votive candles burned on prickets and many-armed candelabra, their golden flames casting a glow across the altar stone and the brightly painted pillars that lined the outer edges of the nave. Though small, its rough-stoned walls ancient, the chapel's interior was richly decorated. There were even a few elaborately carved granite tombs set in alcoves near the altar.

But none of that interested her as she moved deeper into the chapel, her steps echoing against the low, barrel-vaulted ceiling. She searched the shadows, peered into the darkest corners, and even peeked behind startlingly lifelike effigies on the tall, granite tombs. She walked up and down the nave twice, looking everywhere for Sorley.

He wasn't there.

The chapel was empty.

Pausing near the altar, she rubbed her arms and adjusted her cloak. The night's chill damp slipped in through the narrow windows set high in the thick walls. The candles, however plentiful, did nothing to chase the cold.

In truth, her need to draw her mantle closer had more to do with her than the worsening weather.

Sorley's failure to appear sent her hopes plummeting.

She'd been so certain he'd keep his word.

Now . . .

She headed back to the door, wishing the votive lights didn't cause so many shadows to leap and dance across the walls. Sir John Sinclair's face seemed to stare at her from the darkest corner, his hooded eyes glinting in triumph, his mouth quirked in a self-satisfied smile. She knew he wasn't really there, but his imagined expression was just the sort of look he'd give her if her father capitulated, accepting the slippery nobleman's bid for her hand.

Munro MacLaren knew herbs and mosses, healing lore and the beauty of words.

He was easily fooled by men.

And so, it would seem, was she.

Disappointment bit deep. Worry also rose inside her, making her feel slightly faint. It was one thing to undress before Sorley, a compelling, boldly handsome man she was strongly attracted to. She accepted that her proposal meant he would ravish her. The carnal act was her choice, her only means of deterring Sinclair. She'd been fully prepared to pursue her plan to its inevitable conclusion, the ruination of her name and the loss of her maidenly virtue. Indeed, she'd even embrace such a fate.

She was not willing to lie with Sir John.

The possibility, and all its sickening consequences, hit her in the stomach. For a moment, her world tilted, the stone floor seeming to dip beneath her feet. The chapel walls appeared to close in around her, pressing so near it became hard for her to breathe.

Needing air, she reached for the door.

Before her fingers could close on the latch, the door swung open and Sorley stood before her. He filled the arched entry, his broad shoulders and tall, strapping body etched against the silvery mist blowing across the courtyard.

"Lady Mirabelle." His tone was low, deep, and shockingly intimate. It also sent awareness rushing all through her. "Were you leaving already?"

He closed the door and stepped forward, setting his hands on her shoulders. "I was no' able to get away until now."

"I haven't waited long..." Mirabelle stared up at him. Her heart thundered so fiercely, she couldn't think of anything else to say.

He took her breath, robbing her of all thought. Resplendent was the first word that came to her mind. In the chapel's incense-scented dimness, the flickering candlelight showed the intensity of his gaze. His dark eyes shone like clear, night-blackened water. The wind had tossed his hair, blowing it across his brow in a way that made her yearn to reach and smooth back the gleaming strands. His cloak was a deep, rich blue and woven of costliest wool. Through the mantle's opening, she could see a fine silvered belt slung low on his hips, and the great sword he carried with obvious pride. His leather boots were of a higher quality than any pair possessed by her father. He smelled of sandalwood, the exotic scent playing havoc with her senses. Unfortunately, his jaw was hard-set and his eyes held a dangerous glint.

He didn't appear pleased to see her.

Nor did anything about him hint that he'd recently worn the tattered rags of a beggar.

Or that he'd been in the company of a similarly guised man who'd lurched into the narrow lane that ran through the village of St. Mary's Abbey, a supposed leper who'd grabbed her guard's leg, babbling incoherently. She'd seen more chaos in the village, and had witnessed a stew-and-ale hawker suddenly yank a sword from his cart as she and her party had left the abbey's ruined burial ground.

Her father's man had slewed his horse around, blocking her view and then galloping with her and Maili from the strange scene. But they'd heard the shouts and clashing of steel as they'd thundered away. It'd been a fierce, nightmarish affray that shouldn't have involved two penniless beggars, unless they hadn't been what they seemed.

Her eyes, and her imagination, could've tricked her.

Still...

"Has the chapel's cold frozen your tongue, my lady?" He leaned toward her, his breath grazing her cheek. "Shall I warm you?"

"I am fine," Mirabelle lied. "The cold never bothers me. I much prefer it to being hot."

"Indeed?" For a beat, he looked amused.

"Yes. I mean—" She broke off, realizing her gaffe.

"I know what you meant." His levity gone, he looked at her with such a fierce expression that her stomach quivered. "Even so, I would no' be responsible for you catching a chill. I regret keeping you."

"You didn't." Mirabelle straightened, hoping to look more confident than she felt.

It wasn't easy.

Rarely had she found herself in such a state, excited, nervous, and terrified.

"I just arrived." She kept her gaze steady on his, half sure that the heat in his eyes would soon ignite flames to sweep the length of her.

"Did you think I wouldn't come?" He arched a brow, clearly aware she'd spoken an untruth. "You needn't have doubted. I gave you my word."

"You might've been delayed, rendered unable to meet me." She watched him carefully, suspicious. "Much can happen—"

"Nothing would have stopped me from keeping a promise to you." He lifted a hand, smoothed his thumb over her lower lip.

Mirabelle's entire body warmed as he let his gaze drift down her, from the top of her head to the tips of her rain-damped slippers. There was something in his expression that made her feel as if he wasn't just looking at her, but removing her clothes. As if he knew very well what he'd see if he'd done so.

She lifted her chin, not wanting him to guess how powerfully he affected her, that her heart raced from her daring move in meeting him here. She'd crossed a line in doing so.

Now there could be no retreat.

"You promised me nothing." She spoke as calmly as she could. She had to give him the chance to back away. "You weren't obliged."

"I aye keep my word, lass." He held her gaze, his dark eyes like polished jet in the candlelight. "There were too many years when my word was all I had to be proud of. Ne'er do I misuse or break it. Most especially when it is given to a beautiful lady."

Mirabelle swallowed, unable to help herself. "You are a charmer."

A slow smile curved his lips. A darkly seductive smile, as unsettling as how he'd let his gaze slide oh-so-suggestively up and down her body. Yet his boldness made her pulse leap. It also warmed her in indecent places. She touched a hand to her breast, feeling both hot and dizzy despite the chill dampness of the chapel.

He stepped closer, giving her the distinct impression he'd pounce if she so much as blinked. "I am fond of women, aye."

"So I have heard." She kept her head raised, resisted the urge to wipe her palms against her cloak.

"Are you nervous?"

"I am relieved." She spoke true, just not admitting she was indeed jittery. Her emotions were running higher than ever before.

She was also sharply aware of every ruggedly alluring inch of him, including the oh-so-virile bulge she could see through the edges of his cloak. The glow of a wall sconce slanted right there, proving that he wasn't just a tall, strapping man, powerfully built and good-looking.

He was also just as well-lusted as the court ladies claimed.

Sorley the Hawk wanted her.

And he was already prepared to do exactly what she'd asked of him.

She pretended not to have noticed.

"A lady in my position cannot afford the luxury of nerves."

"You are a brave lass." He considered her, his voice so low, so intimate that her heart beat faster. "I'm impressed by your courage."

"All Highland women are strong." Hoping to appear worldly, she let the hood of her cloak fall back, aware the many candles would shine flatteringly on her hair. She'd left her hair unbound and shook it back now, letting the freshly washed curls tumble to her hips. She knew it was foolish, but she couldn't shake the urge to distract him as much as his overpoweringly virile presence rattled her. She could hardly breathe, standing so close to him.

"You should understand my feelings." She prayed only she heard the tremor in her voice. "I did not make my request lightly. After all I've told you, my predicament should be clear."

"So it is." He placed a hand against the small of her back, steering her deeper into the chapel, away from the door. "I sympathize. No matter how highly regarded he is at court, Sir John is a suitor no maid should accept. Even so, I am surprised to find you here.

"What you have proposed will see you rid of more than an unwanted admirer." He stopped before a knight's tomb, releasing her to lean back against the stone gallant's recumbent form. Resting his palms on the tomb's edge, he crossed his ankles. The casual pose made him look as if they were discussing the rain drumming on the chapel roof rather than something as monumental as the loss of her maidenhead. "Given the seriousness, the finality of such an act, some lasses might've reconsidered."

"I am not 'some lass.'" Mirabelle put back her shoulders, trying to ignore how good he looked in the soft glow of the candles.

"I am a MacLaren, Highland born and bred." She pretended not to see how his lips twitched as he fought to hide a smile. "There is little I will not do when pressed to a wall. I am not as mild-mannered or kindly-natured as my sire. I do not allow myself to be cornered.

"And"—she spoke with pride—"there is nothing I fear."

"Except Sir John."

"I revile him. There is a difference."

"Many who have tried to thwart Sinclair are no more, my

lady. You may trust that some of those poor souls have been women."

"Is there no one brave enough to challenge him?" Mirabelle couldn't believe there wasn't.

She was also sure the one man who could was before her.

Proving it, Sorley's gaze chilled. "He knows a sword blade hovers a breath from the back of his neck, that a dirk can be easily slid between a man's ribs when he sleeps. He is aware he's watched, my lady.

"I cannae say more." His voice was cold, the tightness at his jaw hinting at a man very different from the masterful lover who set court ladies' hearts to fluttering. "All you need to know is that I understand why you wish to repel his attentions. He is no man for you to marry."

"That is why I came to you." Mirabelle glanced over her shoulder at the door, sure she'd heard something.

But it was only a mouse scuttling about on the cold stone floor.

When she turned back to Sorley, he was still leaning against the tomb. His hands remained where they'd been, palms flat on the curved edge of the tomb, his feet crossed at the ankles, as casually as before. But his dark eyes were hooded now, his face shuttered. His mood had changed, turning so guarded the air felt different, seeming to crackle with tension.

"Is that your only reason, my lady?" His gaze pierced her. "Because you know Sinclair is capable of anything? Because my reputation—"

"To be sure, I am aware of his villainies." Mirabelle tried to ignore the rushing in her ears, the terrible sense that everything was now ruined. "Your reputation is also—"

"Wicked enough to attract your attention?"

"I didn't mean—"

"Let us speak plainly, Lady Mirabelle." He stood, his sword clanking against the tomb. "You wish me to defile you so that Sir John, my sworn enemy, will lose interest in you. Odious as he is, he is known to be fastidious in all things. He will not follow where I have been. I believe you know *where* I mean?" He had the audacity to flick his gaze to the exact part of her that he meant, as if he could see right through her clothes. "Or do you, in your maidenly innocence, need me to explain?"

Mirabelle bristled, her temper rising.

Knowing her face flamed, she aimed her own gaze at the sword at his hip. "Perhaps I'd rather hear if you always enter holy places wearing arms?"

"There are many sacred places, lady, and"—he swept back his rich blue cloak to reveal his sword in all its gleaming magnificence—"as long as there are men who'd sully the sanctity of such sites, I will keep Dragon-Breath—"

"Dragon-Breath?" Mirabelle seized on the odd name, for he was coming toward her, his steps slow and purposeful.

"Aye, so my sword is called." He stopped, setting his hand on the hilt, his expression still hard. "She is named for the knight who gave her to me. He was overly fond of onions. He was also the first man of noble blood to believe in me and"—his face turned even darker—"he should no' now lie beneath the tainted, weed-choked earth of a ruined abbey's burial ground. He was cut down fighting the English who defiled the site. His death is a reason I keep my sword at my side where'er I go.

"I do so whether entering the King's own chapel or even a Druid's wood, for such places, to my mind, are possessed of an even greater holiness than anything built by man." He gave her a slow, measured smile that didn't reach his eyes. "Does that answer your question?"

"Not all of them." Mirabelle felt unjustifiably shamed, his words weighing heavy on her heart.

But she wasn't about to let him see her vulnerability.

She also had a terrible suspicion that when he'd spoken of

his slain benefactor, he'd meant the neglected burial ground at St. Mary's Abbey. She knew it well, visiting every time she was in Stirling. She placed flowers on the graves of MacLaren kinsmen who rested there.

"What else would you like to know?" Sorley smiled again. This time a touch of warmth did reach his eyes, but in a devilish gleam that sent her heart plunging straight to her toes. He sauntered toward her again, the look on his face making her mouth go dry. "Perhaps you wish to hear my answer to your proposal?"

Annoyed that she was so susceptible to him, she stood her ground, refusing to back away when he stopped right before her, so near that she could feel the dark, masculine heat pouring off him. She was also forced to breathe in his rousing sandalwood scent. Its exoticness, and a subtle, irresistible hint of pure, hot-blooded male, affected her so powerfully that she forgot all reason.

Lifting her chin, she flipped her hair over her shoulder and gave him a piercing look of her own. "With surety, I want to hear your decision. But first"—she challenged him in the strongest voice she could muster—"I'd like to know why you spent the morning garbed as a penniless beggar."

About the same time, but unknown to Mirabelle and Sorley, a woman hovered beside one of the arcade pillars and blessed the chill wet mist blowing across the castle courtyard. Lovely and thick, the shimmering mist hid her well, sparing her pity if anyone happened to notice her.

She'd never been a vain woman. Her path in life, such as it'd been, hadn't given her cause for any such posturing or illusions. She'd always known her limitations and accepted them as her due.

After all, there was more to be said for what dwelled within.

The good of one's soul and how caring one's heart.

Beauty and its attendant frivol was fleeting. But a heart that loved true, loyalties that never wavered, stayed with a body forever.

She knew that well.

Still...

She didn't wish to be mistaken for a beggar, and she'd flinched on hearing the word, the fair maid's voice carrying on the night wind, bringing just that wee snippet of her discourse with the bold, strapping young man who'd joined her in the chapel. She'd watched the arrival of them both, her usual boredom causing her to look on with interest when first the dazzling flame-haired lass crossed the bailey to enter the empty chapel.

A romantic at heart, despite everything, she'd really taken note when the braw, dashingly clad gallant appeared out of the mist, striding purposefully toward the holy site as if he couldn't wait to seize his lady to him, perhaps lifting her in the air and swinging her in a circle before pulling her into his arms for a deep, much-anticipated kiss. Or so she imagined as she'd watched them close the chapel door, shutting themselves inside their candlelit trysting place.

They surely weren't aware of the barely visible cracks in the chapel's ancient window glass.

But she knew.

One such as her had much time to drift about, mostly unseen or disregarded by passersby, while noticing so many things herself.

So she'd allowed herself to slip a wee bit closer to the chapel, driven by curiosity and a yearning for what once was and could never be again.

Hearing the girl accuse the lad of being a penniless beggar surprised and saddened her.

He'd looked nothing the like to her.

Nor had the lass struck her as the shallow sort, despite her vibrant good looks.

Disappointed, the woman drew her rose-colored cloak tighter against the night's chill. Not that she minded the cold or even the light, mizzling rain. Where she now dwelled, such dreary grayness was commonplace. She'd even learned to embrace the bleakness, sometimes feeling an odd kinship with the racing wind and swirling mists. The bone-deep cold that froze one's marrow even on the rare days when the sun shone brightly enough to pick out the worn threads and patches that marred her once-lustrous rose mantle.

Not that she minded the cloak's sad state.

All things considered, she was ever so glad she hadn't lost it when...

She closed her mind, not wanting to remember what had happened to her. How she'd come to be what she now was. Very much a wraith, she spent her days flitting about with only the sorrow that lived in her heart. Memories were too painful to allow.

Yet...

Now and then a glimmer of hope reached her, something that ofttimes seemed too miraculous to be true. Then a tiny part of her, a wee sliver of the happy woman she'd once been, would flare to life and she'd do something reckless like coming here this night.

And almost every time, the great effort it cost her to appear would be for naught.

This e'en was no different.

She'd thought to catch a spark of young love and excitement. Not to spy on the pair. She'd never have stooped so low. She'd only wanted to bask a bit in the glow and warmth of their happiness.

It would've been good for her to have done so.

As things stood...

She huddled deeper into her cloak and sighed, knowing that if anyone heard, they'd mistake the sound for the soughing of the night wind.

It *was* a night for suchlike.

Cold, wet, and full of mist, just like the place in which she dwelled. Great dark clouds even raced across the moon. She felt right at home, though she knew well the path back there was forever barred to her.

So she went where she could, gliding into the chill darkness, embracing the thick wall of mist that soon closed around her.

Once she'd been someone's much-loved wife.

Now she accepted her existence as a wraith.

There was little else she could do.

Chapter Seven

✦

A penniless beggar?"

Sorley let a trace of humor lace his voice. For good measure, he also met Lady Mirabelle's pointed gaze with wide, disbelieving eyes. He was well able to feign astonishment when situations demanded.

If any saints lingering in the chapel objected to his deception, so be it. As the King dutifully kept candles lit and incense burning, Sorley doubted any such vaunted beings would mind. There was even a precious phial of St. Mungo's holy blood hidden away in a gold-and-jewel-encrusted box in a secret wall aumbry.

All that, the King did to honor his God.

Surely the saints wouldn't take umbrage to a wee falsehood to protect men who guarded the King?

Sorley was certain that was so.

Either way...

Dealing with Lady Mirabelle called for caution.

To his horror, she was just as observant as he'd suspected. In his experience, women who were both intelligent and delectable were nothing but trouble. Already, she

stood before him like an avenging Valkyrie. Or perhaps a
firebrand, her flame-colored hair tumbling to her hips, the
unruly curls gleaming in the candlelight. She held herself
as straight as if she'd swallowed a spear shaft. Her lovely
lavender-blue eyes blazed. The rapid pulse beat at the base of
her throat warned she was mightily vexed.

So was he.

But he was annoyed with himself, not her.

The Fenris generally kept their baser urges tethered
around females who could endanger the secret engage-
ments of their carefully-guarded order. A woman too clever
or inquisitive was passed by for one who wasn't. Prickly
women were to be avoided at all costs. Every man walking
knew that once such a female's temper ignited, she could be
trusted to do anything.

Mirabelle was more than a little prickly.

Secretly, Sorley admired how glorious she looked in her
agitation.

A true vixen, she'd be insatiable once her passion was
wakened.

Unable to help himself, he allowed his gaze to skim over
her breasts. They were full and round, lush curves thrusting
beneath her cloak. He was sure her nipples would be pert,
well-tightened with the cold and her irritation. How he'd
love to feel them harden even more, responding to his questing fingers. Better yet, his lips, as he teased and tasted her.

Her nipples would only whet his appetite.

She had other, even more tempting places he'd enjoy
savoring. Deliciously feminine delights at the apex of her
thighs, beckoning with silken heat, honeyed and molten.
Knowing it was madness, he lowered his gaze, looking there
now, imagining.

She noticed and frowned. "Don't try to distract me. You
were garbed as a beggar, this very morn. I know because I
saw you."

Sorley almost laughed. He wasn't the distraction.

She was.

Hoping to turn the tables on her, he flashed his most devilish smile.

"You are mistaken, sweet." He held his arms out to the sides, turning in a slow circle to give her a full and thorough view of his richly worked and costly raiment. "I enjoy garments of as high a quality as coin will buy. Having worn enough castoff and threadbare clothes as a lad, there is nothing on this good earth that could persuade me to don such rags again."

"Perhaps a secret mission?" Brazen as aye, she tilted her head, studying him in a way that would've jellied his spine if he were a lesser man.

The look she was giving him also proved she had sharper wits than most.

She had recognized him at the Red Lion.

He just hoped she hadn't also done so at St. Mary's village.

His gut telling him she had, he did the only thing he could do and leaned toward her, treating her to his own special brand of a penetrating stare.

The kind he hoped would make her wish she'd kept silent with her nosy enquiries.

"My clandestine assignations, lass, have to do with you. Meeting you here is the only secret mission I have indulged in of late," he lied, speaking softly against her ear. Nipping the lobe, he straightened, pleased to see surprised indignation flash across her features. "Or is it no' your wish that we keep this rendezvous to ourselves?"

"This is a business matter, not an illicit meeting." She went to the tomb he'd leaned against and walked its length, trailing her fingers along the stone. "I offered you good coin for the pleasure. Enough siller for you to purchase as many fancy gewgaws and fine clothes as you desire, *Dungal*."

"Dungal?" Sorley's eyes widened.

Not because she'd remembered the fool name Roag had given him in the Red Lion's stableyard, but because she was bold enough to challenge him.

Few women would.

Even fewer men would dare, for they feared his skill with weapons. They also knew he cared naught for the niceties of knightly warfare. If pressed, he'd use any means possible to win a fight.

He seldom lost.

And he only fought when he believed in a cause.

No one would accuse him of allowing himself to be bought. There were names for such men and he'd rather cut his own flesh than join their despicable ranks.

"Yes, Dungal." Mirabelle lifted her chin and straightened her spine even more. "Look surprised all you wish. I know you heard me. There is nothing wrong with your ears, though you do seem a mite forgetful."

I could say the same of you, Sorley almost shot back at her.

Hadn't it slipped her mind that they'd once danced a Highland reel? That she'd left him standing alone in the center of the hall, shaming him before all who'd been gathered there?

Men and women alike had laughed at him. A few good-hearted souls had turned aside, pretending not to have seen. Some had watched in pity, their sympathy cutting deeper than the others' mirth.

Mirabelle was watching him now, one red-gold brow elegantly raised, a challenge in her eye.

Not wanting her to see his annoyance, Sorley leaned against a stone column and crossed his arms as if her use of the silly name meant nothing.

He wouldn't mention the coin.

He'd told her once he didn't want her money, and if she

said the like again, he'd prove it to her in a way that required no words.

Just now, he simply looked at her.

"I saw you at the inn. You were with another beggar." She persisted in bedeviling him. Worse, her remarkable eyes sparked and a tantalizing flush spread across her cheekbones, making him wonder what she'd look like with a delicious tint of pink blooming across her breasts.

He was fond of lust-blushes. They proved a woman's desire. Something told him Mirabelle's passion would blossom more beautifully than that of any other female he'd ever known. It was a thought that set him like granite.

If she lowered her gaze, she'd see.

For once, he didn't care.

He hitched up a corner of his mouth, if only to unsettle her. "Can it be you have an unhealthy interest in beggars, my lady?"

"If I do, it is because I know when someone is making a fool of me." She didn't turn a hair, her lovely lavender-blue eyes so serious he burned to grab her face and kiss her until the ridiculous earnestness was replaced by the fiery heat of urgent, naked desire.

He'd felt a fierce ache to possess her ever since he'd stepped into the chapel. Her agitation just made him want her more. Annoyance not only heightened her color and let her eyes blaze, but her breasts rose and fell so temptingly he could hardly bear to look at her. He was so primed, so hungry for her, that he was near to forgetting what honor he did have.

"I would ne'er make a fool of you." He held her gaze, fought an irresistible urge to seize her, taking her here and now on the cold stone floor of the chapel. Or perhaps he'd rather catch her by the waist, plunk her down on the altar stone, toss up her skirts, and have her fast and furiously, as had surely been done on the stone in pagan days.

The thought made his blood heat even more.

His loins tightened unbearably.

As if she knew and wished to torment him, she paced a few steps away and then whirled to face him. The spin made her lustrous red-gold hair swing about her shoulders, the curling ends bouncing provocatively at her hips. It was a seductress's trick. She employed it expertly, capturing his entire attention, fanning flames that already licked far too hotly at his groin.

"You are a man who would do anything." She gave him a long, assessing look that made him feel almost guilty even though he'd done nothing wrong.

Far from it, he was here to help her.

And he was doing so against his better judgment. It scarce mattered how much he'd enjoy a taste of her. Or that he couldn't wait to thrust his hands into her glossy unbound hair, even rub his face in the silken strands, inhaling deep of her summery rose scent. He'd kiss her thoroughly, too. Pull her so close, hold her so tightly, that her full, round breasts were crushed against his chest.

"So I am, aye." He let a slow smile spread over his face. "I will do most anything. Even when I know I shouldn't. There are times I just can't help myself, see you? This is one of them."

She blinked. "Does that mean you'll do as I've asked?"

"So far as I can, aye." The admission caused another fierce coil of heat to tighten in his loins. It was such an intense, pleasurable sensation that he rushed on, before he could change his mind. "I have conditions. If you agree to them, I will do everything—"

"What can be so difficult?" Unaware of the storm building inside him, she set her hands on her hips and gave him another long look from her great lavender-blue eyes. "It should be a simple matter. Something I'd have hoped you'd do without hesitation, even enjoying the task, given your known behavior at court.

"Folk say you are bold and daring." She looked him up and down, her color rising again.

"I am glad to hear it." Sorley hoped she'd think he meant his reputation with women.

She pounced, proving the sharpness of her wits. "Men say you are a Fen—"

"Men can say what they will." Sorley bit back the urge to curse beneath his breath. His work for the King was the last thing he'd discuss with her

Her chin came up. "I believe you were on a Fenris mission at St. Mary's, along with your bloodthirsty friend."

She kept her chin raised, the gleam of the righteous in her lovely eyes. "He whipped off his beggar's robe in the village and cut down an equally wild-eyed rogue who'd been hawking mutton stew and ale before he drew a sword and leaped to attack your friend. And that's not all I saw."

"Is that so?" Sorley cocked a brow.

She took a step closer, her hands still on her hips. "You argued with a monk in the market square. Maili, the serving girl from the inn, was with me. She needed to return to Stirling and asked if she could ride with us."

Mirabelle leaned toward him, her rose perfume wafting close enough to tickle his nose. "She's my witness."

"Do you no' want to hear my terms?" Sorley ignored her arguments. Lifting a lock of her hair, he rubbed it between his fingers, trying to distract her.

Maili was a good lass, but she was also too soft-hearted and trusting. She'd learned of the Fenris by chance, having once scooted beneath a tall four-poster bed at the Red Lion, hoping to clean away dust and cobwebs. Instead she'd heard an earful. She'd been an unwanted but ofttimes useful Fenris helpmate ever since.

She'd never willingly betray them.

Doing so unknowingly was another matter.

Sorley frowned, not for the first time thinking he could

do well without women in his life. If only they weren't so damned appealing.

Lady Mirabelle drew him more than most.

In truth, more than any other female he had ever known. The ferocity of his attraction to her, and his body's reaction when she was near, stunned him. And he wasn't a man who was easily surprised.

He also knew better than to remain too long with her in the incense-scented, candlelit intimacy of the chapel. If they didn't soon part ways for the night, he wouldn't be responsible for his actions.

"My stipulations," he reminded her, half certain she must've bathed in rose oil for the sole purpose of deliberately arousing him. The scent was witchy, entirely too beguiling. "We must discuss particulars. The sooner that's settled, the faster you'll be rid of Sir John."

"A moment, please." She held up her hand. "The person making a business proposal is the one who decides how it should unfold."

"No' this time." Sorley's frown deepened, becoming a full-blown scowl.

"I need to be sure nothing goes wrong. You're a dangerous man, capable of anything." She stepped closer, her witchy perfume coming with her. "Especially after having seen you at St. Mary's. There was an affray there, with swords. I'm sure you were involved. Fighting someone, likely even killing—"

"You haven't seen me since we spoke on the battlements." Sorley shook his head slowly and reached to cup her face in his hands. "If you doubt me, answer this. Have you ne'er heard what happens to a man after a swordfight or battle? The blood lust clings to him. It races through his blood, firing other urges. The kind that are sharper, more potent, than any blade of steel." He leaned in, so near that he knew his breath warmed her cheek. "When that happens, my lady, a man becomes a ravening beast. His hunger for a woman, for primal release, is so powerful he cannot withstand the temptation.

"So-o-o!" He stepped back, holding his hands palms upward in the air. "If I had fought at St. Mary's, or anywhere, this day, you would no' now be standing fully clothed before me, your maidenly virtue intact."

He heard her breath catch, saw her eyes widen.

"I would've slaked my lust for you." He lowered his hands, using all his strength to ignore how his words tightened his entire body. "All my desires unleashed on you, as soon as I walked in the door. So dinnae push me, lass. I'm no' in the habit of despoiling virgins, but if you persist in provoking me—"

"I am not—"

"You are a minx and were one the moment you drew your first breath." Sorley looked her over, not caring if his gaze burned her. She set him aflame. "A man would have to be stone cold dead no' to want you."

"Is that why you have terms?" She touched his cloak. "Because you desire me?"

"I'd see you safe, no more." Sorley gripped her wrist, removing her hand from his mantle before she drove him to doing something he'd regret. He was a breath away from ravishing her. "I've told you, I dinnae touch virgins. Leastways no' where I'd need to if I agreed to your request."

"But you have."

"No' completely." Sorley shook his head again, hoping he had the strength to keep his own conditions. "I'm willing to help you cause a stir. I will come to you in the hall, plying you with my attentions, kissing and touching you. Before all, I will seduce you. Sir John will see and—"

"That won't help." Mirabelle frowned. "I'm not sure he'd care about kisses and a flirtation."

"Aye, he will. He'll do so because you must appear

to enjoy my kisses, to welcome everything that happens between us. When he's livid, I'll lead you from the hall." Sorley set his hands on her shoulders, aroused already just by how she looked up at him from beneath her thick, gold-tipped lashes. "What he'll have witnessed by then will be more than a 'flirtation,' I assure you. I will put my hands on you, even slipping them inside your bodice. You must dress accordingly, wearing a gown that dips low enough for me to have access." He held her gaze as he spoke, wondering if she knew what such words did to him. "If I deem it necessary, I might lower my head and nuzzle your neck, perhaps even trail kisses across the upper swell of your breasts. So you needn't worry. You will be scandalized, the talk of the court. When we leave the hall, no one will doubt where we are going and why."

She made a soft noise. Her gaze slipped to his mouth, lingering there just long enough to send a hot tide of desire straight to his loins. When she met his eyes again, a shock of heat swept the rest of him. He could take her now, slaking his savage need for her.

"So when we reach your bedchamber, you'll—"

"We'll no' be going there." Sorley ignored the regret that punched through him. "It's enough for Sir John to think so. In truth, I'll escort you to your own quarters, leaving you at the door. We'll part ways there and no one will be the wiser. Above all, your virtue will still be intact when you waken the next morning."

"This is your stipulation?" She gave a slight shake of her head, as if she hadn't properly heard him. "A deflowering that isn't one?"

"It is part of my terms, aye."

"There are others?"

"Two, unless I think of more. I'd know when your father isn't likely to dine in the hall. I'll no' distress him unduly. By the time he hears, he'll be ready to learn the truth about Sir

John." Sorley slid his arm around her, resting his hand on the curve of her hip. "You can then tell him what happened. That you are still a maid, as pure as aye."

"You are most thoughtful." She sounded annoyed.

"I try, my lady." Sorley would bet she'd be even more vexed by what he meant to do next.

Before he could let that worry him, he caught her to him, claiming her lips with a fierceness he knew would stun her. He gripped her nape, thrusting his fingers into her hair while keeping his other arm wrapped tightly around her waist, holding her crushed against him. He kissed her deeply, pure masculine triumph whipping through him when she pushed her hands up between them, digging her fingers into the front of his cloak as she clung to him, her body melting into his, capitulating.

She leaned into him, tilting her head, parting her lips so he could kiss her more thoroughly. She even flicked her tongue against his, seeming to enjoy his devouring kiss, welcoming the stroking of his tongue over hers, the heady intimacy of the soft, warm breath they shared.

Sorley's heart hammered, the pounding at his groin an almost unbearable torment.

She clenched her hands against his chest, the sweetest tremor rippling through her. "Oh, dear saints..." She breathed the words against his mouth, sweeping one hand up his chest and over his shoulder to twine her fingers in his hair. "I never knew..."

The reminder of her innocence hit Sorley like a fist to his ribs. He tore his lips from hers and looked down at her, breathing hard.

"That, my sweet, is why I kissed you." He moved back, took a few more steps, putting an arm's length of space between them.

He didn't trust himself to stand close to her.

She blinked, looking almost as deliciously dazed as if

he'd just made love to her and she lay naked and delectable in his mussed bed. "I don't understand. I thought—"

"That I was overcome with wanting you?" Sorley forced a casual tone.

He *had* been crazed with desire.

But he wasn't about to let her know.

"Appearing to seduce you in the hall will include such kisses, my lady." He made it sound as businesslike as he could. "I needed to be certain you'd return them convincingly. If not, we'd have had to practice your reaction. Sir John will only believe our performance if it looks real."

"I see." The softness left her face, her entire body going rigid as she straightened. She stood tall, almost looking as if she'd swallowed an iron hearthside poker. "I assume I did well enough?"

Sorley winced inwardly at the ice in her voice. "Better than I would've believed, my lady."

She nodded, not a trace of warmth on her face. "Then I should tell you that my father will be returning to the Red Lion in three days' time. He wishes to spend a few nights there, studying the mosses and lichen found on the roof slates and instructing the innkeeper how to make foot powder out of crotal lichen. His absence would be a good opportunity for our staged engagement." She flicked at her sleeve, the high color on her cheeks revealing her annoyance.

"Indeed, lady." Sorley gave her a slight bow. "I will watch for you in the hall."

"I will be ready." She nodded again, even more curtly than before.

Sorley felt more an arse than ever in his life.

But it was for the best, for both of them, to keep their intimate entanglement as straightforward and unemotional as possible.

Indeed, it was crucial.

He held her gaze for a long moment, not liking how every

inch of him burned with the desire to kiss her again. His lust went deep, the urge potent, heightened by how lovely she looked in her high-colored annoyance. He didn't want his body to respond to her. He really didn't like the feeling that he was drawn to her for more than her tempting curves and the gleam of her gorgeous flame-bright hair. Mirabelle MacLaren, if she were allowed to, would turn his world upside down.

She was a complication he couldn't allow.

Not as the King's man, a Fenris Guard with no place in his life for a headstrong, all-too-inquisitive and clever nobly born female.

So he stepped closer again and took her by the elbow, leading her to the door. Unfortunately, when they reached it he couldn't resist lifting her hand and pressing a kiss to her knuckles.

"I will look forward to the pleasure, my lady." He let her go, stepping back into the shadows of the chapel as she strode away across the courtyard, quickly disappearing into the rainy darkness.

The moment the mists closed around her, he swore.

He should be glad to have riled her. There truly was no room in his life for Lady Mirabelle. To be sure, he didn't fit into her world.

The problem was how much that bothered him.

Chapter Eight

❧

Botheration!" Mirabelle heard the chapel door close behind her, the soft fall of the latch proving Sorley had chosen not to follow her. When he'd remained in the open doorway after she left, she'd thought he might do so.

Truth be told, she'd hoped he would.

Instead, he'd simply stood there and watched her walk off into the cold, wet night. She'd known because she'd felt his stare boring into her. She wasn't about to whirl around to be sure. She could tell fine enough. And her resentment grew with each step she took.

She shouldn't be surprised.

Everyone knew he was a rogue, rough-edged and brazen. He lived to please himself, barely accepting the strictures of a civilized society, and then only when it served him to adhere to such constraints.

Sadly, she couldn't make such excuses for her own actions, or for the frustration and disappointment she was now feeling.

She paused to draw her cloak tighter against the wind. Not that she minded its buffeting. The wild wet night suited her mood. Mist and clouds swirled everywhere, great billowing swaths of gray that filled the courtyard and swooped down from the heavens to race across the ramparts. The rain was still little more than a drizzle. But the fog had thickened into a whirling, shimmering mass that cloaked the castle's highest towers, hiding much of the keep from view. Torches did burn in the arcaded walkways around the courtyard, but their flames were mere smudges of yellow against the gloom.

That was fine with her.

Darkness meant chances were good no one had seen her leave the chapel.

Even so, she strove to keep her back straight, her head raised. She might be stepping a mite faster than she'd like, but she felt a powerful need to put distance between herself and the great folly she'd allowed to befall her when Sorley announced his conditions.

She hadn't expected him to kiss her.

Not this night, anyway.

She'd thought to be more prepared when the inevitable kissing began. She knew enough about mating to be aware that kisses would be a prelude to the carnal act. She'd not wanted him to sense her attraction to him. He'd refuse her for sure, if he knew. So she'd meant to detach herself from her body and the natural physical urges that would surely arise. She'd turn her mind to other matters.

Her plan was good.

She'd pretend Sorley's seduction wasn't happening and conjure images of her father's collection of lichens, moss, and sundry other healing goods on display in so many of Knocking's rooms.

She could think of little better to dash sensual arousal than the dried heads of adders, twists of withered eel, and the claw-joints of newts, carefully preserved in full moon-infused sage oil.

She'd also neglected to tell Sorley about the wild-looking Highlander—Grim Mackintosh, by name—who'd called at the Red Lion Inn, asking of him.

And didn't that prove how thoroughly Sorley scattered her wits?

Feeling honor-bound to let him know, she started to turn, thinking to go after him. Before she could, something stirred in the arcade. She blinked, staring at the patch of rose-colored luminosity gliding along the covered walkway, moving slowly and with grace.

Mirabelle's eyes rounded, heart almost stilling.

She forgot the mysterious Highlander.

How could she not when the rose *glow* was taking on the shape of a woman? Mirabelle could see her luminous gown, delicate and fine, a whisper of flowing skirts. She wore a hooded robe or perhaps a shawl draped over her head. Mirabelle could even make out the fullness of her breasts, the feminine shoulders and gently rounded hips.

And even though the rose-hued raiment looked like silk and was molded to her curves, the arcade's walling showed right through the shimmering form.

That could only mean...

She was staring at Stirling Castle's pink lady.

Clasping a hand to her breast, Mirabelle watched as the ghost slid silently along the arcade. Her pink mantle glowed and her cowled head was bowed. The fine hairs on her nape lifting, Mirabelle took a cautious step forward, then another. Now that the famed spirit was so near, she had to get a better look. She'd tried too many times to catch a glimpse of her.

So she edged closer, painfully aware of her footsteps on the cobbles. The pink lady had drifted behind one of the stone pillars and hadn't yet reappeared. Mirabelle bit her lip, willing the ghost to emerge. She crept nearer, trying to step quietly.

"Please..." She was almost at the arcade. "I know you're there."

"I am flattered, fair lady." Sir John Sinclair stepped out of the darkness. He smiled, his teeth flashing white. "Looking for me, were you?"

"Sir John!" Mirabelle started, her heart now thundering for an entirely different reason. His smile didn't waver and as always, something about it made her skin crawl. He wore a dark cloak, explaining why she hadn't noticed him approach. Richly worked, even bearing costly jet along the edges, the mantle didn't match the rumors that he was on the verge of losing his lands and titles. Neither did the gold flashing at his throat and on his fingers.

Dark, lean, and handsome in a smooth, polished way that didn't at all appeal to her, he finally stopped smiling and let his hooded gaze glide over her. Somehow, even with a serious expression, he managed to appear amused.

Mirabelle stood straighter, bestowed her haughtiest gaze on him.

His eyes glinted. "If I'd known you desired my company, I'd have left the hall much earlier, Lady Mirabelle."

"I wasn't looking for you." She hoped her voice sounded stronger than it did to her.

"Then perhaps you are pleased to have found me?"

"You surely know the answer to that, good sir," she dared, irritation bubbling up inside her. It cost her entire will not to hitch her skirts, turn, and stride away. Instead, she kept her chin raised, her gaze steady on his.

"Indeed." He nodded as if unfazed by her rudeness. If anything, the glimmer in his eyes turned unpleasantly appreciative.

She wished her heart would stop racing.

There were folk who aye knew when someone was ill at ease. She was sure Sir John possessed such skill. His hooded eyes said as much, as did the slight lift to one of his brows.

He could see right through her. And he was well aware she couldn't stand him, that he was the last person she would've wished to meet alone, on such a dark, dreich night.

"So you weren't seeking my company?" His tone made her shiver, not pleasantly.

"I thought I saw one of the castle cats." She glanced about as if searching for such a creature.

Nothing stirred.

Mist swirled everywhere, thick and cold. Hazy light spilled from the nearby hall's door and windows, but did little to chase the shadows. Any other time she wouldn't have minded. She would've found the night's silvery cast beautiful, even magical in a wondrous, otherworldly way. She usually appreciated such evenings.

But Sir John was leaning in, reaching for her hand, surely to kiss...

Mirabelle backed away, bumping into a pillar. "What are you doing here?"

"I should ask the same of you, my lady." He stepped closer, his sleek, oiled hair gleaming in the torchlight. Whatever grease he smoothed on his dark, carefully combed hair also glistened in his neatly trimmed beard. It smelled, too, the heavily spiced scent almost overpowering. "A lady shouldn't be out on her own, in the dark."

"Celtic women have more freedoms than others." Mirabelle slipped her hands behind her back, clasping them, before he could seize one and lift it to his lips. "We go where we please, when we wish."

"Then I am most intrigued." If he noticed her hand-trick, he gave no indication. "I admire a woman with spirit. Temperament and courage are alluring in many ways. A woman unafraid to explore her passion is a female highly prized." He caught her elbow, tugging her closer, a suggestive smile curving his lips. "When she accepts a man's guidance, is willing to indulge—"

"I am sure the hall is filled with such ladies." Mirabelle tried to break free, but his grip was like iron. "One of them will—"

"Court ladies bore me." He drew her nearer still, his smile fading into a look of such intense deliberation Mirabelle's blood chilled. Lifting his free hand, he undid the clasp of her mantle so that the edges fell free, revealing the low-cut bodice of her gown.

"That was not wise." Mirabelle bristled. Snatching her brooch, she refastened it and gave Sinclair her iciest stare. "No man touches me."

"So I have observed." He had the audacity to look pleased. "Why do you think I've noticed you?"

"Then pray un-notice me."

His gaze flicked over her, a corner of his lips lifting in a slow, measuring way. "That, sweeting, is as impossible as telling a river to change its course."

Mirabelle narrowed her eyes at him, pride not letting her flinch.

The chill air tightened her breasts, raising gooseflesh and causing her nipples to thrust against the dipping fabric. Thinking of Sorley, she'd chosen one of her most daring gowns. The deep-plunging front verged on indecent, allowing the tops of her nipples to peek above the bodice edging.

Any moment they'd pop free.

She could feel the cold air puckering that sensitive flesh now, knew her agitated breathing already exposed even more of her than the gown's scandalous design intended. One more too-deep, overly long inhalation and her nipples would wink pertly at Sinclair, a possibility he clearly anticipated, for he'd again let his gaze drift lower, latching on to the top swells of her bosom, the rims of the chill-puckered crests. Mirabelle felt his stare as surely as if he'd reached out and grasped her breasts with his long, beringed fingers.

She jerked again, trying to pull away. "Did you know Highland woman carry daggers?"

"I have heard it said." He didn't blink, his gaze riveted to her breasts.

He also didn't release her.

If anything, his grip on her arm tightened.

"It should delight me to discover where you've hidden your ladies' dirk." He looked up then, triumph on his face. "Perhaps you will show me when I visit your father at Knocking Tower. We can take a walk across your heathered moors and—"

"My father would never—"

"Invite me to your home?" He released her at last, stepping back but bracing a hand on the arcade pillar, his outstretched arm blocking her escape. "Dear lady, you truly should spend more time in your sire's company rather than flitting about alone in the cold, dark mist. Your father has asked me to come to Knocking." His confident air rang true. "I told him I've traveled the Hebrides. And that, while there, I was fortunate enough to spend time at the homes of several clan chiefs who give patronage to the MacBeths, the learned order of Gaelic healers. Your father is most interested to hear about—"

"Lies?" Mirabelle didn't believe a word.

Sir John shrugged. "Your father was impressed."

"He will listen to me." She knew he wouldn't.

Not if he thought he could spend hours and days questioning Sinclair about the far-famed MacBeths.

"You will only irritate him." He leaned in, his wine-tinged breath fanning her cheek. "It was his suggestion that I ride north with you when you leave here. And"—he let his gaze sweep her again—"why should I not when such delights await me? A walk in the heather with you, learning the secret place you hide your—"

"I'll show you now!" Mirabelle thrust her hand through

a slit in her skirts and whipped out the thin-bladed dirk she wore strapped to her thigh. Brandishing it before Sinclair's nose, she narrowed her eyes. "Don't make me use it. I'd rather not bloody the King's courtyard cobbles."

To her annoyance, Sir John laughed. "Your fire attracts me, lady. Now I shall truly look forward to my visit to your wild Highland hills. If all the ladies there are such vixens, then I shall—"

"You wouldn't leave alive." Mirabelle tossed back her hair and pressed her dirk beneath his chin. "No one would ever find your body, because we'd toss you in a bog. It'd be a shame if any Highland creature soured his stomach from gnawing on your rotten bones."

"Just how would you kill me?" He seized her wrist in a lightning-quick move, snatching the dagger and flipping her skirts up to reveal the leather sheath strapped high on her right thigh. "Try such foolery again and it is you who will not waken to enjoy the morrow," he hissed, shoving the blade back into its holder and letting her skirts drop. "Be warned and do not test my leniency."

"Then do not expect to sleep well if ever you do come to the Highlands." Mirabelle swatted at her skirts and yanked her cloak back together. "We are not above being sneaky if pressed to a wall, my lord."

He looked amused. "I can well imagine you in such a position. A woman against a wall is a joy to savor."

"A man sleeping is easy prey." Furious, Mirabelle held his gaze. "More than one fool has left this world in the dead of night, his journey to hell hastened by a knife slipped between his ribs as he slumbered."

"How good to see that converse with you will never be wearying." He lifted a hand to pull on the pointed tip of his beard. "I vow your bed play—"

"Her what?"

A tall, plaid-draped man appeared before them, his

shoulder-length auburn hair blowing in the wind, his proud, handsome face stern. "A good e'en, Sir John, Lady Mirabelle," said Alexander Stewart, Earl of Buchan, and King Robert III's wildest, most notorious brother. Hailed as the Wolf of Badenoch after the rugged Highland territory he called his own, he ruled his lands with an iron fist and a brand of leadership not for the faint of heart. The Wolf wasn't a man to counter.

He looked furious.

"Can it be you are giving this maid a poor impression of my brother's court?" His soft Highland voice held warning notes of steel. "My lady and I thought so." He glanced at the beautiful, well-made woman beside him. "Isn't that so, Mariota?"

"I must agree." The woman stepped forward, placing a hand on Mirabelle's arm. A waft of pleasantly earthy musk perfume came with her. She had a welter of lustrous, garnet-red hair that she wore loose and curling about her shoulders and eyes of deepest blue. A heavy gold torque adorned her neck and her dark green cloak flattered her vibrant Celtic coloring.

She looked at Mirabelle for a long moment and then shifted her gaze back to Sir John. "This young maid doesn't appear pleased by your attentions."

Mirabelle recognized her as Alexander Stewart's longtime and much-loved mistress, Lady Mariota de Athyn, or Mackay when away from the Gaelic speakers of her native bounds in Scotland's remote far north.

She lightly squeezed Mirabelle's arm and gave her a reassuring smile. Graced with a full, lush form that made it easy to understand why the earl worshipped her as he was known to do, she also had the kind of smile that held so much warmth you felt embraced from the top of your head clear down to your toes.

"You heard the lady." The Wolf looked away from his

mistress, fixing a fierce stare on Sinclair. He also stepped closer, placing his hand demonstratively on his sword hilt. "I trust we erred?"

Sir John blanched, but he caught himself quickly, bending a deep leg to the earl. "Lord Alex, Lady Mariota. You misheard me. I jested that Lady Mirabelle's eyes must be playing tricks on her." He didn't look at Mirabelle. "She said she came upon a kitten and tripped over the wee creature. I saw no such animal, but gladly offered her my arm, thinking to escort her back to the hall."

The Wolf only arched a brow.

"You are a right gallant." Lady Mariota spoke just as smoothly as Sinclair, her voice rich with the pleasing lilt of the hills.

Straightening to her full height, she pinned Sir John with a look that left no doubt of her opinion of him.

Mirabelle listened, a whirl of thoughts plunging her into momentary silence. The Wolf and his lady could be her greatest allies. Yet in her mind, she also saw Sorley's hot, intense gaze locked on hers; her lips still tingled from the kiss he'd given her in the chapel.

If she begged Alex Stewart's help, there'd be no need to tryst with Sorley.

Could she leave Stirling without seeing him again, spending time with him in the way he'd proposed? Perhaps enjoying even greater intimacies? Ones that—the saints preserve her for such wanton longings—she ached to experience and savor?

She stood straighter, put her shoulders back, the answer clear.

She held her tongue, glancing at Lady Mariota.

The older woman was looking at the Wolf. "I believe we shall accompany Lady Mirabelle to her father's table in the hall. You, Sir John, may go where you please."

"You are kind, my lady." Mirabelle smiled at her.

Sinclair frowned, clearly not fond of being addressed so boldly by a woman. "See here, Lady Mariota—"

"I have." Her tone held all the confidence of a woman well-loved and encouraged to share her views. "We both have."

That she spoke for the earl had Sinclair tightening his jaw, his dark eyes turning cold.

He said nothing.

The Wolf let go of his sword hilt and drew a large Highland dirk from beneath his belt. "Lady Mirabelle," he kept his gaze on Sir John as he addressed her. "Did Sir John distress you in any way?"

"No." Mirabelle gave the only answer she could, the memory of Sorley's wicked smile, his touch, giving her no other choice. "I did see a cat running along the arcade. Sir John appeared just after."

"So he didn't assist you when you tripped?" Lady Mariota touched her arm again, the gesture allowing her to insert herself between Mirabelle and Sir John.

Mirabelle hesitated, glancing toward the chapel. "Everything happened so quickly. Then you and the earl arrived."

"Sinclair." The Wolf looked down at the dirk in his hands and began using its tip to carefully clean his fingernails. "Did you know that no man leaves my Badenoch territory alive if he is known to have insulted a lady? My wild hills and moorlands are a great distance from my brother's hall." His gaze snapped up then, his light blue eyes revealing his swelling rage. "Court manners and niceties have little use there. A strong hand is aye needed in such a bleak, godforsaken place, so full of stone and peat bogs, howling wind and no mercies.

"Men know better than to rile me." He kept working at his nails with the dirk tip, his soft Highland voice low. Those who knew well him would have turned and fled, because the deceptively gentle tone was his deadliest. "If a man's honor means nothing to him, we help him find it by dressing him in his finest mail and armor and tossing him into the loch. Imagine! Most such offenders sink from the weight of their sins before they can swim ashore. If they do, and they're still reeking of guilt, we set fire to their feet and see how fast they can stamp out the flames." He raised his voice then, speaking with relish. "Did you know such malefactors burn brighter than any balefire? That they do, I say you!"

"I have done no wrong, my lord." Sinclair shifted, but held the earl's gaze. "The lady is unharmed and—"

"Other times, if we've no mind to watch them dance," the Wolf went on as if Sir John hadn't spoken, "such varlets have found themselves trussed and roasting o'er a spit. Or"—he lifted the dirk, examining its blade—"we simply hang them, letting their carcasses dangle and rot. The sight warns all that I do not look kindly on the mistreating of women."

"To be sure, my lord." Sir John nodded.

"See that you remember." Alexander Stewart inclined his head as well and then sheathed his dirk. "Dinnae give me cause to warn you again. Badenoch may lie many miles from here, but it is no' so far as the moon."

"Indeed, my lord." Sir John bowed low. His relief was palpable when the Wolf waved him away, toward the rain-drenched courtyard.

He left quickly, disappearing into the mist before the earl even lowered his arm.

"Well done, Alex." Lady Mariota smiled and touched her lover's broad, tartan-clad back.

"I have ne'er liked that bastard." The Wolf turned around, his handsome face softening when he saw his mistress's smile. "'Fore God, I'd love to ken how he stays in my brother's good graces, oily as he is. If Robert would spend even a fortnight in the north, he'd soon learn which men can be trusted and who seeks only to fatten his own purse. And"—he glanced at Mirabelle, his face darkening again—"which men ought to have the root of their evil twisted right off them."

"Alex!" Lady Mariota gave him a look of reproach.

But her eyes twinkled, especially when the Wolf wrapped an arm around her, pulling her close.

"I aye speak the truth, lass, as well you ken." An exceptionally tall man, he bent his head to her brow. "And you, lady"—he straightened and looked at Mirabelle—"should have a care when traipsing about the courtyard of an e'en, bold Highland lassie or nae."

"I shall, my lord." Mirabelle bobbed a curtsy.

"Aye, well." The Wolf jerked his chin toward the hall. The vigorous strains of pipes and fiddle were just beginning to drift out into the night. "I am riding north at first light. I dinnae care to be away from my hills o'er long, nor does my lady." He pulled Lady Mariota even closer to him, dropped another kiss on her shining hair. "We're celebrating our departure in the hall. Will you join us?"

"I . . ." Mirabelle would've loved to do so.

But what she really wanted was another long, hot bath. She felt a powerful need to scrub her flesh until all trace of Sir John's hands on her was well and truly washed away. Her skin crawled from his touch and despite the bravura she clung to so fiercely, her heart hadn't stopped thundering. Worse, his narrow, sharp-featured face lingered in her mind. His slickly combed hair, black as a raven's wing and smelling of heavy spices, the salacious curve of his lips and his hooded eyes, so capable of making her feel as if icy fingers clamped around her heart, squeezing.

She'd rather think of Sorley, even if he had mightily annoyed her.

Mirabelle glanced again at the chapel and drew her cloak against the cold.

"She is tired, Alex." Lady Mariota slipped from her lover's grasp and reached for Mirabelle's hand, tucking it in her arm. "Let us see her safely to the women's quarters and then leave her be for the night."

"Is that your wish, my lady?" The Wolf looked at Mirabelle.

"I would like to retire, aye." Mirabelle nodded.

"So be it!" The Wolf smiled and slapped his thigh. "I am no' one to argue with a lady."

And so the King's brother and his mistress led Mirabelle through the misty dark, past the hall's open door and the revelry within, to a far corner of the courtyard where a torchlit archway marked the entrance to the stair tower to the castle's guest quarters.

They left her, promising to send up a bath, and she went to stand before her room's small fire, stretching her hands to its flames as she waited. The Wolf had been kind. One word from her and he'd have dealt with Sinclair, she knew. He'd have served the noble with his own brand of Highland justice.

She'd said nothing.

Now she released a long sigh, heightened awareness of a very different sort blossoming inside her as the fire's heat warmed her.

How far gone was she in her attraction to Sorley that she'd forgo a means to be rid of Sinclair just so that she could hold on to her one chance to enjoy a night in Sorley's arms?

That was the way of it.

And it was a truth that had the potential to be very damaging.

What folly that she didn't care.

Mirabelle also didn't notice the faint glimmer of pink rippling the air near the room's fine four-poster bed. In that, she wasn't alone, for no one had seen the fine trace of a woman in rose who'd followed her and the King's brother and his lady across the bailey and up the tower stair.

It was better so.

Stirling Castle's pink lady appreciated her privacy.

Indeed, she considered the ability to remain unseen when desired one of the most appealing advantages of ghostdom.

A disadvantage was being privy to things that were none of one's business.

For a soul with little to do but drift and flutter about walls that had once echoed with her footsteps, her laughter and, at times, her sorrows, any such glimpses into the lives of those yet mortal could prove an irresistible attraction. Much as she wished that wasn't so.

It had hurt her heart to see the extravagantly dressed courtier accost the young Highland maid.

Hadn't she suffered the same such unwanted attentions after her beloved husband had been killed in a raid on the castle? It'd been so many years ago, nearly a hundred by mortal reckoning, when the English had come to storm Stirling's gate. Her husband had fought valiantly. He'd fallen with sword in hand, a stalwart to his last breath. A knight of much honor and no small wealth, he'd left her a young widow seen by many as a prize.

When she declined the offers of those eager to claim her—and through her, her late husband's legacy—hadn't some men turned to fouler methods in their hope of trapping her into wedlock?

Unlike the braw Wolf of Badenoch, no man of Stirling had sallied forth to spare her such indignities.

To be fair, those were troubled times in Scotland.

With England's hated Edward I claiming the stronghold and overrunning its proud walls with his own garrison of Sassenach knights and fighting men, she'd had little recourse but to fend for herself.

It hadn't been easy.

She'd gladly shed her earthly mantle when a bowl of spoiled eel soup took her life. In truth, with the wisdom of the crossed-over soul, she now knew the soup had been poisoned. Tainted by those who saw her demise as the fastest means to lay hands on her husband's lands and title, the coffers of treasure folk believed he'd brought back with him from the Crusades and journeys to distant lands.

Rosalind, for that was her name, knew better.

Her husband's greatest treasure was the goodness of his heart and his valor and unflagging loyalty, the love he showered on her every waking moment of their much too short life together. His glory hadn't been in gold, but in his kindness to others, especially those less fortunate. He'd used his influence to protect them. He'd been the best of men and she'd missed him fiercely.

Since then she roamed alone, glimpsed only when she wished someone to see her.

Or by those who were gifted to observe more with their hearts than their eyes.

The flame-haired maid, Lady Mirabelle, was such a soul.

Rosalind had known the moment the lass spotted her floating along the arcade.

It'd been long since anyone had seen her, even though she was about always.

The pity was that so many travails and heartaches awaited the lass. Knowing suchlike was another pesky part of being a bogle.

All manner of wisdom came to ghosts, the onslaught of *knowing* a terrible nuisance, especially in great crowds such as filled the castle hall and other such places where many men gathered. Rosalind suspected she was more susceptible than most bogles, for she'd had a measure of such talent in life. Now she need only flit past someone to sense that person's destined path.

Lady Mirabelle's journey wasn't a bright one.

But she couldn't see its end, which gave her hope and spoke for the girl's strength. For while all things were indeed writ in stone, a living soul still had the choice to ignore fate and keep walking.

And Rosalind was sure Lady Mirabelle was a walker, a strong and proud lass who'd not let the winds of destiny buffet her.

Rosalind wished she'd been as bold.

At least, she'd had manners and still did.

For that reason, she begin to shimmer as fast as she could, allowing the lovely pink haze that surrounded her to lose its glow as she slipped ever deeper into the shadowy world she now called her home.

Lady Mirabelle was undressing, preparing for the steaming, herb-scented bath castle servants had just prepared for her. Rosalind didn't wish to intrude on the maid's well-deserved privacy.

Not that the girl's bared flesh or the intimacies of a bath embarrassed her.

But she'd caught a snippet of thought from the girl's troubled mind and deemed it best to leave her alone to dwell on the problem.

Rosalind smiled as she faded into nothingness.

"How to please a man of insatiable desires" truly wasn't a hardship.

Rosalind was sure such matters would come naturally to the girl.

She decided to watch her from afar, eager to see the man she so fervently wished to entice. If the gods were kind, and she knew they could be for some, the young man would be worthy of her.

She already knew the girl was a treasure beyond telling, and that her life would touch many.

Dashing a tear from her cheek, for such as she could cry when deeply moved, Rosalind cast one last look at the maid, catching her just as she lowered herself into the fragrant water of her bath.

Then the dark mists of her own realm spun faster, claiming her as they always did. And if anyone had noticed a faint glow of pink in the bedchamber's deepest corner, it was no longer there.

Although some might sense what remained behind...

A blessing of love.

Chapter Nine

❖

Lady Mirabelle was a bad influence.

Sorley scowled darkly as he nipped around behind the chapel. Because of her, he preferred the longer, more circuitous route to the castle tower that held his privy quarters. He didn't care to cut across the courtyard. The shorter, more direct path no longer suited him. Not after being with a certain flame-haired minx in the candlelit confines of the chapel. She'd melted against him, returning his kiss and setting him ablaze with her passion.

Now he needed air, the night's chill damp to cool the fire inside him.

She made him burn that hotly.

Her voice alone roused him. Soft and honeyed, each lilting word stirred him like an intimate caress. In truth, as pleasing as it was to listen to her, she didn't need her enchanting Highland accent to render him witless. She could do that simply by standing near him, silent. In her presence, everything else ceased to exist, no longer mattering because he only thought of her. Having a woman affect him so powerfully was a new and discomfiting experience.

He didn't like it.

Nor did he care for the increasing surety that she was a female unlike any other.

He'd aye believed one lass was good as the next, especially once they were naked in his arms, writhing beneath him in the throes of carnal ecstasy. At such times, he couldn't much tell a difference. He took care to tumble only jaded court women and the saucy tavern lasses at the Red Lion, females who enjoyed the glories of the flesh with the same gusto he did. He also kept watch over them even after he'd lost interest in their favor, aye ready to lend support if ever his seed bore fruit. He was not his father.

He didn't despoil innocents.

He'd also come to suspect he was incapable of appreciating a woman for more than the hot, silken delights nestled betwixt her thighs.

Yet he knew from their kiss that Mirabelle's loving would sear him to the soul. She'd do more than slake his desire and deplete him. She'd leave him with a fierce longing to claim her again and again. She'd consume him with the need to sink into her sleek, heated womanliness as often as possible. He'd crave her always.

If he were fool enough to touch her.

Which he wasn't.

Still, she was a disruptive, disconcerting distraction. A bane he didn't need in his well-ordered and most enjoyable life. Even the brief time he'd spent with her in the chapel had given him a raging ache in the head. Elsewhere, too, though he was trying to ignore that particular pounding.

Nor did he appreciate how easily her silly blether about castle ghosts was influencing him.

God's bones, she was turning him daft!

Sure of it, he stopped before the low stone wall of the chapel's once-pagan burial ground and pulled a hand down over his face. Pink ladies, bog beasties, headless pipers, Highland bogles, and who-knew-what-all she believed roamed and moaned about Scotland's fair countryside.

He was having none of it.

Yet...

He *had* seen something.

And what better place for a Scottish ghost to float through the mist than among the tilting, moss-grown gravestones of an ancient Celtic sacred site?

Although the two white-glowing orbs he'd spotted hadn't exactly glided eerily along as he'd have expected such spirits to do.

They'd bobbed up and down, appearing and then disappearing in the darkest corner of the age-old burial ground. It was an uncanny spot, dreary, cold, and full of shadow, even on the brightest summer day.

Some folk swore it was a *thin place*, a spot where the veil between the spiritual and earthly worlds stretched transparent, allowing a communion between the realms of the living and the dead.

Sorley believed that as much as he trusted the moon would fall from the heavens.

Even so, he felt his body tense, his gaze narrow. Especially when the two glowing orbs surfaced again, gleaming through the swirling mist. As before, they rose and fell in ghostly rhythm, perhaps paying homage to a broken grave slab not far from where they kept appearing.

"Saints, Maria, and Joseph!" He borrowed an oath said to have been the favorite of a great Highland chieftain he'd always admired, Duncan MacKenzie, the Black Stag of Kintail. Curious, he stepped over the low stone wall, so worn and crumbled it scarce resembled one. Then he headed for the mysterious bobbing orbs.

It was rough going.

While the holy chapel basked in the King's favor, the interior sumptuous and in excellent repair, the wee bit of ground that held hoary pagan graves didn't enjoy such care. If the truth were known, it was hard to find someone brave enough to tend a spot of ground many believed was still ruled by the old gods. Folk feared the long-buried Celtic dead might rise and take vengeance on the living Scots who now worshipped another God on their sacred land.

Sorley harbored no such worries.

He took care not to step in a rabbit hole or worse. He didn't want to plunge to his waist in the wormy earth of a collapsed gravesite. Grass and nettles grew thickly between the slanting and tumbled tombstones. He wouldn't know he'd stepped wrongly until he'd done so.

O-o-oh...

The thready, high-pitched cry came from nowhere and everywhere, echoing through the mist. Piercing enough to have been a banshee, the wail froze Sorley where he stood. He wouldn't wager on it, but he was fairly sure the mist distorted the sound, making it seem to ripple the air.

He also suspected one of the strange white-glowing orbs had issued the blood-chilling call.

It was a possibility he didn't like at all.

But if he didn't confront the ghosts, seeing for himself if they were or weren't real, he wouldn't sleep that night.

Unlike Lady Mirabelle, he wasn't keen on meeting spirits.

But a man should be a man always, even in the face of the long-departed. Like as not, he'd discover that the shrieking banshee was only an owl.

So he kept on, carefully picking his way through the knee-high grass and around broken graves.

He was almost upon a split grave slab that raged up out of the weeds like a crooked, beckoning finger. It was the stone that hid the two glowing white orbs when they weren't popping up from behind the slab's angled, age-pitted surface to shine through the mist.

At once, the orbs loomed into view.

"God's wounds!" His eyes rounded. He could scarce believe what he was seeing, but there could be no mistaking the bright white forms. Or that they moved with a steady, bouncing rhythm, as if dancing.

Sorley shuddered, half worried that if he took another step he might be swept back in time, finding himself in an older, darker age, right in the midst of a pagan ceremonial circle.

He knew suchlike held human sacrifices.

He also knew they enjoyed orgies, an activity he wouldn't have minded.

But he wanted nothing to do with Druids' darker rituals.

Still...

If Lady Mirabelle was man enough to chase after the pink lady, he could take the last few steps across the grassy ground to the broken grave slab.

A strangled noise rose from behind the stone before he could. It was a sound he recognized. He'd made the same noise often enough, always when on the edge of a thunderous release.

"*Ahhhh...Aye, lass, aye...*" a man's deep voice lifted to the night, confirming his guess.

Sorley nearly choked, trying to hold back his laughter.

Just then, the mists thinned enough for him to get a better look at the two glowing white orbs. There was nothing mysterious about them at all. They were the white-gleaming buttocks of a naked man.

A lusty sort, to be sure. And one who was enjoying himself immensely.

That, too, Sorley knew with surety because the soft sighing he'd believed to be wind through the grass was none other than the excited gasps of a woman on the verge of her own stunning climax.

Sorley's lips twitched and he felt a surge of manly

camaraderie with the fellow responsible for giving the wench such pleasure. Her breathless pants indicated her lover was highly skilled.

A quick tryst on a cold, misty night and in a place of ancient legend wasn't a bad idea.

Sorley might have to try it himself if he could persuade one of his favorite bed partners into risking damp grass and nettle stings.

This night, he'd leave such joys to the fun-seeking pair.

Deeming they deserved their privacy, he started backing away, hoping to leave as quietly as he'd arrived.

One, two, three steps, he made with ease.

Then the rustling behind the slanting grave slab became louder, a touch more frenetic. Sorley froze again, not wanting to disturb a special moment.

He did smile for them.

"O-o-oh, Lyall, I knew you loved me," came the woman's shuddery gasp as she no doubt reached her peak. "And I love you! Only you, Lyall. Oh, o-o-oh..."

Sorley's smile faded as dark, simmering annoyance twisted his gut.

He knew Lyall.

There was only one man by that name at Stirling. He was a good-looking, strapping lad who worked in the stables. More randy than a rutting stag, Lyall tupped as many lasses a night as he could. Some claimed every hour, though Sorley knew that was kitchen blether. It was also rumored Lyall exerted no effort in attracting his conquests. A crook of his finger was enough, a glance, or a suggestive smile that, by all accounting, drew women almost magically.

Sorley knew such tricks.

He was also aware that while Lyall's name meant loyal, the lad aye forgot the lasses even before he flipped their skirts back down.

Sorley pulled a hand over his chin as he looked up at the

cloud-torn sky. Lyall's lusty adventures didn't concern him. The lad's hot-bloodedness and his apparently unquenchable thirst for landing between a woman's thighs were none of his business. Still, an oath rose in Sorley's throat and he bit it back, frowning.

Wasn't he guilty of the same transgressions? Hadn't he tumbled more women than he could begin to count, much less remember?

Still, there was a difference.

He never let them believe he loved them.

If they ever mentioned the word, or gave him the impression they even *thought* it, he backed away, never to seek their company again.

He aye made clear his amorous activities were all about the physical release and pleasure.

No more, no less.

The poor lass beneath Lyall's thrusting hips thought the lad cared for her.

Even now, she was panting more words of love. They stung Sorley's ears as he hastened through the little pagan burial ground. He no longer cared if the pair heard him, knew they'd been observed.

Devils rode him. Hell fiends that stabbed his back with spears of flaming agony, dredging up hurts he preferred to keep hidden deep down in his soul.

But they weren't there now.

Every last one was clawing its heinous way upward, reminding him of the heartless man who'd sired him. Sorley knew the scoundrel was of the same ilk as Lyall-who-raked-muck-from-horse stalls and allowed hapless, trusting kitchen wenches to fall in love with him.

The only difference was that he remained certain his father hadn't been a Stirling man.

He'd bet his sword, his most prized possession, that the blackguard was a Highland chieftain.

He had always felt that in the pit of his gut.

Such feelings never lied.

He didn't either. Well, except in Fenris matters, and then only for the greater cause of the King's will and desire, and Scotland's own weal.

So his demons bit hard as he made for the stair tower to his privy quarters. The orgiastic cries and lovesick words of Lyall's latest tumble-mate followed him. The girl's breathy pants and pathetic avowals of devotion plagued him more with each step he climbed up the winding stair. By the time he reached his landing and gained the refuge of his bed-chamber, his night was well and truly ruined.

Kissing Mirabelle in the chapel had been disaster enough.

Being reminded of his nameless father and his callous deeds had given him the rest.

He wouldn't think of the poor lass who'd soon realize her folly. Lyall wasn't a lad worthy of a maid's heart.

And love was nonsense to be avoided at all cost.

He doubted the like even existed.

Sure of it, he strode across his room—grateful that a servant had lit the wall sconces—and poured himself a healthy measure of uisge beatha, knocking down the fiery Highland spirits in one long gulp.

Perhaps he'd treat himself to another.

Descending into a senseless, mindless sleep appealed greatly. His demons were loose this night. He could feel their talons shredding his resistance, their fiery breath scorching his nape. They wanted blood and usually took a pound or two of flesh as well.

Sorley ignored their snarls and started undressing. He tossed his cloak over the arm of a chair beside his fireplace. His doublet followed, landing on the floor. Not caring, he shrugged out of his shirt, welcoming the room's chill on his bared skin. Anger coursed through him, heating him from the inside out, and not in a pleasant way. He blazed as hotly as if someone had lugged the huge, double-arched kitchen hearth into his bedchamber, complete with a raging, bright-burning fire. And as he rid himself of the rest of his clothes and yanked off his boots, naked at last, he would've sworn he saw his demons dancing in the flames.

For once, he wasn't of a mind to wrestle with them. The morrow would suffice.

He just hoped they didn't follow him into his dreams.

Above all, he didn't want to find Lady Mirabelle there.

Lifelong devils he could handle.

He'd been battling the beasties ever since he'd first learned the true meaning of bastard, what it meant not to have a father in a world where blood and lineage was everything. His devils were a plague, but he knew how to silence them. How to control the darkness he wouldn't allow to invade his life, making him miserable.

He wasn't sure what to do about Mirabelle, or, more specifically, what he should do about his feelings for her.

That they existed couldn't be denied.

Furious that was so, he knocked down the remainder of his uisge beatha, not surprised he felt more like a caged beast than ever before in his life.

The question was how fast Lady Mirabelle could run if he couldn't control his savage desires.

He hoped she wouldn't be put to the test.

Sometime in the small hours, Sorley snapped out of a deep, uisge-beatha–inspired sleep, sure his plaguey demons *were* coming for him.

Fanglike teeth flashing, red eyes ablaze, and with their talonlike claws extended, they scratched at his bedchamber door. Clawing relentlessly, seeking entry so they could finally get their shriveled, leathery hands on him, at last claiming his black, sinful soul.

That he knew, sure as he breathed.

Yet.

Then the skull-splitting haze from too many cups of strong Highland spirits thinned just enough for him to hear the beasties' clawing—*tap, tap, tap*—for what it really was: someone knocking at his door.

The raps were soft enough to scream stealth.

Whoever was out there, trying to waken him, didn't wish to be seen.

And didn't he know only one person who skulked about the castle so late at night, poking her pretty nose into places it didn't belong?

How dare she come to his room again?

"Bluidy hell!" He threw back the covers and leapt from his bed.

Unfortunately, the first thing he then did was to trip over his discarded boot.

Tap, tap, tap!

The knocking turned more insistent.

Righting himself, he cursed again and stormed toward the door, bare-arsed as he was. If the sight of his free-swinging nakedness shocked her—which wasn't likely, as she'd seen him thus before—so be it.

She deserved no better for disrupting his night's rest.

As if his demons wished to disturb *him*, the wall sconces had guttered as he'd slept. Rarely had his room seemed so dark, so full of shadow and gloom. Even his night candle on the table beside his bed had gone out. In his fuzzy-headed state, he couldn't see well and slammed his toe into an iron-bound chest near the door.

"Suffering saints!" He hopped on one foot, clutching his throbbing toe.

Outside, the *tapping* ceased.

"Och, nae, sweet," Sorley growled, "you're no' sneaking away now." He grabbed the latch, yanking open the door before she could flee. "What the bluidy—"

His jaw slipped, and he was stunned into silence to find Maili on the threshold.

"Sakes, lass!" He pulled her inside, closing the door behind her. He grabbed a plaid off a hook on the wall, slinging the tartan—a MacKenzie weave, as he admired that clan—around his hips, leaving his chest bare. "Can a man no' have his sleep?"

"Think you I'd not rather be abed?" She moved deeper into the room, away from the door. She carried a small hand torch and set its tip to several of Sorley's wall sconces, finally placing her torch in an iron hook near a window. "It's been a long day and I'm tired." She met his annoyed gaze, her own earnest. "William sent me."

Sorley blinked. "Wyldes?"

"Himself it was, aye." Maili stood beside his bed, her hands clasped before her.

Sorley shook his head, trying to scatter the last of the uisge beatha fumes. So this was why Maili had ridden back to Stirling with Mirabelle and her guard. The question was why the innkeeper had sent her.

William Wyldes did nothing without reason.

Sorley frowned. He was sure he wouldn't like Maili's tidings.

News that came in the wee hours was seldom good.

"I saw Wyldes this morn." Sorley couldn't help his querulous tone. "Is there a problem at the inn?"

"Not trouble, a visitor." Maili dropped onto the edge of his bed, smoothing her skirts. "A man called in not long after you left. He came asking about you. William thought you should know."

"Did the man say why he's seeking me?"

"Not that I heard. William didn't tell me if he knew."

"Many men stop at the Red Lion." Sorley leaned against the bedpost, considering. He also forced a casualness he didn't feel, not wanting to alarm Maili.

"This wasn't just any man, not a common wayfarer." She lounged against his pillows, her expression anything but troubled.

Sorley's instincts were on high alert.

Wyldes could smell a rat at a hundred paces. He'd think to have whiffed a monstrous one to have sent Maili to pester him in the middle of the night.

So he spoke plain. "I have my enemies, lass. Old ones with long memories and deeper grudges, new foes I make every day." That was as close as he'd go to mentioning the Fenris. "Now and again suchlike surface to challenge me. Did this man give his name? Is he lodging at the inn? If so, I'll head over to the Red Lion in the morning."

He'd welcome a fight.

There was only one pastime he enjoyed more. And as that wasn't possible, leastways not with the lady of his choice, he wouldn't mind breaking the bones of whoever thought to call him out for a tussle.

He could think of no other reason for anyone to look for him.

"I'm not sure he's an enemy." Maili's face softened, taking on the dreamy look she always wore when she fancied a man. "I do think he's a warrior, though. He's a great giant of a man with a thick mane of wild black hair and smoke-gray eyes. He has a beard, too, and wears silver rings braided into it. Ne'er have I seen the like..." Her eyelashes fluttered and she bit her lower lip, clearly smitten. "Handsome he is, in a fierce, hardened way. And he had an amulet hanging around his neck, a silver Thor's hammer."

Sorley fought the urge to snort.

He also bit his tongue rather than tell Maili he didn't care if the man had the Norse god's lightning bolts shooting out his arse.

"His name, lass, that's all that interests me." That wasn't quite true.

From Maili's description, he'd never met such a man. And that mystery caused an unpleasant tension to start building in his shoulders. He didn't expect anything good to come of meeting the stranger. Though he would relish a fight if it came to one, and he suspected it would.

The man sounded like a mercenary, like as not, someone sent by one of his less stout-hearted foes. The kind of man who saw his might in coin rather than his sword arm. Sorley found paid fighters distasteful. He disliked their employers even more. Men should fight their own battles.

Maili was twirling a curl of her dark brown hair around her finger, her lips curved in a smile that could only be called besotted.

Sorley frowned. "He did give his name?"

"He's Grim Mackintosh." Maili leaned deeper into his pillows, linking her hands behind her neck. "He's a Highlander from Nought territory in the Glen of Many Legends. A *Highlander,*" she enthused, saying the word as if such beings had winged ankles, walking without their feet touching the lowly ground.

Sorley's mood darkened.

Once, he'd also been in awe of Highlanders. But that was long ago, back when he'd been a wee gullible lad and hadn't yet learned how cruel such men could be. Hope had still beat in his boyish heart. Secretly, he'd believed his Highland chieftain father would come for him, whisking him away, making his world right, as they'd ride off to the distant hills he dreamed of and felt so drawn to.

That was then.

He was a boy no more.

These days any whiff of tartan put his back up, souring his mood and ruining his day.

There were a few exceptions.

King Robert's brother, Alex, commonly known as the Wolf of Badenoch and as deserving of the name as a mortal man could be, stood in Sorley's highest regard. It was Alex, more than his kingly brother, who truly steered the Fenris. A fearsome but great-hearted man, the Wolf also loved his wild hills and moors above everything and enjoyed nothing better than parading about court in full Highland regalia, his plaid and his pride proudly displayed.

Sorley also excluded MacKenzie plaids from his aversion to tartan. He held MacKenzies in grudging admiration because of their much-famed chieftain, Duncan, the Black Stag of Kintail. He couldn't count the rousing tales spun about the man, or how often he'd heard it said that the Black Stag was even greater than his legend.

So sometimes he wore that clan's blue-and-green tartan, simply because no one would dare tell him not to. He also did so in tribute, though he was not wont to admit it.

"Not many Highlanders visit the Red Lion." Maili's wistful tone reminded him he wasn't alone.

He looked at her, found her twirling a tassel on one of his bed cushions. Her eyes were even dreamier than before. Whoever the Highlander was, he'd turned Maili's head.

He still couldn't place any Grim Mackintosh of Nought in the Glen of Many Legends.

"Nought, aye?" He had heard of the Mackintosh lands. "That's said to be a godforsaken place, all rocky, jagged peaks, mist, and cold winds. Folk claim Nought is wild, remote, and so rugged only mountain goats and fools would dare set foot there. I ken no Nought men."

He did envy them, deep in his heart.

That was a truth that scalded him to the bone. It also clamped around his chest, so tight the longing almost wrung the breath from him.

He could imagine the remote splendor. As a lad, he'd dreamt of belonging to a place like Nought. Somewhere carved of soaring, wind-beaten heights, deep gorges filled with cascading waterfalls, and high moors where the heather rolled on forever, the desolation so glorious it hurt the eyes to behold such grandness.

Sorley set his jaw against the images, pushing them from his mind.

If a Nought man—and a warrior, at that—had gone to William seeking him, it wouldn't be to regale Sorley with the wonders of his home.

"This Grim..." He angled his head, his mind racing. "He's a warring man, you say? Are you sure he's no' a Sassenach in disguise?"

That could be a reason for Wyldes's warning.

Maili looked shocked. "No Englishman could speak so beautifully. I vow"—her cheeks flushed pink—"I nearly *enjoyed* myself just listening to him. Only Highlanders can melt a woman with their voices, making us—"

"Have done, lass!" Sorley scowled at her. "There's more to man than his burr."

Maili sighed dreamily. "Say you."

"I do. I'll also say I'm surprised you aren't in a hurry to race back to the Red Lion. If this Grim is such a paragon"—Sorley didn't hide his annoyance—"I'd think you'd be eager to return to his bed. Sakes, you look close to needing to fan your face each time you speak of him."

"I do fancy him." Maili jumped to her feet, brushed at her skirts. "And I did ask if he required his comforts addressed, his bed made warmer..." She glanced aside, seeming embarrassed. "He wasn't interested, said he just wanted a clean room to sleep and victuals."

Sorley's jaw slipped. "Then he'll be of another bent than most men, sweet."

He wouldn't have thought it, but still...

Maili *was* fetching. She had a cheery, saucy air that drew men, always. Few could resist her. Sorley only did because he loved her like a sister. Otherwise he'd also be tempted, mightily so.

"There are men who dinnae favor ladies." He sought to make her feel better.

"Oh, nae, Grim's not that way." She shook her head, her dark curls bouncing. "He's married, he is. He—"

Sorley snorted. "Most men are, love. A wife rarely stops a man from—"

"Not a wife, perhaps, but love." Maili's eyes warmed, turning dreamy again. "Truest love always stays a man. He may look at such as me, but he'll enjoy only his meal and ale at the Red Lion. Grim Mackintosh is such a man." She stood straighter, squaring her shoulders as if to defend him. "He even told me I'm bonnie and that the bards in his hills would sing of my charms. But he also said that, for him, his lady wife shines brighter than all the stars in the heaven. That her light and warmth is with him always, wherever he goes."

"Long-winded bastard, what?" Sorley snorted again.

Such a man likely had *other* problems keeping him from tumbling a fine lass like Maili.

"He's not a bastard at all. He—" Maili clapped a hand to her lips, her eyes rounding. "Och, sorry! I didn't mean—"

"That I ken, sweeting." Sorley slid an arm around her, drawing her close as he guided her to the door. Releasing her, he set his hand on the latch. "Did William have aught else for me to hear?"

Maili shook her head. "Only that he feels Grim's tidings are important."

Sorley nodded. "Then all I can do is to find out what he wants."

"I can't wait to hear." Maili reached to squeeze his arm as she nipped past him, quickly disappearing down the dimly lit corridor.

Sorley closed the door behind her, his mood now worse than ever. And not because some stranger named Grim blew in from one of the bleakest corners of the Highlands, calling at the Red Lion to ask of him. Whatever the man wanted would be addressed swiftly, with swords, fists, or words, however their meeting fell.

Crossing the room, Sorley climbed back into his bed, huffed an agitated breath. He'd lied out the gills to Maili, and not the Fenris-driven falsehoods that were necessary and acceptable.

He'd stooped to the lowly, despicable kind of lie that would eat into him for days, damning him to the bone.

He'd have never believed it, but he understood Grim Mackintosh's wish to sleep alone. Only difference was that it was lust and not love that diminished Sorley's usually rampant need for a woman.

Since Lady Mirabelle's appearance, he'd lost his appetite for bedding any other lass.

He only wanted her.

Wishing he didn't, he rolled onto his side and resisted punching the bedpost. Busted knuckles would serve him naught. And he'd regret the dent he'd plow into the bed's richly carved oak frame. He'd spent too many years sleeping on a scatter of hay in a dark corner of the castle kitchens as a lad to damage the proud "laird's" bed he'd bought with his first hard-earned coin.

Still, he was furious to have fallen under Mirabelle's spell.

Praise God it was only lust he felt for her.

He just hoped the powerful urges she stirred in him faded once she was gone, that he'd then forget her, his usually ravenous appetite for women returning. All women, in their vast and delightful variety. He didn't relish going through his days primed for the one female he shouldn't desire and could never make his own, no taste remaining for the other lovelies of the fairer sex.

He wasn't made to monk.

Mirabelle appeared to grace the earth for the sole purpose of maddening him.

It was an undertaking she executed with great skill.

She was by turn seductively provocative and alluring in her innocence. She knew how to walk, taking every advantage of the generous curves the good gods had bestowed on her. She teased with smooth alabaster skin that begged to be touched. And—he was convinced—she bathed in rivers of rose oil, the witchy scent too beguiling for any man to withstand.

He refused to consider her remarkable eyes and what happened to him when she swept him with one of her bold, all-too-direct gazes.

Her lips tasted as luscious as he'd aye imagined, while her tongue...

"Hellfire and damnation!" Sorley flipped onto his back and glared up at the bed's intricately-carved oak canopy. For the first time in his memory, he resented the bare-breasted wood nymphs made to look as if they peered down from the panels of black, age-glossed wood.

He had the distinct impression they were laughing at him.

Closing his eyes, he ignored them.

He wasn't as successful putting Mirabelle from his mind. But he did know one thing. And it was a greater truth than anything else.

The sooner he saw the last of her, the better.

Chapter Ten

❧

Much later, in the darkest, most still hours of the night, Mirabelle stood alone in the castle's exquisitely appointed Rose Room. Only a few doors from her guest chamber, the favored haunt of court ladies was lavish beyond her wildest imaginings, the room's sumptuous furnishings so grand she wondered if she was still in bed, dreaming.

Yet she was awake, her inability to sleep having brought her here.

She'd hoped to encounter a few women, having heard their chatter drifting from the room often enough. But apparently Stirling's ladies enjoyed better slumber than her own. No one had greeted her when she slipped into the oh-so-feminine, rose-colored chamber.

In truth, the walls were whitewashed, though so many large tapestries graced the room that its real color couldn't be seen. It was the rose-bedecked wall coverings that drew the eye, each masterpiece shimmering in hues of palest pink to deepest red, the embroidered blooms looking so real that she almost felt as if she'd stepped into a beautiful rose garden blossoming in all its summer glory.

Even the artfully carved fireplace was crafted of smooth and gleaming pink marble.

A dazzle of silken cushions in the same shade adorned the benches in the room's three deep-set window embrasures, while thick, pink-waxed candles glimmered softly in delicately arched wall niches. Never before had she seen such colored candles, and their glow only added to the chamber's magical air of enchantment.

Whoever cared for the room had placed wine jugs, silver-edged cups, and an array of tempting-looking cheeses and oatcakes on a table draped with a rich damask covering in a fetching shade of dark rose.

Mirabelle's belly rumbled, but she went to stand before one of the chamber's tall arch-topped windows rather than indulging in the potent Rhenish wine or the delicious-looking refreshments that she was sure would only sit like rocks in her stomach.

The Rose Room and its fairytale trappings could've sprung from a bard's most romantic storytelling, but her mind was filled with more important matters than admiring fripperies, or even eating.

She couldn't forget Sorley's kiss.

Neither her glimpse of the castle's pink lady, her unpleasant meeting with Sir John, nor her encounter with the Wolf and his lady could banish the heated memory of his lips claiming hers. He was beyond all doubt the most dashing, alluring, and compelling man she'd ever met and she half believed he'd cast a spell on her.

Just thinking about his kiss, how his tongue had slid inside her mouth to tangle with her own, made her breasts swell and ache and sent an embarrassingly wicked rush of hot, damp warmth tingling across her most private places. Any moment she would burst into flame, she was sure.

Worst of all, her wantonness made her forget proper decency.

She should have told him about the Highlander who'd called in at the Red Lion, asking of him.

She'd meant to do so. Something told her the man's business with Sorley was earnest.

But...

He stole her wits. His proximity, even just the way he looked at her, or simply breathing the same air, chased all else from her mind. Nothing remained except her burning wish for him to take her in his arms and ravish her. Not only by kissing her, but entirely.

She'd hoped a bit of converse with another, equally sleep-deprived maid would turn her thoughts to less dangerous musings. That the hours until first light would pass more quickly, once she returned to her bed.

For it was then, at daybreak, that she planned to visit Sorley's quarters.

Not to press him about her proposal and his insulting stipulations, but to warn him about the Highlander.

If early morning found him a bit sleep-befuddled and he then decided to kiss her...

So be it.

She wouldn't complain.

She stepped closer to the window, inhaled deeply of the cold night air. Her shift and bed-robe weren't much protection against the chill, but she didn't mind. In truth, she appreciated the briskness. She also took pleasure in the hour's stillness.

Stirling Castle wasn't often quiet.

So she nearly jumped from her skin when the sound of the door latch echoed through the Rose Room's elegant splendor.

She jolted, awareness sluicing her as the door opened and closed behind her. The beat of her heart quickened, her pulse thundering. She knew without looking who'd entered the room, and it wasn't one of the court ladies. Only one person could provoke such a reaction in her, simply by stepping over a threshold, his presence already flowing around her so potently that she could hardly breathe.

"Sorley." Turning to face him, she wasn't surprised to see that he looked murderous. He made right for her, his stride bold and forceful, the fierce glint in his eye sparking her own ire. "This is a ladies' chamber." She lifted her chin as he neared, meeting his furious gaze. "We are in the women's tower, a place that should be safe from male intrusion, especially at this late hour."

"I ken exactly where we are." He stopped before her, catching her arm. His grip was tight, his expression even darker this close. "What I'd hear is what you are doing here. In the Rose Room, and"—he swept her with a heated gaze, from her tumbled, unbound hair to her slippered toes and back again—"half-dressed in naught but your bedclothes."

Mirabelle kept her chin raised. "I couldn't sleep."

"Neither could I, you little she-vixen." He leaned in, didn't release his hold on her. "My bedchamber looks directly across to this room. Imagine my surprise to gaze this way and see you limned in thon window arch, the light of the moon and the Rose Room's candle glow treating me to a sight no man should be presented with unless he's about to strip down himself and bed a woman. Had anyone else seen you..." He let the implication hang between them, meaningfully.

Mirabelle didn't like his assumption. "Someone else wouldn't have stormed across the bailey and barged into this room, spoiling my night's peace and—"

"Think you?" He released her then and stepped back, shoved both hands through his hair. "Are you so naïve that you dinnae ken this chamber's purpose?"

Mirabelle blinked. "Ladies of quality come here for refreshments. I have heard their chatter, ofttimes late of an e'en." She had, hence hoping to exchange a few pleasantries with one or two this night. "I thought to—"

"You erred badly." Sorley glanced about the lovely room, and even in the soft glow of the candlelight, she could see the agitation in his eyes. When he looked back at her, his jaw was hard-set, a muscle clenching there. "To be sure, fine ladies frequent this room. But they dinnae come here to engage in simple blether."

"I do not follow your meaning." She did, but was too stunned to say so.

"Indeed?" He arched a brow, his piercing gaze warning her that she trod on dangerous ground. "Shall I tell you what goes on here, lass?"

"I am sure you know."

"No' just myself." He indicated the nearest tapestry with a jerk of his chin. It was exceptionally lovely, covered with silk-embroidered roses in full bloom. "Can you guess why the room is called after roses?"

Mirabelle set her hands on her hips. "Because of the wall hangings; each one is covered with roses. They're even on the cushions of the window embrasure benches."

"So they are."

Mirabelle lifted her own brow, holding his gaze. "Why do I have the feeling you're about to say something for the sole purpose of shocking me?"

"I came here to protect you." His face turned even more thunderous. "The roses you see everywhere in this chamber, and the room's name, refer to another type of rose. A wonderfully feminine one much enjoyed by men."

"A female rose?" Mirabelle didn't understand.

Then she did, a wash of heat soaring onto her cheeks. She flashed a quick look about the chamber, at all the pink and red blooms. Dear heavens . . . She lifted a hand and clutched her bed-robe tighter across her breasts, hoping the dim lighting would hide the color she knew must be making her face glow. "Surely you do not mean—"

"I do." His tone was earnest. "Be glad none of the court

ladies were entertaining admirers when you happened in here. Some of the men who hold trysts in the Rose Room are darker-natured than most. Your arrival, so scantily clad, would've invited trouble."

"My robe covers more than the gown I wear at the high table each evening." Mirabelle knew that was true.

She wouldn't have left her guest chamber otherwise.

Sorley just looked at her, his handsome features setting in hard lines as he slowly shook his head. "That may be so, sweet. Until you commit the folly of standing in a window arch with the light of the moon shining on you and the flames of candles limning you from behind.

"Very little of you wasn't to be seen," he told her, his voice deepening on the words, as did the look in his eyes. "You could well have been unclothed."

"Oh." Mirabelle swallowed, the shift between them charging the air, making her tingle in indecent places. She looked up at Sorley from beneath her lashes, wondered if he knew that his words affected her so powerfully. That, despite her innocence, she dreamed of standing before him wearing nothing but desire. Of lying naked in his arms, living the passion she'd savor ever after.

"Dinnae e'er come here again," he fair growled the warning, the heated look that had flared in his eyes once more replaced by anger. Whate'er possessed you to do so?" He took her arm again, leading her away from the window.

"I told you, I couldn't sleep." Mirabelle spoke true. "Indeed, you are the reason I couldn't," she added, becoming as annoyed as he was. It was humiliating that he could admit to seeing her near naked, yet even then, well-lusted as he was known to be, he clearly didn't desire her.

Freeing herself of his grasp, she stood as straight as she could and flipped her hair back over her shoulder. "I'd planned to visit your quarters at first light," she informed him, her tone as cold and clipped as his had been scored by ire. "I had tidings to share with you and grew restless waiting for the sun to rise."

He looked at her, his face expressionless. "You've changed your mind about our plan to thwart Sinclair?"

"Not at all." Mirabelle stiffened at his tone, quite sure his stony features were meant to hide how much he hoped she did want to cancel their agreement. "I meant to tell you that a man came asking for you at the Red Lion Inn when I was there with my father. He was a Highlander, Grim Mackintosh of the Glen of Many Legends.

"He was questioning the innkeeper about you," she rushed on, noting how his expression was closing even more. "I forgot to mention him in the chapel. He seemed so eager to hear of you, I thought you should know."

To her surprise, he shrugged. "Many men come looking for me, lass."

Mirabelle frowned, confused.

She had been so sure he'd be glad to know. She'd even thought...

"He was a fighting man, a battle-hardened warrior by the look of him." She reached to touch Sorley's arm, abandoning caution to put her suspicions to words. "I think he may have heard you're a Fenris—"

Sorley placed two fingers to her lips, silencing her. "There are no such men, sweetness. They are a myth, no more. Legends the storytellers sing of on long, dark winter nights before the fire."

"He knew your name." Mirabelle twisted free, her eyes narrowing suspiciously. "I heard him ask for you."

Sorley wasn't about to speak of the Fenris with her.

He most assuredly wouldn't do so when she was hovering so near, little more than a slip of cloth and her bewitching rose perfume between them, her lush, female warmth beckoning him so fiercely he was set like granite. He'd run full mad to come to her here.

Yet if he hadn't...

"I can't believe you're not concerned." She frowned at him, proving her prickliness.

He could see the dark rims of her nipples through her bed-robe, the tempting shadows at the tops of her thighs. Her rose scent wafted beneath his nose, reminding him of exactly what he'd find if he parted her legs.

Sorley drew a tight breath, in agony.

His manhood twitched, demanding satisfaction.

He slid an arm around her waist, tugging her close. "Did you no' hear me, lass?" He leaned down and spoke against the silken hair at her temple. "It's nothing new for a man to come looking for me. He'll be some saucy wench's father or brother, maybe her uncle or a husband. If he wishes to challenge me, we will fight when he finds me. Until then, I have other cares." Returning her to her room was the great-est. "Come, I'll see you back to your guest quarters. You'll sleep better now, having told me what worried you."

He would spend the night's remaining hours pacing his bedchamber, willing his thoughts on anything but how much he wanted her.

He'd run so hard he'd spill if he wasn't soon rid of her.

Yet he couldn't bring himself to release her.

Instead, he caught her hand and kissed the soft skin of her wrist. "I didnae mean to shock you by telling you about this room." He could see the agitation on her face, the high color in her cheeks.

He'd clearly riled her.

Perhaps it was better so. She'd keep up her guard with him, be wary. And then he'd find it much easier to kiss, touch, and scandalize her when the time came. If their act remained just that, he'd be better able to put her from his mind when she returned to her Highlands.

That *was* how it would end.

Yet...

His jaw clenched, fury swelling inside him when he realized he was still holding her hand, even circling his thumb over the silky-smooth flesh of her palm. Worse, he'd been kissing her fingers.

He set her from him, scowling. "You see, minx, this room has a witchy effect on men. They come here and do things they wouldn't elsewhere."

She colored even more, her sapphire eyes blazing. "The room it is now?" Moving away from him, she went to the refreshment table. She walked its length, trailing her fingers over the fine, rose-colored draping. "I do not believe you. Indeed"—she whirled to face him—"I know enough of coupling to be aware that doing so would be most uncomfortable in a chamber graced only with a victual table, a stone floor, and equally hard stone benches in the window alcoves. The maze of cushions would slip." She strode into one of the embrasures, nudged the pillows with her knee. When the cushions tumbled to the floor, she gave him a triumphant smile. "No one keen on lovemaking would see such uncomfortable surrounds as suitable for their chosen pursuit."

"Well observed, my lady." For the first time since he'd entered the damnable room, Sorley felt a smile tugging at his lips.

A wicked smile, for the devil himself was riding him.

Mirabelle MacLaren brought out the worst in him. But he was a scoundrel already; a rogue not known for his use of fancy words or courtly manners. He was simply himself, so he rolled his shoulders back, appreciating how her eyes shone in the candle glow, aware that his next words might dim their light, perhaps even shocking her.

Still, he wouldn't lie.

"Court ladies and their lovers dinnae enjoy carnal pleasures here." He made a sweeping gesture with his hand, taking in the room in all its rose finery. "You are quite right in your observation."

Her brow furrowed at that, but rather than marring her beauty, she looked so desirable in her perplexity that he didn't care what happened next.

He wanted only her, and the hard beating of his heart warned that he did so in a way much more disturbing than the persistent tug at his groin.

He frowned, dismissing the possibility.

She glanced about, eyeing the chamber's elaborate trappings. "But you said—"

"I told you men and women come here, and they do."

"You implied they do more than talk."

"So I did, and they do, just not in this room." Needing distance from her, he went to the nearest tapestry, lifting its edge to reveal the hidden door beneath. "They slip into secret love lairs where they are ensured privacy. If you look behind each wall hanging, you'll find a similar door." Sorley opened the one before him, revealing another chamber. No candles burned here, but enough moonlight fell through several high-placed window slits to adequately illuminate the room. More lavish than the main chamber, the smaller enclave gleamed in the same rose tones and was nearly filled by a huge four-poster bed. "Here is where Stirling's lofties take their pleasure. Have a closer look if you're curious." He challenged her, expecting her not to budge.

She surprised him by coming forward, again touching his arm as she stood beside him, peering into the little room's opulence. He watched her gaze flick over the sumptuously dressed bed, the small but equally inviting couch, and the low table that held an elaborately worked iron stand upon which an oil lamp waited to be lit. The table also offered an array of earthen jars, each one clearly filled with scented creams and oils to be enjoyed during sensual pursuits.

The way her eyes narrowed on the jars proved she'd guessed their purpose.

"After what you've said, I wonder that these chambers

are not occupied." She glanced back at him, looking more curious than shocked. "I have heard laughter and muted voices through the walls nearly every night."

Sorley shrugged. "The Wolf and his lady were celebrating in the hall this night. Like as no', the revelers became a bit too merry and fell asleep on the floor rushes. It would no' be the first time."

"Then I should like to see more." She tossed a look over her shoulder, toward the Rose Room's main door. "If you think we shall remain undisturbed?"

"I can guarantee it." Sorley pulled a dirk from its sheath on his belt and, without hesitation, thrust it into an iron ring beside the little room's door. When he turned back to Mirabelle, he couldn't keep a corner of his mouth from twitching. "No one will enter a chamber that's been claimed. A man's dagger or his sword, or even his cloak brooch, is signal enough that a pair is within, desiring to be left alone."

"You have been here before." Mirabelle's voice held an edge.

When she slid a glance at him, he would've sworn he saw a flash of jealousy in her eyes.

"To be sure I have," he admitted, ignoring how his heart had leapt to see her annoyance. "I am a man, lass. I wouldn't have hot, red blood in my veins if I didn't desire a comely, willing female."

She frowned, her cheeks coloring prettily.

Sorley felt like an arse.

But he wasn't about to tell her he'd been here with Maili. Not just once, but several times. Or that their activities in the secret enclaves had nothing to do with bed-play, but rather standing at opposite ends of the little rooms, their ears pressed to tiny crevices in the wall, hoping to catch evidence of Sir John's perfidies.

The noble was known to frequent the Rose Room.

And more than one of the ladies he'd visited here had mysteriously vanished thereafter.

That knowledge had been a reason his heart had nearly stopped when he'd glimpsed Mirabelle in the chamber's window arch.

Just now, she stood so near that he breathed in her witchy scent on every inhalation, a heady intoxication that only served to worsen his mood.

If she so much as bumped against his iron-hard, straining manhood, she would see how ready he was for her.

He was that primed.

Equally appalling, he was powerfully pleased by her courage. Most noblewomen of her innocence would fall into a swoon at the sight of such a decadent love lair. If they didn't pinch their lips in disapproval, perhaps even slapping him for presenting them with such a sinful scene, they'd no doubt run from the Rose Room, crying that they'd been contaminated by wicked, abhorrent surroundings.

Mirabelle's curiosity attracted him, earning his respect and admiration.

Too bad those were feelings he didn't want to harbor for her.

So he put back his shoulders and let his frown darken, hoping to appear formidable, untouched by the joy it was to see her studying a den of pleasure with obvious interest and feminine delight.

"It is clear, sir, that you do not find me comely." Her sudden observation almost made him bark a laugh, so far from the truth was her judgment of him. "Though,"—she looked at him, her eyes shining in the dimness—"you surely know I am willing enough for everything, given the request I've made of you. Indeed, seeing how you glare at me, I doubt there is any purpose in the act you propose we engage in, in the great hall." Her tone held a challenge. "Sir John will not believe you're truly seducing me if you find me so distasteful."

This time Sorley did snort. He couldn't help it.

He seized her arms, tugging her against him. "Sweet

lass, if I found you any more delectable than I do now, this moment, you'd be on thon bed with your skirts tossed up about your hips and I would be buried deep inside you, riding you until you cried my name for all broad Scotland to hear the pleasure I'd give you. Be glad I have my honor, such as it is." He set her from him, straightening his plaid before she could glimpse the rock-solid length of him straining to claim her.

Because he was so riled, he glared at her. "Dinnae fash yourself, lassie. Sinclair willnae have a shred of doubt when I take a seat beside you in the hall. He'll believe what we wish him to think. My actions will give him no choice but to do so."

"Say you?" Mirabelle held his gaze, lifted an artful brow.

Moving away from him, she went to the bed, touching its luxurious satin coverlet. "I hope you are right," she said without looking at him. "He has been pressing my father, insinuating himself into his favor with tales about his knowledge and experience with the famed MacBeth healers. Sir John claims to have encountered them during a journey to the Hebrides. He thinks to visit my father at Knocking Tower to discuss herbs and healing.

"I needn't tell you that my father would be swayed by such an offer." She lifted one of the cushions, plumped it, and then returned it to the bed. "Most keen, indeed, if you'd hear the way of it. Little else matters so much to him as medicinal practices."

"His daughter surely ranks higher." Sorley was certain of that.

But she was toying with a thick gold tassel that dangled from the bed curtains, and watching her fingers pull on the heavy threads was making his loins grip so fiercely he could hardly draw a breath.

"You sound pained, my lord." She flicked the tassel, appeared fascinated by its swing.

"I am no lord, my lady." He emphasized her title, needing the formality it put between them.

"I would hear how you know Sinclair's plan." He remained on the enclave's threshold, clenching his fists to keep from seizing her to him again. "You didn't mention this when last we spoke."

She turned to look at him, her gaze direct. "He approached me in the bailey, after I left you at the chapel. It was then that he—"

"Did he touch you?" Sorley was on her with two swift strides, this time gripping her shoulders. "If he so much as harmed a hair on your head, I will—"

"I pulled my lady's dagger on him." Her chin came up, pride ringing in her soft Highland voice. "I would've used it, too, had not the Wolf—"

"Alex? The earl?" Sorley's brows rose. He knew the King's brother despised Sir John.

"Him, and no other, yes. He came along with his lady, Mariota. Sir John made a hasty enough retreat after their arrival. They escorted me back to my guest room, even had a bath sent up for me."

Sorley relaxed. "The earl is a hard man. Good to those he favors, but fierce to any who'd cross him. Sinclair wouldn't dare. But Alex's position as King Robert's brother binds even his hands so long as he is here at court. In his Highlands, he rules with an iron fist. But after he rampaged through Forres and Elgin some years ago, earning excommunication for burning the Elgin Cathedral, even he is cautious in the King's presence." Sorley frowned, glad he wasn't bound by such restraints. "The King still believes Sinclair is a fine enough man, only misunderstood and, at times, unlucky in his dealings. He sees the good in everyone, even the vilest. Sir John takes advantage, aye managing to remain in the King's favor." It was a talent the oily snake had mastered to perfection.

"Then it is even more important that no one suspects

your ruination of me isn't real." Mirabelle drew away from him, forcing herself to be bold. Before her courage fled, she slipped out of her bed-robe, letting it drop to floor and pool around her ankles. She knew the plain linen nightshift beneath would reveal her nakedness.

She didn't care.

She did smile, daring Sorley to notice.

There was no question that he did. A low, most masculine sound rumbled somewhere deep in his chest and his face darkened at once, his eyes turning almost black. Never had he looked more fierce.

"That wasnae wise, lass." He shook his head slowly, his gaze tracking her length, down and back up again. "You dinnae ken what you're doing, the dangers you provoke."

Something leapt inside her, emboldening her even more. "You kissed me in the chapel to test how well I'd react to your mock seduction. Perhaps you should practice your own amatory skills, leastways so that you do not spoil our play acting by glowering at me as you do."

"Dinnae push me, sweet." His voice was low, husky. "I can see your nipples, and more. That wee slip of a gown you've on hides naught. I willnae be responsible if you dinnae cover yourself at once."

He bent to reach for her bed-robe, but Mirabelle placed her foot on top of it, smiling when he straightened to frown at her even more darkly.

"You said in the chapel that your seduction would require you to touch my breasts." She couldn't believe her daring, but he was so big and strong. Something inside her was awakening to the lure of him, urging her on. A hot, passionate female need that thrummed through her like liquid fire, igniting a need she couldn't deny. "I'm thinking we should practice that now. You caressing my breasts."

"I say you've run mad." He didn't budge. But a muscle ticked in his jaw, revealing his agitation.

The bulge at his groin was an even greater indication.

"One touch." She held his gaze, unblinking. "So that I do not appear startled when you do so in the hall."

He inhaled sharply, then released an annoyed-sounding breath. "Holy horned mother of all the heathen gods," he snarled, reaching for her, yanking her hard against him. "You were surely put on this earth to be the end of all men unfortunate enough to set eyes on you."

"As long as one man loses interest in me, I am glad." She didn't say how much *his* regard mattered. That she wanted to make memories, needed to take them home with her to the Highlands, to treasure forever.

"Damn Sinclair!" Sorley's grip tightened on her shoulder, his fingers twisting in the skein of her unbound hair. Then he cursed again and swept his hand down over her breast, clutching her through the thin sheath of her gown. He caught and held her gaze, his own burning as he circled the thrusting peak of her nipple with his thumb. "This is how I will begin touching your breasts in the hall, lady. Take note, feel every rub of my thumb o'er you, and then ready yourself for this…" He let the words tail off, not taking his gaze from hers as he plunged his hand beneath her nightshift and started rolling her nipple between two fingers. When she gasped and bit her lower lip, the pleasure so intense delicious shivers streaked through her, he flashed a roguish smile—his first that night—and then he stopped rolling her sensitized flesh. Instead, he tugged ever so lightly on her nipple. Again and again until she was sure her knees would buckle if he wasn't holding her so tightly against him. "As you see, minx, I can pretend sensual enjoyment as well as you. No one will guess we're acting."

That truth dashed her rising passion as soundly as if he'd dumped a bucket of ice water on her.

"I do agree!" Jerking away from him, she snatched up her robe and swirled it around her shoulders. "And I thank you for indulging me."

To her embarrassment, he nodded almost regally. "The pleasure was mine, my lady."

Neither smiling nor scowling now, his handsome face was expressionless, as blank as stone.

Hers was flaming.

So she didn't object when he placed a hand at her waist, urging her from the love lair back into the Rose Room's main chamber, and then out into the better-lit corridor. But instead of joining her, he leaned against the doorjamb and folded his arms.

He looked arrogant and self-satisfied.

Her heart thundered still, her body responding to him even now.

"Be gone to your room, lady." He glanced that way, then back at her. "I will stay here until I see you slip safely inside. Bar the door once you do. I shall hear the drawbar slide into place and willnae leave until it does. Open to no one, not even me."

"There is no danger of that." She gave him her haughtiest look, then turned and hurried away, walking with as much dignity as she could muster.

It was hard, because she felt his stare boring into her.

She couldn't be sure, but she thought she also heard him curse again.

And in a way that gave her a glimmer of hope, making her pulse flutter anew.

Could it be he did care for her?

If so, it was a possibility that excited her far more than was wise.

Chapter Eleven

❧

Such a fine view and yet…"

Mirabelle heard Sorley's smooth, deep voice behind her and nearly fell from the battlement's crenel notch. She'd foolishly bent over the opening in the wall, leaning forward to a perilous degree. The spot was Sorley's favorite viewing point, which she'd known, but it was later in the morning than he visited the ramparts.

She'd felt safe, sure he wouldn't appear.

Now he'd caught her with her rear quarters in the air. A position that was not just awkward, but also highly suggestive, especially after their ill-fated encounter in the Rose Room the night before.

Still, it couldn't be helped.

She had good reason to peer over the walling.

The very best, to her mind.

So she straightened with as much dignity as she could, trying not to notice how her entire body tightened with embarrassment.

Lifting her chin, she turned to face him. "A good morrow to you."

"So it is." He narrowed his eyes, his expression so intense, so dangerous and predatory, that a rush of heat swept her. "As you're aware, I come up here every morn to enjoy the splendor."

"I thought you made your visits at first light."

"Aye, well. Your troubles of last night seemed to have become mine. I didn't sleep well." He stepped closer, so near his proximity almost seared her. His sandalwood scent surrounded her, teasing her senses and making her heart beat faster. "Now I am glad I wakened so late. Had I been here earlier, I'd have missed such a glorious sight."

His cordial tone didn't match the hardness of his gaze. The firm set of his jaw also bespoke annoyance. So did the way he towered over her with a challenging, anticipatory air as if he sought to provoke a reaction.

He was angry, definitely.

In consideration of how they'd parted in the small hours, she was the one who should be vexed.

His attempt to unsettle her only fired her already simmering agitation. So she stood as tall as she could, squaring her shoulders and hoping he'd credit her flushed cheeks to the wind. She also sent a silent prayer to the gods, thanking them for the height and stature that allowed her to appear courageous when a show of strength was needed.

In truth, a floodtide of awareness rushed through her, vivid images from their encounter in the Rose Room stirring her blood, making her wish she was still in his arms.

She shouldn't desire him.

Hadn't he shown her how little the pleasure had meant to him?

The memory scalded, helped her stand against him now.

" 'A glorious sight?' " She lifted a brow. "I am not lacking in wit. I know you don't mean the hills and the river. There's too much mist this morning to see them." She glanced at the scudding clouds, the mist that hid everything but the boulders strewn down the cliff. "What I don't know is what you meant by 'and yet.'"

"I believe you do." He touched her hair, lifting a curl and rubbing it between his fingers. "Why else would you have posed yourself—"

"I wasn't posing." Mirabelle refused to bat his hand away, not wanting him to see how much his touch affected her. "I wouldn't do—"

"Lady, I already ken you will do anything." He didn't release her hair, the slow rubbings of his thumb doing terrible things to her belly. "You're a brave and daring lass. And just now, you're upset because I proposed a plan that differs from yours."

"That's not true."

"Aye, it is." He let go of her curl, smoothed his knuckles down her cheek. "You're intelligent enough to ken that the man hasn't been born who can resist a comely woman's bottom waving in the air, beckoning him. After last night, you're surely aware how dangerous it is for a man to be exposed to your charms. I only wonder how you knew when I'd come out onto the ramparts. Were you lying in wait, listening for my steps on the stair?"

"I did no such thing!" Mirabelle felt the heat score her face. "You—"

"I ken women." Leaning in, he pushed back her hair and placed his lips to her ear, speaking low. "You should ken ne'er to try such a trick again. It won't work, no' with me, sweet."

That did it.

Mirabelle's temper snapped. Whirling away, she set her hands on her hips, her breath coming hard and fast. "Aye, you have the right of it."

He cocked a brow, showing he also had the nerve to look pleased.

Mirabelle frowned at him. "I am annoyed and disappointed.

My life, everything in my world, depends on keeping myself from Sir John's clutches."

"He'll no' touch you, lass. I promised you that and it's true."

"That doesn't change that it's shaming to know you find me of all women not desirable enough to bed." She couldn't believe she'd been so blunt.

But she'd expected him to accept her wishes, executing them in every way she'd requested, including the carnal aspects he supposedly enjoyed so much.

"To be sure, your refusal frustrates and humiliates me." She let her tone dare him to say she had no reason to feel as she did.

For a heartbeat the night before, in the corridor on her way back to her room, she'd half believed he'd stride after her, catching her to him, swinging her about, and kissing her hotly. Ravishing her then and there, until her very toes curled with wanting him.

But he hadn't budged.

He'd let her go.

She shouldn't care, but she couldn't keep her scowl from darkening. She knew her eyes blazed, felt the heat of annoyance coloring her cheeks.

"My suggested plan to address your difficulties should make you happy." His answer wasn't the one she'd wanted. "I regret it drives you to such silliness as I just witnessed."

Mirabelle's jaw slipped. She could only stare at him.

He still believed she'd posed at the rampart wall.

She took a deep, shuddery breath, not caring if he saw her vexation. Tremors of agitation rippled through her. He was only half the reason. Though, indirectly, he was completely responsible.

"I was not leaning over the crenel to entice you." She held out her hand, warding him off when he started toward her. Furious, she threw a glance at the ramparts' notched wall, her heart thundering. "I saw—"

"Dinnae tell me you were looking for the pink lady, down

on the rocks?" He followed her gaze, shaking his head. "Thon slope is too steep for even a ghost to flit down. If one dared, she'd stub her gauzy toes on the rocks. There's stone piled on stone from this wall"—he thumped a merlon—"all the way to the bottom, where the haint would find an even greater sea of boulders. Aye,"—he hooked his thumbs in his sword-belt and rocked back on his heels—"you'll no' be seeing a bogle by peering over the battlement wall."

Mirabelle bristled. "You are insufferable."

"So many say." He had the audacity to smile.

Mirabelle began tapping her foot. "You're also unable to think of aught but coupling with jaded court women and taunting me about ghosts."

He lifted his hands, palms outward. "You have me there, sweeting."

"I am not your—"

"Indeed." He inclined his head, his smile gone. "You are no' mine and that is good so, my lady. That shall remain the way of it no matter how much you tempt me, how luscious I find your lips, how pert your nipples, or how many times you wriggle your delectable bottom in my face."

"I wasn't 'wriggling my bottom' at you." Mirabelle would think about his other observations later. She didn't trust herself to do so now.

She did turn back to the crenel notch, peering through it as best she could without leaning into its opening as she'd done before. This time, much to her sorrow, she saw only broken rocks and a few threads of thin, blowing mist.

Nothing else stirred.

And that made her heart squeeze.

Straightening, she took a deep breath and turned back to Sorley. "I was watching a wee kitten. I saw him from my room's window when I opened the shutters. He was down on the rocks, beneath the battlements. I've never seen a tinier kitten, so thin he couldn't weigh more than air. He looked injured, was favoring his back leg. I worried about him, so I nipped out here to see him better." Mirabelle swallowed the sudden thickness in her throat, not wanting him to see how much the kitten meant to her. "I wanted to know where he was heading so I could circle around the base of the curtain wall and find him. He's why I leaned into the crenel. Now he's gone." She didn't hide the accusation.

"A kitten?" Sorley arched a brow. "Are you sure he wasn't a bird, small as you say he was?"

"I can tell the difference between a bird and a kitten." Mirabelle wasn't surprised he didn't believe her. "Or have you ever seen a gray-striped bird with big pointy ears, huge round eyes, and a furred tail?"

"So it was a kitten." He didn't sound concerned. "His mother will have been about somewhere."

"He was alone." Mirabelle's heart began to hurt again. "He was lost and hungry. Frightened—"

"Sweet lass, do you ken how many cats and kittens roam Stirling?" He strolled over to her, cupping her face in his hands. "There are plenty, and they take good care of themselves, I promise you."

"Not this one." Mirabelle could tell.

She'd also named him already, thinking of him as Little Heart.

"So you weren't wagging your bottom in the air to tempt me?" Sorley released her and stepped back, a note of humor in his voice. "I am disappointed, fair lady, for I was sure that was so."

Mirabelle glanced again at the wall, the now-empty crenel. She thought she heard the kitten crying, but then realized the sound was only the wind whistling round the tower. She also knew Sorley was trying to lift her spirits, make her forget Little Heart. Although she knew she wouldn't—she'd felt an immediate and powerful bond with the kitten—she was warmed by his effort.

"Sorley..." She started to thank him, but the words slipped away when he gave her a smile that curled her toes.

"Aye?" He angled his head, waiting. "Are you ready to admit it was the pink lady you were staring after, down on the rocks?"

"No, there really was a kitten."

"You can tell me true, Mirabelle." He spoke her name in a way she'd never heard before, his voice stroking her like an intimate caress.

"I did. Tell you true, I mean." She shivered and drew her cloak tighter against the wind, protecting herself from him. The excitement he stirred inside her, a thrill of expectancy that made her breath catch and her skin hot.

"I wished to tell you..." She broke off again, barely able to string words together.

"Aye?" He was looking at her with his dark, intense eyes, his gaze both unnerving and causing her pulse to skitter. It was difficult not to squirm.

If she didn't know better, she'd believe he'd cast a spell over her. That he wasn't who he appeared to be at all, but a dark sorcerer who'd conjured the most potent love elixir in the world. That he'd somehow administered it to her, rendering her helpless against his will.

He surely knew her thoughts. Was aware that she couldn't stop remembering his kiss and how the urgent, open-mouthed plundering of her lips, the madly-arousing thrusts of his tongue, had fuelled her own passion. She'd been ravenous for him, and she wanted more.

Here on the battlements in the cold morning air and with the mist blowing all around them.

In truth, she desired it fiercely. She ached to feel his hands on her, to be held in his arms, and have him initiate her in all the pleasures of the flesh that would follow. Her yearning made clear how foolish she'd been to approach him with her proposal. She might as well have stepped into the flames of a balefire. Their kiss in the chapel had scorched her, awakening her to passion. What happened in the Rose Room had branded her, irrevocably. Should anything else occur between them, she'd be haunted by the memories for all her days, never again whole.

The longing would eat her alive, making her miserable.

She knew that.

Which brought her guard back, praise the heavens.

"I'm sure you have much to do, so I won't keep you." She held his gaze, wondering how he would fill his day. She hoped it wouldn't be with a woman. "Perhaps you hope to meet the man who asked for you at the Red Lion?" The possibility sat better with her than imagining him in some wanton's bed. "He did seem eager to speak with you. The Highlander named Grim—"

"Aye, Grim Mackintosh, from the Glen of Many Legends." He surprised her with his openness. "I am on my way to seek him."

Mirabelle blinked. "You didn't seem concerned about him last night."

"I'm no' that now either." He gave her a slow smile. "I'd just hear what he wants. By all accounts, he's different from the usual sort who come round, asking for me."

"By whose account?" The question slipped off Mirabelle's tongue before she could catch herself.

Sorley's smile deepened. Winking, he reached to tweak her cheek. "Sweet lass, did you no' ken that a wise man ne'er reveals his sources?"

It was then that everything was clear.

"Maili told you. She came back with me."

He shrugged, his smile still in place. "Maili is aye full of blether."

His answer-that-wasn't and the way his eyes warmed as he said the girl's name sent a stab of hot green jealousy straight to her heart.

He clearly cared for Maili.

He also had no wish to discuss the stranger with her.

"I've no idea who the man is or what he wants." His words proved her wrong. "As you said as well, he's a warring sort. Like as no', he's an old enemy I've forgotten. Or a paid fighter employed by someone I've grieved. Either way, I'm expecting a scuffle with him. So"—he stepped close again, once more placing his hands on her shoulders—if you hear of aught happening to me, stay near to your father and his guards. At the worst, if Sinclair plagues you after you leave here, send word to Alex Stewart, the King's brother, up in Badenoch. He has a fierce reputation, but is great of heart and loves women. He'd no' hesitate to rid you of any problems Sinclair might give you. Indeed, he'd make sure the bastard would ne'er trouble anyone ever again, male or female. Remember that, if I dinnae return."

He took his hands from her shoulders, stepping back. "Though I fully expect to, ne'er you worry."

"I wasn't." She knew he'd be back.

She also had the strongest feeling the Highland warrior's wish to speak with him had nothing to do with fighting.

She didn't feel it was her place to say so.

But she did wonder about one thing. "How will I know when you've returned?"

"Och, you'll know. Everything will unfold as you desire." He took her hand, lifting it to his lips. "Leave it to me."

Before she could ask what he meant, he squeezed her fingers and then strode off into the mist, leaving her to stare after him.

Much later, but in a distant place, far from Stirling and many other places as well, hard rain lashed at the stout stone walls of a clifftop stronghold. The wind also rose, howling past the towers and rattling window shutters. Somewhere near, thunder rumbled, deep and bold, as if the floor-shaking booms came not just from the dark, angry heavens but also the bowels of the earth. Such days of wild wind and icy, spitting rain were common in these parts.

Some claimed the sheer, soaring peaks that held the stronghold needed fierce weather as sustenance. That such cold majesty could thrive only on gray, bleak days and nights of impenetrable blackness.

That the gloom even stole the light out of Scotland's shimmering summer skies, daring the sun to shine.

Others whispered the darkness was a curse. Punishment rained down on the laird for his many transgressions and sins.

The truth would likely never be known.

Few visitors made the treacherous journey, so not many men had opportunity to ponder the possibility.

Regrettably, the clan who dwelt here had a long history of being at odds with their neighbors, far off as most of them were. That sorrow was slowly changing. Leastways some erstwhile foes had visited at the last Yuletide.

Otherwise, those who called this place home mostly walked alone.

For the stronghold was Duncreag, "fortress of rock," though its aging chief, Archibald—Archie—MacNab thought of it as a castle of sorrow.

The most charitable description of Duncreag was a massive, wind-lashed eyrie, daunting and formidable. It was perched high atop a sheer, rocky crag, and clouds and mist often hid the stronghold from view. Unlike other, similarly situated holdings, Duncreag lacked a stone stair leading to its lofty door. Anyone wishing to visit had to climb a threadlike goat track that wound its way up the treacherous bluff.

That being so, not many would-be guests bothered.

And that suited Archie fine.

For he knew he was cursed. With the wisdom that comes

with age, he regretted his sins and had no wish to burden others with his ill fortune.

It didn't matter that he was lonely, a shadow of the lusty, life-loving, always-smiling man he'd once been.

He'd reaped what he sowed, after all.

And he had only himself to blame that he now sat alone at his high table, Duncreag's vast great hall empty save for the ever-smoking torches and the scores of hounds who, remarkably, loved him despite his damnable past.

Firming his jaw, for it shamed him too much to show his sorrows, even when no one saw, he sat straighter in his high-backed laird's chair and continued feeding tidbits of fine, roasted beef to his dogs.

Slipping his meals to his much-loved and trusted four-legged companions made the beasts happy. Besides, who would care if lack of food shriveled him to bone?

He was fine with turning into one of the ghosts he was sure haunted his cold and stony stronghold, so full of darkness and gloom.

Of course, there were a few exceptions…

A small number of garrison men, Mackintoshes mostly, were currently gathered in one of Duncreag's solars, drinking ale and casting dice. Duncreag men for the now, the Mackintosh warriors were good-hearted souls from Nought in the neighboring Glen of Many Legends.

Led by Grim Mackintosh, a battle-hardened warrior if ever there was one, the Nought men were generously helping Archie rebuild his lost garrison. Some of the Mackintoshes had agreed to stay on at Duncreag indefinitely, claiming an affinity to the territory's rocky bleakness. Others were here only until Archie's few remaining kinsmen, young lads mostly, had been trained as stout enough fighters to adequately defend the formidable stronghold.

It'd fallen once, taken by a now-dead dastard, Ralla the Victorious, and his war-band.

Rough, clanless men, they'd slaughtered nearly all of Archie's kin and left the proud stronghold a shambles. Even Archie's beloved wife, Rosalie, had perished. Mackintosh warriors from Nought, led by their chief, Kendrew, and his captain, Grim, had used stealth to gain the stronghold walls, reclaiming Duncreag for Archie.

Unfortunately, no one could repair his broken heart.

So Archie took a long, deep breath—he wasn't as strong as he'd once been—and pushed carefully to his feet. Slowly, so as not to trip over the dogs clamoring after him, he crossed the hall to the lovely harp that had once belonged to his late wife, Rosalie.

Archie set his hand on the harp, stubbornly pretending he didn't need its support.

He also knew it was the smoky haze from the hall torches that stung his eyes, making them water. His fool throat wasn't thickening simply because he'd dared to pluck a harp string.

"You're all I have left of her, eh?" He touched another string, then blinked hard when his vision blurred, making it difficult to see.

Not that he needed his eyes to appreciate the harp's grace and beauty.

A wedding gift he'd ordered specially made for his bride, the harp was carved of beautifully polished wood and stood at a respectable height. Its tallness had delighted Rosalie, as her first harp had been a small, hand-held instrument. This one had twenty-four gut strings, enabling her to play the most enchanting music of an evening.

Blissful nights that were no more and never would be again, as the sorrow in Archie's chest dutifully reminded him.

Truth be told, everything brought back his memories.

He couldn't even sit at his high table, in his own laird's chair, without remembering how, at night's end, he and Rosalie would walk arm in arm from the hall. How they'd climb the turnpike stair, often pausing at the alcove on the third landing for a long, deep kiss, a joy they'd allowed themselves even when his hair had started to turn gray and the first fine lines began appearing around her eyes.

Theirs had been a love like no other.

Didn't he know, having loved so very many women?

Leastways in the carnal fashion!

That wildness, his youthful follies and sins, along with the terrible consequences, was the reason he was cursed. That he knew, and he would never believe otherwise. Not in a thousand lifetimes.

Just now, though, he was an auld done man.

And hadn't he been foolish to cross the hall without his walking stick?

But pride didn't diminish with age and hardship, not even with heartache.

So there was nothing for it but to return to his chair the same way he'd reached the harp, one slow and tedious step at a time.

He was halfway to the dais when his world's only ray of sunshine burst into the hall. Breena, she was, a young Irish lass taken during Ralla's raid on her village. She'd stayed on at Duncreag after the Mackintoshes reclaimed the stronghold for Archie. She'd married Grim, the Mackintosh chief's captain of the guard, now in charge of rebuilding Archie's fallen garrison.

The union between Grim and Breena pleased Archie greatly.

He didn't wish to pester them, but was eagerly awaiting bairns.

Duncreag had been empty and silent too long. The laughter of children would do the old, cold-steeped stones much good. And Archie as well, though he was reluctant to admit any such hankering for wee ones.

He was cursed that way, after all.

His own sons, all six of them, were dead, cut down by Ralla's sword.

His one daughter...

His heart clenched, warning him not to think of what Ralla and his men did to her.

Breena was like a daughter now. So he stood as straight as his aching bones would allow and gave her the best smile he could muster.

"I didn't think to see you this e'en," he greeted her as she neared. "Wasn't Grim due back from Nought this day? I'd have thought you'd be up at the highest tower window, watching for his return."

"Oh, he'll be away a while yet, he will." She stopped before him, her lilting voice as always a comfort. "His chief, Kendrew, is keeping him busy, last I heard. I don't truly mind."

"Tired of him already, eh?" Archie knew that wasn't so.

"Not at all." She winked. "The longer he's away, the happier he'll be to see me."

"That he will." Excepting his sweet Rosalie, Archie could think of no finer lass a man could come home to.

Lithe and lovely, Breena had a cascade of burnished red hair that shone like autumn leaves in the sun and the creamiest skin Archie had ever seen. Her eyes were deep green and, in certain lighting, gleamed with golden flecks. She moved with grace, loved to dance, and Archie was hard put to say which was more beautiful, her singing voice or the music she made when she put her talented fingers to Rosalie's harp.

Old and feeble as he was, Archie would break Grim's bones if ever he hurt the lass.

"He'd best be hieing himself back here soon." Archie swelled his chest a bit, trying to appear lairdly. "I've seen some of the other braw Mackintosh warriors eyeing you when Grim wasn't looking."

"You haven't!" Breena saw right through him. "Even if

one of them did fancy me, they'd sooner cut themselves than cast a glance at Grim's lady. Aren't I blessed to be her?"

"Humph. I'm saying that's him."

"He's fond of you, too." She hooked her arm through his and began leading him gently across the hall, back to the empty high table. "It's a fine night to be inside, enjoying a well-burning fire."

"I haven't noticed." Archie would sooner crawl naked to Glasgow and back than admit he did appreciate the huge fire roaring in the hearth.

He also loved the howling wind and the rain battering Duncreag's wall. An affection for wild weather came with being a MacNab.

What a pity there were so few left of them.

"One night is as much as the other," he grumbled, pausing when his favorite dog, Rufus, trundled over to lean his bulk into him. He reached down to rub the old dog's head. "I scarce note what day it is, much less if it's a good one for hall-sitting."

"I do not believe you." Breena leaned round to kiss his cheek.

Archie kept on petting Rufus. "I cannae make you, can I?"

"Indeed, not." She laughed then, the light, airy sound secretly delighting him.

His Rosalie had a similarly pleasing laugh.

He missed her cheeriness, he did.

He missed his sons and his daughter. And—he shut his mind to their loss—he wasn't going to think about them anymore this night.

"You miss your family terribly, don't you?" Breena's soft voice made his fool throat ache again. When Rufus pushed away from him, letting out a long, mournful old dog's groan, his eyes began to sting as well.

There were times he'd swear the beast could see into his soul.

Hadn't he reared Rufus from a wee whelp? Rosalie had hand-fed him spoonfuls of mush when the poor mite's mother died when Rufus and his littermates were just days old. Only Rufus survived. The two of them were nigh inseparable. The old dog knew him well, including his secrets.

Sometimes Archie needed to speak of them, and Rufus made a good, and safe, listener.

Rufus didn't judge, either.

Dogs only loved a man. And wouldn't the world be fine if folk were as accepting?

Archie scowled, knowing that wasn't so.

If he was silent long enough, Breena wouldn't mention his family again. It was a trick he'd perfected with her, learning quickly that she felt a need to comfort him. She just didn't understand that his way of soothing his sorrows was to ignore them and keep to himself.

"I lost loved ones, too." She paused before the dais, waiting for him to set his foot on the first low step. "Ralla and his men killed nearly everyone in the village, burning everything. Yet through his bringing me here, I met and married Grim."

"I know, I know." Archie let her help him into his laird's chair, not even grousing when she smoothed a plaid over his knees. "Fate is inexorable."

"So it is." She stepped back, dusting her hands. "My people believe that."

"That's because you Irish have so much Viking blood." Archie bit back a smile, imagining her as a Valkyrie.

She had the heart of one, for sure.

But slight and graceful as she was, he could better see her as a Highland wood nymph. Or perhaps a water sprite, sitting high on the rocks beside a tumbling waterfall, the glistening mist haloing her as she played her harp and sang. Such an image fit her well.

"Scots have no less Norse in them." She winked as she

poured him a cup of ale. "Vikings raided near and far, eventually settling the lands they'd first plundered. They intermarried everywhere."

"Humph." Archie lifted his ale cup to his lips, took a long sip.

He wasn't of a mind to think of marriage, Viking or otherwise.

Not with Rosalie so heavy on his mind.

She, too, had loved nights such as this. She'd stand at the window, stars in her eyes and awe on her face, claiming the wind and rain entertained better than any troop of dancers and tumblers at the royal court.

And wasn't that a place that sent a dagger straight into his heart?

As if she knew, Breena's smile faded. "The men should be in here with you, not casting dice in the solar."

Archie thrust out his chin. "Who do you think sent them there?"

"They shouldn't have gone."

"They had no choice. I'm still laird. My word is law, however old and feeble I am."

"You're nothing the like." She slipped her arm around his shoulders, gave him a squeeze.

"There are many who'd argue with you."

"I'd welcome setting matters aright." She straightened, smiling again.

"You see to keeping that man of yours happy." Archie thumped his hand on the table. "About time he returned. It isn't natural for a husband of less than a year to stay away from his lady wife so long."

"Seeing this empty hall, I must agree it'll be good to have him back. You know"—she set her hands on her hips, her green eyes flashing—"were he here, he'd not have stood for the men leaving you alone."

"Aye, he can be as cantankerous as me, what?" Archie

lifted his cup in mock salute. "Here's to thrawn men, the more stubborn the better."

"Grim means well, always." Breena glanced about the hall, surely noting he'd put out some of the torches, allowing the shadows to deepen.

"And you, my lord"—she turned back to him—"will not spend the rest of the night alone. I'm away to the solar now and bringing the men back with me."

"Och, nae, you willnae, lassie!" Archie leaned forward, gripping the table edge, moving with startling speed, considering his ancient, moldering bones. "I want my peace."

"I do not believe you." She raised a hand, silencing him when he tried again to protest. "I'll sing and play the harp. You know you enjoy listening."

"I like sleeping, too," Archie huffed. "That's what I'm a-wanting. Rufus is also ready for his bed. We're both tired."

The dog was at Archie's chair, his rheumy eyes as bright as an old dog's eyes could be, his scraggly tail wagging.

He didn't look at all sleepy.

"Some help you are, laddie." Archie scowled at him.

Breena laughed. "A bit of music and song will do you good. Didn't you enjoy our Yuletide feast?" She lifted a brow, clearly aware he couldn't argue. "There were lots of folk here then, plenty of cheer and revelry."

"That was Yule, and an exception." Archie busied himself scratching Rufus's ears. "It was also long ago, nigh onto a year now.

"And"—he snapped up his head, fixed her with a narrow-eyed gaze—"the folk who came only did so because you and Grim rode about the hills for days, bribing them. Dinnae think I don't know what you did. You paid them all to make merry to please an auld done man."

"We reminded them what a good neighbor you are and that Christmastide should be celebrated with cheer." She gave him the same nonsense she'd offered him since the day. "No other persuasion was necessary."

"Pah!" Archie hooted. "Some of them were my most evil-tempered foes. They wouldn't have come for naught. I'll ne'er believe it."

Breena leaned down and kissed the top of his head. "Does it matter why they were here? They remained friends, and that's a blessing."

"No' the kind I need."

"Friends are aye treasures." Straightening, she reached to smooth back his hair. "One never knows when we'll need them. Or when they might need us." She angled her head, giving him a look that would've scared him if he wasn't so fond of her. "Love and forgiveness have more power than the sword. Even Grim believes so."

"Humph!" Archie jutted his chin. "Sounds like wedded life has addled his wits."

"Could be." She shrugged, looking so pleased he was suspicious.

But before he could question her, she winked and dashed from the hall.

She'd be on her way to fetch the men as she'd vowed to do. The few kin he had left and the Mackintosh fighting men from Nought, who he was sure would rather keep playing dice in the solar.

He'd rather trudge up the stairs with Rufus, seeking his bed and pulling the covers up to his chin.

Scowling, he took a bit of cheese off a tray and gave it to Rufus.

He leaned down as Rufus ate it, whispering in the beast's ear. "It's a sad thing when a man realizes he's no' just old and feeble, but a liar as well, eh?"

Rufus licked his face in answer.

And Archie leaned back in his chair, secretly eager to hear footsteps nearing the hall.

Chapter Twelve

❖

Sorley stood at the edge of the road, looking at the candlelit windows of the Red Lion Inn. It was later than he'd hoped to arrive, the afternoon damp and fog-shrouded. The woods were already dark, the chill air scented with wet pine needles, wild thyme, and the peat smoke rising from the sprawling inn's chimneys. Indeed, gloaming was nigh. But certain matters had kept him overlong at the castle.

A greater folly than he'd e'er engaged in, for sure.

Yet...

Wouldn't a man do anything to please a lady?

Knowing it was so, he blew out an annoyed breath. Praise be, the MacKenzie plaid he'd flung across his shoulder, and the sleeves of his shirt, hid the scratches on his arms. Regrettably, there wasn't much he could do about the ones criss-crossing his hands.

He was fairly sure his beard concealed the wee, but oh-so-irritating slash on his jaw.

If anyone was bold enough to comment on his appearance, he'd give him a slow, commiserating smile and hope he'd assume he'd enjoyed a particularly vigorous round of bed-sport.

Sadly, no such lusty female had given him these scratches.

Not a female indeed, if he was a judge of such things.

"Ungrateful wee bugger!" Feeling a fool, he rolled his shoulders and then straightened his plaid, well aware he was stalling.

Now that he was here, the Red Lion only a few paces away, his feet didn't seem to want to leave the road.

He knew in his gut that the Highland warrior waiting inside was trouble.

Anyone named Grim had to be.

If he was still at the inn, late as it was. He'd sent word to William that he'd arrive before midday, and that was long past. If he were waiting on someone he didn't even know and the wretch didn't show for hours, like as not he'd have left before now.

Or he'd assume the day's wet gloom kept the man away.

Not many ventured out in such miserable weather.

A glance up and down the road proved it. Nary a soul moved anywhere, only the thick, drifting mist. He could scarce see the deep piney woods behind the inn. Across the road, low, heavy clouds crouched over the rolling hills and pasturelands, hiding them as well.

And didn't the day's dreariness pose another problem?

Such weather was good for William's trade, always drawing a crowd to the inn.

The place was surely packed.

Wyldes kept a huge fire blazing on days when the mist rolled in, and everyone within a hundred miles knew it.

Wayfarers turned up in droves, wishing a rest from their travels, good ale, a filling meal, and a clean bed for the night. Locals also looked in. Farmers mostly, strapping, rough-hewn men who worked hard and enjoyed gathering at the tables to drink ale, laugh, curse, and warm themselves before they trudged home to their wives.

Now and then the guests were strangers, men from afar, unknown hereabouts, their reasons for calling at the Red Lion a mystery.

Others, like Munro MacLaren, came to clamber about on the inn's roof, poking at slate moss and pondering its healing properties while their she-vixen daughters set about to bewitch any man who happened across their path. Sorley scowled, annoyed that it took but the space of a heartbeat for Mirabelle to claim his thoughts. Worse, he could still see the tempting fullness of her breasts, pressing against the linen of her nightshift, feel the silky-hot thrill of her peaked nipples between his fingers. Forcing her from his mind, he adjusted his plaid, then blinked to find that somehow his feet had carried him away from the road and up the well-trodden path to the inn's door.

He didn't want to go in.

His gut warned him, tightening to a cold, hard ball as he reached for the latch.

As he'd expected, he opened the door to a swell of voices and the clatter of cutlery and tankards. Too late for retreat; he stepped into the Red Lion's low-beamed and crowded long room.

Trade was better than he'd guessed, the inn noisy, smoke-hazed, and with every available table occupied. Sorley stood where he was, letting his eyes adjust to the dimness as the familiar blend of smells assailed him: peat and wood smoke, roasted meats and savory stew, fresh-baked bread, and the richness of ale.

The Red Lion was a grand place to be on a chill and wet afternoon.

It just seemed that a certain wild-haired, bushy-bearded Highland warrior said to wear a silver Thor's hammer amulet didn't agree.

Such a man was nowhere to be seen.

Sorley pulled a hand down over his own beard, torn between relief and annoyance.

Moving deeper into the room, he looked about, trying to peer into the dark, murkier corners without noticeably doing so. He saw no one but the expected assortment of travelers and farm men, until he looked toward the table nearest the open archway to one of William's smaller rooms.

Three men sat there, each one doing his damnedest to appear invisible.

They failed miserably.

They also increased Sorley's perturbation, for he knew them well. They were none other than his three archfiends and fellow Fenris, Roag the Bear, Andrew the Adder, and Caelan the Fox.

Caelan sat beneath a wall sconce. The flickering light burnished his rich, dark auburn hair so that he stood out even though he busied himself tucking into a large bowl of William's famed venison stew.

Andrew appeared fascinated by the bannock he was smearing with way too much butter. Dark as Sorley and Roag, he held his head lowered, his gaze fixed on his task.

Only Roag caught his eye and grinned. He lifted his pewter ale tankard in salute, confirming the first thought that popped into Sorley's mind when he'd spotted the three of them: They knew why he was here.

They'd come to spy on him.

Sorley knew that Caelan and Andrew should've ridden north with Alex Stewart, the Wolf. Their presence here, instead, indicated they'd heard rumors about Grim Mackintosh and his quest. They deemed his business with Sorley important enough to postpone their journey to the earl's distant Badenoch.

Sorley headed their way, their chosen table telling him where Grim waited.

The Highlander would be in William's smaller room, the one that offered the most privacy.

A pity he'd have to sit alone a few moments longer.

Not feeling at all guilty, Sorley strolled up to his arch-rivals' table and plucked Caelan's spoon from his fingers. For good measure, he also nabbed his bowl of venison stew, holding it out of reach.

"Dinnae tell me our good friend, Alex, doesn't serve just as tasty victuals in Badenoch." Sorley flicked a glance at the thickly buttered bannock in Andrew's hand. "Or did the two of you have another reason for no' riding north with the earl when he left Stirling? With so much clean, fresh air up his way, and bountiful grazing, I'd think a Highland venison stew would be even better, wouldn't you say?" Sorley set down the bowl and spoon. He braced his hands on the table, leaning in to meet each man's gaze. "The truth is, you're no' here because you prefer William's stew.

"And you"—he flashed a glare at Roag—"can wipe that smirk off your face."

Roag's expression didn't change. "I dinnae understand your upset." He gestured to Andrew and Caelan. "We're sitting here quietly, enjoying a meal, and minding our own business, behaving—"

"You dinnae ken how to behave." Sorley straightened, wishing, not for the first time that day, that he'd stayed in his bed.

"Have you seen the sky?" Caelan pushed aside his buttery bannock, his tone reproachful. "Full of woolly clouds, it is. Today like sheep, tomorrow come the wolves. You ken what that means."

"Aye." Sorley did.

He didn't like it all the same.

While he might agree that the coded Fenris warning applied to his meeting with Grim Mackintosh, he didn't see it as a reason for Roag, Andrew, and Caelan to sit guard outside the inn's small room.

Nor did he need their help.

As if he read Sorley's mind, Andrew leaned over and gripped Sorley's arm. "No need to get riled. No' when you'd be playing sentry, too, if one of us was about to walk into that room." He glanced at the shadowed archway, lowering his voice. "Thon's a mean-looking brute. Big enough to take on all four of us with one hand tied behind his back."

"The more pleasure to fight him." Sorley broke free of his grasp and swatted at his sleeve. "I face my challengers alone."

The looks his rivals exchanged said they didn't care how he saw it.

They weren't budging.

"Stay if you will." Sorley stepped back from the table. He looked round for William, not surprised to find the inn-keeper hovering right behind him. "William, give these loons all they wish to eat and as much ale as they can drink. Even a lass or two if they desire such entertainment. I'll pay, and gladly. Just keep them out of my way." He shot a warn-ing look at the table. "If I see them again before I leave, if I suspect their flapping ears are pressed to the wall, fists will fly. House rules or no'."

"Nae bother." William's light blue eyes twinkled as he made a slight bow. When he straightened, he gave Sorley a comradely nudge toward the archway. "Be glad you have friends. There's lots who dinnae, the gods pity them."

"That I know." Sorley turned to him, meaning to say more, for he liked the innkeeper, appreciating his good humor and honesty. But William was already moving through the closely set tables, heading for his kitchen.

And somehow, with the surprising ease of many big, burly men, he'd done more than give Sorley a friendly push toward the small room.

He'd maneuvered him right into it.

Sorley blinked, for the small room, in truth a private

parlor, was awash in golden candlelight. Every wall sconce was lit and slender tapers stood on the linen-draped tables. The glow shimmered on the walls and spilled across the polished flagstone floor. Even the ceiling rafters glistened, the age-smoothed wood as black as a midnight sea reflecting the light of the stars.

Any other time Sorley would've appreciated the sumptuousness, especially the fine hint of peat in the air, the earthy-rich scent coming from a small, handsomely tiled hearth on the far side of the room.

It was there, at a lavishly set table, that the Highland warrior sat.

"I didnae come here to fight you." The Highlander stood, proving himself every bit as large and fierce-looking as everyone said.

Still, he didn't strike Sorley as hostile.

Unfortunately, his greeting indicated he'd heard Sorley's quip to Roag, Andrew, and Caelan.

If he'd caught anything else, he gave no sign.

He just looked across the room at Sorley, almost measuring him. Leastways, that's the impression he gave. He had a gaze that seemed to peer deep, and his eyes were the same dark gray as the mist rolling past the room's small-paned windows. His face was a good one, strong and open. But his expression was hard to read, not friendly or unfriendly, though the silver warrior rings he wore braided into his beard proved that he wasn't a man to anger.

"Grim Mackintosh, of Nought in the Glen of Many Legends." He extended a hand, waiting for Sorley to come and clasp it.

When Sorley did, he discovered Grim's grip was as firm as his own. "Sorley." He nodded once, annoyingly ashamed that he couldn't state a surname. The lack hadn't bothered him in years, but Grim's steady, assessing gaze made him uncomfortable. "Men call me the Hawk."

"That I ken." A touch of warmth lit Grim's eyes and he flicked a glance over Sorley. "All the men hereabouts speak highly of you. And"—he quirked a half smile—"so do the women."

"We've agreed you aren't here to fight, which much surprises me," Sorley returned, gauging his words. "But I dinnae believe you're here to praise me either. I'd know why you've been asking about me."

"Aye, well..." Grim's levity vanished and he pulled out a chair, patting its back. "Will you no' join me for a meal and ale? There is much we must speak of, important matters that'll go down better with good food and libations."

Sorley remained standing.

He didn't like Grim's answer.

And the man's soft, Highland voice, its deep richness and lilting tones, wore on his nerves.

"I have ne'er been to the Glen of Many Legends." Sorley crossed his arms, not ready to claim the offered seat. "Nought territory is a place I've heard of often enough. There are many tales, saying it's wild and bleak."

"So it is!" The Highlander's face warmed. He even smiled, his glance going to the fire as if the red-glowing peat bricks could take him home. "There is nowhere more grand than Nought." He turned back to Sorley, his gaze intent. "Imagine a place so breathtaking, so heartwrenchingly beautiful that each time you walk there, your awe is as great as if you're seeing it for the first time. That is Nought, my friend." He sat back, a corner of his mouth hitching up as he reminisced. "It is a place like no other."

"Yet you tore yourself away to come here." To Sorley's amazement, he was sitting.

He didn't recall taking his seat.

Grim met his eye, nodding once. "See you? Even just hearing of Nought has spelled you."

"I am nothing the like." Sorley took an oatcake and a bit

of cheese, not wanting Grim to sense his discomfiture. I ken that Highlanders love their land." He met Grim's strange gray gaze, hoping he wouldn't guess his lifelong fascination with rugged, heathery hills, empty moors, and soft Highland mist. "All Scots ken how the men of the north feel about their glens."

"We are blessed, I'll no' deny." Grim lifted his tankard, tapping it to Sorley's.

Seeing no course but to return the courtesy, Sorley raised his own ale and took a sip.

William's famed, frothy ale tasted like sawdust.

"I'd rather hear what you want." Sorley set down his tankard. "Most men seeking me wish a fight. It's no' every day a man asks round about me, wanting to talk. I dinnae care for it."

"I'd feel the same." Grim held his gaze. "Though I wouldn't have minded your friends joining us." He glanced at the archway, now empty and in deep shadow. "Such stalwarts are worth all the world's gold. A man needs loyalty. It's times of turmoil and doubt that show us who our true friends are. Thon men are yours."

Sorley now knew that he didn't like Grim.

No' at all.

The man wasn't just a Highland warrior. He was a warrior-poet.

They were the worst of the lot.

He knew it well, because Caelan fancied himself as such. With his rich chestnut hair and blue eyes, he aye boasted that his good looks and silvered tongue made him a great favorite with the ladies.

Sorley believed true men didn't need words to win a lass's favor.

He was a man of action.

He also had honor. His own brand, anyway. And for that reason, he'd never have plunked himself down at a table so close to a supposed friend's should-have-been-secret meeting with a stranger.

Some men simply lacked scruples.

Before he could say so, William came through the archway wearing his big leather apron and an even larger smile. He carried a huge tray of smoked fish from the river, a house specialty, bread and cheese, more bannocks and butter, and a dish of smoked oysters.

As he placed the offerings on the table, a young kitchen lad brought bowls of venison stew, the same much-praised recipe that Caelan was spooning. The lad's tray also bore still-warm gooseberry pasties fresh from the oven. There was even a little pot of bramble preserves, another house favorite and made by William's widowed great-aunt, Berengaria, who claimed a spoonful cured all ills.

Sorley eyed the preserves, considering eating half the jar.

Turning to the lad, William took the bowls of stew and set them before Grim and Sorley. The stew was well-seasoned and rich, the rising steam mouthwatering. Seeing their appreciation, William patted the table and grinned. "This should last you a while. There's more. Sorley knows my stew kettle is bottomless."

Sorley noticed William was making no move to disappear as he usually did after serving a table.

Apparently he'd turned as long-nosed as Roag, Caelan, and Andrew.

So Sorley sent a pointed look at the shadowed archway. "Good trade this day, William. Glad to see thon tables so full for you."

"That they are." Wyldes shrugged, the twinkle in his eye hinting he already knew Grim's tidings.

"Aye, well." He set his hands on his aproned hips, his face creasing into a warm smile. "I'll be leaving you. Ring the bell if there's aught you need." He tipped his head toward a small beribboned bell affixed to the wall not far from their table. "Loud as it gets in the long room, I aye hear a summons and will come."

He left them with a half-grin on his face, his steps jauntier than usual. Ever a good-natured soul, his increased joviality was still suspect.

Sorley addressed Grim as soon as Wyldes vanished into the long room. "Can it be that everyone in this inn kens why you're here?"

"That I doubt." The Highlander didn't turn a hair. "Some may have their own ideas. It was necessary to make enquiries. Such questions aye raise others, don't they? Men love secrets."

"I dinnae care for them." Sorley's patience was waning. "I'm also no' fond of waiting. So"—he pushed aside William's tantalizing stew bowl and leaned across the table, into Grim's black-bearded face—"tell me what you want or I'm leaving now."

"If you knew Highlanders, you'd understand we love telling tales." Grim dipped his spoon into the stew and took a leisurely bite. After what seemed forever, he set down the spoon and carefully dabbed his mouth with a white linen napkin. "Words matter to us. Our ancestral homes, our hills and glens, all our history, are the threads that weave our past and carry us into tomorrow. Ours is a different world, and it shapes us." He paused, glancing at the windows where nothing could be seen but swirling mist. "We take our time. With how we say things, and many other matters. There are sennachies who take days to recite their clan chief's lineage. Such bards are greatly prized and envied by those with less skilled storytellers."

Sorley watched him from stony eyes. "Some might say such a love of blether means you're all a bunch of bluidy windbags."

"We can be that, for sure." Not looking at all offended, Grim lifted his tankard, took a healthy sip.

Sorley didn't touch his.

"I've little patience with Highlanders, less with their myths and legends." Sorley sat back in his chair, trying to ignore the heat inching up his nape, the throbbing tightness forming between his shoulder blades.

"Yet you wear a MacKenzie plaid." Grim flicked his gaze over the proud blue and green tartan.

"I like the colors."

"Do you have MacKenzie blood, then?"

"I dinnae ken whose blood runs through my veins, as you're surely aware." Sorley wasn't about to admit his admiration for the MacKenzies and their almost-mythic chieftain, Duncan, the Black Stag of Kintail.

He did reach for another bannock and more bramble preserves. "I dinnae care either. Bloodlines and lineage have no meaning for me. It also doesn't matter to me whose tartan I sling across my shoulder." He held Grim's gaze, knew his own was hard and cold. "If the colors and weave suit me, the wool keeps me warm and dry, I'm fine."

He felt anything but.

He snapped his brows together, took a too-large bite of brambly bannock.

"Perhaps you have a touch of MacKenzie in you?" Grim studied him, critically. "You have their coloring. The dark hair and eyes, though"—he rubbed his bearded chin, making his warrior rings clink together—"some have startling blue eyes, especially the women."

"I've ne'er seen a MacKenzie woman."

"Can you be so sure?"

"Indeed!" Sorley again leaned toward the Highlander, ominously this time. "I ne'er forget a lass. No' the ones I take to my bed, nor the ones I merely wish a 'good morn.' That, too, you'll ken, seeing as you've been slinking around asking about me."

Grim only smiled. "MacKenzies are a hot-blooded race.

They lose their heads easily, giving in to their temper." He spoke as if Sorley didn't have steam shooting out his ears. "They're known to have grand passions. The ladies—"

"I dinnae give a flaming heap of heather about MacKenzie women."

Grim lifted a brow, his expression saying he should.

Sorley was tempted to shove away from the table and storm from the room.

All that kept him from doing so was knowing his three archfiends and Wyldes would see him go. They'd laugh in his wake, ribbing him for weeks.

So he reached for Berengaria's special bramble preserves and smeared a heaping spoonful onto a bannock. He didn't really believe the brambles cured all ills, but he was annoyed enough to try anything.

The bramble preserves were delicious, anyway.

Grim . . .

He was a worse annoyance than Sorley would've believed.

"See here, Grim of Nought," he resented that his bitterness slid into the place name, but he couldn't help it. "You're a fighting man." Sorley let his gaze dip to the silver warrior rings in Grim's beard. "Perhaps you enjoy kicking a man when he's down. Be warned, I kick back and worse. Truth is I love a good clash. If you—"

"I'm no' here to fight." Grim spoke so evenly, Sorley disliked him even more. "And I ne'er kick a downed foe. No man I ken would do so. No' if he's a good warrior. My beard rings"—he lifted a hand, fingering one—"were made only from the swords of the most valiant enemies I cut down. Men who fought well and died better. I honor them by wearing the rings."

"I did wonder." It was all Sorley could think to say.

He also frowned harder. Rarely had anyone made him feel so callous with a few deft words.

Softly spoken, *lilting* words that only worsened his mood.

"Aye, well…" Grim was watching him with a razor-sharp gaze. "I'm no' here to speak of my warring days. Nor did I come to spin bluidy tales, though the truth is often as disturbing. I wish to tell you of Duncreag, a holding in Glen Creag, the glen of rock."

Sorley cocked a brow. "I thought you were from Nought, in the Glen of Many Legends?"

"So I am." Grim helped himself to another spoonful of venison stew. "Nought is my home. Just now, I'm helping a neighboring chieftain rebuild his stronghold, Duncreag, and his garrison.

"A war-band of broken men took the castle about a year ago, doing much damage. Worst of all"—he paused, dabbing the napkin to his lips again—"the brigands slaughtered almost every soul at Duncreag. The chief's sons and daughter, most of his kin, and even his beloved lady wife all perished."

"I've heard such feuding is rampant in the Highlands." Sorley took a bite of bramble-laden bannock. He needed to occupy himself and didn't want Grim to see that his tale affected him. No stranger to fighting, he did feel sick inside whenever he heard of women mistreated.

To learn of innocent ladies slain made his gut twist painfully.

So much so, that he forgot his dislike of Grim.

"Even in Stirling, we hear tell of the clan warfare, the rampaging—"

"The tragedy that befell Duncreag and Archibald MacNab had naught to do with clan feuding." Grim was watching him even more intently now. "Archie's stronghold was raided because the attackers thought to find a hoard of treasure hidden there. They also hoped to use Duncreag as a base for their depredations in the surrounding glens. Duncreag is remote. You'd be hard put to find a better-suited hideaway for such a purpose." Grim took a long sip of ale, his gaze never leaving Sorley's face. "The stronghold sits atop a sheer bluff, a great soaring one even higher and more rugged than Nought. The only access is a thread-thin goat track that winds up the cliff face. Duncreag should be impregnable, and will be better defended once I've trained and settled Archie's new garrison."

"The MacNabs weren't good fighters?"

"Duncreag was taken by stealth. But, aye, the men weren't the stoutest warriors. The MacNabs' strongpoint has ne'er been swinging a sword."

"What then?"

"They're a race of poets." Grim sat back, a small smile playing at the corners of his mouth. "Seldom have I heard words and song of such beauty as can be enjoyed in Duncreag's hall of a cold, dark night, the fires blazing and good ale flowing at the tables."

"Humph." Sorley snorted, his resentment of Highlanders returning with a vengeance.

Hadn't he dreamed of spending his nights thus, as far back as he could remember?

He also finally grasped what Grim wanted of him. Leastways he had a suspicion.

"You're in charge of manning the chief's new garrison?"

"I am, aye."

"Can it be you're asking me to help you?"

"No' quite, though it'd be a boon for Duncreag if you would."

"Alas, I cannae." Sorley ignored the stab of regret his denial brought. "I'm a Stirling man as much as you're a Highlander. My life and work are here, no' off in your hills fighting for men I dinnae ken."

"And if I told you they are men you should know?" Grim swirled the ale in his tankard, studying the frothy brew as if it held all the world's wisdom. "If I told you the chief, Archie MacNab, is a broken man? That, as I believe, it would heal him greatly if you ride north with me?"

Sorley frowned.

Something wasn't right, a word, a twist of phrase, a puzzle he wasn't seeing.

He set down the spoon he'd been about to dip again into William's delicious venison stew. "Why do I have the feeling there's more to this than needing a good fighting man to help rebuild a garrison?"

"Because there is." Grim leaned forward, his face earnest. "I am as much Archie's friend as the acting captain of his new garrison."

"That's no' an answer."

"It is if you agree that when you love a man, you want the best for him."

"That makes even less sense." The fine hairs on the back of Sorley's neck were beginning to rise. Worse, he had the most uncanny sense that his plaid was stirring, moving about his shoulders and arms almost like the gentle, caressing hands of a woman.

He gave Grim the driest look he could muster, not wanting him to guess his ill ease. "Any seasoned warrior could train a garrison. Surely there are enough stalwarts in your hills for such a task?"

Grim didn't blink, his steady gaze making Sorley feel under assault. "The garrison is only part of it. To be sure, we have braw fighters in the Highlands. I want the man who will no' just join me in strengthening Archie's defenses, but also make him whole again. He needs and deserves his peace. I mean to give it to him." He offered Sorley the slightest of nods. "No' what he's lost, but something else to lift his heart again."

"You're that close to the MacNab?"

"I care about him, aye. He's a fine chieftain, a good man who made mistakes." He gestured with his stew spoon, pointing it at Sorley. "We all do, or will you disagree?"

"Nae." Sorley shook his head, not sure if the odd rushing

in his ears was his blood or the wind racing past the inn's windows. "There isn't a man walking who doesn't carry regrets, sorrows, and guilt."

He wasn't sure where the words came from, or the sympathy he felt for this unknown Highland laird.

For some reason, his throat was thickening and he felt an odd pain in his chest. His heart thumped slow and hard. And each breath was a struggle. He almost felt lightheaded.

Reaching for his ale, he drained what was left in the tankard.

He'd always heard Highlanders had a touch of the fey about them, and Grim was proving it. Even the din from the nearby long room seemed to be fading, his whole world contracting to the Highlander's strong, black-bearded face, the bitterly earnest look in his eyes. The intangible sense that a hint of pleading lurked in his gaze's smoke-gray depths.

"I'm glad you see it that way." Grim's words seemed to come from a great distance.

They also made Sorley damned uncomfortable.

"I still cannae go north with you." Sorley wished William would return with more ale. He could do with a barrel. "I'm no' the man you need."

"Mayhap," Grim agreed. "But you are whom Archie needs."

Sorley's eyes narrowed. "Whom he needs?"

"As I see it, aye."

His words rushed over Sorley like flood waters, knocking the breath out of him and making him feel as if he reeled, even though he was in a chair. He shook his head, not liking the notions rising in his mind.

It couldn't be possible.

His wild imagination was running free, mocking and teasing him...

"What are you saying?" He reached across the table, grabbing Grim's wrist. "Speak plain."

"Can you no' guess?" Grim's question made Sorley's entire body still.

"Nae, I cannae." Saints o' mercy, was that his voice? "Tell me."

"Archibald MacNab is your father," Grim declared. "I'd like to take you to him."

Chapter Thirteen

❦

That cannae be." Sorley stared at Grim in stunned disbelief. He clutched the table edge, his temples pounding. "I ken all the Highland chieftains who come and go at court. No' just now, but in past years. MacNab of Duncreag is no' one of them." He shook his head. "You err."

"Nae, he was, for sure." Grim looked certain. "You wouldn't know his name because the late King Robert banished him from court. He ordered Archie struck from memory, forbidding anyone to speak of him."

"Then how do you know he's my father, if no one dares voice his name?" Sorley leaned forward. "Did he tell you of me? Send you here?"

"He doesn't even know." Grim reached for the earthen jug on the table and poured the remaining ale into their tankards. "I came on my own. And that's of no import. What matters is that Archie will heal if you'll return with me to Duncreag, assume your rightly place as—"

"What, his heir?" Sorley came to his feet, then wished he hadn't, for the room seemed to be spinning. "That's howling mad. If I e'er meant aught to him, if he even knew I existed, where was he all these years?"

Grim raised his tankard, took a long swallow. "We agreed all men make mistakes, have regrets."

"No' living, breathing ones!" Sorley dropped back into his chair, grabbed his own ale. He tipped it to his lips, annoyed the tankard only held a sip.

He glared at Grim, vaguely aware of whoops and table thumping in the long room. The raucous sounds were so close they could only stem from one corner. And he knew exactly where it was, right outside the open archway. He also knew who sat there, making merry at his expense. Not that he cared. His three archfiends could strip naked and dance a jig on the table and it'd be nothing to him.

Their revelry was the least of his worries.

What plagued him was his curiosity.

He wanted to know more about Archibald—Archie— MacNab of Duncreag.

At the same time, he didn't like feeling a jot of sympathy for the man.

That he already had, before he'd known Grim's secret, was a problem.

"The day is a fine one, eh?" William strolled up to the table, smiling ear to ear as he set down an even larger jug of fresh, frothy ale and a small pewter tray with two cups of uisge beatha.

"I'm thinking something stronger than ale is welcome?" William rapped the table. He also gave a Sorley a friendly whack on the back. "Indeed, I'm passing round a few flasks of my best spirits in the long room."

"I wouldn't know why." Sorley didn't touch the little cup.

He did lift his head to glare at the innkeeper. "If the ruckus out there has aught to do with me, we are no longer friends. You'll have proven yourself spawned in the depths of hell and no' the man I aye thought you were. One who kens when to keep his lips sealed."

William raised his hands, palms outward. "I told everyone we're celebrating the year-day of this inn. That's no' far from the truth, as the day passed a sennight ago.

"Ten grand years"—his smile deepened—"since I took o'er the Red Lion from my father and his father before him."

Sorley nodded once, in polite recognition. "I still dinnae want your uisge beatha."

"Knock it back, my friend." William rested a hand on his shoulder, gripped hard. "Remember, the view down a road aye depends on the direction you're looking. Think on that. My fine Highland spirits will help."

"They'll give me a sore head in the morning," Sorley grumbled, taking a nip all the same.

When he plunked the cup back down on the table, William was gone.

Grim was watching him, looking mightily pleased.

"What?" Sorley glanced down, wondering if he'd dribbled uisge beatha or Berengaria's bramble preserves in his beard or onto his plaid.

"You have the devil's own temper." Grim sipped his uisge beatha, his observation seeming to amuse him even more. "Did you ken that the MacKenzies' greatest—"

"I dinnae ken that lot at all." Sorley leaned across the table, clamping his hand across Grim's wrist before he could lift his cup for another sip. "I told you, I like the colors of their tartan."

A plaid that—he noted to his horror—once again seemed to be shifting lightly across his shoulders and back, as if an unseen female hand were touching him. Stroking him not in a sensual way, but gently and soothingly.

The sensation made his skin crawl.

Lady Mirabelle, were she here, and he praised the gods she wasn't, would say a ghost was caressing him.

"Have you aye been drawn to the MacKenzie tartan?" Grim didn't seem to care at all that he was gripping his arm so tightly. "Aye been so hot-headed? Truth be told, I'm no' surprised."

Sorley let go of Grim's arm and sat back. "I dinnae see what my temper, or the MacKenzies, have to do with you and Archibald MacNab of Duncreag."

"Nae?" Grim arched a brow. ""Were you no' aware that Clan MacKenzie's greatest hero chieftain, Duncan, the Black Stag of Kintail, was also known as 'the Devil'? He, too, had a raging temper." Calmly finishing William's uisge beatha, Grim raised the empty cup in salute and set it back down, quietly. "One could say such outbursts of fury run in the blood of that house."

"I wouldn't ken." Sorley reached for old Berengaria's bramble preserves only to discover he'd already emptied the little pot.

"Your mother was a MacKenzie." Grim spoke as easily as if he were commenting on the mist whirling past the windows. "Daughter of a cousin several times removed from the mighty Black Stag himself."

The words slammed into Sorley, stunning him so thoroughly the impact nearly knocked him off his chair.

"My mother?" He stared at Grim as though he'd stood and turned into Duncan MacKenzie himself.

He couldn't say more because his heart had stopped, his world crashing in on him. His jaw slipped, his chest tightening fiercely.

"I ken it's a shock." Grim was sympathetic.

Somehow he'd procured more uisge beatha, a fresh wee cup, which he slid in Sorley's direction. Wyldes must've crept into the parlor, unseen as he so oft managed to be, bringing more of the fiery spirits. "I wish I could've lessened the blow," Grim owned, looking on as Sorley drained the cup in one quick gulp.

"I dinnae have a mother." Sorley wiped his mouth with the back of his hand, set down the empty cup. "I ne'er knew her. I cannae believe you."

"Och, it's true enough. Her name was Gavina and by all accounting she was exceptionally beautiful. Unfortunately, she was also high-spirited, and in her most tender, vulnerable years, she lost her heart to the wrong lad, a roguish squire passing through Kintail with his liege lord."

Grim paused, waiting for Sorley's nod before he continued. "Your mother quickened with child. By the time she knew, the lad who'd compromised her was gone. His name is lost to history, no one remembers. Fearing reprisals from her family, Gavina fled, making her way south through the Great Glen. She eventually found sympathetic farmers, MacDonalds of Glencoe, who took her in, caring for her and then comforting her when the child was stillborn. She stayed on with them, helping with chores and looking after the smallest bairns and children."

"A servant, then?"

Grim shrugged. "Perhaps some would say so. But the MacDonalds treated her with kindness. They respected her secrets and never sent word to her father, a possibility she greatly feared."

"The MacKenzie temper?" Sorley could imagine.

"Their rages and passions are far-famed, aye." Grim spooned up a bit of gooseberry pastie. "That hot blood became your mother's worst enemy, heralding her downfall, and yours."

Sorley stiffened. "I'm still no' convinced she was my mother. The MacNab was a MacNab, no' a MacDonald. Glencoe is a great distance from Stirling. I do ken I'm a court bastard, sired at the castle."

Grim arched a brow. "You weren't aware Scottish Kings love hunting? That their wish for the most magnificent stags takes them far and wide, even into the wilds of Glencoe?"

Sorley comprehended. "She caught the eye of one of the King's men?"

"Nae, it was King Robert who claimed her."

"The King?"

"King Robert II himself." Grim took another bite of gooseberry pastie. "I couldn't learn what he told the Mac-Donalds, or perhaps paid them for her, but he took her with him to Stirling. Once at court, he made her his mistress."

"The King?" Sorley couldn't believe it. Never had he heard the like, and hadn't Grim sworn Archibald MacNab sired him? "You're no' making sense. If I was the King's by-blow, I'd no' have slept on a bed of straw in the kitchens as a lad."

Grim set down his spoon. "I didnae say the late King fathered you. I said he made your mother one of his most favored mistresses."

The truth hit Sorley like a punch in the gut.

He winced, imagining Lady Gavina's dilemma.

Looking Grim square in the eye, he voiced his suspicion. "Archibald MacNab seduced her. That's what you're saying, right? Her waist thickened with me and the King's wrath was great, aye? He banished her, or had her killed. That'll be why I ne'er knew her."

The possibility chilled his liver.

"Tell me that's no' true." He hadn't expected to feel anything, but his heart was splitting, a terrible heat burning the backs of his eyes.

He wanted to wring the MacNab's neck.

"I wish I could say otherwise, my friend." Grim sounded genuinely regretful. "More or less, that is the way of it. Leastways, from what I could gather of her sad tale. You did know her, though. You—"

"Nae, I ne'er—"

"Aye, you did, but only as a wee mite." Grim was fingering one of his beard rings, as if the telling bothered him.

"The King meant to have her walled up alive, great-bellied as she was, so tremendous was his rage. But his own lady wife, who knew of his many women and was a caring soul, persuaded him to simply send her away. A lesser noble with connections in the Hebrides arranged for a deep-pursed Islesman to take her. Once she'd birthed you, that is. The Islesman, a Barra man, I believe, came for her and you, and there you lived for nearly two years. On the far isle of Barra, until your lady mother perished after eating seabird eggs that had spoiled."

"So she took me with her?" Sorley could hardly speak for the thickness in his throat.

"She did, and she loved you fiercely. With all her Mac-Kenzie passion." Grim closed his eyes as if the tale pained him. "Sadly, the Islesman had fallen so hard for her, he couldn't bear having you around as a reminder. It's said you resemble her greatly.

"And so..." He let the words tail away. "I was returned to court to be raised as the unwanted bastard of Archibald MacNab."

Grim looked embarrassed. "I wouldnae put it that way, but aye."

"Be glad I cannae go with you to Duncreag." Sorley couldn't believe the fury burning inside him. "I would kill the MacNab with my bare hands."

"He's a good man." Grim's gray eyes met his, and there was a hint of pleading in them again. "Broken, sorrowful, and regretting his past. He is alone. No man should be denied forgiveness—"

"If his Duncreag is as remote and wild as you say, what was he doing at court?" Sorley needed to know, though he could imagine. "Few Highlanders are greeted in Stirling's vaunted hall."

"The King invited him."

"To steal his mistresses?"

Grim cleared his throat. "The King and a party of nobles were journeying through the Highlands, making sure of the clan chieftains' loyalties. The party called at Duncreag for a night's lodging.

"Archie was a bonnie lad and a fine storyteller. His father had him entertain the royal party at the feasting that e'en and the King was greatly taken with Archie's talent. He urged Archie's father to allow him to return to Stirling with him, to be employed as royal bard. And so—"

"He did more than sing and spin tales before the royal hearthside!" Sorley disliked the man more and more. "That is the way of it, aye?"

Grim looked pained. "He suffers much regret."

"He should!" Sorley slapped his hand on the table. "I have ne'er heard of a greater craven." It was all Sorley could do not to roar.

But the long room was still in a tumult, the laughter and shouts louder than ever. The last thing he wanted was to draw a throng of swivel-necked, long-nosed onlookers into the small room, their stares and—he winced—pity making him feel worse than he already did.

Taking a deep breath, he flattened both hands on the table, making ready to stand, to turn his back on Grim Mackintosh, late of Nought in the Glen of Many Legends. To walk out of the Red Lion, never to think of the man again. Most especially, not to dwell on the callous, black-hearted rogue who'd sired him.

There was just one other thing he wanted to know.

Leaning forward, he spoke coldly. "I'd hear how you learned all this. Tell me so I can then put you, your friend, MacNab, and the rest of this misery from my mind. I've spent years trying to puzzle together who my father and mother were. I cannae believe men would speak to you, a stranger here, while refusing me the truth." That suchlike had happened galled him.

"Aye, well…" Grim pushed back his chair and stood. "Perhaps you will now think just as poorly of me as you do of Archie, for I used a method that some might well call a bit unfair."

To Sorley's astonishment, Grim took his great wolf pelt off a nearby chair. Lifting it high, he shook out the folds to reveal a worn-looking leather pouch tied by a strap to the cloak's lining. Unfastening it, he brought the pouch back to the table and gave it to Sorley.

"Open it and you'll see how I oiled tongues." Grim stepped back and folded his arms.

"Humph." Sorley looked down at the lumpy pouch in his hands. Curiosity alone made him untie the leather strings and pull apart the top. A tinge of cold stone and the sea rose from the bag's depths. The scent, heady and very different from anything he knew at Stirling, let his pulse quicken despite his annoyance.

He shot a glance at Grim, who simply nodded. Sorley thrust his hand into the pouch, withdrawing what appeared to be a twist of fossilized root, age-smoothed and blackened.

The bag was full of them.

"What's this?" Sorley carried the thing to one of the wall sconces, turning it this way and that in the candlelight. "A stone root?"

"Indeed." Grim's lips twitched as if he was amused by Sorley's astonishment.

There was also a hint of pride on him.

That only stirred Sorley's interest. He also forgot his anger, much to his surprise. Rolling the stone root between his fingers, he glanced at Grim, sure he was pulling some kind of trick.

"I cannae believe such a thing loosens tongues." He placed it on the table. The stone root gleamed, its satiny surface catching the light. "Is it spelled, then? I ken you have powerful wise women in your hills."

"No' charmed by a cailleach, nae." Grim's pride was swelling. "The stone roots are blessed. But it's the glory of Nought that gives them their strength, the power that makes them so valuable."

"How so?"

"They come from a jutting promontory at Nought called the Dreagan's Claw." Grim returned to the table and reached into the pouch, taking out another of the stone roots. He twirled it between his fingers. "The Dreagan's Claw is a high, windblown place that ends in a tangle of rock neither man nor beast should dare tread upon. All sides of the promontory fall straight to the sea, and there are great, gaping crevices that could send false-stepping souls hurtling to the rocks beneath the cliffs. Where the Dreagan's Claw isn't clogged with huge, broken boulders, stumps of smooth, age-darkened wood litter the ground."

"Wood in such a stone-choked place?"

"Aye." Grim nodded. "They are twisted tree roots, ancient and fossilized, and they prove that long ago, a thick forest covered the mighty cliffs we of Nought call the Dreagan's Claw." He leaned toward Sorley. "It is from those hoary, once tall and proud tree stumps that I gather the stone roots, carrying them with me always."

"Aye, well." Sorley was unimpressed.

Grim smiled and tucked both stone roots back into his pouch. "They are good for making men speak."

"I cannae guess why." Sorley watched him tie the leather string and fasten the pouch inside his wolf-pelt cloak.

"If you understood the Highlands"—Grim straightened— "you'd ken we dinnae just love our land fiercely. It is our greatest strength, nourishing us and making us who we are: hale, hardy, invincible men, all our living days. And beyond, or so we believe." He took both tankards off the table, handing one to Sorley. "A stone root from a place as powerful as Nought can work wonders for a man. Think hard, my friend . . ."

He smiled as he knocked his tankard against Sorley's. "The ancient fossil-trees at the Dreagan's Claw once stood tall and proud, but no longer do. Some men have the same problem."

Sorley almost choked on his ale. "Nae! I willnae believe it."

To his astonishment, he started to laugh. "Dinnae tell me you carry around stone roots, letting men believe they cure such an affliction?"

Grim slung an arm around Sorley's shoulder. "A man quickly spills secrets if he thinks possessing a wee bit of Nought's *strength* will let him once again stand proud."

Sorley shook his head. "I have ne'er heard the like."

"You could learn many more such wonders if you'll ride with me to Duncreag." Grim stepped back, serious again. "You should ken the Highlands, even if you have no wish to forgive Archie."

Sorley set his jaw, the man's name sparking his ire.

"Nae, I cannae go with you." He shook his head, furious that somewhere, deep inside, he was considering just that. "I dinnae have a horse."

The excuse slipped off his tongue before he could stop it.

Grim pounced. "The innkeeper has a good stable. I have seen his beasts. I will buy you one for the journey."

"I have my own coin." Sorley wouldn't accept charity, nor did he need it.

"Then you'll join me?" Grim made it sound as if he'd already agreed.

"I didnae say that." He was tempted.

And not just because he'd always yearned to see the Highlands. This was the opportunity he'd been waiting for all his days.

His chance to avenge himself on the father who'd spurned him.

Now, knowing of the fiend's treatment of his mother, he was even more eager to repay the man in kind.

Unfortunately, he was beginning to like Grim.

He didn't want the Highlander to think poorly of him.

His need to confront Archibald MacNab was greater.

So he took a long breath, hoping he wouldn't regret his decision. "When are you heading north?"

"This is joy!" Grim beamed, his beard rings clinking as he clasped Sorley's shoulder, gripping tight. "We can ride at first light on the morrow, if it suits you?"

"It doesn't." Sorley wasn't leaving Stirling until he'd dealt with Mirabelle. He'd sworn to help her, however much doing so would brand him forever. He'd feel worse if he rode away and she fell into Sinclair's clutches. "I've an important matter looming and cannae leave until it's settled. Can you wait a few days yet? If so—"

"As long as you need." Grim stepped back, grinning. "Though my lady wife will no' be pleased!"

"Aye, well." Sorley glanced at William's fine feast, much of it untouched. "Shall we celebrate our agreement by finishing William's meal?"

"Indeed." Grim followed him back to the table, his pleasure making Sorley feel guilty.

But only until he remembered everything he'd discovered about his father.

The man might be auld and done, broken and alone. But he was also a greater bastard than Sorley ever would be. As such, he deserved what was coming to him.

And it wouldn't be the loving, long-lost son Grim meant to deliver.

It'd be vengeance, and served as cold as Sorley could make it.

Never would Sorley have thought he possessed even a drop of Highland superstition. He scoffed at bogles, banshees, loch beasties, and any other heather-spun foolishness. Yet now that he'd left the Red Lion to walk along the empty, mist-drenched road back to Stirling, he was tempted to accept such possibilities.

For sure, never did the damp, dark mist seem so malevolent. Though to be fair, the foulness of his mood could be a reason. It shouldn't have, but it had irritated him that Roag, Andrew, and Caelan hadn't acknowledged him when he'd left the inn's small room.

Deep in their cups, they'd not even glanced his way.

Sorley frowned, knowing he shouldn't care.

Yet...

He knew they'd heard at least some of what Grim had told him. He'd thought their hoots and whooping had been in comradely jubilation. Even if there was little to be pleased about, all things considered.

So he marched on, secretly wishing the outskirts of the town would soon appear. He'd welcome a glimmer of light in the distance, something other than the dense, impenetrable mist blowing everywhere.

He couldn't see a single star through the thick pall of clouds. Even the moon was nowhere to be glimpsed. What *was* about was a strange rustle of movement that seemed to keep pace with him. He couldn't make out anything lurking in the darkness on either side of the road, but he had the uncomfortable sense of being observed.

The fine hairs on his nape were lifting and that was always a bad sign.

"Saints, Maria, and Joseph!" he snarled Duncan MacKenzie's favorite curse beneath his breath and quickened his pace.

For good measure, he also set his hand on his sword hilt.

Though, in truth, he doubted Dragon-Breath would frighten a ghost.

If something worse than a spirit was in the wood along the roadside, he didn't care to know.

He wished he'd left the inn sooner.

He had certain matters to attend at the castle. An important errand that would mean slipping unseen into Lady Mirabelle's quarters.

And he could only do that when the night was yet young enough for her to still be in the great hall, dining on the dais with her father.

If he entered her room when she was present . . .

A fierce scowl drew his brows together. Such was a hazard he didn't want to risk. She plagued him enough already. Indeed, getting away from her and putting her from his mind, once and for all, was one of his reasons for agreeing to journey with Grim to Duncreag.

It scarce mattered that if he had his way, he'd stay with her for as long as she remained in Stirling, even longer, if the gods were kind.

They weren't, as he well knew.

And he wasn't quite so depraved as to snatch her out from under her father's nose, stealing her away into the night as in times of old.

He was tempted.

And something big was shifting in the mist ahead of him.

He also caught a distinct skitter of pebbles, then the odd rustling from earlier.

Halting, he tilted his head to listen. But he heard only the whisper of the trees and the gurgle of a burn deeper in the wood. The road curved here, following the shoulder of hill. A low stone wall ran along the wood's edge.

He could just make out the wall through the mist.

Low as it was, it wouldn't offer a hiding place to anyone wishing to ambush him. But in the fog, someone crouching beside the stones did have an advantage. And that he couldn't allow.

For sure not when he heard the rustling again, this time bringing the unmistakable chink of steel, then the soft creak of leather that could only be a sword's scabbard slapping against a man's thigh.

Sorley's entire body prickled with a warrior's instinct.

He eased Dragon-Breath half out of her sheath and rounded the bend in the road as three trolls loomed up before him. Their short, squat bodies were dark smudges against the mist.

"Sakes!" Sorley stared at the beasties. He'd known evil was about this night.

He pulled his sword free, swinging the blade around to point at the trolls. "Stay there, and I'll leave you be. I've no' quarrel with your like, though I will—"

"Do what?" came Roag's deep voice as he sprang off the low stone wall, straightening to his full height. "Cut us down for coming to congratulate you?"

Andrew and Caelan likewise leapt to their feet, no longer trolls, but the tall, strapping men they were. They strolled up to Sorley, clearly amused.

"Seeing ghosties in the mist, eh?" Andrew stopped before him and hooked his thumbs in his sword belt. "Can it be your newfound Highland blood has turned your wits already, letting you see haints and bog-beasts in the dark?"

"Fooled you good, we did, didn't we?" Caelan slung an arm around Sorley's shoulders, squeezing tight.

"Aye, you should've kent us better." Roag shook his head in mock reproach. "As if we'd drink ourselves blind when there's such grand news to celebrate. No' even William's finest lassies could've kept us from following you."

"You shouldn't have." Sorley resheathed his sword, wished the mist was just a bit thicker so he wouldn't see how broadly Roag, Andrew, and Caelan were grinning. "There was more to make merry about back at the Red Lion, lusty wenches and good ale. My news, as you surely heard, wasn't much to be joyful about. Save that I'll be riding north with Grim in a few days, to meet my father."

For some reason he couldn't name, he didn't mention Archie's failings.

That was personal, and he'd handle the matter in his own way.

"So your mother was a MacKenzie." Andrew sounded awed. "To think you've aye been drawn to that clan, as if you somehow knew."

"What I know is that my mother is dead." Sorley was glad for the dark, hoping none of his friends could see the muscle jerking in his jaw.

"We didn't just come after you because of Grim's news." Roag's tone revealed he had seen the leaping muscle. "We wanted you to know we're glad about you and Lady Mirabelle. We were there when you first saw her, the Highland reel—"

"There's nothing between us," Sorley denied, his jaw muscle working even faster. "She doesn't remember that night. It was long ago and—"

"We're three trolls a-sitting on a wall!" Caelan laughed and punched Roag's arm.

"Aye, well." Roag drew himself up, clearly preparing to speak for them all. "We kent this is the patch of road with the old pagan well off in the trees, at the burn." He glanced that way, then winked. "Have you forgotten the Beltane morn you swore there'd be naked lasses there, bathing their breasts and thighs to keep their beauty forever?"

"Aye." Sorley chuckled; he couldn't help it. "I'd climbed down in the well shaft and wailed like a ghoul when you loons arrived, looking for the lassies."

"It did seem a good place to waylay you." Andrew also threw a look at the low stone wall, barely visible through the mist.

Many memories lived in the shadows beyond, especially around the old sacred well.

They'd all made their own Beltanelike merry there over

the years. Leastways when they'd been lads and not minding a tumble on cold, damp ground.

"That doesnae change that there's naught between me and Mirabelle MacLaren." Sorley felt a need to set that straight. However much he appreciated her lush curves and other charms, no matter that he admired her boldness and her courage, or that her concern for a wee kitten touched something deep inside him. She remained the last female he ought to allow close to his heart. No highborn lady would ever tread there, not so long as he had a jot of wits.

He rolled his shoulders, not liking the tension building there. He also didn't care for the white-hot jolt of jealousy that pierced him on knowing that, someday, somewhere down the road, another man would claim her, making her his bride. That truth put a fierce scowl on his face.

"She means nothing to me." He turned his frown on the others, not missing how their fool eyes glinted in the darkness. He laid on his hardest tone, "I'll take the head off the first one of you who says so. She's a virgin." Sorley hoped that declaration would wipe the knowing looks off their faces.

It didn't.

Indeed, the loons exchanged glances as if deciding who should share a secret.

Sorley crossed his arms. "Speak true. What is this about?"

"We ken what you did for her." Roag answered first.

"Och, aye?" Sorley cocked a brow.

"Chasing all o'er the rocks beneath the curtain wall, looking like a buffoon racing after his shadow. And all for a wee kitten." Caelan caught Sorley's hand, lifting it up to expose the red scratches everywhere. "No man would do the like lest he'd fallen hard."

Releasing Sorley's hand, he glanced round at the others. "Agreed?"

They all grinned.

"Naught ails me except a wish to see the last of you." Sorley glanced pointedly in the direction he'd been heading, toward the town. With luck, the three of them would melt back into the mist.

Instead, their faces sobered. "Aye, well..." As so often, they spoke as one.

Roag stepped forward, gripped Sorley's arm. "That's the other reason we followed you. To make our farewells."

"I'm no' staying at Duncreag." Sorley looked around at the others. They still weren't smiling. "My business there willnae take long."

"You're mishearing us as aye." Roag tightened his grasp on Sorley's arm, then let go, stepping back. "We're the ones leaving."

Sorley blinked, looking at him. "You?"

"Aye, all three of us, though I'm away on my own." Roag glanced at Andrew and Caelan, then back at Sorley. "You ken, when the wind whistles..."

"A wolf is sharpening his teeth," Sorley finished the Fenris code words, wondering what Alex Stewart, the Wolf, was planning for his friends.

"So it is," Andrew spoke up, his chest swelling a bit. "You didn't think you were the only reason we didn't ride away with Alex when he left Stirling, did you? Truth is," he lowered his voice, "he wanted us to leave later and ride up through the hills as cattle drovers. He doesnae trust some of the lairds selling beasts at the Crieff cattle market. Two of them have disappeared mysteriously, and we'll be looking for them."

"They're either dead or guilty," Caelan added, stepping forward. "The Wolf wants to know."

"And you?" Sorley turned to Roag, not liking the fool's grin.

"Och, I'm off to the Hebrides!" He hooked his thumbs

in his sword-belt and rocked back on his heels. His chest puffed out even more than Andrew's. "'Tis a great chieftain of the Isles I'll be guising as." He winked, clearly amused. "Alex isn't at all fond of Hebrideans and wants someone in place to keep an eye on the bastards.

"There's piracy, rapine, and worse going on in thon waters. And"—he glanced about, his voice dropping dramatically—"Alex and his brother, the King, suspect some of the chiefs are planning a campaign to take the crown. The gods ken those Islesmen are bold enough to try."

"I wouldn't doubt it." Sorley agreed, secretly envious of his friends' adventures, especially Roag's. "Then you'll be gone a good while."

The three of them nodded in unison.

Sorley inclined his own head, feeling oddly sorry to see them leave. He stepped back, instinctively knowing they were about to fade into the mist again. "God go with you, all three of you."

"He wouldn't dare." Roag laughed and leaned in to punch Sorley's arm. "No' if He doesnae want his eyes catching fire. I, for one, willnae just be after scheming Hebridean chieftains. I hear the women in those Isles ken how to kindle a heat that blazes hotter than the sun. And I dinnae mean a hearth fire." He winked, his grin flashing when the others laughed.

Only Sorley didn't.

For some inexplicable reason, he didn't even make a rude quip when they announced they were heading back to the Red Lion, wanting to finish what they'd started with William's waiting lovelies.

By the time he did open his mouth to make such a jest, they were gone.

It was then, listening to their cloaks rustling through the mist, their footfalls growing fainter, that he realized why he felt so strange.

This night was the first time he'd ever thought of them as true friends.

Frowning darkly, he set off down the road again, hoping to be back at the castle within the hour. No matter how he viewed Roag, Andrew, and Caelan, he should be glad to have his peace from them for a while.

To be sure, he wouldn't miss them.

Nor would he miss Mirabelle when he took his farewell of her. Far from it, he'd be relieved to see the last of the trouble-making lass.

For all her witchy enchantments, she was the last female he needed in his life.

She could bring utter ruination to a man.

One glance from her sapphire-blue eyes would suffice, a mere crook of her finger. A single whiff of her heady rose perfume and all good sense fled.

She was danger, walking.

For a man in his position, a vixen to be avoided at all costs. Leastways, where a man's heart and deeper emotions were concerned.

Pausing, he lifted a hand and glared at the damage to his skin. The scratches were livid red and many, some of the welts even swelling. The wee kitten was a fighter, had spirit.

Roag, Andrew, and Caelan had the right of it.

No man suffered the like gladly.

But wouldn't he do anything for the woman he loved?

Chapter Fourteen

❦

*S*he tempted him.

Mirabelle savored that small triumph as she entered her small but well-appointed bedchamber in the castle's ladies' quarters. It was late evening, but she still remembered every word she and Sorley had exchanged on the battlements that morning. She also couldn't forget how he'd looked at her, raking her with heated glances, from head to toe, his boldness scorching her everywhere in between. She'd melted, feeling his gaze as surely as if he'd touched her. Wishing he had, she closed the door behind her and rested her weight against it. In truth, too much excitement, and hope, prickled inside her to trust her feet to carry her deeper into the room.

She felt positively giddy.

Who would've thought Sorley the Hawk would admit the like?

It wasn't in his nature to desire a virtuous maid.

Yet...

He'd declared that he found her lips luscious and her bottom delectable. Such admissions were beyond her wildest expectations. Mirabelle shivered, her entire body tingling, her heartbeat increasing. She just hoped she could make him feel more than lust for her. At the very least, she hoped he'd give her a chance to tell him why she'd walked away at the Highland reel all those years ago. Why she'd left him standing alone.

She might also tell him that she wanted his passion for the memories she could cling to on cold, dark nights in distant days when, as she knew would happen, she'd be compelled to wed a man of suitable station and breeding.

That she believed remembrance of his touch would then sustain her. If he knew, perhaps his heart would soften toward her.

Not sure that was possible, considering Sorley was, well, Sorley, she lifted a hand to her breast, letting her eyes adjust to the room's dimness. She could see that a small fire still burned in the grate, though the flames were weak, the peat bricks beginning to fall to ash. But someone had lit her bedside night candle and two of the wall sconces, although they also flickered and smoked, their flames not even casting a glow onto the floor rushes.

It scarce mattered.

The room was functional, not grand. There weren't any lavishly carved chairs, tables, and gew-gaws set about, waiting to trip her in the darkness. Only one sturdy trestle table, safely pushed against the far wall, a single straight-backed chair, a few hooks for her clothes, and a plain wooden chest to hold her bulkier goods. Even the bed was unadorned, a simple oaken four-poster bearing nary a swirl of decoration. Still, it was welcoming enough, with clean sheets, soft pillows, and warm woolen blankets.

Dark blue covers that were moving!

"Holy sainted heather!" Mirabelle pushed away from the door, her eyes rounding. The bedding rose and fell as if a disembodied fist punched up through the mattress, perhaps hoping to seize her.

She clapped both hands to her cheeks, her heart hammering. The *cover-jumps* increased, now racing up and down her bed, out of control.

"Saints have mercy..." She took a slow step backward again, reaching behind her for the door. Her fingers trembled and her palms were damp, so slick she couldn't properly grasp the latch.

Her legs were less help, feeling leaden, making it impossible to run even if she could open the door and flee. Taking a deep breath, she silently vowed to light a hundred candles in the chapel if only whatever devil was in her bed would leave.

Surely wanting Sorley's assistance wasn't a great enough sin for the gods to send demons after her?

She'd loved him for years, after all.

He was the one man in the whole of the world she'd ever wanted. The only soul she knew she'd never forget, not for all her days, nor even beyond. He'd affected her that strongly when they'd been younger. Seeing and knowing him as a man confirmed the depth of her feelings.

Whatever force had seized her bed was also powerful.

The covers jigged and leapt, as if damning her for the truth in her heart. Condemning her for the way her breath hitched just to think of him, how his dangerously handsome face, his kisses, occupied her always, even following her into her sleep, claiming her dreams.

To her mind, true love was never bad. It was certainly not deserving of such a terror as possessed coverlets.

"Mercy!" She pressed her back into the solid wood of the door, her gaze fixed on the bed as something else struck her: What if Sorley was being equally punished?

He'd gone to meet with Grim that day and as far as she was aware, he hadn't yet returned.

No one knew anything about the rough-looking Highlander from Nought in the distant Glen of Many Legends.

What if he'd been sent by the gods to strike down Sorley?

Mirabelle shuddered, icy chills racing along her spine. She couldn't bear it if that was so. She'd feel especially dreadful if the deities' wrath came because he'd agreed to help her out of her quandary with Sir John.

Aid her in a limited way, that was.

Kisses in the hall and—her face flushed and a rush of heat swept her secret places—a few touches of his hands to the bared flesh of her breasts. That was all, she was sure. They wouldn't advance to any deeper intimacies. Hadn't their encounter in the Rose Room, and on the battlements, made that clear?

Suchlike was sinning enough.

Leastways it was for Scottish gods below the Highland line. Lowland folk were less tolerant than Highlanders in matters of the heart and fleshly delights. Such goings-on as she and Sorley meant to perform in the hall were an unpardonable wickedness. Wanton behavior beyond all decency and grace. Leastways if the lady involved was a virgin of noble blood, born of a good house and name.

Mirabelle frowned, released a shuddery breath.

Keeping her gaze on the jumping covers, she again tried the door latch. But her grip only proved more clumsy than before, as if the gods wished to trap her.

She bit her lip, her pulse racing.

There were times she envied such lasses as Maili. The freedom they had to love where, and with whom, they desired. Although even if she could indulge herself thus, she'd want only Sorley.

He'd been branded on her soul from the moment she'd seen him across the raucous great hall at her uncle's feasting celebration so many years before. When she'd gone to him for a dance and their gazes had locked, she'd been lost, his forevermore. He'd dazzled her with a glance, his dark good looks, even then. He'd stolen her heart, claiming it with his bold, flashing smile, his swagger and pride.

Sadly, what happened next had made him revile her. She couldn't blame him. After all, wasn't that exactly what she'd set out to do? Leastways, after she'd spotted her fierce-eyed, man-hating great-aunt and her father's brawniest, most bull-like champion storming across the cleared space of the dancing area, both of them bent on murder.

The brutish guard would've beaten Sorley to a pulp, perhaps worse. She couldn't have allowed that to happen. But sparing him a thrashing had broken her heart.

Now...

She only wished she knew he'd returned safely from the Red Lion.

She also wanted her bed to stop moving. She usually didn't fear aught, but devils and demons did exist, as all Highlanders knew.

However...

The evil eye was also real, so perhaps if she stared fiercely enough at the bed, the jerky movements would go away. So she fixed a fearsome scowl on her face and glared at the bouncing covers.

They stilled at once.

"Praise be!" She took a few steps forward, her gaze not leaving the rumpled sheets.

"Yeoooooow!" A tiny gray head with huge white-rimmed eyes and large pointy ears popped up between her pillows, the kitten's blue gaze latching on hers as it yowled again, this time even louder.

"Little Heart!" She ran across the room, her own heart bursting.

"Dear heavens!" She dropped to her knees beside the bed and reached for him, hoping to cuddle him to her breast.

She didn't need to, because he flew at her, landing on her shoulder and clinging fast, purring a storm. Mirabelle stood, holding him against her, blinking hard to chase the heat stinging her eyes.

"Oh, you sweet wee mite!" She stroked his velvet fur, wincing at his airlike weight, his thinness that let her feel every one of his ribs. "You will never be hungry again, I promise," she vowed, kneeling to place him on the rushes, her heart swelling to see his wobbly steps bringing him right back to her.

His limp was gone.

He seemed to know her, appeared just as happy to be hers as she was to have him.

She scooped him up against her cheek, turning her head to kiss his soft little face. "You won't have to ever worry about anything ever again. You're mine now and your name is Little Heart."

He pressed into her, purring as if he knew.

And she knew how he got here.

There was only one explanation, and it filled her with as much joy as finding the kitten in her bed.

Sorley had caught him for her. That meant he'd returned safely from his meeting with Grim Mackintosh. Unless he'd retrieved Little Heart before he'd left Stirling to make his way to the Red Lion.

She wouldn't have known, as she'd spent the day with her father in the castle scriptorium.

But she meant to find out, and soon.

She also needed to thank Sorley. She'd consider the meaning of his rescue of Little Heart later. She didn't want to get her hopes up. She did have to fetch food for the kitten.

"You darling..." She lifted him back onto her bed, hating to leave him. "I'll be back anon, I promise."

Then she bent down and kissed him again. "Till soon."

As he mewed in answer, she turned and slipped from the room, closing the door gently behind her.

Sorley knew the moment Mirabelle entered the great hall.

Much to his annoyance, Sir John also noticed.

He sat not far from where Sorley stood in the shadows of a window embrasure. Two court beauties flanked the noble, each one famed for how generously she shared her charms. Even so, Sir John turned his head as Mirabelle passed his table. Stroking his pointy black beard, he let his hooded gaze follow Mirabelle's progress down the hall's broad center aisle. With a grace all her own, she was heading for the raised dais where her father dined with his guardsmen.

She glowed, looking happier than he'd ever seen her.

He could guess why.

And her delight affected him so deeply that he lost all awareness of everyone and everything else in the hall. He saw only her sparkling eyes, the pleased flush on her cheekbones, and the soft curve of her lips, her smile warming him clear to his toes.

He should be admiring how her glorious hair gleamed in the torchlight. Or that her deep blue gown displayed the creamy top swells of her breasts and clung to her waist and hips, leaving little doubt how lushly she was made. He half believed he caught a tantalizing hint of her rose perfume floating in the air behind her.

The length of her skirts flattered her long legs, so slender and shapely. The kind of limbs a man loved having wrapped tight around his hips. Better yet, her tempting thighs, when parted, would offer a succulent feast.

He'd glimpsed the shadow of those curls in the Rose Room, knew they'd be burnished and glossy. Rich with the heady scent of her deepest femininity, her secret places drew him fiercely. His urge to touch her there, to taste her, almost consumed him.

Indeed, he wanted her so much that just the sheen of the torches on the exposed half-moons of her breasts sent hot blood rushing to his nether regions, quickening his desire, setting him like stone.

That he ached to lie with her stood without question.

Yet...

Watching her enter the hall caused his heart to start a slow, hard beating.

And that was a problem.

Heart thumpings meant something more than simple lust.

Pure carnal need could be slaked in a shadowed alcove of the hall or on a quiet stair landing. Plenty other places would do as well. Many were the kitchen lasses and laundresses eager to lift their skirts. Wyldes's Red Lion wenches were aye eager to sate such urges.

In desperation, his hand would serve.

Regrettably, none of those options would ever satisfy him again. He shifted, uncomfortable with the notion. But there was no denying the unaccustomed tightness in his chest each time he saw Mirabelle, the way his pulse leapt when she looked at him. He couldn't speak to her without wanting to touch her flame-bright hair, or better yet, grab her and pull her to him, kissing her soundly and more.

Most alarming, she made him wish for things that could never be. Like the pleasure of waking beside her in the morning, seeing her sleep-mussed and soft-eyed, all warm and pliant in his arms. The new day theirs to claim, any way they wished to enjoy the hours.

Such thoughts were new to him, and disturbing.

He was well used to desiring a woman, but he'd never before *adored* one.

Frowning, he lifted a hand and rubbed the back of his neck, aware he could've used a much stronger word.

Truth was, no female had ever stirred him so thoroughly, to the bone and deeper. Mirabelle was a poison in his blood, and he doubted he'd ever be able to purge himself of her. Especially since he would soon do everything to and with her that was possible without taking her maidenhead. It was a fool plan and dangerous. But she'd made the offer and he couldn't resist.

Besides, he had a few plans of his own. Wasn't it a Fenris truth, even carved into everything he was, that a man never gained aught unless he fought for it? He might be the last man who'd qualify as a suitable husband for Lady Mirabelle, but he damn well could protect her from landing in the arms of an even worse choice.

Feeling a need to use Sinclair's belly for spear practice, Sorley sharpened his gaze, turning it again on Sir John. The noble still sat with two of the court's most accommodating harlots, his attention blessedly once more on easier conquests than Mirabelle.

Even so, just looking at the snake sent bile rising in Sorley's throat, made his sword hand itch.

How he'd love to spill Sinclair's guts here and now.

He would make certain the fiend never laid a finger on Mirabelle. Not here, and not in her beloved Highlands. That, he could do for her.

He also had another task to undertake in her interest, something he knew would please her.

So he looked toward the dais end of the hall where she now sat beside her father.

He wanted to see her face, be sure she was at ease. But so much bustle and tumult filled the hall that he couldn't clearly observe the dais tables from where he stood.

Huge fires blazed in the hall's double-arched fireplaces, each one sending showers of sparks, smoke, and low-drifting haze into the air. Noblemen and their ladies packed every table while knights and squires, garrison men, and the ever-present visitors vied for any available perch. Many had to settle for standing in the hall's pillared aisles. The cacophony was deafening, made worse by the scores of laughing, screeching children and romping dogs.

Sorley was lucky to have enjoyed the vision that was Mirabelle MacLaren for as long as he'd managed to keep her in sight.

He hadn't been so fortunate in choosing the right window embrasure.

This was the third he'd tried, seeking the alcove that offered access to a hidden passage. No matter, he'd keep looking until he found the one he needed.

He just wished he'd paid more heed when, as lads, he and Roag, Caelan, and Andrew had flitted in and out of the passage and its secret turnpike stair. Determined, he once again backed against the embrasure's window seat. He carefully reached down and lifted the cushion. Just as had happened when he'd tried a few moments before, the seat failed to rise when he slid his fingers along the cold, smooth stone of its edge.

There was no hidden lever.

He was beginning to think he and his friends had dreamt the dark, dank tunnel-like passage. A castle secret known only to a few, supposedly, the passage was said to have once given a particularly lusty prince discreet access to the ladies' quarters. The same prince was said to have built the Rose Room. His day was long ago, in times so ancient no one could now recall the hot-blooded royal's name.

Fortunately, the hidden passage led directly to the guest room assigned to Mirabelle.

Sorley meant to gain access to the room while she supped with her father. He wanted to deliver a sack of kitten-care goods that he'd gathered with the help of the castle cook, the kitchen lads and lasses, and even William Wyldes's aunt Berengaria.

Now...

Frowning, he hitched the strap of the heavy leather bag over his shoulder. Bulky and unwieldy, the bag would prove awkward to carry up the passage's tight, winding stair. Who would've thought a wee kitten could require so much *weight* for his comfort?

He didn't quite agree that a wooden crate and a bagful of river sand was a necessity.

Berengaria had insisted, and as the old woman was considered an authority on cats and kittens, who was he to argue?

He stepped back out into the hall to survey his options. There were many more window embrasures lining this side of the great hall. And he was certain the alcove with the trapdoor window seat was along this particular wall.

One embrasure had been claimed by a woman in a shimmering cloak of rose.

Sorley was sure the lady sat upon the window seat he needed.

As if the woman knew and agreed, she turned her head to look his way. He couldn't quite make out her features because of the smoke haze in the air, but he could tell she was young and beautiful.

She was also smiling.

He started toward her, ready to encourage her to leave so he could see if the window seat accessed the secret passage.

That, too, she appeared to know for, still smiling, she patted the seat cushion.

And then she disappeared.

Chapter Fifteen

❧

Sakes!" Sorley's eyes rounded. He stared at the empty window embrasure, the stone bench against its wall where, only a moment ago, a beautiful lady had sat amongst the pillows, smiling. For sure, she wasn't there now. Sorley shook his head, disbelief sluicing him. The sack of kitten goods slid from his shoulder, dropping to the floor.

He rubbed his eyes, sure the woman would be there again when he reopened them.

She wasn't. So he blinked several times, but that also failed to bring her back. She simply wasn't there. Or rather, she never had been.

Deciding that possibility suited him best, Sorley picked up the cat pouch and strolled over to the now-empty embrasure, doing his damnedest to forget what he'd just seen.

Ghosts didn't exist, after all.

Not in his world.

But Mirabelle was enjoying dinner with her father. Now was the best time to take the kitten supplies to her room. He wouldn't disturb her. The secret passage would allow him to deliver the sack without compromising her.

No one would see him enter her bedchamber.

He just hoped the wee hissing, scratching beastie would be asleep. He didn't fancy another tussle with the kitten, especially as he knew who would win.

Above all, he wanted to be sure Mirabelle was happy, and that meant seeing to the bugger's needs. So he stepped into the embrasure and eased up the sumptuous cushion and a folded plaid, surely meant as a knee warmer.

He found the lever at once, pushing it with practiced ease.

The stone seat creaked open, the lid rising slowly to reveal a gaping black hole. Thanks to the torchlight from the hall, it was possible to make out rough-hewn stone steps cut into the castle's rock. A bit of the stone-flagged floor of the passage below was also visible. He gripped the opening's edges, then lowered himself into the passage's entrance, pulling down the seat lid behind him.

Darkness claimed him when the seat fell into place, but there was a hand rope along the short length of stair. He knew the way and was soon down the steps and in the passage, trailing his hand along the wall to guide himself. He swiftly reached the secret turnpike stair and mounted the curving stone steps, soon gaining the top of the winding stair. Now, nothing but a concealed stone door and its opening-lever stood between him and his goal.

On the other side, a tapestry covered the passage's secret entrance.

Or exit, depending on one's direction.

His, of course, was the latter. So he once again adjusted the kitten sack strap on his shoulder and opened the secret door. Pushing aside the wall tapestry that hung on the other side, he stepped into the bedchamber, and froze.

Mirabelle stood in the middle of the room.

She was naked.

"Sorley!" Her eyes flew wide and she clapped one hand

to her breasts, the other to the burnished red curls at the apex of her thighs. "What are you doing here?"

"I could ask the same of you." Sorley dropped the sack, not hiding the wicked smile that tugged at his lips. He let his gaze flick to her breasts, the sweet curve of her hips. "Last I looked you were in the hall, heading for your father's table."

"Clearly, I am not there now." Her shoulders went back, the motion doing wondrous things to her breasts, making them sway despite the hand she'd clutched before them. "I am here and you shouldn't be."

"Say you?" Sorley felt his smile becoming a full-blown grin. He couldn't help it. "Some might think the gods arranged this meeting. That it's their way of evening the field. After all, you did slip into my private chamber, finding me unclothed on my bed..."

He let the words hang in the air, appreciating how agitation put a lovely flush on her cheeks and the lush top swells of her breasts.

"I entered your quarters with good reason." She turned, showing him her back, her delightfully rounded arse fully displayed for his delectation. "I was preparing for bed. You should leave."

"Och, sweeting, that I cannae do." He started toward her, unable to help himself.

Not caring even.

A man could only take so much temptation and his blood ran redder, hotter than most. He hadn't come here to seek her arms, naked or otherwise, yet...

Happening on such a serendipitous delight...

He could only let his gaze sweep over her, sure he'd never seen a more exquisite woman. After they parted on the morrow's eve, he might never see her again. It was a prospect that tightened his innards, bringing a sharp pain as sure as if someone had thrust a white-hot poker into his chest, splitting his heart.

Honor bound him to let her go. She deserved a good husband someday, a better man. Besides, he was also the King's sworn servant, tied by his oath to ever perform duties that could make a wife a widow.

Still...

He had to touch her.

Strolling the rest of the way over to her, he gripped her by the waist and lowered his head to press a kiss to the smooth skin of her shoulder. She gasped, a slight tremor racing through her. But she didn't break away from him, not even when he slid a hand down over her hip and lower, savoring her soft, warm skin. He spread his fingers across the luscious curve of her buttocks and squeezed for a moment, relishing her, stunned by how good she felt beneath his greedy, questing palm.

"Precious lass, so sweet." He shook his head slowly, letting his gaze again glide over her lush and tempting shapeliness. "You are a prize beyond all telling, a treasure. You ken it's no' possible for me to walk away. No' when you're standing naked before me."

She turned to face him, remarkably calm, her hands not hiding any of her. "You didn't say what you're doing here."

"Losing my restraint, wouldn't you say?" He leaned closer, only a breath away from her oh-so-kissable lips. "Every last shred of it, be warned."

If she so much as blinked, he'd forget his damnable honor, his lifelong determination to never despoil a virgin, and give himself over to the raging in his blood. He'd kiss her long and deep, ravishing her until she melted against him, unable to stand on her own, possibly not even able to breathe.

He wanted her that fiercely.

Driven by his desire, he slid a hand down over the bottom curve of her buttock, letting his fingers glide perilously near to an even greater temptation. "I cannae resist you, Mirabelle, no' for all the world's gold."

"Is this another test?" She jolted when one of his fingers touched her feminine heat, the sleek, slick wetness beneath her curls. "A new practice session, to see if you can arouse me? So that our performance in the hall looks real?" Her voice rose, tinged with anger. "If so—"

"Lady, we practiced enough in the Rose Room." Sorley frowned, but removed his hands from her. "The truth of it is, play-acting wasnae needed. No' then, and for sure, no' now." He looked at her, glad to see her chin lifting, admiring the spark in her eyes. "I am scorched by the heat of you, sharply aware of the delicious, satiny wetness..."

Again, he let the words tail off, their portent most plain on her face. In the visible quickening of her breath, how her pulse beat so seductively at her throat. She was a vixen bred and born, her boldness and spirit proving everything he'd ever heard about hot-blooded Highland lasses.

How fearless they were, how passionate.

"You see the fires you stir, lass. Such flames blaze too dangerously for a lady." He straightened, his heart thundering, his loins uncomfortably tight.

He shouldn't be so out of control, but everything about her played havoc with him.

She drew him to her as if by a powerful, inexorable cord that he knew would circle round and hang him.

"Indeed,"—he thrust his fingers into her hair, letting his hand glide through the glossy skeins—"you would've been wise to stay in the hall."

"I couldn't—"

"So I see." He leaned close, so near that he knew she'd feel the warmth of his breath across her ear.

She shivered, the reaction rippling through her. "Please."

"I aye do, lass." He lifted his head, nipping her earlobe before stepping back, raging need for her pumping through him, the hammering of his heart warning how much he wanted her.

Nae, he loved her.

That he knew with the certainly of the stars in the heaven, the moon and the sun. All of which he'd pull down to earth, serving them to her on a silver platter if only he could. If doing so would make her love him.

But just now...

He touched her hair again, trailed the backs of his fingers down her cheek. "You take my breath."

And she did.

Her full, round breasts gleamed in the candlelight, and her nipples, so temptingly taut, peeked boldly at him as if begging a nip and lick. Her glossy red feminine curls beckoned at the apex of her thighs. And the longer he looked there, the harder he grew. In truth, his entire body tightened.

He'd never wanted a woman more.

Any moment he'd—

"Owwww!" He blinked, swatting at his neck to dislodge the hissing kitten who'd apparently sprouted wings and flown at him from the bed to sink his damnably sharp claws deep into his skin.

He'd completely forgotten the wee beastie.

"Little Heart!" Mirabelle rushed forward, grabbing the kitten, cuddling the lucky bugger to her breast. She also snatched her undergown from a chair, gripping it before her like a fluttering linen shield. "All is well, my darling," she crooned to the kitten, who now purred loudly, the image of fluffy innocence.

"Nae, it isnae." Sorley aimed a glance at the room's shuttered windows. The wind was rising and howled past the tower, icy air seeping in through the wooden slats.

"Sinclair was in the hall earlier. I didnae care for the way he watched you. We'll have to be more careful than we thought in the hall. He's no' a man to be fooled." He didn't want to frighten her. He also shouldn't say what he was about to, but he wanted to reassure her. "I'll be taking other measures as well. Even after you leave Stirling, he'll no' bother you."

She frowned, bent to place the kitten on the floor rushes. "You're not going to kill him? I've heard whispers that he doesn't fight fair. He might—"

"Sweet lass, he wouldn't live to draw a second breath if he challenged me." Sorley strode a few paces away, not wanting her to see the bloodlust her words surely put on his face. He'd love nothing more than use his sword to send Sir John from this world. "For the now, just be assured I'll be watching him. And that where I cannae be, others—"

"So you are a Fenris." She circled round to stare at him, awe on her face. "I knew it, was sure that—"

"Men dinnae speak of such matters, lass." He could hardly talk now, for she'd slipped on her gown and stood fumbling with the bodice laces. He didn't dare offer to help. He'd rip the clothes right off her again, caution be damned.

He drew a tight breath and clenched his fists to keep from reaching for her. "It could be there are some men worthy of Fenris legend. Dedicated warriors who fear naught and will no' allow harm to come to innocents."

"So you do admit it." Her smile almost unmanned him.

"I'm owning to naught. I'd only have you know I'll aye see you safe." The gruffness of his voice shocked him, and he hoped she wouldn't guess how much the wonder on her face affected him, or how powerfully it roused him to see her hands working at her bodice laces. "I didnae come here to pounce on you. I brought you something." He reached beneath his plaid, retrieved a small leather pouch that hung from his sword-belt. Untying its strings, he dug inside the bag, finally producing a good-sized Celtic brooch.

He held it to the light of a nearby wall torch, turning the pin so its age-smoothed bronze gleamed as if alive. A fierce-looking stag's head adorned the piece, the proud antlers and the beast's ruby eyes leaving no doubt that the brooch had once belonged to a man of great worth. Turning back to her, he held out his hand, the pin winking at her from his palm, an offering he hoped she'd accept.

She came closer, touching the brooch with a finger. "It is very fine, and valuable. Surely you are not giving this to me?" She looked up at him, her eyes asking more than her words. "Where did you find it?"

"Nowhere. It was offered to me in exchange for coin, many years ago, in a dockside tavern near Glasgow." Sorley spoke true, his heart clenching on the memory. "The man was a Highland clansman, a MacKenzie who'd fallen on rough days. He claimed the brooch was once owned by his people's greatest chieftain, Duncan MacKenzie, the Black Stag of Kintail.

"I'd heard of him. He's a legend, after all." Sorley took her hand, placing the brooch on her palm and closing her fingers over its beauty. "Some say the Black Stag lives still, that he guards Kintail to this day, invincible as the glory that clings to his name. Whatever the truth, it is known the pin now belongs to me. Keep it and take it with you to your Knocking Tower. If e'er you need me once we've parted, send the brooch back to me and I'll come to your aid."

"You are generous." She was peering at the brooch, sounding oddly disappointed, as if she'd expected him to say something else. "But I cannot accept your gift."

"Aye, you can and must." Sorley was firm. He didn't tell her why he also wanted her to have the piece: that, as he now knew, he had blood ties to the great Clan MacKenzie and its half-mythic chieftain.

He would rest easier in his bed of a night once she left Stirling if he knew such a meaningful part of him had gone away with her.

He wasn't a man of poetic sentiment.

But he did want her to have a means to reach him.

There was also another reason...

"You must wear the brooch in the hall on the morrow's eve." If she didn't, he would pin it on her himself. "I've heard your father will be off to the Red Lion by midday. If that is so, the brooch will let me know the path is clear for our plan. Anyone who sees the pin will know it was a gift from me. Sir John, too, will notice. He'll believe my seduction of you is real."

Sorley hoped that would be the way of it.

If not, Sinclair would learn just what a bastard he could be.

Mirabelle tilted her head, watching him closely. "You've thought of everything."

Clearly, he had no idea that he'd seduced her many years before. In this very castle, in the same great hall, his dark good looks and swagger catching her eye, his roguish smile and bold spirit winning her heart so completely no other man could ever hope to claim her affection.

She was his, then and now.

Yet he didn't even guess.

"So that is why you are here." She finished dressing, as calmly as she could, and brushed at her skirts. "I thought perhaps it was because of Little Heart. I know you rescued him." She glanced at the kitten, now rolling about on the floor rushes. "I meant to find you in the morning to thank you. I'll never forget that, not all my days. It was so good of you. But I never thought you'd appear in my bedchamber"— she glanced at the secret door, once again hidden behind the tapestry—"arriving by a hidden passageway I knew nothing about."

"Few people do. Some friends and I played in the passage as lads." He went to the tapestry, picked up a bulky leather sack and brought it to her, setting it at her feet. "These are goods for the kitten. Things William's aunt and the folk in the castle kitchens said you'd need for him."

"Supplies for Little Heart?" She looked at the sack and felt her face softening, the most wondrous warmth spreading through her.

Sorley shifted, looking uncomfortable. "Aye, well. The wee bugger deserved a good start with you. I could tell you wanted him badly."

Mirabelle raised her head, meeting his gaze. "You could've brought this later. Little Heart is fine, as you can see. He's not even limping anymore." She scooped up the kitten, holding him to her breast. "I think knowing he's now safe and loved made the hurt go away. I couldn't find any injuries. I looked and— "

"He had a thorn in a hind paw."

Mirabelle glanced at the kitten, then at him. "You removed it?"

"I did." Sorley lifted his hands, showing her the backs of them. He also rolled up his sleeve, revealing a few livid red welts. "The mite didn't understand I meant to help him."

"Oh, Sorley!" She set down the kitten and rushed over to Sorley. She wrapped her arms around his neck, leaning up on her toes to kiss his cheek. "Thank you so much!"

"Humph." He disentangled himself and began unpacking the kitten sack, lifting out the food, bowls, and a water flask. Next came a cushion and a soft, worn plaid, cut down to kitten size, plus the other odd bits. He glanced at her, flashing a smile. "Berengaria and everyone else swore the kitten would require suchlike."

He shrugged as he set a wooden crate and bag of what could only be river sand on the rushes. "I was told this would be most handy, especially as you'd surely be keeping the kitten in your room until your return to Knocking."

Mirabelle looked at him, her heart clenching that he could mention her departure so casually.

"O-o-oh! How thoughtful." She spoke as lightly as she could and nudged the crate with her toe. "I'd not have considered such a thing." She clasped her hands before her as she comprehended the crate-and-sand's use.

It was clear Sorley wasn't at all bothered by her imminent return to her hills.

Like as not, he couldn't wait for her to leave, was counting the hours, glad to be rid of the nuisance she surely was to him.

The thought ripped her in two.

She couldn't say for sure, but she'd swear the already dim light in the chamber darkened. That the wind's howl suddenly sounded more thin, hollow as the emptiness she could feel opening inside her.

It was colder, too. The chill, damp air so biting she doubted all the covers in the castle would warm her when she slipped into her bed.

Gooseflesh rose on her arms, but she refused to rub it away. Just as she fought hard not to shiver. And why should she? For the ice wasn't born of the dark, storm-chased night. It came from within her, deepening and worsening the more Sorley busied himself with the kitten goods.

The longer he failed to see past her eyes and into her heart.

"William Wyldes's aunt gave me this." He was setting a braided wicker basket on a chair, showing her how the wooden lid could be securely tied into place.

Mirabelle scarce noticed.

He remained oblivious. "She said it'd be useful for securing the kitten when traveling."

"It's perfect." She joined him by the chair and examined the basket. "You know much of my doings. It is true, my father's work here is almost done. When he returns from the Red Lion and his last look at the moss slates on the inn's roof, he wishes us to be away to Knocking."

She watched him carefully, hoping to see his brow furrow or some change of expression. But nothing altered. He simply looked sure and strong, a big, strapping man she wanted so badly that even now her heart was leaping, just standing so near to him.

Did he not care for her at all?

Surely he must, for he'd rescued Little Heart to please her.

In truth, she'd heard he always looked after the vulnerable and needy, man or beast. Saving a kitten was likely just that, an act of compassion he would've performed for anyone upset about the kitten's plight.

Mirabelle glanced behind her to where Little Heart now slept before the hearth fire. On his back, he'd stretched his little legs to the ceiling, looking so dear that she melted. She turned to Sorley, emotions of an entirely different sort making her bold.

"You could have brought me these goods another time." She lifted her chin, challenging him. "Can it be"—she flipped back her hair, held his gaze—"you had another reason? For coming now, so late in the night?"

She tightened her fingers around the bronze MacKenzie brooch, hoping he'd admit that more than a wish to protect her had spurred him to give her such a gift.

But he only reached out and stroked her arm, his gaze lighting on her lips and then dropping to where her breasts pressed against the thin linen of her night-robe. When he again met her eyes, his own once more held the roguish charm that she found so irresistible.

"I could stand here until all eternity's morrows dawned and faded and ne'er list all the things that would make a man seek your door, my lady." He caught her hand, the one holding his brooch, and gave it a squeeze. "Indeed, Berengaria told me cats are swift. She worried that Little Heart might dart out, disappearing, when you opened the door."

"I see." Mirabelle tamped down her disappointment.

His words, while flattering, could've been made to any halfway fetching female.

She'd hoped he'd open his heart to her.

She wouldn't embarrass herself by baring her own.

So she kept her chin raised, her back straight. "It was good of you to help me with Little Heart. And"—she uncurled her fingers, glanced down at his brooch—"I shall wear this pin proudly, and gladly make use of your offer of protection if ever the need arises."

"Then all is well, my lady. I'll no' be here long after our meeting in the hall." His features were hard now, revealing little. "I have urgent matters calling me away."

"You're leaving Stirling?" Mirabelle blinked, stunned. "So soon?"

"Aye, mayhap I'll go tomorrow e'en, after we've parted." He went to the hidden door, turning back at the concealing tapestry, already distancing himself from her. "I cannae say how long I'll be away. But you'll be fine. Sinclair willnae even glance at you once he's seen us together in the great hall."

"But I thought..." Mirabelle bit her lip and glanced aside. The kitten was yowling at her feet, batting her skirts for attention. "It might have been useful for us to be seen together after tomorrow night. Strolling the castle gardens, enjoying the rise of the moon from the battlements, or—"

"Such are pastimes for lovers, my lady." His words ripped her heart.

She scooped up her kitten, holding him to her breast. "I know, but—"

"I dinnae ken that word, my sweet." He touched two fingers to her lips, silencing her. "Be in the hall at the gloaming hour tomorrow e'en and we'll settle the matter troubling you. Thereafter..."

He lifted the edge of the wall hanging and opened the secret door. "I will wish you a good life, Lady Mirabelle."

"And I you," she offered, her tone as cool as she could make it. "May you meet much success on your journey."

"That I shall, for I will be repaying a much overdue debt." He stepped into the dark passage, his eyes glinting in the shadows. "I ride north with Grim Mackintosh. His reason for seeking me was astonishing. He came to fetch me to meet my long-lost father."

Mirabelle stared at him, feeling the words like a physical jolt. She forgot all else, a wave of happiness for him washing through her. "But that is wonderful. What a joyous reunion you will have—"

"I shall see you in the hall on the morrow, lass." He gave her a slight bow, ignoring her words, not looking at all glad-hearted about his father.

Her own brow crimping, Mirabelle started to ask him who the man was, but Sorley was already descending the spiral steps of the hidden stairwell, disappearing into the deepness of the shadows.

He was gone, and she already felt his absence as if they'd parted forever.

Chapter Sixteen

✤

Early the next morning, Sorley approached Stirling Castle's scriptorium, sacred haven for the King's scribes, bards, and other learned men. Claiming nearly the whole top floor of one of the main stronghold's highest towers, the King's much-prized library was a lofty, airy place. Even here in the corridor, the pleasant whisper of clean, cold wind slipped through tall, narrow window slits, and shafts of sunlight slanted into the passage, turning the whitewashed walls and well-swept floor a bright shade of gold.

Sorley scarce noticed, for his mind was on something much more sacred than the King's collection of ancient tomes and parchment scrolls.

If he knew he was the last man who'd make Mirabelle a suitable husband, an equal truth was that he'd damn well ensure her safety. No matter what Highland dotard chieftain someday gained her as a wife.

That, he would do for her.

So he quickened his pace through the sunlit corridor, sending a silent prayer to his gods that he'd find her sire,

Munro MacLaren, hard at his transcribing work in the King's scroll-filled sanctuary.

One more curve of the passage, and he'd be there.

Then he was.

Two royal spearmen guarded the scriptorium's door, but they made no effort to halt Sorley's approach. Indeed, one of them nodded infinitesimally and stepped aside at once, freeing the way for Sorley's entry.

"Did you hear the wolves howling near the castle walls earlier this morn, Hawk?" The man greeted Sorley in Fenris code, his presence not surprising Sorley at all, for men of the secret brotherhood were well able to blend unnoticed in any group, even the King's guard. "Could be the beasts will breach our walls one of these days."

"That would be a sight never forgotten." Sorley returned the man's nod, giving him the coded alert that no word should be spoken of his visit to the scriptorium.

The fellow Fenris's eyes acknowledged the message, then the man reached to open the door for Sorley, both guardsmen stepping back to allow Sorley to cross the sanctuary's threshold. They closed the door quietly behind him.

For a beat, Sorley was near blinded by the light within the vast, many-windowed chamber. Rows of tall, stone-edged arches cut deep into the walls allowed the sun to flood the room. Just across from the door, the largest window of them all framed the same sweeping view of the distant Highland hills that Sorley drank in from the battlements every morning. Those ever-longed-for peaks reared before him in all their sun-washed glory, their magnificence slamming into him like an iron fist, piercing his soul, squeezing his heart.

Mirabelle rose before him, too, his mind's eye seeing her astride a fast-running horse, galloping toward those blue-misted hills, her lustrous, flame-bright hair streaming out behind her, each muscle-packed bound of her steed's racing hooves carrying her away from him.

At the thought, an unreasonable fury swept him and he blinked hard, forcing his eyes to adjust to the room's dazzling brightness. Besides the many windows, candles burned everywhere, braziers cast additional light, and several bronze oil lamps hung on gold-painted chains from the room's high, raftered ceiling. Where the walls weren't covered with shelves of countless scrolls and precious books, every spare inch was colorfully painted in gleaming blue and shining gold, the brilliance scarce to be believed.

Unfortunately, the scriptorium appeared empty.

Leastways of occupants.

Or so Sorley thought until he strode deeper into the oversized room, into the crowded maze of scroll-and-parchment-cluttered tables.

Munro MacLaren perched on a stool before one of the tables, his slight form hunched over a scroll, his quill scratching noisily across the unfurled parchment. An ancient-looking tome was propped open before him, clearly the much-revered book on healing that he'd been called to Stirling to transcribe from the Gaelic into English for the King.

Bernard of Gordon's invaluable *Lilium Medicinae*, penned over a century ago.

Only such a treasure would keep Mirabelle's scholarly father from noticing Sorley walk right up to where he sat scribbling so industriously.

Sorley couldn't imagine a man having such a fascination with books and healing.

He had other interests.

So he placed both hands flat on the table and leaned in, knowing a direct approach was the only way to break the older man's focus.

"Knocking," he used the laird's proper title, "I'd have some words with you."

"I am busy with words now." Munro MacLaren glanced

up with obvious irritation. "Orders were given that I'm no' to be disturbed." Looking right back down at his work, he began scribbling again. "By anyone, and the command was given by the King."

"Was it now?" Sorley reached across the table and plucked the quill from Munro's ink-stained fingers. "Be that as it may, I'll still be having your ear."

"Who are you?" Munro snatched back his quill, his scholarly-pale cheeks reddening. "There be two guards outside, how did you pass them?"

Sorley straightened and hitched a hip on the edge of the table, folding his arms. "Could be they are my friends. Or"—he stretched out the word—"they ken better than to stand in my way when I wish to speak with someone."

"Are you a MacKenzie?" Munro was glaring at him from beneath beetling brows, just now noting the MacKenzie plaid Sorley wore with such pride, especially since learning his mother was of that race.

"I am called Sorley the Hawk," Sorley answered, as coolly as MacLaren's voice was agitated. "If you paid more heed to the folk moving about this court, you might have heard tell of me," he added, not surprised Mirabelle's bookish sire didn't know him. For the same reason, he'd be unaware of Sir John's perfidious nature.

"But you gleaned rightly, I have ties to the MacKenzies." Sorley hadn't planned on making the claim, but the words left his tongue as if he'd said them often, feeling so right, a wash of pride swelled within him. "My mother, rest her soul, was a Kintail woman."

"And your father?" Munro narrowed his eyes at him, his question underscoring the Highlanders' obsession with blood and lineage. "Surely he didnae go by the name of 'the Hawk'?"

"My father is Archibald MacNab." Sorley struggled to keep the distaste from his voice. "I'm his by-blow."

"Are you now?" MacLaren looked at him with new interest, some of the suspicion fading from his face.

To Sorley's surprise, he waved a hand at the bread, cheese, and ale at the far end of the table. "A son is a son is a son, lad," he said, wriggling his inky fingers at the refreshments. "Help yourself to a bite or a nip of ale, and tell me what's so important you'd disturb my work."

Sorley ignored his hospitality. "That's a sentiment I wouldn't have expected from you, a Highland chieftain. Some might say a bastard is what he is, born on the wrong side of the bed linens."

"Aye, well..." Munro glanced at his ink-smeared fingers, picked up a cloth, and rubbed at the worst of the stains. "Could be that's true. But"—he looked up swiftly, his blue gaze measuring—"once a man's been a bit seasoned by life, he kens what truly matters, laddie. Blood is blood, where'er its wellspring."

"You are generous." Sorley returned the older man's gaze, sure the aging chieftain didn't recall once sending his largest, meanest guardsman after a cheeky lad with too much swagger and not enough sense.

Or he meant what he'd said and was too tactful to own to the truth.

Highlanders were known to bend their words in favor of politeness.

Not that it mattered either way.

Sorley reached for the offered ale jug and poured out two cups, sliding one in MacLaren's direction. The other he lifted in silent salute, draining his measure in one long gulp.

"To the MacNab, then. My errant sire." He set down his empty cup with a clack and drew the back of his hand over his mouth. Only he knew he was trying to wipe the taste of the name off his lips.

Munro's gaze was piercing, thoughtful. "Archie is an old friend and ally. I saw him last Christmastide, at his yearly

Yule feast, though he didnae mention any bastard son that I can recall."

"He wouldn't have done." Sorley saw no reason not to speak true. "He doesn't know I exist."

"Ach, well! That changes everything." Munro slapped the table, stirring his parchments. "You should journey to Duncreag Castle and make yourself known to him." He spoke lightly, as if such a feat were easy. "He'd rejoice to see you. He's an auld done man these days, could use a lift of heart."

"I'm no' here to speak of him." Sorley leaned across the table again, bracing himself on his arm. His plan to accompany Grim Mackintosh north and seek long overdue vengeance on his father was something best kept out of this discussion. He was here for matters of much greater importance. So he drew a deep breath and used his most earnest tone. "I'd warn you no' to allow Sir John Sinclair to ride with you to Knocking Tower, or to e'er let him visit you there. He is dangerous and no' to be trusted."

"Sir John?" Munro looked skeptical. "He has knowledge of the MacBeth healers. Spent time with them in their own domain, he did, the wildest corners of the Hebrides. He's offered to share their wisdom with me, herb lore and healing methods he observed during his stay with them." He glanced at the precious tome before him, the much-famed *Lilium Medicinae*, and then looked again at Sorley. "Such insight, straight from Scotland's most renowned healers, would be invaluable. Perhaps even more so than this book."

Sorley bit back a snort, not wanting to offend him. "If Sir John even dipped a toe in the great Sea of the Hebrides, the stars and the moon will fall from the sky. If he's ever met a MacBeth healer, all the heather in Scotland will pull up roots and run south to England.

"He is only telling you such tales to win your trust, to gain access to your hall." Sorley didn't warn him of the fiend's reason: to claim Mirabelle's hand. If he did, he'd have to disclose Sinclair's dark and bent nature, and doing so would surely cost the laird weeks, if not months and years, of sleepless nights, worrying for his daughter's safety.

A matter he meant to address.

It was enough for MacLaren to bar his door to Sir John.

Already, the older man looked discomfited. Blinking, he peered at Sorley, the candlelight revealing how watery his aged eyes were.

"Knocking is a fair place." Munro's brow pleated. "But I dinnae see why Sir John—"

"Would lie to you?" Sorley could name many reasons. But his mind raced for ones odious and believable enough without bringing Mirabelle into it. "He has great debts, difficulties deeper than even the King's knowledge." That much was true. "I've heard he's plotting to entertain you with false accounts of his supposed stay with the MacBeths and that while he has your attention, his men will gather in your grazing lands, stealing away your cattle and taking them to the great markets in Crieff and Falkirk. By the time you'd note their absence, the beasts would be sold." Sorley spun the tale as he went, not feeling guilty, for he knew Sinclair had committed even worse crimes. "No one would suspect him, because at the time of the cattle thievery, he was standing before your hearth fire, regaling you with his stories of the Macbeth healers."

"Bluidy hell—who would've thought it!" Munro looked scandalized. "To think I believed the fork-tongued, flat-footed scoundrel."

"You are not alone," Sorley sympathized. "Many at court favor the man, even King Robert. So you mustn't say aught of what I've told you."

"How do you ken suchlike?" Munro cocked a brow, a thread of doubt creeping back into his voice.

Sorley shrugged and glanced aside, letting the growing

silence weight the air, lending credence to what he didn't say aloud.

"Perhaps the same way I gained entry to this room even though two of the King's guards stand outside." Sorley used a meaningful tone, the closest he'd go to revealing his true position at court. "Some men aye see and hear more than others, my lord. Men who aren't noticed, as unseen as a bird in a tree or a dog scrounging in the floor rushes beneath a hall's high table."

"So you're a spy, then." Munro's gaze was sharp.

Sorley almost laughed, liking the man. "I am Sorley the Hawk, no more, no less."

"Humph." Munro didn't look appeased.

"Who or what I am doesnae matter. Only that you decline Sir John's petitions to ride north with you. And"—Sorley gave him a fierce look—"keep your gates closed to him if he should journey to Knocking on his own."

"So I will, aye then." Munro finally conceded. "Because you're Archie's lad. For sure, I was looking forward to hearing the MacBeths' secrets."

"You'd have been fed nonsense." Sorley was sure of it. "But I can offer you something true, and much more interesting, I vow."

Sorley reached beneath his plaid and withdrew a lambskin pouch, carefully untying its opening. As Munro looked on, he produced a cloth-wrapped stone root, a gift from Grim Mackintosh, and placed it on the table.

"This is a prize worthy of study," Sorley declared, whipping away the cloth with a flourish. "It is a fossilized tree root, now harder than stone and blessed with much strength and power, or so I was told by the man who gave it to me, a Mackintosh of Nought territory in the Glen of Many Legends."

He didn't mention the stone root's best-known use. Nor was it necessary, because Munro had slipped off his stool to lean over the stone root, his eyes a-gleam, his excitement clear.

"A stone root, you say?" He touched the length of polished black stone, awe in his voice. "I have heard of such wonders, but ne'er seen the like. Indeed, I doubted their existence." He straightened and looked at Sorley. "They are said to cure many ailments, even straighten the back of a soul bent by too much hardship and care. One need only place the stone root in a kettle of boiling water, then drink a cup when the stone broth has been steeped in the dark of a moonless night.

"I will surely recall other uses after pondering on it a while." He scratched his beard, his gaze again on the stone root. "I thank you for showing it to me."

"You may keep it, lord." Sorley felt generous.

The older man beamed at him, his happiness touching Sorley in a way he wasn't accustomed to feeling.

"I shall treasure it, I will." Munro's hands actually shook with reverence as he carefully rewrapped the stone root.

"Aye, well." Sorley nodded, stepping away from the table. "I'll no' keep you from your work any longer. I ken you'll be heading out to the Red Lion Inn later this day, then leaving these parts soon thereafter."

"So you are a spy, what?" Munro gave him another sharp, assessing glance, but this time the look was leavened with good humor.

"I am myself, lord, nothing more." Sorley strode to the door, not liking how his throat thickened, how the old chieftain's kindness tightened his chest. He paused on the threshold and looked back over his shoulder. "Remember my words about Sinclair. And"—he made a slight bow—"perhaps someday I will call at Knocking myself, take you with me to Nought and its famed Dreagan's Claw promontory where there are many such stone roots. For the now, I wish you well, lord." Sorley stepped from the scriptorium, closing the door before Munro MacLaren could respond to him.

Not that it mattered.

He'd seen the eagerness on the chieftain's face. More than that, he'd caught the admiration in Munro's watery blue eyes. His own misting unaccountably, he blinked hard and set his jaw, striding past the two guardsmen with only a gruff farewell. He'd been sure MacLaren would heed his warning about Sir John, but he hadn't expected to win the man's regard.

Above all, he hadn't thought doing so would affect him so powerfully.

A whirl of new and not necessarily welcome emotions swirling inside him, he made his way down the sun-bright corridor, grateful when he reached the dimness of the stair tower.

The night would bring an even greater test to his heart when he met with Mirabelle in the hall.

He was no longer certain he could do as he'd said.

He wanted more than a few kisses, neck nuzzles, ear nips, and nipple tweaks.

He wanted all of her.

And he strongly suspected he'd claim her, too. His restraint was gone, his good sense and every reason he shouldn't love her flown out the window.

The consequences be damned.

Much later, deep in the gloaming hours, Mirabelle made her way into Stirling Castle's great hall and took her accustomed seat at one of the honored tables on the dais. She hadn't seen Sorley since the night before, in her bedchamber. Nor did he appear to be anywhere near now. Sitting as straight as she could, nerves allowing, she lifted a hand to touch the stag-headed MacKenzie cloak brooch she'd pinned so hopefully to her gown's shoulder.

Now, more than ever, the pin held tremendous importance for her.

Wondering if her secret knowledge showed, she looked about, searching the crowd. The hall blazed with the light of roaring fires and countless torches. Chaos reigned throughout the vast, smoke-hazed space, the gaiety and noise at a fever pitch. A feast was in full swing, the long tables filled and the aisles between crowded with celebrants. In one corner, a harpist played and sang, her voice sad as she mourned ill-fated lovers and praised the lonely beauty of empty, heather-swept glens. Not far from her a piper strutted proudly, his jaunty tune at odds with the woman's heart-wrenching song.

In the center of the hall, in a cleared space, a troupe of jugglers performed, tossing burning staves high into the air and catching them again, much to the delight of the cheering onlookers.

The din rose and fell, made more deafening by the barks of the castle dogs. The beasts dashed everywhere, streaking beneath the tables, bounding through the aisles, ever hoping for fallen scraps and then fighting over the prize when a choice bone was found.

Her own treasure...

Mirabelle pressed her fingers more tightly to her stag-head brooch, her breath catching when she finally spotted Sorley in the throng. She stared, her heart swelling, awe sweeping her like a blaze.

She knew at once that something had changed.

If he had been bold and dashing before, now...

He was magnificent.

Still a good distance from her, he differed from all other men as if every candle, torch, and fire in the hall burned only to light his glory. He stood tall and broad-shouldered as always, his dark hair gleaming and the sword at his side—called Dragon-Breath, she knew—shining as if its steel had captured the light of the stars. Gold and silver rings banded his powerful upper arms and his sword-belt was slung low about his hips where it was clasped by a beautifully worked silver wolf's head. He wore the MacKenzie tartan with a bold, roguish flair, the blue and green weave vibrant beneath the torches. He didn't look anything like a bastard.

He looked as if he ruled the hall.

Apparently he also commanded her heart, because it was hammering so fiercely against her ribs, she was sure everyone present must hear its thunder.

Then his gaze locked onto hers and he started toward her, his stride purposeful and proud.

Mirabelle sat rigid, her blood rushing, her stare fixed on him as he neared the dais, not even needing to elbow his way through the crowd, because men and women alike leapt aside, clearing his path to her.

All around them, the hall was in an uproar, but she scarce noticed, seeing only Sorley.

She couldn't breathe.

Then he was right beside her, claiming the seat a noble relinquished with haste, nearly tripping over the long drape of the table linen as he jumped up and scrambled away, freeing the bench for Sorley.

He edged nearer at once, slinging his arm around her shoulders, his gaze intense, seeing no other. "Fair lady, your beauty shines brighter than any light in this hall." He lifted her hand, turning it to press a kiss to her palm and then nip the soft skin of her wrist before releasing her. "Nae, I err. You put the very sun to shame."

Mirabelle swallowed, moistened her lips. "You speak flattering words, sir." She forgot the carefully rehearsed lines she meant to say to him. Somehow his approach wasn't what she'd expected. "All know you favor the ladies and—"

He touched his fingers to her lips and shook his head. "There are no other women, lass. I see only you. Here in this hall and here"—he pressed a hand to his heart, his gaze burning into hers—"where it matters most. I speak but the truth, sweetness. Indeed"—he leaned in, nuzzled her neck, and lightly bit her earlobe—"I have ne'er in my life been more honest. No' with anyone, no' in all my days."

Mirabelle was stunned into silence.

She couldn't form words, for her fool throat was turning awfully hot and thick. And her wretched eyes were beginning to burn, a terrible stinging heat pricking madly at the backs of her lids.

This was not the deal they'd made.

Not how she'd expected him to ravish and scandalize her.

Though folk *were* staring, their heads craning and whispers made behind quickly raised hands. But no one seemed shocked or appalled. The men appeared amused and even encouraging, while the women just looked envious.

And—Mirabelle shivered—from the hall's darkest corner, Sir John Sinclair glared at them, fury glittering in his dark, hate-filled eyes.

"Ignore him." Sorley hushed the words against her ear, his lips doing sinfully wicked things to the sensitive flesh along the side of her neck. "I have taken measures to protect you from him. The rest will wait until we've enjoyed this evening together."

"I wasn't aware you saw it that way." Mirabelle regretted the words as soon as they left her tongue, but Sir John's stare unsettled her. Sorley's convincingly real attentiveness scattered her wits. "I thought you were eager to have done with our performance."

"You think I'm acting?" He pulled back, looked at her levelly.

Mirabelle forced a smile, more sure than ever that the wind had turned. She knew instinctively that it wouldn't ever swing round and blow the other way again. What she said next would seal her fate.

So she lifted her chin, meeting his bold gaze. "If you aren't, then admit who you now know you are. My father told me of your visit to him this morning. We are close, despite his preoccupation with herbs and healing." She took a breath, steeling her backbone. "Your father is Archibald MacNab, chieftain of Duncreag, and your late lady mother, God rest her soul, was a Kintail woman, belonging to the great Duncan MacKenzie's clan. He was known as the Black Stag of Kintail, hence your affection for this brooch."

She touched the pin, taking strength from its cool bronze, fastened so close to her heart.

"All that you know?" He lifted a brow, smiled at her.

He didn't look a whit surprised or uncomfortable.

"So you admit it?" She didn't blink, though his smile was causing the sweetest warmth to swirl low inside her, deep in her belly, low by her thighs.

"I'll tell you anything you wish to know, lady." He lifted his hands in surrender, turning them palm out.

"I'd hear the truth." Mirabelle felt a flush coloring her cheeks.

Folk were still staring at them, some even chuckling now, a few nudging elbows and leaning in, angling their ears to catch every word.

"Honest words might frighten you, my lady." Something in his tone warned that was so.

"I am a Highland lass, don't forget." Mirabelle sat up straighter, her heart racing again. "We do not scare easily. Indeed, some say not at all."

Sorley's smile deepened and he swept his arm around her again, this time pulling her onto his lap. "Then brace yourself, lassie, because the names of my parents are no' the most important truths here. That honor stands between the two of us only." Something flared in his eyes, an uncompromising intensity that made her pulse leap. "It has to do with our plan and why we're sitting here just now."

"We had an agreement." Mirabelle shifted on his lap, keenly aware of a certain hot ridge of hardness nudging the bottom of her thighs, burning her even through the layers of her skirts.

"Aye, we did." He took her face between his hands then, kissing her long and deep. When he pulled back, breaking the kiss, his eyes were darker than she'd ever seen them, and he was breathing hard. "I still have a plan, sweetness. And I hope I'll gain your agreement."

Mirabelle just looked at him, sure she hadn't heard rightly.

But she must've, because all along the table, and even elsewhere on the dais, people were grinning, looking on with rapt interest.

Mirabelle ignored them, but she did frown. "Our plan doesn't seem to have the effect I'd desired."

To her surprise, Sorley grabbed her to him again and kissed her even more hungrily than before. It was a wild and heated open-mouthed kiss, full of breath, tongue, and desire. He thrust his fingers into her hair as he ravished her lips, holding her firmly to him, giving her no choice but to return the kiss with equal fervor.

She did so gladly, feeling bereft when he finally tore his mouth from hers. She hadn't wanted their kiss to end, and the delicious tingles rippling through her left no doubt that she wanted more.

Sure he could tell, she met his gaze, thrilled and excited, but also worried that her heart and not her good sense was guiding her.

"That was indeed better." It was all she could think to say. "A most convincing display, certainly."

"Indeed." He leaned in and kissed the tip of her nose. "Though my purpose has changed, or have you no' heard anything I've said this e'en?"

Mirabelle blinked. "I don't understand."

"Then I shall make it clearer." He cupped her face, slanting his mouth over hers again, his tongue thrusting sure and possessively.

She melted beneath the onslaught, gripping his shoulders to keep from sliding off his lap. Then he pulled back, breaking the kiss as swiftly as he'd seized her. But he kept hold of her face, looked deep into her eyes. Clearly stirred, his chest rose and fell, heavily. His gaze wasn't just piercing, but blazing with something that made everything else around them fade to nothingness, as if they were alone in the hall, perhaps in all the world.

"This isnae a planned seduction, Mirabelle," he spoke her name as if it held gold. The rough softness of his tone weakened her knees.

The look on his face...

Her eyes started burning again just seeing the adoration there, and the other, more fierce expression that she didn't dare hope to decipher.

"No deliberate attempt to scandalize you." He leaned close to say that, lowering his voice so no one else would hear. "A man doesnae bring shame to the woman he loves."

"Oh!" Mirabelle jolted, the heat in her eyes spilling free, rolling down her face. She dashed at her eyes, swiped a hand across her cheek. "What are you saying?"

"Only what should be obvious, you precious minx." Sorley grinned, using the side of his calloused thumb to wipe away her tears, "I didnae come here tonight to cause a stir. I'm here to claim you."

Chapter Seventeen

❦

Sorley and Mirabelle approached her guest chamber just as muted laughter, and other highly suspicious noises, drifted into the corridor from the lavish confines of the nearby Rose Room. The sounds hinted that they weren't the only ones to have left the hall's feasting at its most lively, raucous hour. He glanced at Mirabelle beside him, aware that waiting any longer would've been impossible.

Hadn't he spent a lifetime yearning for her?

"Sweet lass, hear me well before we enter this room." He put all the love he felt for her into the endearment as he set his hand on her door latch. He didn't open it. "No one below will doubt that you are mine. Leastways, everyone in the hall now kens that I want you." He let his gaze flick to his MacKenzie stag's-head brooch, pinned so proudly to her gown. "Men have seen that my intentions are honorable and earnest. Even so, I will leave you here, to your night's rest, if you wish."

"You know what I want." She looked up at him, her lustrous hair spilling around her shoulders, gleaming in the light of a wall sconce. Her cheeks were flushed, Sorley hoped with pleasure and excitement. Her eyes sparkled like sapphires, lovelier than ever and filled with an emotion that humbled him, or would have if he weren't so damned proud to see it there.

"I'll not change my mind." Her voice was strong, clear. "Not this night, not ever." She touched his face, his beard. "This is about more than my asking you to ruin me for Sir John, it always has been."

"So I have hoped." Sorley still didn't open the door.

"I believe you know my feelings." She held his gaze, her courage as beguiling as her beauty. "I did not hide them in the hall, nor ever."

Sorley lifted a brow, almost reminding her that once, long ago, she had indeed done so.

Or so he'd come to believe.

Not that it mattered.

Past deeds might make someone who they were, even marking them, but what truly counted was the path stretching ahead, the tomorrows to come, and he meant to spend every one of his with the woman he loved.

"If I cross this threshold, there'll be no going back. No restraint." He gave her a final chance. "I will ravish you in there, as I have e'er dreamt of doing. Thoroughly, completely, and until we are both so replete, so sated, that we cannae move. Then we shall begin again."

"And I shall see my most fervent desire fulfilled." She placed her hand atop his on the latch, pressing down so they opened the door, together.

A fire burned low on the grate, casting the room in a rosy glow. Someone had lit a brazier in the corner, its small flame and warmth having drawn her kitten, who slept curled before it, the sight of the kitten's ease making Sorley more glad than ever that he'd fetched the wee creature. Mirabelle was watching the mite, the look on her face enough to send him out to rescue every poor cat in the land.

Indeed, he might—if she asked it of him.

He set a hand on her waist, turning her back to him, intending to kiss her, then remove her clothes, bit by bit, until everything she wore slid down her lush body and pooled on the floor around her feet.

As if she knew, she glanced at his hand, and then met his gaze, her beautiful eyes shimmering with happiness. With great care, almost reverence, she unclasped his brooch and moved away to place it on the table. The way she handled it, as if the pin was crafted not of somewhat-battered, age-worn bronze, but costliest jewels, did terrible things to a place deep inside his soul.

Indeed, if he'd ever known love could beset a man so roundly, he might never have crossed that crowded hall at her uncle's feast all those years ago. For truth, emotion rode him so hard, he could feel his eyes misting, so powerful were his feelings for her.

"Lass..." His voice was rough, his chest tight. "Come here, I would hold you, kiss you."

"More, I hope," she spoke boldly. "We have waited overlong, I think." She glanced at his brooch again, a smile playing about her lips. "I'd have you know that you won my heart years ago, at my uncle's celebration. It never mattered to me that you couldn't name your parents. I left you because my father's guard was a brutal man. A clan champion who, back then, would've loved nothing more than taking you out into the courtyard and—"

"I ken that, sweet." He did, the surety of it having come to him in recent days. He did know women, and Mirabelle's heart aye shone in her eyes. "Though I vow I would've put a few bruises on him, even then."

He flashed his best smile, striding toward her, not wanting to speak of that distant night. "He matters no more, my heart. Naught else is of importance, but that we—"

"Well..." She came to him and slid her arms around

his waist, leaning into him. "It is a grand thing that you've learned who your mother was, and that you'll meet your father when you ride north with Grim. I hope you'll take me with you." She lifted up on her toes and kissed him, lightly, expectantly. "That would be wonderful."

"You are wonderful, lass." He stepped back then, knowing she wouldn't like what he was about to say. Setting his hands on her shoulders, he spoke plainly. "I dinnae think you'd enjoy journeying with me. You wouldnae be pleased by what happens when I meet the man who sired me. I've waited long for the day, and there is much that must be said to him. My words willnae be kind." He stroked the curve of her cheek, using his knuckles to soften her frown. "There is no place in my world for a man who caused such grief, especially to my mother."

Mirabelle's chin came up. "He will be older now, and surely regrets the past. He'll want—"

"I want you." Pushing Archibald MacNab from his mind, Sorley's need for her raged. His blood heated, his restraint gone.

She surely sensed the change in him with a woman's sensual instinct, for she placed a hand to her breast as she watched him. The return of her smile, a tremulous, excited one, stirred him more than if she'd reached out and seized his aching hardness.

"You know I yearn for the same, for you, Sorley, only you." Her words sealed their future.

He'd never let her go. Not for her father, the King, or even a greater power.

"May I?" He flicked a glance at her gown, sharply aware that he'd never in his life asked a woman's permission to unclothe her.

Nor had he ever felt a need to prolong the pleasure, removing garments slowly, for the pure joy of savoring each new inch of bared skin.

He wanted to do more than savor Mirabelle.

He intended to worship her.

"You may do anything," she spoke softly, her acquiescence setting him like granite.

"Sweet lass, you dinnae ken what you do to me." He began untying her bodice laces, his need flaring even more when her breath caught and a tremor rippled through her. His fingers brushed the top swells of her breasts, their soft, smooth warmth making him mad for her. "I may no' last until I've undressed you."

"Then I should warn you that we'll be done here anon, for you shan't need long to do so." She smiled as he loosened the ties and her gown began to slide down, freeing her breasts, her hips. "I am naked beneath."

"By all the gods!" Sorley's entire body tightened, his pulse roaring, as the gown fell to her feet and she kicked it aside to stand fully unclothed and proud before him, her back straight, and the rest of her...

"You will be my end, lass." He could hardly speak, scarce heard his own words for the blood pounding at his ears. Other parts of him throbbed in a worse way, but he used all his strength to ignore the fire raging at his loins, the rampant desire that made the hard length of him strain against its confinement.

He gripped her chin, lifting her face to his, looking deep into her eyes. "Never have I desired another woman more than you, Mirabelle. I wanted you from the first moment I saw you, those many years ago. My need for you hasnae diminished in all that time. If anything, it's worsened, consuming me so that I hoped for nothing else than to someday claim you, to make you mine at last."

He thrust a hand into her hair, lifting it back from her face, twining the thick, glossy strands through his fingers. "I just ne'er thought the day would come, ne'er would've believed such a blessing."

"No, that is you, Sorley." She held his gaze, the truth ringing in her words making his heart thunder.

Sure no gift under the heavens could be greater, he scooped up her gown and draped it over a chair. When he turned back to her, she hadn't moved, made no attempt to conceal her nakedness.

How glorious she was!

He let his gaze glide over her, appreciatively. He looked his fill, loving the smooth sleekness of her skin, almost rosy in the firelight. She stood perfectly still, proud and beautiful. Her wild flame-bright curls were delightfully tousled, temptingly framing her lovely face and shoulders, a skein of wonder tumbling to her hips. Other curls, of a deeper bronze, beckoned at the top of her shapely thighs. She was graced with the most exquisite breasts he'd ever seen. Full, round, and creamy, their lushness made his jaw clench and his manhood burn even hotter.

When her already-pert nipples tightened beneath his gaze, he could withhold himself no more.

"You are more beautiful even than I imagined." He swept an arm around her, pulling her to him. He touched his free hand to her shoulder, brushed back her hair. "I would ravish you, lass. I must."

"Then do," she urged, her eyes darkening as she slid her arms around him, holding fast to his sword-belt as if she'll fall otherwise.

Sorley needed no further encouragement. "I would kiss every inch of you," he vowed, cupping her breast, kneading and squeezing her ripe curves, loving how responsively her nipples pebbled beneath his palm. His need blazing, he lowered his head and captured one of them with his lips, drawing deep, circling the puckered tip with his tongue. He licked and suckled, again and again until he could feel her melting against him.

She gasped and swayed, as if her knees buckled. He

tightened his arm about her waist, still suckling her, swirling his tongue around and over her luscious nipple.

"Dear saints." Mirabelle clung to him, gripping his belt as she stared at his dark head, his shining black hair swinging across his plaid-draped shoulder as he kissed and licked her breasts.

Sensations spiraled inside her, racing everywhere like rivers of tingling, molten fire. The secret place between her thighs pulsed and warmed, feeling heavy and aching, deliciously. Never had she felt such unrestrained bliss, need and desire so intense that she bit down on her lip, so hard she almost tasted blood.

Sorley pulled back, his gaze locking on hers as he smoothed his hand down from her breasts, across her belly, and then right between her legs. He cupped her there, the firm pressure of his palm against her hot and needy female flesh almost too wondrous to bear.

"What are you doing?" She knew, but even daring as she believed herself, she couldn't put words to how his questing fingers stroked her so intimately, rubbing her oh-so-gently. How could such a light touch make her feel as if she would shatter any moment?

"Such a caress is only the beginning." He drew one finger along the center of her slick, swollen flesh, his gaze wicked, burning. "The pleasure will spike when I do this..." He let the promise hang in the air, touching the tip of his finger to a tiny, highly sensitive spot, circling with slow deliberation, driving her wild.

She gasped, half frustrated, straining toward something she could feel spinning to a brilliant, dazzling conclusion, while the other half of her hoped the whirl of heady sensation wouldn't stop.

"Open to me, let me see all of you." His voice was rough and deep, the purpose of his words sending another floodtide of lush, languid heat streaming across her most womanly place.

"Spread your legs, wider. Let me see more, so lovely are you." He knelt before her, steadying her by placing his hands on her hips. "That's my lass..." He coaxed her, his finger still circling, the slow, sensual rubbing good beyond anything she'd ever felt. She started rocking her hips, running her fingers through his hair, pushing herself against his bliss-spending hand. "More, lass, I cannae see enough."

"I vow you can." She glanced aside, sure she was about to hurtle over a glittering, looming precipice. Liquid tingles, hot and urgent, pooled at her core, delicious quivers rippling all through her, the pleasure searing. "You are seeing more of me than anyone ever has."

"Nor shall any other man enjoy such a privilege," he returned, his stroking fingers more insistent now, skilled and possessive. "Only a bit wider, sweet, for ease..."

Mirabelle dug her hand in his hair and felt her world dipping, spinning away from her.

"Open to me," he urged again, using the edge of his thumb to circle her now, his other fingers teasing the soft skin of her inner thighs.

"Aye, just so," he sounded pleased when she did as he bid.

She stood with her legs parted, too swept away by desire to feel shame at the intimacies bared to him, his breath even warming her there.

"Oh!" She looked down again, sure he wouldn't put his mouth on her.

He was watching her, his roguish smile, the hunger in his eyes, chasing the last shred of her modesty. "Dinnae refuse me this pleasure, lass." His breath tickled her again, stirring her intimate curls. "You are tastier than any delicacy at the King's most lavishly spread table. I could feast on you for hours, even days, and still want more. So ravenous am I for you." Proving it, he leaned forward and dragged his mouth across her belly, nuzzled his face against her damp curls, inhaling as he did. "Your scent sets me afire. So rich, so good..."

Mirabelle shivered at the provocative appreciation in his low, deep voice. Flames of her own licked across her skin, melting her inside.

Then he did what she'd known he would, kissing her there where she burned the hottest, tingled so maddeningly. He opened his mouth over her, licking her most lasciviously. And still, he circled the pad of his thumb over that one spot that seemed the center of all pleasure.

Her heart raced, everything in her tightening as he kissed and licked her, ravishing her indeed. He looked up at her as he did so, his dark eyes gleaming in the firelight. His gaze held passion and want, raw desire that made what he was doing to her an even headier delight.

Or so she thought until he replaced his circling thumb with his tongue, flicking its tip back and forth over her tingling, pulsing flesh, the tiny nub that quivered with such intense sensation it was unbearable.

"Relax." He slid a hand behind her, splaying his fingers across the curve of her bottom, holding her steady. "Let me give you this, show you how much I want you."

"You are." She couldn't say more. She was breathless, falling into an abyss, the room darkening as his tongue lashed at her, licking the length of her, swirling over that one maddening spot.

Then he stopped there, taking that place into his mouth, drawing on her, gently. She cried out, her entire body trembling with her release, the unexpected rush of such intense, all-consuming bliss.

Sensation swept her, endless waves of dizzying pleasure. She felt her hips arching, knew she was pushing herself against him. As if from a great distance, she heard a sound, almost a deep, dark growl, purely masculine. It was hard to tell because she was melting into him, disappearing as surely as morning sun banishes mist.

As she floated, she was vaguely aware of him scooping

her into his arms and carrying her across the room, where he lowered her carefully onto the bed. Half sure she was dreaming, she opened her eyes to see him standing a few feet away, undoing the shoulder clasp that held his plaid.

He was looking right at her, his gaze dark and fierce.

Mirabelle's heart started pounding again, her blood heating anew. As long as she could remember, or so it seemed, she'd dreamed of this moment. Seeing Sorley before her now, his magnificence limned by the firelight, so much passion and love on his face, was almost more than she could bear. She trembled, her breath quickening as he pulled off his plaid and let it fall to the floor. His shirt followed, disappearing in an eye-blink. His eagerness to be naked with her excited her so much that the hot tingling between her thighs returned, the sensations almost overpowering. She shifted on the bed, so in love, so impatient to be in his arms. She burned for him to make her his at last, in all ways.

"I dinnae do this lightly, lass." He set his hand on the wolf's-head buckle of his sword-belt. "You ken I have ne'er lain with a virgin, ne'er despoiled a highborn lady." He unhooked his belt, threw it aside, coming forward to stand right before the bed's edge.

"I'm no' ruining a lady now either." He shoved down his hose, stepped out of them. "I am claiming you, Mirabelle. I am taking what is mine and what I've wanted for so long. There is no shame, no scandal in what we are about to do. You shall be my bride, my lady wife for the rest of our days. All that is happening now is that I'm about to show you how much I love and desire you, as I have always done."

"Oh, Sorley, you know I lost my heart to you that long-ago night." Mirabelle pressed a hand to her mouth, unable to say more. Her throat was too thick, her joy too great. She opened her arms to him, awed to see how ready he was to do as he'd vowed.

His darkly wicked smile alone curled her toes.

His big, strong body, now fully naked and so near to her, stole her breath. His skin gleamed, the soft glow of the fire playing over his hard-muscled form. She saw the scars he'd taken in battle. Her heart squeezed to see them. She meant to caress and kiss each one, erasing the hurt they must've caused. She also ached to touch the dusting of his dark chest hair, to trail her fingers over such pure male glory, trace the arrowing line of that crisp hair straight to where his long, thick manhood strained so proud against his abdomen, his desire apparent.

Mirabelle drew a breath, so pleased that he stood there, bold and glorious, letting her look her fill of him. She'd never tire of gazing on him, so heady was the sight of his raw male beauty.

"Enough, lass. It's no' easy to stand here, you studying me as you are." His words, the implication behind them, sent a new barrage of tingles sweeping across her most tender flesh. "For truth, I'd rather look at you," he said, the roughness of his voice exciting her even more. Reaching down, he eased her thighs apart, his eyes darkening as he gazed at her. He stepped closer, trailed his fingers over her damp curls. "Ne'er have I been more roused."

"O-o-oh..." She leaned back against the pillows, barely breathing as another floodtide of delicious shivers raced across the soft, sensitive place he stroked so expertly.

"Sweet lass, sweet precious lass." He cupped her hard, squeezing. "You dinnae ken what you do to me, but I'm about to show you."

Then, with the same speed with which he'd removed his clothes, he was on the bed, stretched out beside her. He pulled her into his arms, holding her tight against him as he slanted his mouth over hers, kissing her deeply. It was a hard, rough kiss, full of breath and tongue, and so savage that her entire body quivered. She returned the kiss with equal fervor, twining her arms around his shoulders, gripping tight as he plundered her lips, the sensations so intense, so pleasurable, she didn't want him to ever stop.

She cupped the back of his neck, clutching him to her, melting into his kiss. But he tore his lips from hers and caught her hand, bringing it to his mouth. He nipped the flesh beneath her thumb, and then kissed her wrist before he raised her arm, stretching it over her head.

"My heart," he hushed the endearment against her shoulder, pressed his lips there as he rolled on top of her. He reached down between them, guiding the hard, hot length of him to her entrance. "I'd no' hurt you for the world."

"You won't—only if you do not claim me now." Mirabelle grasped his face with both hands, turning him to her for more kisses.

He obliged, sealing his mouth over hers in a hungry, open-mouthed kiss, the glory of it proving again that she could never live without such pleasure, without him.

Then all thought vanished when she felt him tense and begin pushing his maleness slowly, carefully inside her. She kissed him more deeply, swirling her tongue round and over his, savoring the intimacy, not minding the hot, tight, pinching sensations clenching at her center. The pressure did hurt, but it was also thrilling. A union with the man she'd loved and wanted since girlhood.

"My love..." She thrust her fingers into his hair, holding him tight, kissing and kissing him as he eased ever deeper into her, claiming her innocence, her heart, body, and soul, granting her heart's desire.

"You are mine." He pulled back, breaking their kiss to push up on his arms and look down at her, his expression almost feral.

"Only yours." Mirabelle held his gaze as he pressed deeper, now fully inside her, riding her. She soared, wrapping her legs about his hips, needing, craving the closeness of being one with him.

"My precious lass." He tipped back his head, staring up at the rafters, the cords of muscle in his arms and neck straining, his jaw clenched. "My sweet Mirabelle..."

Then he stilled, a great shudder passing through him as he jerked and called out her name, a flood of heat filling her as he released his seed.

"Sorley..." Mirabelle lay perfectly still, half afraid to move, not knowing what to do.

She felt awed, humbled, and blessed to have brought him such intense pleasure.

"You unman me, sweet." He eased off her, drawing her gently into his arms, nestling her head against his shoulder. "I should have lasted longer, but"—he slid his hand between her damp thighs, his thumb once again finding that wondrous knot of sensation he'd rubbed before. He began circling the spot now, slowly and gently, his touch so light that it could've been a butterfly wing.

"Just lie still, let me pleasure you." He kissed the top of her head, his circling thumb rubbing round and round. Melting her until, as before, the waves of bliss washed over her, rushing her into that dark, glittering place where nothing existed except the ecstasy he gave her.

She closed her eyes, felt herself falling as the room spun away and all she heard was the thunder of her blood in her ears, the beating of her heart.

And, though she couldn't quite be sure of this, Sorley's softly muttered praise. Thanks for all she'd given him.

Of course, she saw it differently.

And the more she came back to her senses, the more she knew that was so. Words of love and endearment weren't all he'd said as he'd made her his.

Taking a deep breath, she opened her eyes, still too drained to slip from the bed. She did note that Sorley had done so. He stood across the room, at the small table that held her water jug and wash basin, pouring water, delightfully at

ease in his nakedness. Indeed, she enjoyed the view of his
strong back, his legs and buttocks, so much that she almost
wished he wouldn't turn around. But she needed to clarify
something, so she scrambled up against the cushions and
pulled a pillow before her.

Not to hide herself, but because the hearth fire had
dwindled to little more than a flickering red glow of ash,
and the night's chill was biting now, the room's cold raising
gooseflesh on her bared skin.

"Sorley..." Her voice was hoarse, her lips tender from
their kisses. "Did I truly hear you say you wish to marry me?
I didn't think—"

"That I'm the marrying sort?" He turned, striding toward
her with the basin and a few linen cloths clutched in his hand.
His manhood hung loose and free, relaxed now, yet still so
beautiful to behold that another faint wash of tingles rippled
across the still-throbbing flesh between her legs. "That I am
no', as anyone will tell you. In truth,"—he stopped before
her, setting the bowl and cloths on the night table—"you
couldnae land a worse husband, there's no denying. But
no man will ever love or want you more." He dipped one
of cloths into the basin, wringing it out before he planted a
firm hand on her belly, holding her still as he slid the linen
between her legs, wiping the blood smears from her thighs,
her aching female flesh.

Mirabelle felt herself flushing at his ministrations, but...

They also roused her—that he would tend her so intimately, his gaze on that exposed part of her, thrilling and
exciting her. It made her want him to claim her again.
First with his bliss-spending fingers and mouth, then—she
shivered—once more with all of him, again and again.

She bit her lip and glanced aside, wondering if she wasn't
the one unsuited for marriage.

Surely she'd turned wanton?

"You are a prize any man would give his soul to claim,

Mirabelle." He parted her thighs a bit more, rubbing her with the cloth. "So beautiful, so responsive, so proud and true, courageous. You are caring." He glanced at the corner brazier where Little Heart slept contentedly. "So many good things that I'd need the whole of our lives to count them all."

"You do not think I am brazen?" There, she'd said the word aloud.

"You are perfect." He tossed aside the damp cloth and reached for a dry one, dabbing her gently. "I wouldnae want you any other way.

"I am the one no' bent for marriage." He didn't sound as if he objected, though. "We'll just have to think on where to wed, where to live, how to shape our lives. We'll manage. I should warn you that I have a stubborn streak. I am no' dissuaded by difficulties or challenges. Indeed, I aye find a way to master the first and welcome the second.

"The King will surely want us to marry here, at Stirling." He finished drying her and dropped the linen to the floor. Sitting beside her on the bed, he pulled her against him. "William will ne'er speak to me again if we dinnae hold a wedding celebration at the Red Lion. Your father, once I have spoken to him, may wish for a further feasting at Knocking."

"My father..." Mirabelle felt a pang of doubt, tamping it down before Sorley noticed. "He has always wished me to settle in the Highlands. He is eager for grandchildren and—"

"He shall have them, and plenty." Sorley took her face between his hands, kissing her deeply. "I will purchase or build a small tower house somewhere between here and your beloved Knocking Tower."

"Such a site would be near to your father's Duncreag." Mirabelle touched his cheek, not liking how his expression hardened on her suggestion. "I know Archibald. He is a good man, old and cranky at times, but—"

"I will deal with him in my own time, lass." He gripped her wrist, lowering her hand. "First, I'll postpone my journey north with Grim Mackintosh. That can wait. I've other, more important matters to attend. For the now, I will leave you be." He stood and began gathering his clothes off the floor, dressing as quickly as he'd disrobed. "You'll need a good night's rest and I'll no' have folk wagging their tongues if a servant should enter and find me naked in your bed."

She wanted him to stay. "But I'd rather—"

"I told you once, sweet..." He came back to the bed, leaned down, and dropped a quick kiss to her brow. "I dinnae use the word 'but.' "

Already clothed, he stepped back and slung his sword-belt low about his hips. The flame of the night candle caught the jeweled eyes of the belt's wolf's-head buckle, making them gleam as if the beast lived.

Mirabelle shivered, rubbing her arms against the chill that swept her. "What of the Fenris? Will you not be missed if you leave Stirling?" She surprised herself by mentioning the secret brotherhood.

But the wolf's-head buckle brought the myth to mind.

The way Sorley's gaze sharpened on her was even more telling.

She scooted from the bed, went over to him and gripped his arms, challenging. "I know the name hails from Fenris the Wolf in Norse mythology. He was a troublemaker, the son of Loki the trickster."

"Aye, and Thor shoots thunderbolts at every man who displeases him." Sorley broke free of her grasp and wrapped his arms around her, drawing her close. He stroked her hair and smoothed his hand down her back, cupping her buttocks. "The Fenris are a legend, love. If I was one, I'd be oath-bound no' to speak of them."

"You wear a wolf's-head belt buckle." She lifted her chin, met his gaze. "I have never seen it on you before this night. There must be a reason."

"There is." He squeezed her bottom, and then slid his

hand beneath her, between her thighs, lightly teasing her intimate curls. "I like the buckle. It was a gift from the King's
brother, Alexander Stewart, the Wolf of Badenoch. Truth is I
wore it to impress you. It is a fine piece of workmanship." He
glanced down, his gaze on the wolf's head. When he looked
back up at her, his face was serious. "This, too, I will tell you.
Listen hard for I'll no' say the like again. I'll aye protect you
as fiercely as a Fenris would guard his lady."

He took her face between his hands, something in his
eyes almost frightening her. "Woe be to any man who'd dare
try to harm you. Or when they come, our children. I'd follow
such a fiend to the ends of this earth for vengeance, even into
the coldest pit of hell."

"I know you would." She did, she'd always known.

"If aught should e'er happen to me, send the buckle to
the earl." He released her and strode to the door, where he
turned back, fixing her with a level gaze. "Alex will then
set guardsmen to watch o'er you for life. That, sweet lass, I
promise you. Remember it always, for that truth is the reason
I wore the wolf buckle. To make sure you're aye safe." He
cracked the door, glanced left and right down the corridor
before opening it wider. "I will come for you in late morning. By then, I will have made plans for us."

"Can you not stay…" Mirabelle let the words tail off, for
he'd stepped into the passage, closing the door behind him.

She hurried across the room, opening the door again
and peering out, but he was already gone. She couldn't even
hear his retreating footsteps, which shouldn't surprise her.
Wouldn't a Fenris be able to disappear swiftly and silently
into the shadows?

She was sure that was so.

Just as she was certain he'd done exactly what he'd sworn
never to do. He might not have broken an oath verbally, but
he had let her know the truth.

He'd done so because he loved her.

His trust only made her love him more.

Her heart swelling, she returned to her bed, smoothed the rumpled coverlets. As she did so, a hint of sandalwood and pure male musk rose to tease and tantalize her. She closed her eyes for a moment, inhaling deeply. Images of everything they'd done together swirled across her mind, exciting her so much she wondered if she'd catch fire.

Shivers of delight rippled through her.

She just hoped her heart was big enough to hold her happiness.

That she'd be able to wait until he returned for her the next morning. It seemed like ages away, and she already thrummed with anticipation.

Chapter Eighteen

✤

Sometime in the small hours the next morning, Mirabelle sat up in her bed, knowing something was wrong. She just didn't know what had wakened her, pulling her from a deep slumber. Sorley had been right, she'd needed the rest. Even now, she felt dazed from their lovemaking. Sated and sweetly replete, though a lingering soreness did throb between her legs. But that slight discomfort wasn't what had disrupted her sleep. It was much less tangible, an inner knowing. The kind of sensation Highlanders thought of as a "stirring in the air," even when not a breath of wind blew.

She pushed back her hair, glancing about, seeing nothing unusual. Sorley's sandalwood scent still clung to the bedsheets, as did a trace of heady masculine musk. His powerful physical presence had also left a mark on the chamber, branding it so soundly, she could almost imagine him standing before her now, bold and gloriously naked, ready to pull her into his arms and ravish her awake.

Regrettably, he wasn't here.

It was much too early for him to come calling for her.

Not the grayest sliver of light crept through the shutter

slats, though across the room, peat ash still glowed in the hearth. All was still and quiet, even the corner brazier no longer burning. The few furnishings in the chamber stood out black against the softer gray of the night shadows.

The room was also bitterly cold.

Settling back onto her side, Mirabelle started to pull the covers over her shoulders, deciding it was the chill that had disturbed her, when she realized the truth.

Little Heart was gone.

He'd slept curled into the crook of her neck, his wee head resting on her shoulder. His soft, sweet warmth, tiny and light as he was, had soothed her, helping her drift into her dreams after Sorley left. She'd felt the steady rise and fall of his breaths, heard his gentle snores. She'd appreciated the comfort of his nearness.

Now he wasn't there.

Blessedly, he couldn't have gone far.

Like as not, he'd hopped off the bed to visit the crate and its layer of river sand, thoughtfully recommended by William Wyldes's aunt, Berengaria, and delivered by Sorley, his kindness to her kitten touching her deeply. She waited for the now-familiar *scratching* to alert her that Little Heart was again ready to join her on the bed.

The sound didn't come.

Indeed, she didn't hear him at all. That was strange. He'd taken a fierce liking to her, never leaving her side except when he slept before the brazier. Already feeling at home with her, he purred, trilled, or hopped about like a flea when he wasn't snuggled against her. There was none of that now.

Worry niggled at her, dread creeping in as the stillness lengthened.

"Little Heart!" She sat up again, this time flinging back the covers and swinging her legs over the edge of the high mattress. "Little Heart, where are you?"

She looked about, straining to see in the dark as she slid

off the bed, the rushes cold and prickly on the bare soles of
her feet.

Naked, for she always slept so, she wrapped her arms
around her waist for warmth and hurried about, searching for her precious wee kitten. Her mouth went dry and
her heart raced in alarm. She feared he'd slipped out and
couldn't bear if something had happened to him.

It was then, as her eyes grew accustomed to the shadows,
that she noticed his new braided wicker travel basket was
missing.

She frowned, turning in a circle, searching to see if she'd
put it somewhere else, in a place she'd forgotten.

But she hadn't.

The basket wasn't in her room, and that meant . . .

"Oh, Little Heart!" She dashed from corner to corner,
hoping she was mistaken. Dropping to her knees beside
the bed, she lifted the heavy dressings and peered into the
blackness beneath the four-poster. "Where are you, my
sweet one?" She didn't see anything, only gloom. Nothing
stirred. "Did Sorley come back and take you away?"

She couldn't imagine he would, not when he'd promised
to fetch her later that morning. For sure, he'd been good
to Little Heart, but she also knew he wasn't overly fond of
him.

Yet the kitten and his basket couldn't have vanished into
thin air.

Mirabelle pressed a hand to her cheek and drew a long
shuddering breath, terrible heat stinging the backs of her
eyes, thickening her throat.

Little Heart couldn't be missing.

She'd already given her heart to him.

"The bastard doesn't have him, fair lady." Sir John's
deep, smooth voice sent chills all through her. "That questionable honor falls to me. If you wish to see your pet again,
you won't scream."

Mirabelle spun around, fury replacing her fear. "Where is he?" She grabbed her night-robe off the bed, throwing it around herself as she ran at him. She grasped the front of his cloak, fisting her hands in the costly folds. "What have you done with him? Give him back now, at once!"

With ease, Sir John grasped her wrists and lowered her arms. "Are you aware, my lovely spitfire, that you are almost unclothed?"

"Did you know you're a greater bastard than one whose birth made him that way?" She glared at him, thankful to know her night-robe was thick enough to shield her from his lecherous gaze.

"How dare you enter my room, take what is mine!" She stood straight, her shoulders squared. She wouldn't give him the satisfaction of showing fear. "If it's coin you seek, I have coffers of silver. You can have as much as you wish, just give back my kitten."

"You know what I desire, Lady Mirabelle." He didn't release her arms, keeping them pinned to her sides. "Likewise, you're surely aware that I am no longer interested in your bride money or lands."

She raised her chin, narrowed her eyes. "Where is Little Heart?"

"He's in his basket outside the door, hidden in the shadow of a wall niche. No harm will come to him if you do as I say. Be warned"—he leaned in, his eyes cold and unblinking—"if he brings a single flea to my fair Dunraine, I shall crush him beneath my boot. A worse fate will then befall you." He straightened, his hooded gaze drifting over her. "But not until I've tired of you. Seeing you now, in all your fury, I vow that won't be for a very long time. I enjoy a spirited woman. The lash of their fire is invigorating, breaking them a welcome challenge. Of course, then I lose interest. Would that displease you?" He curled his lip, mocking her.

Mirabelle let her distaste burn in her eyes.

Her blood was turning to ice. "You wouldn't dare attempt to take us from here."

"I dare anything I please." He glanced at the door she'd forgotten to bar after Sorley left her, his voice smooth as he turned back to her. "Doesn't my presence here prove that? If you doubt me, you won't when we reach Dunraine."

"You're mad." Mirabelle's chest tightened, her breath starting to come in short gasps. She tried to remain calm, to think.

"So some say." A dark smile spread over his face. His eyes were soulless. "You can decide at Dunraine."

Mirabelle shivered. She didn't know of such a holding, but she'd heard whispers that Sir John held a distant keep, half in ruin, where he took women to lock away and use until he wearied of them. Once that happened, they disappeared, never to be heard from again.

He was said to deny the keep's existence, and its nefarious purpose.

She knew from his tone that Dunraine was this nightmare place. She also knew he wouldn't mention it unless he saw her as no threat.

That meant...

"You plan to kill me." She could feel herself paling, the blood draining from her face.

"Not for a while, perhaps never, if you can hold my attention that long." He jerked his pointy-bearded chin at her clothes. They were draped over the room's one chair. He also glanced at her cloak, hanging from a peg on the wall. He released her, giving her a shove. "Dress, and quickly, for I have men and horses ready."

"Men, or snakes?" Mirabelle used her iciest tone as she hurried into her gown, pulling it on while keeping her night-robe wrapped about her. She also struggled to pin Sorley's MacKenzie brooch on the inside of her gown, which wasn't an easy task. She wasn't going anywhere without it and he'd surely snatch it if he saw.

"They are guards, my lady." He went to the door, leaning against the jamb, his arms crossed as he waited for her to dress. "Even one such as I has stalwarts. Trusted men and skilled fighters, they will circle back and cut down your hawkish bastard should he be smitten enough to follow us, hoping to rescue you."

"He wouldn't bother. He doesn't care that much for any woman, all know it." She gave him her haughtiest look. "It won't matter to him what you do with me. You err." She hoped he'd believe her.

He laughed, proving he didn't.

"He would eat you with a spoon, and all of you." He strolled over to her and gripped her arm as soon as she swirled her cloak around her shoulders. Then he pulled her to the door. "He would slay his own King if Robert glanced sideways at you. I saw how he looked at you in the hall. He was all over you, kissing you, pulling you onto his lap." His gaze swept her, disdainfully this time. "Everyone present saw him take you abovestairs, knew what then happened."

"You're obsessed." Mirabelle forced down her fear. She didn't like the glint in his eye, was becoming sure he was mad, completely crazed.

"Nae, I am doing you a service." He inclined his head slightly, as if he expected thanks. "You shan't be soiled by a lesser man, but honored by the skilled and vaunted touch of a noble. I shall keep you not as my wife, but as one of my Dunraine mistresses. It's a much more fitting role, wouldn't you say?"

Mirabelle felt bile rising to choke her.

Before it could, she drew herself up to her full height. "I'd sooner lie with a toad."

"So you did." He looked at her squarely. "I have spared you further soiling."

"Pah!" Mirabelle's temper was swelling. "You are soured because you've been hounding my father, pressing him to agree—"

"Ahhh…That was then, Lady Mirabelle, and is no more. I'm no longer desirous of your hand." He shook his head in seeming regret. "Even so, you're too fetching to suffer the taint of a nameless bastard whose ambitions and pride are greater than his station."

"Do you speak of yourself, my lord?"

"See you? Even your wit amuses me."

"A dagger passed between your ribs won't." Mirabelle stood as straight as she could and put back her shoulders. "Surely you haven't forgotten my warning?"

"You are not wearing a lady's dirk now." The corner of his mouth twisted up again. "I watched you dress, or have you already forgotten?"

She glared at him. "There will be knives at Dunraine. I will find one. You will never know when it's hidden in the folds of my skirts."

He shrugged. "Then I shall observe you all the more closely. It will be an especial pleasure."

"My pleasure," Mirabelle muttered as he opened her door.

"It could be once you adjust to life at Dunraine. There are other ladies to keep you company. Although…" He shrugged again, looking amused. "Some of the Dunraine women are quite witless, poor creatures. I can't imagine what drove them to such a state."

His grip on her elbow like iron, he peered left and right down the dimly lit corridor.

"Come now," he hissed, pulling her from the room. "We'll fetch your kitten and be on our way. Just remember what I told you. One cry or an attempt to run, and Little Heart will meet the sole of my boot."

He jerked her to a stop beside a shadowed niche in the

wall, reaching in to retrieve Little Heart's basket. He thrust it at her, then dusted his hands as if the braided wicker had soiled his skin.

"Little Heart..." Mirabelle hugged the basket to her chest, relief sluicing her when she felt the kitten shifting about inside. Hearing her voice, he yowled and thrust a paw through a gap in the weaving.

"Be still. Keep him quiet." Sir John gave her a warning look. "I meant what I said, especially about him. Doubt me at your peril."

She didn't.

She believed every word.

Before the first glimmer of sunrise even touched the eastern hills, Sorley stood at his favorite spot on the battlements. The morning air was cold and wet, smelling of damp stone and the rich, black earth of the vales and woodland stretching away from the castle. The view he most loved. The rolling hills and distant Highlands couldn't be seen, everything in that direction lost in heavy mist.

Still, he braced his hands on a merlon and stared hard into the whirling gray, imagining himself riding north to meet the father he'd never known.

A man he didn't wish to know now.

So why could he so easily see himself on such a journey?

He did, the notion even making his throat constrict with emotion, not because somewhere in that distant land of cloud and mist, Archibald MacNab waited, his father by blood if nothing else. Nor were his thoughts born of knowing that even farther north than MacNab's Duncreag Castle stretched the wilds of Clan MacKenzie's Kintail, home of his late mother and where, likewise, his forebears had walked, breathed, loved, and died amongst the hills and heather.

His heart beat strongly at thinking of such a journey, because Mirabelle would ride beside him. They'd go together, as man and wife. And even though he was chilled by the damp wind, that knowledge warmed him to his soul, filling him with such gladness he could feel the strength of that wonder beating all through him.

She mattered more than his lifelong plan to avenge himself on the old chieftain, returning the hurts of ages. He now had other wishes, more important considerations than striding into MacNab's windblown and rocky home for the sheer pleasure of shunning him.

The hills in the distance, always such a beacon, now represented Mirabelle.

Not his wish for vengeance.

Soon, he and Mirabelle would be wed. It was a truth that upended and changed his world, but one that also filled him with pride, triumph, and love such as he'd never known. Someday, their children would walk those distant hills, playing, laughing, and growing strong there. For their sake, and Mirabelle's, he'd make his peace with Archibald MacNab, if grudgingly and without any feeling of kinship on his part. Mirabelle apparently liked the man, and their bairns deserved to know their grandsire, to enjoy their birthright that was Duncreag Castle.

So he stared out across the familiar countryside, looking in that direction, blinking against the steely glint of the Forth as the river began to catch the first light of the day.

A small party of horsemen followed the river's course, cloaked and hooded men racing along the foreshore, the rider in the lead carrying something in front him, draped like a bundled sack across his galloping steed.

Frowning, Sorley narrowed his eyes, lifting a hand to his brow to see against the rising sun.

Fury swept him, swift and boundless.

The *bundle* before the rider was a woman, held facedown by her captor.

He was sure she was Mirabelle.

"Saints, Maria, and Joseph!" He ran along the wall, his heart thundering, the edges of his vision turning red as he stared at the hard-riding party.

If the woman's streaming, burnished red hair, shining like a balefire in the morning light, didn't prove she was Mirabelle, then the familiar wicker basket tied to the horse's saddle horn did.

There could be no doubt.

Mirabelle and Little Heart had been taken.

And he knew their captor.

Sir John had seized her. There was only one place he'd take her: Dunraine, in its deep, dark wood of no return, where the only living females were either servants to his twisted lusts or full crazed from having endured them.

"By the gods!" Sorley raced for the tower stair, hurtling down the winding steps.

He burst into the hall, tearing down the center aisle, dodging tray-laden servants and leaping over sleeping men and castle dogs. When he gained the bailey, he made for the stables, shouting to the first sleepy-eyed, stumbling stable-lad he saw.

"Lyall!" He grabbed the lad, shaking him to wakefulness. "A horse, saddled now! The best and fastest you have, a destrier or charger!"

Lyall blinked, rubbing his eyes. "I don't know…" He frowned. "You ne'er ride such—"

"I'll ride a damned lightning bolt to hell and back!" He gave the lad a shove into the stables, keeping on his heels. "Make haste, then find Munro MacLaren. He should be at the Red Lion. See he's told that his daughter's been taken," he ordered as Lyall hurried a spirited charger out of a stall, quickly saddling the beast. "Alert the King, his guards. Riders have her, heading along the river." Sorley swung up into the saddle, keeping Sinclair's name to himself. He'd have done with the bastard singlehandedly,

making sure he never again had the chance to hurt Mirabelle, or any woman.

He grabbed his steed's reins, vaguely aware of Maili
emerging from the shadows in the back of the stables.

"Sorley! What's happened?" She started toward him,
looking confused, mussed, and just as sleepy as Lyall.

Sorley waved her back and kneed the horse so that the
powerful beast surged forward in a great burst of speed,
almost flying away from the stables and out across the open
countryside, tearing up the earth as Sorley spurred him ever
faster toward the river and the woods beyond.

"Sinclair!" He roared the fiend's name again and again
as the charger splashed along the river's foreshore and then
pounded into the trees, low branches from the thick-growing
pines slapping against him. He scarce noticed, only urged on
the speeding horse.

"Mirabelle!" He shouted for her even louder, lifting his
voice above the roar of his blood in his ears.

No one answered him.

And the only thundering hooves he heard were those of
his own horse.

They plunged on, deeper into the forest, man and beast
as one. Mist swirled everywhere, the trees a rushing blur of
darkness against the gray. Half-sure the devil had given him
wings, Sorley crouched low over the horse's neck, determined
to pursue Sinclair to the ends of the earth, farther if need be.

Then the mists thinned and he saw he had, as a deep
chasm opened before him.

"Hell's fire!" He hauled on the reins even as his horse
reared and swerved away from the yawning abyss. Sorley
would've sent the beast pounding along the gorge's length,
seeking a way around it, but there was no need.

He'd found what he wanted.

Sinclair and his men were riding out of the trees, surrounding him on three sides.

Mirabelle was still with them, slung facedown over Sir John's horse, her head turned away from him, which was a good thing.

If she saw him now, his rage would surely terrify her. He could feel fury rising, his jaw clenching so tightly, his muscle tensing with such anger, he'd swear he was turning to cold, deadly steel.

"You're a dead man, Sinclair." He drew Dragon-Breath, couching her like a jousting lance. He rode forward slowly, keeping his gaze on his foe. "Release Lady Mirabelle and the kitten or I'll run you through, skewering your belly, pinching out your life."

"Sorley!" Mirabelle's cry was muffled. "I knew you'd come!"

"As did I." Sir John sneered at him, reached to clamp his hand over Mirabelle's mouth, silencing her. "Now you, you soiled vixen, will watch him die.

"It is your life that's forfeit, *Hawk*," he spoke Sorley's by-name like a slur. "Or will you fight me and six well-armed men? There's no escape." He glanced at his companions, sitting their horses in a ring around Sorley. River mist swirled everywhere again and a thick layer of pine needles slicked the ground. Where the six mounted warriors didn't block the way, the dense trees and mist did the rest, making a fast run for it impossible.

"So it appears," Sorley agreed, hedging for time, his mind racing.

Sinclair didn't have to know that he never took anything on appearance.

Even so, he cast another glance over his shoulder at the chasm behind him. His assessment was confirmed; the bottomless-looking abyss was a death pit, for him and the valiant charger.

One false step and...

Doom.

Even if he could reach Sinclair, maim or kill him in passing, and pluck Mirabelle and Little Heart off Sinclair's then-riderless horse, there'd be nowhere to go.

He could fight two men, even three, and walk away without a scratch. He'd done so enough times. Taking on six, though he would, wasn't a promising option.

Still, he had no other choice.

So he edged closer to Sinclair's horse. He went slowly, leaning forward to stroke his charger's neck, pretending ease, possibly surrender. If the gods were with him, only he knew that in a moment either he or his foe would die in a fast, bloody clash.

"Mirabelle..." Sorley caught her eye and inclined his head infinitesimally, letting his gaze flick to her left. "The reel, lass," he looked back at her, holding her gaze. "The night of your uncle's celebration, the feast when we met. Where was I, after you left?"

He'd been alone, surrounded by a ring of gawkers, but on his own, apart from the rest.

That's where he needed Mirabelle now.

He hoped she understood. She couldn't answer because of Sinclair's cruel grip on her jaw, his foul fingers pressed over her mouth.

But her eyes lifted his spirit, for even now she looked more angry than afraid. He also saw love on her face, her silent message that if all went horribly wrong, she'd given him her heart, gladly.

As she held his—and now he meant to save her, and would.

His gaze locked on her, he inched closer, Dragon-Breath's hilt already singing in his hand, craving blood. He kept urging the charger forward, nudging him to take a few more steps, slow and easy.

Sinclair looked amused, his sword ready, the blade gleaming brightly in the mist.

His men sat still, watching. Only two of them drew their steel.

"Mirabelle," Sorley said again, inching even closer. "Remember the reel."

He willed her to respond.

She did, twisting round to bite Sinclair's arm before she flung herself to the ground. She rolled to a stop only to spring to her feet, spin about, and snatch Little Heart's basket off the saddle horn.

She sped into the woods, clutching Little Heart's basket and running faster than Sorley would've believed a woman could move.

"You whore!" Sir John roared after her, rising in his saddle.

"Those were your last words," Sorley snarled, the fury in his voice echoing as he kicked back his heels, sending his horse charging forward. He let the beast hurtle on, leveling his sword like a spear, striking the noble before he could finish his cry, plunging Dragon-Breath right through him. Slewing the horse round, Sorley grabbed the blade and pulled it free, not waiting to watch Sinclair crash to the ground. The rush of blood and gore from his belly left no doubt of his death.

Yelling protest, Sinclair's men surged forward, their swords drawn and slashing. Sorley galloped straight at them, arcing left and right with Dragon-Breath. He caught the first man to reach him with a fast slice across the back of the guard's neck, almost severing it. Clearly dead, the man slid from the saddle as his horse bolted into the trees.

"Come, you worms!" Sorley let the charger rise and toss his great head, cleaving the air with his huge, iron-clad hooves. "Prove what it takes to steal a helpless woman. I challenge you to show me!"

"You'll rot for cutting down a lord," taunted a big, heavy-muscled man. He circled Sorley, coming closer with each pass.

"I define a man of worth differently." Sorley cut the air with his sword, the blade gleaming red in the mist. "Fight for thon miscreant"—he flicked a glance at Sinclair's body—"and your guts can join his. The price for your loyalty." On the words, Sorley lunged, sweeping Dragon-Breath in a lightning-fast blow that would've sliced the man in two if he hadn't veered away with equal speed.

"No man has ever cut me," he taunted, wheeling his beast back at Sorley, his sword raised again. "Yield now and I'll make your end swift."

"I cannae, for my blade is too thirsty." Sorley swung again, so fast that Dragon-Breath's steel was a blur of silver and red before it grazed the giant's shoulder, breaking his record and sending spray of blood fountaining in the air.

The big man bellowed and stood in his stirrups, taking a mighty swing, his blade hissing past Sorley's ear, missing him by a hair.

They clashed again and again until Sorley drew back his sword, sweeping it round for a scything blow to his opponent's midsection. Just as the blade struck, a spear pierced the man's shoulder and his eyes rolled back in his head, his sword slipping from his fingers as he toppled to the ground.

At that, two of his companions fled, galloping off the way they'd come, racing through the trees, heading for the river.

Two yet remained and they still looked bloodthirsty, their swords held high. Sorley flashed a glance at the trees, hoping to see who'd thrown the long spear so well. He knew only one man who could.

William Wyldes.

Then the warrior-innkeeper was there, bursting through the trees. He held a second spear couched at the ready, his red hair unbound and flying behind him, his face murderous.

"I had a time of it catching up with you," he shouted to Sorley. "Glad you left me some o' the work!"

Spurring his horse, the innkeeper made swift slaughter of the man who'd turned to challenge him.

"You haven't lost your skill," Sorley called after him as he raced off again, seemingly to follow the two riders who'd escaped into the woods.

It was then that Sorley caught the clashing of two swords coming from the edge of the ravine. He glanced round to see Grim, in full Vikingish war gear, parrying his opponent's sword swipes not with a blade, but with a huge Viking war ax. Grim clearly didn't need help, so Sorley swung down from his saddle and thrust his own sword into the earth, resting his hands on the hilt as he watched the Nought man fight with Sinclair's henchman.

Then, as if weary of circling round with the swordsman, Grim raised his great Norse ax and with one swift downward slash nearly cleaved the man in two.

"Ne'er did care for swords," he called to Sorley as he pulled his ax free from the deep gash in the dead man's shoulder. He wiped the ax-head on the slain man's tunic and then strode over to Sorley, clapping him on the back. "I knew there was another reason I felt a need to come down here. Fate, we say at Nought, is inexorable, my friend.

"No' that you needed the help." Grim stepped back, looking around. "Or perhaps you do? Thon spear-throwing innkeeper"—he jerked his bearded chin in the direction William had disappeared in—"will surely be back anon, bloodied from putting the other two out of their misery. We spoke on the way here and thought, as your usual friends are away, he and I might be of assistance clearing up this fine wood for you. Unless you'd rather we go looking for your lady instead, and bring her back to her father?" Grim cocked a brow, waiting. "That might be best, eh?"

"Try and you'll have a fight with me, my friend." Sorley glanced at the trees, hoping to see Mirabelle returning.

But the woods were empty, quiet now, though the mist was thinning.

It was then that William returned, grinning ear to ear. "Sakes, lads!" He swung down from his horse, his spears notably missing. "That was a fine day's work."

He strolled up to them, taking a leather-wrapped flask from his sword-belt. "It's been a while since I've had cause to wield a long spear. I'd forgotten how much I enjoy a good fight."

"Did Sinclair's two men feel the same?" Sorley knew the answer.

Wyldes winked and handed him the uisge beatha. "They felt the wrath of my spears, they did." He looked pleased as Sorley took a swig of the fiery spirits, then passed the flask to Grim. "Just now, they're enjoying a swim down the Forth. By nightfall they'll be fish fodder."

"Aye, well, that's two less to be rid of." Sorley glanced at the others, not wanting Mirabelle to see the carnage if she returned before he could find her.

"Sorry, lads..." Sorley never let others do work he should do himself, but he couldn't stay a moment longer. "I have to find Mirabelle. A word, before I go..." He jerked his chin toward the slain men, the ravine behind them. "Sinclair has a family, and a good one, save for him. I'll speak to the King myself, and the Wolf. Otherwise, I'd have no one learn of what happened here.

"Or"—this galled him, but felt right—"of Sinclair's other transgressions."

Grim and Wyldes exchanged glances.

Grim spoke first. "We of Nought are well used to ridding the land of pests, leaving no trace to mar the beauty of our glen." He rested his ax-head on the ground and settled his hands at the top of the long hilt. "If you ken what I mean?"

"I do, and I thank you." Sorley meant more than riding up to join a fight.

"Aye, well." Grim nodded. "Then I'll see you at first light on the morrow?"

"Nae, you willnae." Sorley shifted in his saddle, eager to be away. "I've other, more urgent matters to address, though"—he reached down and gripped Grim's shoulder—"I'll make the journey when I can."

At that, William grinned. "I was thinking he'd say that.

"If you're wondering how Grim and I came to be here, you can thank Maili." He winked. "She's a lass of many talents, she is! Ne'er have I seen a woman ride into the inn's stableyard at such breakneck speed and with such a flourish. Looked like a fury, I tell you."

He chuckled, glanced at Grim, who also smiled.

"That she did." Grim shook his head and touched his Thor's hammer. "Though I'd have likened her to a Valkyrie. Be glad she was at the castle stables when you ran down there. She said the lad—Lyall?—fell asleep again as soon as you rode away."

"She was at the stables because I'd sent her there," William put in. "One of the stable dogs has a new litter and I'd asked Maili to pick out a whelp for the Red Lion."

William leaned in, affection in his tone. "She's a sensitive lass and would be offended if you thought she'd have aught to do with Lyall."

"I ne'er did." Sorley wasn't about to admit otherwise.

"Och, one other thing." William grinned. "Your lady is waiting deeper in the wood, in the clearing where the two burns come together.

"I gave her a plaid and some oatcakes and cheese, two good-sized flasks of my best Rhenish wine." He winked, glancing at Grim. "Should the like be needed."

"You're a good man." Sorley grinned, picked up the reins.

Then he lifted a hand in salute, spurred his horse, and galloped away.

Not toward the river and the castle beyond, but deeper into the wood.

Mirabelle was waiting there.

And once he reached her, he wasn't ever going to let her from his sight again.

Chapter Nineteen

❧

If Mirabelle thought she'd been filled with happiness when Sorley made love to her, admitting his feelings for her, the joy inside her nearly burst her heart when he galloped out of the trees and into the clearing where she'd waited for him, fear and worry nearly maddening her.

"You remembered the reel, lass," he called to her even as he reined in, leaping down from his saddle. "Praise all the gods for your wit."

"I thank them for you." She pushed to her feet, running to him, her arms spread wide. Relief and exultation swept her, her heart beating hard against her ribs.

"I am the lucky one." He strode toward her, his own arms outstretched, his smile flashing so broadly, so triumphantly, that she almost melted there and then.

She stopped where she was, pressing her fingers to her lips. She stood in the middle of the grass-grown clearing, just staring at him, the love and hunger for her on his handsome face so wondrous she could scarce breathe. Her pulse raced, her emotions whirling. She didn't know what she'd have done if he hadn't come for her. For sure, she wouldn't have been able to live without him. Overcome, she was also sure he'd never looked more magnificent.

His MacKenzie plaid was still flung proudly across one shoulder, but it was mussed and bore the stains of battle, of shed blood. But not his, she thanked the gods, aware he wouldn't be coming at her so boldly, so powerfully strong, if he'd been injured. His sword was sheathed at his hip, the leather-wrapped hilt likewise dark with remnants of a hard fight, won. As if the gods indeed were smiling on him, the mist was thinning and cold autumn sun spilled across him, gilding him like a pagan Celtic god of old. His hair swung loose about his shoulders, the morning light giving the rich raven strands a gloss of ebony-blue.

Mirabelle's heart fluttered. "I feared for you, worried—"

"You had only to wait." He was almost upon her, his smile gone now, replaced by an expression so fierce, so possessively claiming, that her soul soared. "Think you I'd let a coward like Sinclair keep me from making you my bride at last?"

"Oh, Sorley..." Mirabelle blinked, her entirely body quivering.

Then he reached her, grabbing her to him so swiftly she only knew that, of a sudden, she was crushed against his chest, his arms like iron around her as he slanted his mouth over hers, kissing her hard and fast. It was a bold, devouring kiss, savage in its ferocity, and so thrilling she could only cling to him, returning his hunger with equal fervor.

"Ne'er forget this day." He tore his lips from hers, took her face between his hands. "No man, nothing under the heavens, will keep me from you, Mirabelle. So long as I live and breathe, no one will e'er harm you." He pulled her closer, kissing her again, long and deep.

"You were outnumbered." Her voice was shaky, emotion thickening her throat as she pulled back. "Sir John had men—"

"Did you no' hear a word I said?" He set his hands on her shoulders and looked down at her. "The true mark of a man is no' how many stalwarts ride under his banner, carrying their swords and spears into battle with him, but when he will fight against the odds, accepting any outcome, because he's doing what he kens is right. I would gather every stone in Scotland and toss each one into the sea if you asked it of me, lass." He touched her cheek, lit his knuckles along her jaw. "I'd draw my sword on the Horned One himself to protect you. Though..." He stepped back, taking her hand and tugging her along with him to the plaid by the two burns where she'd waited for him. "As you saw, my friends did ride in to stand with me."

"William didn't seem too worried." Mirabelle remembered her relief to see the big-bearded innkeeper thunder up to her in the wood, leaning down with one strong arm to snatch her onto his saddle as he stormed past.

She glanced at Sorley as they neared the spread tartan, quickly telling him of his friend's rescue. "He said he was riding back to you 'for the joy of a good fight, not because you needed an extra sword.'"

"Aye, Wyldes would say the like." Sorley stopped before the plaid, glanced down to where Little Heart slept on his back in the middle of the tartan, his wee legs sticking up in the air. "I'd no' speak of him just now, or thon Grim Mackintosh who accompanied him. I've other matters on my mind." He bent to scoop up her kitten in one big hand, holding Little Heart against his chest as he used his other hand to unclasp the brooch at his plaid's shoulder.

Striding a few paces away, he dropped to one knee and swirled his plaid across the grass at the edge of one of the burns where wild thyme and orchids swayed in the chill autumn breeze. Lowering the kitten onto his new bed, he stood and dusted his hands, a wicked smile curving his lips as he strolled back to her.

"I'd no' crush the wee bugger if I rolled on him when I'm kissing you." He winked, glanced at her kitten before taking her in his arms again. "But first"—he reached for the small leather pouch that hung from his sword-belt, untying its string to retrieve his bronze stag's-head brooch—"I'll return this to you. It must've fallen when you ran into the trees." He took her hand, placing the MacKenzie pin on her palm, then closing her hand around it. "I'll have the clasp fixed. It must be broken."

"The clasp is fine." Mirabelle tightened her fingers over the beloved brooch. "I dropped it on purpose, hoping you'd find it and know the way I'd gone." She looked down, carefully fastening the pin to her cloak. "Should anything have happened to William and he hadn't been able to tell you where I was."

To her surprise, Sorley threw back his head and laughed. It was a deep, rich sound, its masculine warmth delighting her, melting her to the core.

"William was ne'er in danger." He pulled her down onto the plaid with him, drew her onto his lap. "I swear he's invincible. Or mayhap the gods think he's too full of himself to allow him to die and enter the Otherworld. You ought to know"—he touched a finger to the stag's-head brooch, his eyes darkening as he held her gaze—"I would find you if you were trapped on the far side of the sea, lass. I wouldn't have needed the pin to track you. All I'd have done was to follow my heart."

"Will you tell me what happened?" She didn't really want to know, but felt she must.

"Later, sweet, then I will recount every detail of the fight if you so desire." He smoothed her hair back off her face and dropped a kiss to her brow. "For now, it's enough that you know Sir John is no more, and neither are his men. None of them will threaten you again, nor any woman."

"I would like to hear..." Mirabelle glanced aside, glad

for the clearing's beauty. Its splendor chased the last of the day's horror. The morning was perfect, the mist and clouds shimmering, while a scatter of autumn leaves dotted the dew-kissed grass. The surrounding beeches glowed red and the chill air held the first hint of the winter to come. Mirabelle smiled, imagining those long, dark nights. How she and Sorley would spend them...

Sure she couldn't conceive a greater bliss, she reached to pour two cups of the fine Rhenish wine the innkeeper had left for them.

First, they had this day to celebrate, here in such a fine, blessed place. So she breathed deep of the clean, fragrant air and started to hand Sorley his wine, but a terrible thought struck her before she could. Setting down the cup, she looked at him, her heart seizing.

"Sir John is gone, I know," she voiced her concern, gripping Sorley's arm, "but what of the poor women he kept at Dunraine? No one knows they're there. They are prisoners, may wallow there all their days."

"They'll be fine, ne'er you worry." He caught her hand and pressed a kiss into her palm. "They'll be freed anon, returned to their families or otherwise cared for, depending on their circumstances. I've already set their rescue in motion; they'll no' suffer much longer."

"I am so glad." Mirabelle was.

She lifted a brow, delicious shivers rippling through her because of the stream of light kisses he was planting up and down the inner side of her forearm. "Why am I not surprised? I should have known you'd thought out a plan to help them. You're good at that, aren't you?" She watched him carefully, noting how his expression changed, turning shuttered. "Can it be your friend William and a few others will ride with you to free the Dunraine captives?"

He glanced aside, his gaze on the red-leaved beeches. "I didnae say I'd be doing aught, only that I—"

"Arranged a rescue," she reminded him, watching him draw a tight breath.

When he exhaled gustily, she knew she'd won.

That she'd guessed rightly.

"You're planning a Fenris mission to save those women." She saw a muscle twitch in his jaw. "It's one of the reasons you delayed our departure from Stirling. You and your Fenris friends meant to—"

"What we do"—he looked at her, his fierce gaze locking with hers—"is ne'er spoken aloud, though I'll ne'er hide anything from you," he said, doing just that, his promise warming her to her toes.

"Nor shall I." She leaned over and kissed his cheek.

"Aye, well, as my soon-to-be-wife, you ken fine why I postponed any travel." He stood and tugged his shirt over his head, tossing it onto the grass. "Arrangements must be made for our wedding, plans for feasts and celebrations, decisions about where to hold such revels. One faction will approve, another may feel slighted."

"No they won't." She rose and went to him, smiling. They—"

He touched a finger to her lips. "You dinnae ken the King or Alex as I do. The earl, especially, loves a wild and raucous feasting. Then there's William at the Red Lion." He stroked her cheek, rubbed one of her curls between his thumb and forefinger. "There's your father as well. We've much to consider if no one's toes are to be stepped on."

"We'll think of something." Mirabelle would just as soon they ran off into the heather, pledging themselves to each other in the old way, a tradition still held in the Highlands and as binding as a churchman's mumbling. "For now, I love you all the more for helping those women at Dunraine. I did worry about them. You have a good heart."

"I am nae saint, lass." He made light of her praise. "Whether I participate or no', the Wolf—"

"Ahhh!" She nodded. "I knew the earl was involved in the Fen—"

"He is our leader." Sorley was unlatching his sword-belt, whipping it off as swiftly as he'd done in her bedchamber. He cast the heavy belt, brand and all, onto the ground. "If e'er you breathe a word, I shall—"

"Kiss me and my lips are sealed." Mirabelle dropped back down on the tartan blanket and opened her arms. "Do more and I may not speak again ever, so happy will I be."

Sorley flashed a smile as he stripped off the remainder of his clothes. "Pleased so easily, are you? A few kisses, a bit of stroking, and a man's—"

"Not any man," she corrected, eyeing him appreciatively. "It is your loving I crave, and badly."

"Then I shall no' keep you waiting." Gloriously naked, he moved with speed, stretching out beside her and hitching her skirts up about her hips, rolling on top of her before she could blink. "I love you, Mirabelle, with all my heart and soul, and have aye done so. But just now, it's your sweet womanly heat calling to me."

"So it is," Mirabelle agreed, his brazen words exciting her, filling her with tingly warmth. Twining her arms around his shoulders, she sought his lips, eager for his kisses. She also parted her legs, lifting her hips and rocking against him, sure she'd never tire of his loving. How could she when she loved him so much that just thinking of him made her feel feverish?

But then he was easing deep inside her, and she forgot to think at all. Everything spun away except the man she loved so fiercely and the wondrous joy it was to know that he was hers at last.

Or rather, that they finally had each other.

"I do believe word of your heroics preceded you, my Hawk." Mirabelle twisted round to smile over her shoulder at Sorley as they rode up to Stirling Castle's gates. "Rarely have I seen such a crowd gathered, so many lit torches, unless a great feast was planned. Or"—she turned back to admire the glory—"when a King's champion was to be honored."

Behind her Sorley chuckled low. He also tightened his arm around her waist, giving her a squeeze. "Like as no', they will have heard of your abduction and wish to celebrate your safe return. You are much loved, my lady."

"Or they are glad-hearted for Sir John's demise." Mirabelle shivered lightly, unable to help herself. "Perhaps now that he is no more, men will openly speak the truth about—"

"No' if I can help it." Sorley leaned down and dropped a kiss to the top of her head. "Sinclair's lady wife and family have done no wrong and deserve no such taint. If William and others act as planned, Sinclair willnae be missed for days. Men will think he is off hunting or away to Glasgow. When he is set upon by robbers and killed, his body 'tossed into a river, forever lost,' no one will ken otherwise. He will be properly mourned as is his due as a nobleman, his family no' hurt by shame." He spoke just above her ear, for they were passing ranks of spearmen now, entering the great torchlit pend of the gatehouse arch.

"And the ladies at Dunraine?" Mirabelle spoke equally low. "Will they not revile him, poisoning his name?"

"Perhaps, though they will be urged otherwise." Sorley nipped her earlobe, pressing a kiss to the side of her neck. "A good marriage with a kindly man, a safe home, and the promise of a carefree future is persuasive, lass. As will be no' hurting other innocents."

"You are a good man." Mirabelle's heart swelled and she placed a hand over his arm where he held her, squeezing tight. "The greatest of heroes, just as I knew."

He chuckled again. "Did you now?"

"Always." She blinked, lifted her hand to dash a tear from her cheek.

"I am glad to hear it." He drew rein just inside the bailey, swinging down and reaching up for her, setting her lightly on the cobbles. "Though"—he unfastened the strap that held Little Heart's basket to the saddle horn—"I aye thought it was my swagger that caught your eye."

"It was." Mirabelle didn't lie, but she'd also seen his goodness even then.

She'd recognized it in his gaze. Just as she saw it there now as he gave a coin to the stable lad who ran up to take their horse. He told the boy he'd earn a second coin, or more, if he saw the kitten safely delivered to Mirabelle's guest chamber in the ladies' tower.

"So, lass!" He turned to her, offering her his arm as the lad dashed away, carrying the wicker basket as if it were made of gold. "Shall we see what's afoot here?"

"Indeed." Mirabelle slipped her hand through his arm, let him lead her into the crowd thronging the bailey.

In truth, she couldn't remember ever seeing so many people gathered at the castle. The atmosphere was joyous, excitement in the air. Although it was near to gloaming, the sky already dark with evening clouds—she and Sorley had stayed in the clearing longer than intended, *enjoying* themselves too much to break away any sooner—so many torches blazed on the ramparts and throughout the courtyard and pillared arcades that the castle shone brightly. The walls and even the bailey cobbles gleamed red and gold, the mail and steel of the gathered warriors and nobles, reflecting the flames, adding to the brilliance.

Townsfolk were there, too, filling the courtyard and spilling out through the open gatehouse where men and women milled about beneath the curtain walls, carrying on as if at a gay and festive fair.

"Look! Some people have climbed onto the rooftops of the outbuildings, even the chapel…" Mirabelle tugged on Sorley's arm, nodding toward the little sanctuary, memories of their heated encounter there making her quiver with love for him. She glanced up at him, very proud, for he'd never looked more handsome than now, with the flaming torches making him shine like a Celtic hero. "Folk are even in the old burial yard, standing on the walls—"

She broke off, her breath catching, when she spotted a group of Highlanders standing in the shadows of the chapel wall. Big, heavy-bearded men, they wore polished mail coats and low-slung silver-studded belts hung not only with long swords but also with the wicked war axes of the North. Several had wolf pelts tossed across their massive shoulders, and every one of them was adorned with glittering arm rings and what, at a distance, appeared to be silver Thor's hammer amulets glinting at their throats. Blinking, Mirabelle narrowed her eyes at the warriors, sure of it.

She also suspected who they were.

Didn't they bear a strong resemblance to Grim Mackintosh of Nought?

The fine hairs on her nape lifting, her heartbeat quickening, she flashed a glance at Sorley, relieved to see he hadn't yet noticed the Highlanders. She could only guess why they were here.

She was spared further speculation when the innkeeper, William Wyldes, strode up to them, the crowd parting to let him through.

"About time you returned!" He stopped before them, his feet wide apart, hands on his hips, his grin huge. "What's a grand day without the guests of honor, eh?"

Laughing, he stepped forward and threw his arms around Mirabelle, crushing her in a tremendous hug before turning to Sorley. He punched him in the arm, good-naturedly. "'Tis a night o' wonders, it is!" He grinned even wider, looked from one of them to the other. "Who would've thought—"

"What?" Sorley didn't return his friend's smile, something in his gut warning him he wouldn't like the reason for it. "Dinnae tell me all this revel has aught to do with me. That folk would rejoice to see Lady Mirabelle safe, I'll accept. But I'm no' wonder—"

Wyldes laughed, his merriment only increasing Sorley's suspicion. "Be that as it may," his tone confirmed Sorley's gut feeling, "you are a part of a miracle, true enough. The King has pardoned a man his father banned from court ages ago, even welcoming the rascal's return."

"What *rascal*?" Sorley's blood chilled, an icy cold rushing through him as if a great fist had plunged through his chest, snatching all the warmth in his world. "Who has come to Stirling to earn such a welcome?"

In answer, William made a sweeping gesture with his hand, indicating a group of big-bearded, rough-hewn Highland warriors standing beside the chapel. Sorley eyed them, at first thinking they were Alex's Highlanders, men known to be a wild and rowdy lot.

Sadly, he knew most of the earl's followers, and a second look proved they weren't Alex Stewart's men.

"By the gods," he ground out, frowning. He couldn't say for sure, but looking at them now, he had a fairly good notion whence they'd come.

Turning back to William, he scowled even more. "Those can only be Nought warriors, from the Glen of Many Legends, Grim Mackintosh's men."

He purposely didn't say what he knew: that Grim's men were now lodged at Archibald MacNab's stronghold, Duncreag Castle, rebuilding the raid damage, training a new garrison for his errant sire.

"So they are!" William beamed, his tone jubilant. "And guess who rode in here with them? Looking for you and—"

"By all the gods!" Sorley's rage near choked him. "How dare he come here now, on such a day. Just when—"

"Sorley, please..." Mirabelle leaned into him, slid an

arm around his waist, even her goodness and warmth not lessening the cold boiling inside him.

"Stay out of this, lass." He set his hand over hers, squeezing her fingers, hard. He kept his gaze on Wyldes. "I cannae believe my ears. Tell me I'm no' hearing rightly, I urge you."

"Aye, well..." William shrugged, his smile slipping only a bit. "Truth is, he didnae hie himself down here from his wild Heilands to—"

"Isn't it a joyous night?" Maili appeared around the edge of a clutch of excited-looking matrons, bearing an armful of mead horns.

She offered one to Sorley, her pretty face alight. "Drink, laddie," she urged him, winking. "A bit of mead and the world is right again."

"That I doubt!" Sorley frowned at her, ignoring the proffered mead horn.

"So-so!" Maili kept smiling, her high spirits undimmed as William and Mirabelle accepted their mead, knocking the horns together before lifting them to their lips and drinking.

Sorley folded his arms, waiting until Maili sashayed off, not surprisingly in the direction of Grim's Nought warriors.

As soon as she disappeared into the throng, Sorley fixed his fiercest look on William. "Archibald MacNab is here, feted by our King?"

"So he is!" William boomed the unwanted reply, looking not a whit unapologetic. Tipping back his mead horn, he took a long swig before once again grinning. "Though all this"—he waved the horn at the chaos—"is also about you, and your lady's rescue. You ken her sire is much revered by King Robert." William glanced at Mirabelle, admiration on his bearded face. "The King knows no man could better transcribe his prized *Lilium Medicinae* from the Gaelic than Munro MacLaren. He was outraged that MacLaren's daughter was taken from this castle, right out from beneath his nose. Having the lady Mirabelle and her father here as his honored guests worsened matters." William took another long drink of mead, tossed aside the empty horn. "His relief was great when word came that you'd found and rescued her. So, with your father here, his son such a hero—"

"You were there as well," Sorley minded him.

"Aye, well . . ." William stretched his arms over his head, cracked his knuckles. "When was the last time I had a chance to throw a spear?"

Sorley frowned again and glanced about, looking for any man who might be Archibald.

Not that he cared to spot the dastard.

"Why did he come south?" Mirabelle stepped between them, voicing the very question Sorley was too annoyed to ask again. "Did he hope to meet Sorley?"

For the first time, William looked uncomfortable. "No' exactly," he hedged, hooking his thumbs in his sword-belt and rocking back on his heels. "Truth is Grim Mackintosh's wife, Lady Breena, missed him and insisted on making the journey down here to join her husband. The MacNab is fond of her, supposedly looks on her like a daughter. He came with her. Once they reached my Red Lion, Grim told him the real reason for his quest—"

"To find me, what?" Sorley lifted a hand and rubbed the back of his neck.

He should be pressing his hands to his temples, because his head was beginning to throb. The morning's events and the bliss of his hours in the clearing with Mirabelle were now replaced by a terrible, growing ache between his damned ears. His chest felt oddly tight, too, as if he couldn't breathe.

"You may like the man." William's face turned earnest, the caring in his eyes not sitting at all well with Sorley. "I have met him. He isnae what you'd expect."

"I dinnae care if he walks on water or can sprout wings and fly to the moon." Sorley folded his arms, more angry than he could ever recall being.

"He is o'er there, in thon sheltered arcade, in the shadowed corner with Laird MacLaren." William jerked his head that way, stepping back to free the view. "You'll see, he is no' water-walker or moon-flyer.

"Go now, my friend." He gave Sorley a nudge and nodded at Mirabelle. "Give him a chance."

Sorley clamped his jaw, his fool throat somehow too thick to answer as he'd wished.

He did reach for Mirabelle's hand, twining his fingers in hers. "Come, lass," he managed, his voice rough. "Let us be done with this nonsense."

"Indeed!" Looking most traitorous, her lovely blue eyes suspiciously bright, Mirabelle started forward, tugging him along with her.

Behind them, he heard William slap his damned thigh and bark a ridiculously cheerful shout of encouragement. Unfortunately, Sorley couldn't catch the words, because, for some strange reason, his ears were buzzing.

Then the crowd around them started moving aside, clearing the way so he and Mirabelle could pass through the throng more easily to reach the small cluster of Highlanders gathered in a corner of the arcade.

"Damnation..." Sorley stopped, staring at the group. For sure, his eyes were fooling him.

Munro MacLaren, small and slight as he was, had never appeared more chiefly, or proud. Mail-clad as the Nought warriors, Mirabelle's father stood next to Grim, the steel links of his armor shining like silver. His great tartan was draped nobly over his shoulder and, belying his scholarly heart, a fierce-looking sword was strapped to his hip. A beautiful young woman was speaking to him, her fiery-red hair gleaming in the arcade's shadows. She could only be Lady Breena, Grim's much-loved lady wife.

But it wasn't Munro's transformation or Grim and his lady who held Sorley's attention.

It was the man standing a bit apart from them, gazing out across the throng as if searching for someone. Blessedly, he wasn't looking toward Sorley and Mirabelle.

Sorley was gladdened by that turn of luck, because the Highlander, clearly a chieftain, could only be his father, Archibald MacNab.

"Dear saints, there he is." Mirabelle squeezed his fingers, confirming his dread.

Sorley froze where he stood, staring at the man.

He *couldn't* be his sire.

To be sure, his tartan finery and his proximity to MacLaren and Grim and his wife said he was. There any speculation ended, because the man standing in the shadows of the arcade was a shadow himself.

"He is ill." Mirabelle tugged on his hand and glanced up at him, concerned.

"He is old, is all." Sorley kept his gaze on the fiend, not wanting to feel any sympathy for him. "I'll wager he kens well what I mean to say to him. That will be the reason he looks so pale and worried."

And he did.

More than that, he was leaning on a crummock, a long Highland walking stick, clearly needing the support to stand. Worse, he appeared to have dark shadows under his eyes, and his hair stood up in tufts, the sparse white strands catching the torchlight, making him look ghostly. He didn't appear at all like the dashing, silver-tongued poet he was reputed to have been in his youth.

He looked like a wretch.

Or so Sorley had thought until his vision blurred and he could hardly see the bastard, because, for some reason, his eyes were burning, filling with stinging moisture he refused to acknowledge as tears.

"Mother of Thunder," he swore, swiping the back of his hand across his cheek. "That cannae be my father."

"I vow he is. I know him, you forget." Mirabelle slid her arm around him, urging him toward the arcade. "I think he's seen us."

"Nae . . ." Sorley didn't want it to be true.

But when he looked, the man had turned to Mirabelle's father, who nodded solemnly, as if confirming a question. Then, as if he sensed Sorley's stare, the apparition who could only be Archibald turned to look at Sorley. They locked gazes, neither moving, not even blinking.

Sorley cursed again, or thought he did.

He wasn't sure, because the old man's face lit then, glowing brighter than a balefire. He started forward, using his walking stick to maneuver the few arcade steps and then tap-tap his way toward Sorley and Mirabelle.

He gained a few paces across the bailey before he tripped, stumbling, his walking stick flying from his hand to clatter to the cobbles.

Archibald would've landed on the ground as well if, somehow, Sorley's feet hadn't sprouted wings, letting him race forward. He caught and steadied the old man before he could fall to his knees.

Righting him, Sorley reached to adjust Archibald's plaid and found himself holding his father's arm, supporting him.

"So you are MacNab." It was all he could think to say.

That was a fine thing, because surely the hoarse, full-of-emotion voice wasn't his own, especially when he added, "I've aye hoped to meet you."

That was true enough.

But he meant the words much differently now, little as he could believe it.

"You do me honor, lad." Archibald's voice quivered and he cleared his throat, noisily. As Sorley had done a moment before, he lifted a hand and swiped at his cheeks. Only unlike Sorley, Archie was unable to stem the flow of tears spilling from his eyes.

He waved away the crummock when Mirabelle, equally damp-eyed, tried to thrust it at him. Instead, he gripped Sorley's hands, met his gaze. "I ne'er kent who you were, or where, or if you even lived," he said, his voice shaky. "No one told me, and I didn't dare come seeking you. Those were bad times, lad, another world. I've regretted the loss all my days, ne'er dreamt to someday meet you." He glanced down, fished beneath his plaid to withdraw a small piece of linen, blew his nose.

Sorley swallowed hard, blinking as well.

He was not going all misty-eyed.

This man meant nothing to him. But his heart pounded more strongly, more joyously with every beat, proving him a liar. As did how easily he slid an arm around Archie's thin shoulders, guiding him back to the shelter of the arcade. He pretended not to see the equally bright eyes of the Highlanders waiting there: Mirabelle's father, Grim and his lady wife, a few others Sorley didn't know.

He did know that he couldn't recall a single one of the accusations he'd meant to hurl at his father.

Nor did he want to, and that should've alarmed him.

But it didn't.

He didn't even mind when Mirabelle hooked her arm through Archie's, beaming at him as if he'd just pulled the moon from the heavens for her.

"Have you heard we're to wed, sir?" She leaned in, kissed the old man's bristly cheek. "You're the first to be told." She glanced at Munro, winking. "Unless my father has objections, of course, which would mean we'd simply run off into the hills, marrying in the old way!"

"You'll have a proper wedding at Knocking Tower." Munro came over to join them, clapped a hand on Sorley's shoulder. "I did have a suspicion this was coming." He nodded, then broke into a smile.

"You cannae trick a learned man, lad." He wagged a

finger at Sorley, smiling. "I kent you brought me thon stone root as a bribe for my gel's hand."

"I didnae..." Sorley let the words tail off, for his father was gripping his arm, looking up at him with such hope shining on his face that Sorley's heart clenched.

"Can you forgive me, son?" He spoke clear, not ashamed to voice such a plea before his friends.

"There is no need." Sorley was surprised by that truth. "I already have."

"Oh!" Mirabelle pressed her hands to her face, her tears leaking through her fingers. "I have so hoped for this day."

Sorley frowned, not liking the crowd gathering round them, cheering and hooting and some even clapping. Others were raising ale cups and mead horns, calling for pipers and dancing, a proper celebration.

"Aye, well..." Sorley ran a hand over his hair. He swallowed hard, hoped he wasn't dreaming. "It would seem this truly was a day of wonder," he finally said, glancing up at the heavens, not surprised to see the clouds part to reveal a scatter of stars. They shone down on them all, perhaps even smiling, congratulating.

It wouldn't surprise him.

Indeed, he doubted anything ever would again.

"Son..." Archie gripped his arm again, his voice stronger now, confident. "My stronghold, Duncreag, is a fine place for a wedding," he declared, standing a bit taller. "We host the grandest Yuletide festivals every year." He cast a glance at Mirabelle and her father, Grim and Lady Breena. "Ask them and they'll tell you. They were all at last year's celebrations. There be nowhere more fitting for you two to.—"

"We will think on it, Father," Sorley nodded, using the endearment to sweeten his words.

Not an "aye" as Archie had surely hoped to win.

He would dwell later on why calling Archie his sire felt more right than wrong.

Indeed, it filled him with joy.

But not as much as when Mirabelle lifted up on her toes and slipped her arms around his shoulders, kissing him roundly, in full view of everyone.

"I love you so," she whispered in his ear. "But I think we should head into the hall now. Maili told me the King has set a festive table for us, called in his pipers—"

"Another grand feast, aye?" Sorley didn't miss the poignancy. His heart thundering, he offered his soon-to-be wife his arm, triumph and love sweeping him when she took it proudly. "Perhaps this time we can finish our dance?"

"Oh, we shall, for sure," she agreed, her beautiful eyes shining.

And so they made their across the courtyard to where the great hall's door stood wide.

Many were the reels they danced that night.

Into the small hours, truth be told.

But the true celebration happened when they finally slipped away and climbed the tower stair to Mirabelle's guest chamber.

Once there, he showed her every wicked delight she had to look forward to in the long years they'd spend together as man and wife.

And much later, as she lay sleeping in his arms, he knew for sure that he was no longer a bastard.

He was the luckiest man in the world.

Epilogue

❖

The Red Lion Inn
A Night of Celebration
Autumn 1399

*C*an *you believe it is time to say farewell?"*

Mirabelle edged closer to Sorley, glad for the arm he held so firmly around her. They stood near the hearth fire of the tavern's long room, the warmth of the flames and the wood's soft crackling lending cheer to an already joyous evening.

"I have come to love this place." She glanced up at her soon-to-be husband's handsome face, not caring if he saw the shimmer of tears in her eyes. "Your friends..." She let the words tail off, looked out across the crowded tables, each one filled with smiling, laughing revelers. "I will miss them when we're gone."

Sorley chuckled low and leaned down to kiss the top of her head. "I will keep you too occupied to do so."

Mirabelle smiled softly, knowing that was true.

Indeed, the promise filled her with tingly excitement. Especially when he brushed back her hair and whispered against her ear, "William has outdone himself laying out a fine feast this night, but I vow I am hungry for an entirely different delicacy."

"You are wicked." Mirabelle's pulse quickened, for she knew exactly what he meant.

She also knew it would be a while before he could treat her to such bliss.

She wasn't sure she could stand the wait.

"I ken what you're thinking, lass." His words proved he knew her well. "You err greatly if you think I'm so debauched as to ravish you thusly whilst riding to distant Kintail with such an entourage as will accompany us." He caught her chin, tipping her face to his. "Once we're well and duly wed at the MacKenzies' Eilean Creag Castle, I'll make up for lost time."

"I will hold you to your word," Mirabelle teased, sure there'd be no need.

Sorley was ever ravenous for her, as she was for him.

"Did you proud, didn't I?" William strode up to them, his innkeeper's apron tied around his girth, a grin splitting his bearded face. "Cannae let Clan MacKenzie outdo my hospitality, what?"

He winked and tossed a glance at the linen-draped tables, the sumptuous victuals and plentiful ale. "Legends are sung about their feasts. Seeing as we're all riding north with you for the wedding, I'll no' be shamed."

"You are the best innkeeper in the land." Mirabelle lifted on her toes and kissed his cheek, knowing Sorley wouldn't mind. "You're also the greatest friend," she added, stepping back. "We'll never forget it was you who made it possible for us to marry at Eilean Creag."

"Aye, well . . ." William looked embarrassed. "More like Grim Mackintosh had a hand in that." He slid at glance at the Nought warrior, who sat supping and drinking with his lady wife and Munro and Archie. "Grim kens a MacKenzie or two. I only put a wee burr beneath his saddle, letting him know all and sundry were fashed o'er where you should wed. Seeing as Sorley's mother was a MacKenzie, 'tis only right for you to marry in Kintail." He clapped a big hand on Sorley's shoulder, nodding once as his gaze flicked to the stag's-head brooch pinned so proudly to Mirabelle's breast. "You'll do the lady honor that way."

"Indeed, we shall." Mirabelle slid her arm around Sorley, leaning in against him.

If he knew her well, she knew him better.

The sudden glint in his eye wasn't a reflection of the fire glow. He was deeply touched the MacKenzies were hosting their wedding, welcoming them home as if they truly belonged to their much-vaunted clan.

Which, truth be told, they now did.

"Do you truly mean to hold celebratory feasts at Duncreag, Knocking, Alex Stewart's Badenoch stronghold, and Stirling, after the wedding?" William was shaking his head, looking from one of them to the other. "That's a great deal of carousing, my friend. We'll be traipsing across the land for weeks, mayhap months."

"So we will." Sorley grinned and punched his friend's arm. "It'll be a grand adventure."

"I do hope so," Maili tossed in, hurrying past with a tray of delicious-smelling roasted meat. "I'm thinking to catch me a wild Highland man," she called over her shoulder as she disappeared into the throng.

Sorley and William grinned after her. Mirabelle said a silent prayer, hoping the girl's wish came true.

"There will be much merrymaking," she agreed, turning back to the men. "We didn't want to leave out anyone."

"That may be," Archibald approached them, coming slowly for he'd forgotten his walking stick, "but none of the revels will be as rousing as those at our Duncreag." He looked at Sorley, his sparse, white-tufted hair mussed as ever, his face beaming. "I was just reminding Munro and Grim that no castle hosts a finer feasting than we do."

He stopped before Sorley, swept out an arm, taking in the joyous throng. "We've room for all thon folk and more. Your home, laddie, is a place like no other." The pride in his voice, the hope in his words, squeezed Mirabelle's heart. "Truth be told, you may wish to stay on there."

"We may well do so." Sorley slid a discreet hand beneath his father's elbow, steadying him when he wobbled a bit after making such a flourish. "Come, Munro is glancing round searching for you. Like as no', he wishes to argue the glories of his Knocking Tower." He flashed a wink at Mirabelle and then led his father away, guiding him back to his seat, keeping his hand firmly on Archie's arm as they went.

When Sorley returned, Mirabelle knew they needed to nip outside. Giving him a significant look, she tugged him with her, skirting the young stable lad from the castle whom Sorley had employed to look after Little Heart during their journeying. The boy sat near the door with the kitten, laughing as Little Heart leapt about like a flea, chasing a feather the lad had tied to a stick.

"You didn't have to hire him." She glanced back at the boy when they stepped outside. "Little Heart has his basket, and you know I'd never let anything happen to him. He's my kitten and I will care for him, always."

"So you will, I ken." Sorley took her hand, drawing her farther away from the noisy inn.

The area facing the road was lit with blazing torches and here, too, tables were spread with victuals and ale, enough so that any passing townsfolk or wayfarers could join the merrymaking. Off to the side, beneath the trees, a large number of horses were tethered, beasts that couldn't be stalled in the inn's now-full stables. A few baggage carts were there as well, piled high with canvas-draped travel supplies, all in preparation for the wedding party's departure for Kintail at first light on the morrow.

"The lad has a purpose beyond guarding your precious

kitten." Sorley took her by the shoulders, turning her to him, scattering her thoughts of their pending journey. "Did I no' tell you once that cats are faster than lightning? I'll no' have you aye fashed about what the wee bugger is up to, no' at the times I mean to slip away with you and—"

"Ah-ha!" Mirabelle laughed. "So you do plan to ravish me before we reach Kintail?"

"I intend to always ravish you." His smile flashed, his tone dark with teasing devilry. "Dinnae you e'er doubt it. Though, I'll own we may have to sneak away into the heather and make love on my plaid, during the journey. I'll no' scandalize you before our friends, our fathers. I'd no' risk shocking our redoubtable elders." He winked and ran a hand through her hair.

"Have you truly forgiven Archie then?" Mirabelle needed to know.

Sorley shrugged and glanced aside, torchlight limning his strong profile, glinting in his beard. "If the King can, so can I."

It wasn't the answer she'd wanted.

Or the one she believed.

"As I know you," she said, reaching to touch his face, "you'd have forgiven him anyway, King's pardon or not."

He turned to her, arched a brow. "Is that so?"

"It is." Mirabelle smiled, triumphantly.

"Sakes o' mercy!" He frowned and shook his head. "What e'er am I to do with a wife who kens me so well?"

"Love me?" Mirabelle looked up at him, knew her heart was in her eyes.

"That I already do, lass." He grabbed her hand and pulled her to him. "I have aye done so and have no intention of ever stopping. No' for all our days." And then he did what he did so well, crushing her to him and kissing her long and deep, so masterfully she didn't want him to stop.

But he did, breaking their kiss to nip the sensitive skin

just beneath her ear. "You are my heart, Mirabelle, the whole of my world."

"Oh, Sorley..." Mirabelle lifted a hand and dashed at her eyes.

She could hardly speak for the hot thickness rising in her throat, the hammering of her heart. "Do you have any idea how much I love you?"

He took her hand, bringing it to his lips, kissing her fingers one by one. "I vow I do, praise the gods."

"And I..." She glanced back at the well-lit inn, heard the joyous laughter, the merriment within. "I do wish this night could go on forever."

"My sweet Mirabelle." He cupped her face, kissing her softly this time. "This is no' the end, I promise. It is a grand beginning."

Author's Note

Stirling Castle is one of Scotland's most shining tributes to an ancient and heroic past. Throughout the ages, the mighty fortress has commanded a bluff high above the plain of the River Forth, so guarding one of Scotland's most strategic locations, a place where several vital sites converge: the Forth's most navigable point, access through the hills to and from the Highlands, and important routes leading east and west. Not surprisingly, Stirling Castle was respectfully known as the "Key to the Kingdom."

The castle explored by today's tourist is not the stronghold as it would have appeared in the time period of this book. Modern-day visitors see a castle that has been built and rebuilt over many centuries. Much of this refurbishment was done by James V in the mid-1500s and also James VI later that same century.

Even so, glimpses of much older times remain if one looks closely. Although no archeological evidence exists, many believe the site's occupation dates to the Iron Age. Certainly, ruins of ancient Celtic forts have been discovered. The great Roman general Agricola kept a garrison here. The

truth is there has been a fortress on Stirling's bluff since days
so distant the original defenders have long since faded into
the mists of antiquity.

Therefore, I used my own explorations of Stirling Castle,
my passion for Scottish medieval history, and my imagination to craft the setting as I believe Sorley and Mirabelle
would have known the castle.

The chapel they visit was not the famous Chapel Royal
known to today's visitor. That chapel was built in 1594 by
James VI. However, there are indications that the Chapel
Royal incorporates parts of a much more ancient holy site.
Indeed, the earliest recorded mention of a chapel at Stirling
dates to 1124. There are foundations marked on the courtyard, near the north curtain wall, that may be this older
chapel. If so, it could well have stood atop an even more
ancient site of pagan worship.

The infamous secret love lair, the Rose Room, and the
scriptorium are my creations. Even so, these chambers could
have existed. Scriptoriums were common in great castles
and strongholds, especially royal ones. Likewise, hidden
rooms and passages are a staple in such proud edifices.
Some can be enjoyed today, at the well-preserved properties
of Historic Scotland and the National Trust for Scotland.

Sorley's favorite view from the ramparts is real and can
be appreciated by anyone who cares to climb up to the eastern side of the Stirling Castle battlements.

The ruins of the Abbey of St. Mary, with its wee village
and wharf, were also real. More commonly known as Cambuskenneth Abbey, this important Augustinian site was built
in 1140 at the request of Scotland's King David I. Of tremendous importance because of its proximity to the castle
and the river, the abbey held royal favor and was repeatedly ransacked by the English from the end of the 1200s
and throughout the Scottish Wars of Independence. By the
time this book takes place, the late 1300s, the once-majestic

abbey and its surrounding settlement and riverside wharf stood in complete ruin. I have visited Cambuskenneth and used my time there, and my imagination, to paint the ruin and its village as I believe Sorley and Mirabelle would've known it.

Cambuskenneth was restored in the early 1400s, but never retained the full glory it once enjoyed.

Munro's fascination with the *Lilium Medicinae* could well have happened, as the much-famed text truly existed. "Flower (or Lily) of Medicine" in English, its origins are hazed by time, but the Gaelic work mentioned in this book refers to the version penned by Bernard de Gordon, a fourteenth-century Scottish physician.

The renowned Highland healers, the MacBeths (also known as Beatons), prized their copy so greatly that one of their most revered healers did indeed engage servants to carry the book by land when journeying. It was feared the priceless tome might be damaged by water.

Stirling Castle does have a pink lady ghost. She is the wife of a Scottish knight who died when England's Edward I captured the castle in June 1304.

Mirabelle's home, Knocking Tower, as well as Archibald MacNab's Duncreag, exist solely in my imagination. They are, however, loosely modeled after similar strongholds I've explored in Scotland.

Clan MacKenzie's holding, referred to as Eilean Creag Castle in the epilogue, first appeared in my debut title, *Devil in a Kilt*. The castle's real name is Eilean Donan, and it is one of Scotland's most well-loved and romantic castles. It stands in Kintail, near the beautiful Isle of Skye.

When Donell MacDonnell
disappeared, Lady Gillian MacGuire
thought she was free. She hated
her arranged betrothal.
Yet when Donell returns, Gillian
knows something has changed.

For now he takes her breath away...

Please turn this page for a preview of

To Desire a Highlander

Chapter One

✤

Laddie's Isle
Spring 1400

Lady Gillian MacGuire knew the moment the gods abandoned her.

They'd fled as soon as she'd set foot on this much-maligned island. Perhaps they'd deserted her earlier, not approving of her father's plan to bring her here to await Donell MacDonnell's arrival. Even her brothers had made the sign against evil as they'd climbed aboard their father's ship. Good men didn't sail these waters.

Not if they valued their lives.

The currents were too strong; the seas wild and rough. Unpredictable winds blew always, cutting as knives and colder than hell.

No one could blame her long-lost betrothed for leaving the place. Having lived here, Donell MacDonnell knew Laddie's Isle better than most. Gillian shivered and drew her cloak tighter. She could almost believe the tales that the rocky little island was haunted. That it was cursed because of its dark and sad history.

Yet if the legend was true, shouldn't the Old Ones have stayed at her side? Rallied to protect her?

Instead, they'd left her alone.

Disappearing as swiftly as mist before the sun, or at least as quickly as her father and brothers had strode away to seek out Donell's ruinous hall.

Her father had declared it was necessary to ready the place for Donell's return.

Her brothers agreed.

The gods had simply looked on, perhaps amused by her quandary.

Not pleased with any of them, Gillian stepped closer to the water's edge. Behind her, sheer cliffs loomed high and black. Everywhere else, the sea boiled and churned, lashing against the jagged shore as if to scold each stone that'd dared to break the foaming, white-crested waves.

Gillian ignored the danger. She did take care not to slip on the wet and glistening rocks. The spray dampened her skirts and misted her skin. Above her, seabirds wheeled and cried, and the chill air smelled strongly of the sea. The salty tang quickened her pulse, stirring her Hebridean heart even as her world threatened to crash down around her.

How strange that the day was so glorious to behold. A light mist swirled above the water, luminous silver against the clouded sky. Wind whipped around her, and everywhere she looked, above or before her, she was awed.

Still...

The wild beauty rankled.

The day Donell MacDonnell returned to Laddie's Isle should have dawned dark and gloomy, with sideways-slanting rain marring the magnificence.

And she would rather be anywhere but here, waiting to greet him.

Then again, when had life been fair?

Hers had certainly never been easy, if she cared to admit the truth. Yet she'd always fought against hardships, strife, and disappointments. Tears and pity weren't for her, a chieftain's daughter. She preferred to stand tall, shoulders squared and chin high, always. A brave young woman with long centuries of noble blood in her veins, she prided herself on her strength.

She was equally proud of her by-name, the Spitfire of the Isles.

Secretly, she'd also believed she held the gods' ears.

That they even favored her, looking on her kindly and guiding her in times of trouble.

Now she knew differently.

Somewhere beyond the horizon, Donell MacDonnell was beating his way home. Coming back after five years, to reclaim his remote and windswept corner of the Sea of the Hebrides, and—Gillian knew—to have the bride promised to him by her father only months before he'd disappeared.

Gillian didn't blink as a wave broke over the rocks, the icy water sluicing her feet. She had other concerns of much greater importance.

She was the MacDonnell's bespoken bride.

Yet wedding him was the last thing she wanted.

While not quite an ogre, he was many summers her elder. She doubted he'd ever washed his great black beard, which was bushy enough to house at least three nests of mice. His arms and legs were thicker than trees, his girth immeasurable. Worse, he suffered onion breath.

His meaty hands bore scars, something she'd admire and honor in most warrior chieftains.

After all, a leader unwilling to fight beside his men wasn't worthy of his status as a commander. But Donell MacDonnell's hands weren't just marked by battle. The skin around and beneath his fingernails was black with grime. If his breath smelled of onions, his flesh reeked of things she didn't want to name.

She shuddered, a chill sweeping her despite her determination to remain calm.

Despair and panic were emotions she refused to embrace.

Besides, she had hope of avoiding marital *un*bliss as Donell MacDonnell's wife.

Where he'd gone was a mystery. He'd simply vanished, his men with him. He'd sailed away from Laddie's Isle, leaving his already half-decayed tower to fall even further into ruin. No one had heard of him since, until a passing galley dropped anchor at her father's island home, Castle Sway. The ship's crew begged, and received, hospitality for the night. Plied with generous viands and free-flowing ale, and warmed by the hearth fire, the seamen spoke freely, sharing news from afar.

These tidings included their meeting with Donell at a well-visited seafarers' tavern on the mainland coast.

Unaware that their words chilled Gillian's blood, even upending her world, they claimed he was journeying back to his isle, that he'd vowed he was eager to resume his duties as chieftain of his watery domain.

His arrival was imminent. Or so Castle Sway's friendly and loose-tongued guests had asserted.

Gillian fisted her hands, clutching the folds of her skirts. She welcomed the chill numbness of her fingers. Focusing on the bone-deep cold and the sharp needle pricks racing up her wrists and along her arms kept her from thinking how opportune it would be if Donell MacDonnell's galley were to spring a leak, sinking into the sea.

She might not want to marry him, but she didn't wish the man ill.

Even so...

She bit her lip, remembering how his big, dirty-nailed hand had gripped hers on the day of their betrothal. How he'd lifted her fingers to his lips, his greasy beard tickling her skin as he'd kissed her knuckles.

The hunger in his eyes as he'd done so, the way his gaze had swept her head to toe, was a memory she wished she didn't have.

His slow smile, which revealed the yellowish stain of his teeth...

"Mother of all the gods." Gillian gathered up her every shred of strength and narrowed her gaze on the sea. She lifted a hand to her brow, peering out across the deep blueness of the rolling waves. To her relief, there was no sign of Donell's galley.

Still, her heart beat in her throat and she could feel a subtle shift in the air. As if her world were about to slip from her grasp, the soft tendrils of mist seeming to shimmer with the change.

It scarce mattered that wherever she turned her gaze, nothing but the empty sea stared back at her.

That didn't mean Donell wasn't coming.

The mist was thicker near the horizon, spoiling her view. He could be out there now, his ship slicing through the troughs and sending up fans of spume, his crew's well-plied oars speeding him toward the steep-sided spit of rock known as Laddie's Isle.

Tamping down her ill ease, Gillian reached inside her cloak and slipped her hand through a slit in her skirts. She let her fingers curl around the small leather pouch that hung from a narrow belt slung low about her hips. She took comfort in her secret treasure's solid weight and bulk, the hope its presence gave her.

"So eager for his arrival, are you?"

Jumping, Gillian whipped her hand from within her cloak and spun about to face her oldest brother, Gowan.

He stood less than an arm's length away, towering over her. He'd crossed his well-muscled arms over his chest and planted one booted foot firmly on a wet, weed-draped rock. His deep russet hair, the same rich red as her own, blew about his shoulders, and he was eyeing her intently, peering at her as if she'd grown two heads.

"You startled me." Gillian lifted her chin, ignoring his question.

"And you surprise me." He flicked a glance at the sea. "I wouldnae hae thought you were so keen to greet the man."

"Who said that's why I'm out here?" Gillian tossed her head, knowing her cheeks were flaming. "Could be I'm hoping his galley doesn't appear."

"You ken it will, lass." Gowan stepped closer and set his hands on her shoulders. "That's as sure as the morrow's dawn. No' liking it will change naught."

Gillian drew a tight breath, saying nothing.

She kept her chin high, hoping Gowan—her favorite among her eight brothers—wouldn't hear the racing of her heart, the dread churning in her belly. He might sympathize with her, to a degree. But as a man, born and bred of the Isles and with their ways and traditions carved into his bone, he wouldn't understand her displeasure.

She held his gaze, stubbornly, not liking what she saw.

He'd disapprove of her objections, making light of them, however much he loved her.

"Anything can be changed if the will is there." She stood even straighter, forcing herself to believe her words. "Even the highest mountain can be torn down if you take away one rock at a time."

"Aye, and by the time you're done, you'll be so auld and addled, you'll no longer remember why you started such a fool's errand."

"It's not foolish to me."

Her brother frowned and shook his head slowly. "You dinnae ken what you're saying."

"I do." And she did.

She'd empty the sea with a thimble if doing so would keep her from becoming Donell's bride.

"All lasses must wed, as well you know." He lifted a hand, tucked her hair behind her ear. "That is just the way of it, how life here has e'er been and aye will be. You could do worse than the MacDonnell. He has his own isle, small though it is. His tower will be sound enough, once repaired. The prospects are grand." He swept out an arm, taking in the endless stretch of the sea, the shimmering mist. "Magnificent enough to swell the heart of any Hebridean."

"I've nothing against Laddie's Isle." Gillian spoke true. "It's Donell I cannot abide. You weren't at Sway when he came for the betrothal ceremony. None of you were there," she reminded him, sure that if her brothers hadn't been away at sea, and had been home, in their father's hall, they'd have argued against the match.

"He is a toad." She raised a hand, wagging her finger at him when he started to protest. "He's also ancient, older than any graybeard I've ever seen."

"Lass..." Her brother took her hand between both of his own, his grip warm and firm. "Donell MacDonnell is no more than ten summers older than you. That much I know. The last five years have fogged your memory."

"I wish that were so."

"I'm sure it is."

"Did Father send you to find me?" Gillian slipped her hand from his grasp, suspicious.

Wasn't it in their sire's best interest to be rid of her? A good enough natured man, but much too lusty for his age, Mungo MacGuire had a new young wife. Lady Lorna wasn't even as old as Gillian. If the clan tongue-waggers were to be believed, she was just as hot-blooded as her adoring husband. It was whispered that she'd vowed to give him more sons than the eight he already had.

Lady Lorna also didn't much care for sharing her new home with her husband's daughter.

Gillian frowned, her blood heating even more.

Gowan angled his head, watching her with eyes that missed nothing. "Da is too busy ordering our brothers about, making them brush away cobwebs and sweep stone dust from corners, to even notice you left the hall. He didnae send me to look for you."

"If he did, he needn't have bothered. I'd almost rather stay here." She waved toward the cliffs, and the nameless tower that claimed the promontory's best vantage point. "What awaits me at Sway, but Lady Lorna's peevish glares and taunts? I'm hard-pressed to say which ill is worse. Sharing a hall with a shrew or being shackled to an ogre."

To his credit, Gowan looked embarrassed.

But he held his tongue, still not siding with her.

"You should've stayed in the tower, enjoyed a few ales with our brothers." Gillian held his gaze, seeing no reason for anything but the truth. "There's nothing you can say to make this day a good one."

"Aye, well." Gowan glanced again at the sea, then back to her. "Could be you'll find Donell to your liking." He sounded hopeful. "The ship's crew spoke well of him. They said he wore a fine mail shirt and more arm rings than the Viking warlords of old."

"Indeed?" Gillian was sure they were mistaken.

Gowan nodded. "They sang his praises after you retired for the night. Had you still been in the hall, you'd have heard them."

"They must've been in their cups when they met him." Gillian could think of no other explanation.

Her onion-breathed, great-bellied betrothed could never be likened to a Viking warlord.

Gowan frowned. "Will you no' give him a chance?"

Gillian flicked at her sleeve. "Do I have a choice?"

"In truth, nae." Gowan gave her a long look, somehow managing to look both sympathetic and annoyed. "You're duly promised to him, oath-bound. Such a pact is binding, and cannae be easily undone."

"That I know." Gillian turned to the sea, another truth giving her strength.

She took a deep breath, pretended to smooth the folds of

her cloak so she could touch the small, heavy pouch hidden beneath her skirts.

"I will greet Donell MacDonnell as is expected of me." She forced the words, her hand resting on her secret treasure. "I shall take his measure then, and not before."

"I am glad to hear it." Gowan sounded relieved.

Gillian didn't say that she already knew how the dice would fall.

She'd seen the hunger in Donell's eyes the day of their betrothal ceremony.

To be sure, he'd looked at her in lust. Even young and innocent as she was, she'd recognized the male need burning in his gaze.

More than that, she'd seen the blaze of greed.

However much she might have pleased him, her father's riches, so proudly displayed in Castle Sway's great hall, had impressed him more.

Donell MacDonnell desired coin above all else.

The knowledge helped her summon a smile. "All will be well." She reached to squeeze her brother's arm, hoping to reassure him. "But I would like to be alone now. I need the fresh air and sea wind to prepare myself to meet my future husband. You surely understand?"

Gowan looked at her sharply, perhaps not so easily fooled as she'd thought. Then he stepped back and flashed a grin, once again looking relieved.

"As you wish." He looked off into the distance, toward the still-empty horizon. When he turned back to her, he leaned forward, his gaze piercing. "Dinnae think you'll e'er be alone, lass. Your brothers and I sail past here often enough. We'll look in on you, make certain the MacDonnell is treating you right."

"I know you will." Gillian didn't doubt him.

She just wanted to believe there'd be no need for such concern.

Gowan nodded once, then reached to pat her shoulder comfortingly before he turned and started back up the steep cliff path.

Gillian watched him go, her hand still on her hidden treasure. She rubbed the lumpy pouch, grateful for its bulk and weight. The silver coins and cut-up brooches it held. The armlets and rings, ancient bits and pieces of a Viking hoard her great-great-grandfather had discovered buried in a riverbank many years ago, in his youth. Riches well preserved in a lead-lined chest.

The portion in her leather pouch was all that she could claim.

Her share was enough, she was sure.

Wealth untold, which she hoped would buy her freedom.

She wouldn't be given to a man she abhorred, whatever tradition and duty demanded of her.

Resolve cloaked her like a shield, and she could feel her pulse slowing. The racing of her heart returned to a strong, steady beat as she pushed her worries away. Her breath came easier and the cold began to leave her bones. She was strong and brave, courageous. She wasn't called the Spitfire of the Isles for nothing.

She'd stand against Donell MacDonnell.

She'd walk away the victor. The silver in her secret pouch would pave the way for her escape.

But then, as if the gods resented her boldness, the wind quickened, blowing harder. The gusts shrieked and howled, whipping her hair and tugging at her cloak. Not to be outdone, the sea rose, turning angry as white-capped waves hissed past the rocks, flinging icy spray onto her. Salt stung her eyes and she blinked and rubbed her fists against the burning. It was then, as she struggled to see, that chills raced through her, prickling her skin. The fine hairs on her nape lifted and a terrible cold swept her, worse than a dark winter night before the onslaught of a blizzard.

"By all the gods..." She shivered, still blinking furiously. In truth, she didn't want to clear her vision.

She knew what would greet her when she turned her gaze on the sea.

Even so, the shock slammed into her, her eyes widening at the sleek galley racing so fast toward Laddie's Isle. The ship cleaved mist and waves alike, seeming to fly across the water. A fierce dragon's head glowered from the prow, minding her of Viking ships. And even at a distance, she could see that the twin banks of oars were lined with big, powerfully muscled men. Their mastery of the oar-blades sent up plumes of white water so that the serpent-headed ship didn't just appear to bear down on her, but seemed to froth in hunger.

Most alarming of all was the huge warrior at the prow.
Donell MacDonnell.

His dark hair blew in the wind, and mail glinted at his broad, plaid-draped chest. A true giant, he was every inch as big as she remembered. Only now he looked even more formidable. Thick-bearded and frowning, he could've been Thor swooped down from Asgard to put fear into the hearts of mortal men. Most surprising of all, his girth of old had somehow shifted so that rather than a great ale-belly, what now drew her eye was the width of his shoulders and the many silver rings lining his muscular arms.

He looked stronger than six men. His scowl—a dark one surely aimed at her—left no doubt that he wasn't a man to cross. She could see him whipping out his sword in a heartbeat, swinging with deadly skill.

She pressed a hand to her throat, finding it difficult to breathe.

In her memory, wielding such a great blade as the one strapped low to his hip would've winded him. He'd have huffed and puffed, his face turning red with the effort.

Now...

The five long years away must've hardened and strengthened him.

Gillian inhaled tightly, not knowing what to think.

She did know he was staring at her. She could feel his gaze slamming into her, branding her with the same shock and disbelief stunning her.

Their gazes locked, the impact intense and disconcerting.

Her breath caught again, snagging in her lungs.

But before she could lift her chin and narrow her eyes, showing she wouldn't be intimidated, the sea mist thickened and billowing sheets of gray swirled around the ship's prow, hiding Donell and his galley from view. But she could still hear the creak and splash of the oar-blades, the steady beat of the gong as the ship sped closer.

Any moment, it would flash up onto the nearby landing beach. She could almost feel the sand trembling now, the very cliffs shaking with the fury of Donell's arrival.

She also knew, deep in her bones, that he was more than a changed man.

She'd only caught a glimpse of him, but it'd been enough.

He wouldn't be bought.

He'd claim her and seize her little leather pouch of ancient treasure. Then he'd devour her whole and spit out her bones. Laughing, he'd crack his knuckles and glance about for his next victim.

His ruthlessness left her with one choice.

She'd have to be just as bold.

Better yet, even more so.

THE DISH

Where Authors Give You the Inside Scoop

♥ ♥ ♥ ♥ ♥ ♥ ♥ ♥ ♥ ♥ ♥ ♥ ♥ ♥ ♥

From the desk of Lily Dalton

Dear Reader,

Some people are heroic by nature. They act to help others without thinking. Sometimes at the expense of their own safety. Sometimes without ever considering the consequences. That's just who they are. Especially when it's a friend in need.

We associate these traits with soldiers who risk their lives on a dangerous battlefield to save a fallen comrade. Not because it's their job, but because it's their brother. Or a parent who runs into a busy street to save a child who's wandered into the path of an oncoming car. Or an ocean life activist who places himself in a tiny boat between a whale and the harpoons of a whaling ship.

Is it so hard to believe that Daphne Bevington, a London debutante and the earl of Wolverton's granddaughter, could be such a hero? When her dearest friend, Kate, needs her help, she does what's necessary to save her. In her mind, no other choice will do. After all, she knows without a doubt that Kate would do the same for her if she needed help. It doesn't matter one fig to her that their circumstances are disparate, that Kate is her lady's maid.

But Daphne finds herself in over her head. In a moment, everything falls apart, throwing not only her reputation and her future into doubt, but her life into danger. Yet in that moment when all seems hopelessly lost…another hero comes out of nowhere and saves her. A mysterious stranger who acts without thinking, at the expense of his own safety, without considering the consequences. A hero on a quest of his own. A man she will never see again…

Only, of course…she does. And he's not at all the hero she remembers him to be.

Or is he? I hope you will enjoy reading NEVER ENTICE AN EARL and finding out.

Best wishes, and happy reading!

Lily Dalton

LilyDalton.com
Twitter @LilyDalton
Facebook.com/LilyDaltonAuthor

♥ ♥ ♥ ♥ ♥ ♥ ♥ ♥ ♥ ♥ ♥ ♥ ♥ ♥ ♥

From the desk of Shelley Coriell

Dear Reader,

Story ideas come from everywhere. Snippets of conversation. Dreams. The hunky guy at the office supply store with eyes the color of faded denim. THE BROKEN, the first book in my new romantic suspense series, The Apostles, was born and bred as I sat at the bedside of my dying father.

In 2007 my dad, who lived on a mountain in northern Nevada, checked himself into his small town's hospital after having what appeared to be a stroke. "A mild one," he assured the family. "Nothing to get worked up about." That afternoon, this independent, strong-willed man (aka stubborn and borderline cantankerous) checked himself out of the hospital. The next day he hopped on his quad and accidentally drove off the side of his beloved mountain. The ATV landed on him, crushing his chest, breaking ribs, and collapsing a lung.

The hospital staff told us they could do nothing for him, that he would die. Refusing to accept the prognosis, we had him Life-Flighted to Salt Lake City. After a touch-and-go forty-eight hours, he pulled through, and that's when we learned the full extent of his injuries.

He'd had *multiple* strokes. The not-so-mild kind. The kind that meant he, at age sixty-three, would be forever dependent on others. His spirit was broken.

For the next week, the family gathered at the hospital. My sister, the oldest and the family nurturer, massaged his feet and swabbed his mouth. My brother, Mr. Finance Guy, talked with insurance types and made arrangements for post-release therapy. The quiet, bookish middle child, I had little to offer but prayers. I'd never felt so helpless.

As my dad's health improved, his spirits worsened. He was mad at his body, mad at the world. After a particularly difficult morning, he told us he wished he'd died on that mountain. A horrible, heavy silence followed. Which is when I decided to use the one thing I did have.

I dragged the chair in his hospital room—you know the kind, the heavy, wooden contraption that folds out into a bed—to his bedside and took out the notebook I carry everywhere.

"You know, Dad," I said. "I've been tinkering with this story idea. Can I bounce some stuff off you?"

Silence.

"I have this heroine. A news broadcaster who gets stabbed by a serial killer. She's scarred, physically and emotionally."

More silence.

"And I have a Good Guy. Don't know much about him, but he also has a past that left him scarred. He carries a gun. Maybe an FBI badge." That's it. Two hazy characters hanging out in the back of my brain.

Dad turned toward the window.

"The scarred journalist ends up working as an aide to an old man who lives on a mountain," I continued on the fly. "Oh-oh! The old guy is blind and can't see her scars. His name is . . . Smokey Joe, and like everyone else in this story, he's a little broken."

Dad glared. I saw it. He wanted me to see it.

"And, you know what, Dad? Smokey Joe can be a real pain in the ass."

My father's lips twitched. He tried not to smile, but I saw that, too.

I opened my notebook. "So tell me about Smokey Joe. Tell me about his mountain. Tell me about his *story*."

For the next two hours, Dad and I talked about an old man on a mountain and brainstormed the book that eventually became THE BROKEN, the story of Kate Johnson, an on-the-run broadcast journalist whose broken past holds the secret to catching a serial killer, and Hayden Reed, the tenacious FBI profiler who sees past her scars and vows to find a way into her head, but to his surprise, heads straight for her heart.

"Hey, Sissy," Dad said as I tucked away my notebook after what became the first of many Apostle brainstorming sessions. "Smokey Joe knows how to use C-4. We need to have a scene where he blows something up."

And "we" did.

So with a boom from old Smokey Joe, I'm thrilled to introduce you to Kate Johnson, Hayden Reed, and the Apostles, an elite group of FBI agents who aren't afraid to work outside the box and, at times, outside the law. FBI legend Parker Lord on his team: "Apostles? There's nothing holy about us. We're a little maverick and a lot broken, but in the end we get justice right."

Joy & Peace!

♥   ♥

From the desk of Hope Ramsay

Dear Reader,

Jane Eyre may have been the first romance novel I ever read. I know it made an enormous impression on me when I was in seventh grade and it undoubtedly turned me into an avid reader. I simply got lost in the love story between Jane Eyre and Edward Fairfax Rochester.

In other words, I fell in love with Rochester when I was thirteen, and I've never gotten over it. I re-read *Jane Eyre* every year or so, and I have every screen adaptation ever made of the book. (The BBC version is the best by far, even if they took liberties with the story.)

So it was only a matter of time before I tried to write a hero like Rochester. You know the kind: brooding, passionate, tortured . . . (sigh). Enter Gabriel Raintree, the hero of INN AT LAST CHANCE. He's got all the classic traits of the gothic hero.

His heroine is Jennifer Carpenter, a plucky and self-reliant former schoolteacher turned innkeeper who is exactly the kind of no-nonsense woman Gabe needs. (Does this sound vaguely familiar?)

In all fairness, I should point out that I substituted the swamps of South Carolina for the moors of England and a bed and breakfast for Thornfield Hall. I also have an inordinate number of busybodies and matchmakers popping in and out for comic relief. But it is fair to say that I borrowed a few things from Charlotte Brontë, and I had such fun doing it.

I hope you enjoy INN AT LAST CHANCE. It's a contemporary, gothic-inspired tale involving a brooding hero, a plucky heroine, a haunted house, and a secret that's been kept for years.

Hope Ramsay

♥ ♥ ♥ ♥ ♥ ♥ ♥ ♥ ♥ ♥ ♥ ♥ ♥ ♥ ♥ ♥

From the desk of Molly Cannon

Dear Reader,

Weddings! I love them. The ceremony, the traditions, the romance, the flowers, the music, and of course the food. Face it. I embrace anything when cake is involved. When I got married many moons ago, there was a short ceremony and then cake and punch were served in the next room. That was it. Simple and easy and really lovely. But possibilities for weddings have expanded since then.

In FLIRTING WITH FOREVER, Irene Cornwell decides to become a wedding planner, and she has to meet the challenge of giving brides what they want within their budget. And it can be a challenge! I have planned a couple of weddings, and it was a lot of work, but it was also a whole lot of fun. Finding the venue, booking the caterer, deciding on the decorating theme. It is so satisfying to watch a million details come together to launch the happy couple into their new life together.

In one wedding I planned we opted for using mismatched dishes found at thrift stores on the buffet table. We found a bride selling tablecloths from her wedding and used different swaths of cloth as overlays. We made a canopy for the dance floor using pickle buckets and PFC pipe covered in vines and flowers, and then strung it with lights. We spray-painted cheap glass vases and filled them with flowers to match the color palette. And then, as Irene discovered, the hardest part is cleaning up after the celebration is over. But I wouldn't trade the experience for anything.

Another important theme in FLIRTING WITH FOREVER is second-chance love. My heart gets all aflutter when I think about true love emerging victorious after years of separation, heartbreak, and misunderstanding. Irene and Theo fell in love as teenagers, but it didn't last. Now older and wiser they reunite and fall in love all over again. Sigh.

I hope you'll join Irene and Theo on their journey. I promise it's even better the second time around.

Happy Reading!

Molly Cannon

Mollycannon.com
Twitter @CannonMolly
Facebook.com

♥   ♥

From the desk of Laura London

Dear Reader,

The spark to write THE WINDFLOWER came when Sharon read a three-hundred-year-old list of pirates who were executed by hanging. The majority of the pirates were teens, some as young as fourteen. Sharon felt so sad about these young lives cut short that it made her want to write a book to give the young pirates a happier ending.

For my part, I had much enjoyed the tales of Robert Lewis Stevenson as a boy. I had spent many happy hours playing the pirate with my cousins using wooden swords, cardboard hats, and rubber band guns.

Sharon and I threw ourselves into writing THE WIND-FLOWER with the full force of our creative absorption. We were young and in love, and existed in our imaginations on a pirate ship. We are proud that we created a novel that is in print on its thirty-year anniversary and has been printed in multiple languages around the world.

Fondly yours,

Sharon
& Tom Curtis

Writing as Laura London

♥ ♥   ♥

From the desk of
Sue-Ellen Welfonder

Dear Reader,

At a recent gathering, someone asked about my upcoming releases. I revealed that I'd just launched a new Scottish medieval series, Scandalous Scots, with an e-novella, *Once Upon a Highland Christmas*, and that TO LOVE A HIGHLANDER would soon follow.

As happens so often, this person asked why I set my books in Scotland. My first reaction to this question is always to come back with, "Where else?" To me, there is nowhere else.

Sorley, the hero of TO LOVE A HIGHLANDER, would agree. Where better to celebrate romance than a land famed for men as fierce and wild as the soaring, mist-drenched hills that bred them? A place where the women are prized for their strength and beauty, the fiery passion known to heat a man's blood on cold, dark nights when chill winds raced through the glens? No land is more awe-inspiring, no people more proud. Scots have a powerful bond with their land. Haven't they fought for it for centuries? Kept their heathery hills always in their hearts, yearning for home when exiled, the distance of oceans and time unable to quench the pull to return?

That's a perfect blend for romance.

Sorley has such a bond with his homeland. Since he

was a lad, he's been drawn to the Highlands. Longing for wild places of rugged, wind-blown heights and high moors where the heather rolls on forever, so glorious it hurt the eyes to behold such grandeur. But Sorley's attachment to the Highlands also annoys him and poses one of his greatest problems. He suspects his father might have also been a Highlander—a ruthless, cold-hearted chieftain, to be exact. He doesn't know for sure because he's a bastard, raised at Stirling's glittering royal court.

In TO LOVE A HIGHLANDER, Sorley discovers the truth of his birth. Making Sorley unaware of his birthright as a Highlander was a twist I've always wanted to explore. I'm fascinated by how many people love Scotland and burn to go there, many drawn back because their ancestors were Scottish. I love that centuries and even thousands of miles can't touch the powerful pull Scotland exerts on its own.

Sorley's heritage explains a lot, for he's also a notorious rogue, a master of seduction. His prowess in bed is legend and he ignites passion in all the women he meets. Only one has ever shunned him. She's Mirabelle MacLaren and when she returns to his life, appearing in his bedchamber with an outrageous request, he's torn.

Mirabelle wants him to scandalize her reputation.

He'd love to oblige, especially as doing so will destroy his enemy.

But touching Mirabelle will rip open scars best left alone. Unfortunately, Sorley can't resist Mirabelle. Together, they learn that when the heart warms, all things are possible. Yet there's always a price. Theirs will be surrendering everything they've ever believed in and accepting that true love does indeed heal all wounds.

I hope you enjoy reading TO LOVE A HIGHLANDER! I know I loved unraveling Sorley and Mirabelle's story.

Highland Blessings!

Sue-Ellen Welfonder

www.welfonder.com